HALLOWED GROUND

HALLOWED GROUND

REBECCA

YARROS

Entangled Publishing, LLC
644 Shrewsbury Commons Ave., STE 181
Shrewsbury, PA 17361
rights@entangledpublishing.com

Amara is an imprint of Entangled Publishing, LLC.

Visit our website at www.entangledpublishing.com.

Edited by Karen Grove
Cover design by Bree Archer
Cover images by vvvita/Getty Images
Interior design by Toni Kerr

ISBN 978-1-64937-569-8
Ebook ISBN 978-1-63375-392-1

Manufactured in the United States of America

First Edition December 2023

10 9 8 7 6 5 4 3 2 1

ALSO BY REBECCA YARROS

The Last Letter
Great and Precious Things
The Things We Leave Unfinished

THE EMPYREAN SERIES

Fourth Wing
Iron Flame

THE FLIGHT AND GLORY SERIES

Full Measures
Eyes Turned Skyward
Beyond What Is Given
Hallowed Ground
The Reality of Everything

THE RENEGADES

Wilder
Nova
Rebel

To CW2 Phillip A. Johnson, CW2 Ian D. Manual,
their families, and the rest of the Witchdoctor 11 Medevac
crew, who chanced a hot LZ to medevac my husband,
only to give their lives a few months later in Fallujah, Iraq.
There is not a day that I am not eternally grateful
and humbled by your sacrifice

At Entangled, we want our readers to be well-informed. If you would like to know if this book contains any elements that might be of concern for you, please check the back of the book for details.

PROLOGUE

EMBER

My hand hovered over the signature line.

Ephesus was almost six thousand miles away. A foreign country. A language I didn't speak. But at least I'd be within three thousand miles of Josh. The same continent for two whole months.

My fingers tightened on the pen, and my name unfolded onto the line with sure, fluid strokes. There. Done. I would be the youngest member of the Ephesus Excavation Fall Team. I sealed and stamped the envelope before I could change my mind.

Five knocks sounded in Paisley's signature rhythm on the front door. She was right on time, as usual. Then again, living next door made for quick travel. I tightened my ponytail and stuffed the spare house key into the tiny pocket of my workout capris before I answered.

"Morning, sunshine!" she drawled with a grin. "You ready to hit the trail?"

"I signed." My tone suggested I'd just committed murder.

"It's about time! Really, it's the right choice, and I'm so excited for you! Let's celebrate with some chai afterward?"

"If by chai, you also mean going to a coffee shop, then I'm game," I answered, dropping the letter in the mailbox and then turning to lock the door behind me. Besides, a four-mile hike deserved a caffeinated treat. Damn, the freaking key stuck in the lock. Again.

"Oh my God, Ember." Paisley's broken whisper sent chills racing from my scalp to my stomach.

I abandoned the key and turned slowly, my tennis shoes catching lightly on the concrete of our shared porch.

That feeling—the one I'd left behind in Colorado—swept over me, sickening my stomach in less time than it took to close my eyes...and I knew.

I...just...knew.

I faced our sidewalk, and the air rushed from my lungs in a soundless sob. This was how my world would end, on a cloudless Saturday morning. *God, no. Josh. Please.* His name was the sweetest prayer in my mind, the desperate call of my soul to his...wherever he might be.

Paisley shook as she took my hand, intertwining our fingers and grounding me. *Which one? God, which one?* There was no right answer.

My world paused, as though my mind knew to take in every excruciating detail of this moment—the sunshine filtering through the hanging baskets of flowers we'd just planted, the sounds of laughing children one house over, and the somber expressions of the two officers who walked steadily toward us...

In dress blues.

CHAPTER ONE

Four Months Earlier

"I'm just saying that not all of us are six-foot-four, Joshua Walker." I tilted my head to the side as he put another cooking gadget Mom swore we needed onto the top shelf of the kitchen cabinets.

Josh turned that damn smile on me and shut the door with a flick of his hand before caging me between his hips and the counter. "Okay. When you need something from the top shelf, I'll race over and get it down for you."

"Not the point." I fought back the smile that had been a nearly permanent fixture during the last two days that we'd lived together.

You live together. No more long distance. No more missing him.

I looped my arms around his neck, letting my fingertips graze over the newly cut hair at the base of his head. "What about those times you're not here?"

His gaze dropped to my lips. "Well, then maybe you could simply choose not to fondue for lunch?"

My stomach warmed at the look in his eyes—the one that seemed to ignore that we'd just gotten out of bed an hour ago. His arms tightened around me, bringing our lower bodies flush, and my pulse leaped.

"But maybe I like melted chocolate," I whispered. "It has all kinds of uses."

Those smoldering brown eyes locked on to mine, and I saw it there—the longing that had been our companion these last two years, waiting to finally be together, the intense chemistry that never failed to turn my body pliant the moment he so much as whispered my name.

"December."

That did it. I was a puddle before his lips even touched mine. His mouth brushed them once, twice, before settling over me in a languorous kiss that had me arching against him. I opened for him, and Josh took advantage, stroking his tongue against mine with enough friction to set me on fire.

My heart soared, pouring so much emotion into me that I wasn't sure my body could handle it. A laugh burst free, and I felt him smile against my mouth in response.

"Kissing me is funny?" he asked, lifting me to the counter to bury his nose just beneath my jaw.

"No!" I giggled again as he growled.

His face lifted, the light in his eyes reflecting the sheer joy I couldn't contain. "What then?"

My fingers traced the lines of his face, catching on his rough morning stubble. God, he was just so freaking gorgeous. Somehow he'd gotten hotter in the last two years, time stripping away the last vestiges of boyhood from this glorious piece of man. "I'm just happy."

"Well, that's the idea."

"I keep thinking about the hours we spent driving between Nashville and Fort Rucker, and the stolen weekends, and the good-byes..." And the times we both wondered how long our relationship could stay this strong without living in the same zip code.

He kissed me softly. "No more good-byes."

"Promise?" A tremor slipped into my voice.

He cupped my face and looked so deeply into my eyes that I knew he was reaching for my soul. "I will never leave you again by choice, December. This is it. We made it through the worst, and now we're here."

I sighed and nodded. "So now what? Everything we've done has been to get to this point."

A breathtaking smile swept over his face. "Now, we're just happy. You and me, and this townhouse full of boxes."

Bam! Bam! Our shared duplex wall carried the noise from our neighbors. "It's a little early for a hammer, Jagger," I muttered.

"But maybe not too early to get nailed?" Josh wiggled his eyebrows and swallowed my laugh with a kiss.

If happiness had its own electrical current, we could have powered the whole city of Clarksville.

The alarm blared on my cell phone, and I reached for it, randomly slapping the counter in search while trying not to break from Josh's mouth. *Oh, screw the phone.*

I wound my arms around his neck and threw myself into the kiss, angling the way I knew he liked and sucking his tongue into my mouth. He groaned, sinking his fingers into my hair, and then drove me wild with every lick, nibble, and caress. Josh pulled back with a gentle bite on my lower lip and then silenced my phone.

"Fun time's over, Ms. Howard. You have class in an hour and ten minutes." He waved the phone.

"And?" I questioned, sliding my hands under his PT shirt to feel the delectable ridges of his abs.

With a muttered curse, he retreated. "And it takes one hour and seven minutes to get there, which means it's time for you to go."

I threw on my best pout. "I can skip."

He took my messenger bag and travel coffee mug and thrust

them both into my lap. "No. We had a deal. Normal life, which includes you going to class, no matter how badly I'd like to take you back upstairs and listen to you scream my name as you come."

Need slammed into me, and my breath left in a rush. "That's really not the best argument to get me to leave."

He put the kitchen island between us. "We don't have to fight for time together anymore. This is our normal, babe. So you go to class, and I'll go to work. And if you're a good girl..."

I hopped off the counter and slung my bag over my shoulder, stalking him until his back hit the counter. "If I'm a good girl?" My fingers dipped into his waistband.

His eyes darkened, and his gaze dropped to my lips. "You'll find out when you get home."

Home. I lived with Josh. A fresh wave of euphoria bloomed in my chest. "You have a deal. Whatever will you do while I'm gone?"

"Oh, the normal. Go to work, maybe hang those pictures you marked for the upstairs hallway. Seriously, who frames the Gettysburg address?"

"An avid historian who happens to love that speech." I pushed up on tiptoe and kissed him. "I'll see you later, love."

He tucked my hair behind my ear. "Send me a text and let me know you made it."

"You bet."

I grabbed my coat out of the front closet and zipped it up, barely remembering my coffee as I ran out the door with my books.

"December!" Josh called from the doorway as I slid the key into my car.

"Josh?"

His smile stole the very sun from the sky. "These have been the best three days of my life. I love you."

"I love you, too. Just wait until you're sick of me." I winked, and he laughed.

"Not going to happen. Have a nice day, dear!" he sang, waving and stepping through our front door.

I pulled out of our shared driveway, slightly jealous that Paisley's car was still parked. She'd completed everything she needed face-to-face last semester and was finishing her degree with online courses. We'd all decided on a little neighborhood on the outskirts of Clarksville, Tennessee, and lucked out that the new development had both sides of a duplex open.

Jagger declared the gods of realty had smiled upon their bromance, and we'd signed the leases. I loved being so close to our friends.

Driving an hour to Nashville twice a week to finish at Vanderbilt was more than worth it to sleep next to Josh every night. Besides, it gave me a chance to call Mom, or catch up with April or Sam. As mild as this January was going weather-wise, it was an easy trip.

I made it to a parking space with seven minutes to spare and ended up sprinting to class, taking the first seat along the U-shaped conference table. My laptop fired up as our professor walked in.

"Good morning, seniors," Dr. Trimble said, placing his coffee on the small podium. He glanced at each of us in turn. "Welcome to Thesis. It's good to see so many familiar faces. For those of you who don't know me, I'm not sure how you made it through Vanderbilt without being subjected to my rambling, but bravo."

A small murmur of laughter passed through the twenty or so of us.

He ran a hand over his balding head and adjusted his houndstooth bowtie. "Before we get started, I'd like to introduce my TA." He motioned with his hand, and I turned with the class toward the back of the room. "Mr. Graham is working on his masters, and is doubling as my research assistant."

The corners of my mouth lifted when Luke stood and waved, offering me a smile and a nod. He mouthed, "Coffee?" and I gave a small nod before turning my attention back to Dr. Trimble.

"He'll also be handling the applications for the dig I'm overseeing this fall in Ephesus, Turkey. For those of you continuing on to your masters and doctorates, it would behoove you to apply, as only those who are accepted on the dig will be considered to start in a special spring opening in those programs. Now, let's get down to business."

An hour and a thick syllabus later, Luke and I headed toward the coffee shop.

"How's it going, Red?" he asked, nudging me with his shoulder.

"Good," I answered as we walked. "Josh and I moved in together, and it's pretty perfect so far."

"Ah, the hockey star returns." He held the door open for me, and the welcoming smell of espresso filled my lungs.

"The hockey star never left," I elbowed him. "How is David?"

Luke snorted. "Still leaving his boxers on the floor, but I love him, so what can I do?"

"It's a pretty small problem in the scheme of things, right?"

"There are worse problems to have," he answered. "Hopefully the line isn't too long. Our spot is open."

Once our coffee was in hand, we took up seats on the small loveseat in the corner that we'd claimed during study sessions my junior year. "What are your plans after graduation?" Luke asked, brushing an errant piece of blond hair out of his eyes. He was still trying for the surfer look, but it was growing on me.

"Well, Josh is stationed at Fort Campbell now, so I'm throwing around the idea of getting my masters...maybe my doctorate?"

"Ooh." He leaned forward with an indecent grin. "Talk academia to me."

I laughed and shook my head. "I…I have…"

"Spit it out."

"I kind of want to start focusing more on the writing aspect, really dig in historically, maybe publish something? It's probably not going to happen. I should teach. That's the practical answer."

Luke raised his eyebrows. "You kept a long-distance relationship thriving, and you want to talk about practical? You're a romantic at heart, honey—you can't fool me. You also do whatever you set your mind to, so if you'd like to be the next David McCullough, I think the world is ready."

"What about the next Howard Zinn?" I suggested. "Revolutionize what everyone thinks they know. Look at history from another side and not just the victor's?"

He tapped his fingers on his paper cup and tilted his head. "You need to apply for the Ephesus dig."

I sputtered, nearly spewing coffee all over his cream sweater. "What? That's in Turkey."

"Well, I don't think we can move the location, so yes, you'd have to come to Turkey."

"You're going?" That was definitely an incentive.

"Seeing as my dad funded it, I kind of have to."

"Did he get tired of buying hockey teams?" I joked.

"Hey, it's just the one, and technically since it's an expansion team, he didn't buy it, he started it. Stop changing the subject and think of all the opportunities. Putting your hands on arguably the most untouched Roman ruins in the world… You're still emphasizing in European History, right?"

I nodded slowly, trying to process his suggestion. "I just moved in with Josh. I can't up and leave."

"Red, it's like two months, which is a blip on the radar to you guys, and you'd earn mad street cred with Dr. Trimble toward getting into whatever program you want."

"Okay, you don't get to say 'street cred' again without me laughing."

"Fine, but you need to apply. You'll get accepted. Your grades still stellar?"

"Yeah."

Could you really spend two months away from him when you've been apart for so long?

"Then I think this is something you really need to consider." He rummaged though his messenger bag and brought out a stapled packet. "This is the application. It's not due until spring break. You'd really be an asset, Ember. Plus, if you're just now thinking about your doctorate, you're behind the power curve. The dig would let you into the spring program. Without it, you're behind a year. Plus, it's not like you didn't love the one we did last year, and that was a baby dig compared to this."

Ephesus. A real dig. A chance to discover something—a new theory, a new fact, something I could sink my teeth into and maybe even publish. A real-life use for all the work I'd put into my college career. But not seeing Josh? Voluntarily being long distance again? Madness. I pushed the application away. "I just can't."

He shook his head and stuffed it into my bag. "Yes, you can. You're a brilliant woman, Ember, and if he loves you the way you say he does, he'd never dim your light. Don't become one of those women who forget who they are just because they're in a relationship. At least think about it."

"I will," I promised.

He filled me in on his relationship, and I gave him the short version of how the move had gone, until it was time to head to another class. I'd loaded my schedule last semester, so all I needed were three this go-round, thank God.

I called Josh from the car on my way home. *Home!* I'd never been so excited to see what a normal evening could hold. "Hey!"

"Hey, babe." His tired voice came through the car speakers.

"How was your first day at the unit?"

"Mixed, I guess. You headed home?"

"It's never easy being the new guy, and yeah I'm on my way. GPS has me fifty-five minutes out. Are you in the same company as Will?"

"Yeah, Carter and I are both in Charlie. Jagger's in Bravo with the other attack guys. You concentrate on the road, and I'll work on getting us some dinner, how does that sound?"

Something shifted in my stomach, an unease that crept up my throat. "Everything okay?"

"It will be once you get here." He tried to sound upbeat but didn't quite make it.

"Okay. I love you."

"I love you so much it hurts. See you in an hour."

We hung up, and I cranked some music, but I couldn't shake the crappy feeling that settled in my chest, or help but think about that Ephesus application in my bag.

I walked through our front door five minutes earlier than the GPS predicted. Our living room was partially put away, some of my books haphazardly stacked on the white bookshelves, and a few framed pictures were laid on the square coffee table.

My fingers grazed over Dad's face and that familiar ache returned. Two years, and I still missed him every day.

"I thought you might want to decide where to hang them," Josh said, coming from the small dining room where our four-person table from my old apartment was a cozy fit. He kissed the side of my head and pulled me into a hug, chasing away the sadness with his love.

"That sounds great," I answered, wrapping my arms around his back. He'd already changed into a pair of jeans and a Henley. I had to admit, I liked my Josh better than Lieutenant Walker. "What is that heavenly smell?"

"Takeout from the Italian place down the street. I grabbed your favorites," he said, leading me to the table after I took off my jacket and dropped my bag.

We sat and my mouth watered at the tortellini Alfredo in

front of me. "This looks so good." I shot him a sly grin. "Is this what I have to look forward to at the end of my school days?"

He laughed. "Day three and you're ready to divvy up the household chores."

My cheeks flamed because...

"Don't worry, I know you already have a color-coded chart somewhere dictating what needs doing and when. Just stick it on the fridge, and we'll get it done." His smile melted me more than the wine he'd poured.

He knew me way too well. "The chart isn't color-coded, but that's not a half-bad idea."

"There's a fresh pack of highlighters waiting for you in the desk drawer. Now tell me everything about the first day of your last semester of college."

I filled him in on everything about the classes but paused when I thought about the application. "There's...there's a dig."

"Another one? That's awesome. Where are you going?" he asked as if it was nothing, simply taking another bite of his food.

And I loved him all the more for it.

Josh would never hold me back, never discount my dreams to pay for his own. That's why I couldn't abuse that love. "It doesn't matter. I'm not going. I don't even know if I'd get in."

"You'll get in. Why don't you want to go?"

"It's not a two-week trip this time, it's two months, in Ephesus, Turkey, and I don't want to be away from you that long."

"Turkey?" His fork paused on the way to his mouth.

"Yeah, and not the bird." I shook my finger at whatever smart reply he was thinking. Jagger had rubbed off on his sense of humor.

He quirked an eyebrow. "You should go. That's huge."

"We just clawed our way through a very complicated two years, Josh. This is our time, our chance. You're too important to me to press pause so I can play with some dirt." *Some really cool, very rare, historically badass dirt.*

"You really should go." His voice dropped an octave, and his gaze fell to the tablecloth.

"Oh no, you're not going to be all selfless and Joshy about this. I want this time with you—barbecues with our friends and sneaking off to watch you fly. I can do research from here. I don't need to go to Turkey. I need to be with you."

His fork hit the plate, the clanging obscenely loud in our bare house. "We won't have the summer together, December. You should go, because I won't be here."

I carefully set my fork down, a sickening foreboding settling over us. My food turned over in my stomach as my heart jumped.

"Why? Why won't you be here?"

"God, baby. I'm so sorry."

And just like that…I knew.

"Say it." *Don't say it. Deny it.* I glanced over to where the double-star service flag hung in our window. Paisley and I had thought they were so cute when we'd bought our matching set. But while Paisley's were both blue, one of our stars was gold for Dad. I ripped my eyes away, refusing to think of stitching any other color onto it, and locked eyes with the man who owned my very soul. "Tell me, Josh."

"We're on deployment orders."

My eyes slid shut, like I could block this out, hide from it. It could be Honduras, Guatemala, hell, even Korea. It didn't have to be over there, to that country that had nearly killed him and had ultimately taken my father from me.

"Where?" Our eyes locked, every ounce of the love we'd worked so hard for pouring between us, trying to fill the cracks that would soon become a canyon of distance.

"Afghanistan."

So much for being *just happy.*

CHAPTER TWO

JOSH

The word flew from my mouth, and I would have paid anything to take it back, to wipe the look of total and abject fear off her face. She didn't deserve this.

Any of this.

Life dealt Ember a shit hand, and rather than being the prince, I'd just turned myself into the joker—some sick act of irony. "Babe."

"When?"

"It's complicated. I have to progress through some helicopter training before I'm ready to fly with the unit, and they want me to do that here before I leave."

"Josh. Stop making me ask you things twice, and just be straight with me. You can't hide this from me or protect me from it, so just be honest and tell me when."

God, those eyes, they destroyed me. They were wide, wild, even though the rest of her was composed. "A month."

Her little whimper broke my fucking heart. Her eyes focused on her wineglass, and her spine straightened. I witnessed that moment in the grocery store two years ago all over again, watching her take on a burden she shouldn't have to and stand even taller for it. "Okay. For how long?" Her voice grew steadier.

She was magnificent.

"Nine months. Maybe longer." Nine fucking months without seeing her. Kissing her. Feeling her wiggle closer to me while she slept.

December nodded. "I thought they told you that your battalion wasn't on the patch chart?"

That awful chart, the one that stated which units were up for deployment rotation, was about as trustworthy as a politician. "Right. When I got the welcome call from the unit, we weren't. A different battalion was. But then they decided to go with a task force and pull different companies from different battalions—"

"I know what a task force is," she said quietly, reminding me all too clearly that she was no stranger to this life.

"Right. Sorry. They pulled three of us. Medevac leaves early, but they're leaving me here this month to progress. The rest of the company leaves next week."

She sucked in her breath. "So soon."

"Yeah." An ominous silence settled over our table, the food growing colder by the minute.

"Jagger? Will?"

"Jagger leaves with me. Carter will rotate in a couple months after us, and stay a couple months later. They're trying to make sure medevac doesn't end up with the year-long version of this hell." She nodded but didn't speak, still absorbed in the glass in front of her. I reached for her hand, covering it with my own and squeezing gently. "Babe, this will be okay. I'll be okay."

Her head snapped toward mine, those blue eyes lit with a fire that was as beautiful as it was intimidating. "You. Don't. Know. That." She spat out each word through closed teeth.

Wrong thing to say. "I know that I love you."

She shook her head. "That country nearly killed you last time, and it did kill my dad. All the love in the world can't save us from that." She pulled her hand from mine and buried her face.

"Hey. I know this is scary—"

"I'm trying, I swear. I know I signed up for this. It's not like I didn't know what you were going to do, and I still chose you—*choose* you—but God, Josh. This...I can't wrap my head around it."

I pushed my chair out and reached for her, lifting her tiny, curved frame onto my lap. Her head tucked beneath my chin, and she curled into me, fitting right where she was always meant to be. My arms closed around her. "We have a month."

"It's not long enough." Her fingers gripped my shirt like she could keep me here if she just held on tight enough. God, what I wouldn't have given to stay with her.

"Forever isn't long enough for us, December, but that's what we're going to have. You and I have never chosen the easy path. This is just another hurdle." I rubbed my chin over her soft hair and tried to soak in every detail of holding her—the sweet way she smelled, the smooth texture of her skin beneath my hands.

She leaned back in my arms and cupped my face. "I can't lose you." Her voice broke, and tears pooled in her eyes.

I'd never hated myself more than I did in that moment. She'd made it through a nightmare no one should have to face, and I was about to ask her to chance that fire again. My breath hitched, barely passing the lump in my throat. "You won't. It would take something a hell of a lot stronger than a war to keep me from you."

I sealed that promise with a kiss, tasting her fear and desperation as she responded. She opened underneath me, and I fused my mouth to hers, surrendering to the heat between us to pull us through this moment. There was nothing hotter or sweeter in this world than kissing December, feeling her go soft and pliant.

We'd fought so fucking hard to get here, to be together. This wasn't fair, and we both knew it. But we also both knew it didn't matter. Fair wasn't exactly in the U.S. Army vocabulary.

I retreated just enough to whisper against her lips, "I'll

come home. I swear it."

Her chest trembled as she sucked in a stuttered breath. "Don't make me a promise you can't keep, Joshua Walker."

"I'll spend my life keeping it," I vowed.

Her fingers skipped over my face, like she needed to memorize me. "You don't get it," she whispered. "That's what I'm terrified of."

I pulled her to me the second her tears slipped down her porcelain cheeks, and held her long past their end.

The week had passed too quickly. The days did that now, too, no matter how I tried to slow them down, to savor every second I had with her. It seemed daylight slipped through my fingers.

"I'd almost forgotten how much paperwork there was," I muttered, flipping through the stack.

"God, I thought college applications were bad," Jagger muttered next to me.

The SRP site was packed with orderly lines of soldiers picking up their papers and checking their immunizations, all preparing to deploy.

"What is this?" Jagger waved a paper at me.

I grabbed my own. The DD93 stared up at me, the most macabre piece of work I'd seen since the last time I did this shit. "It's for your next of kin."

"Well, until I marry Paisley, that's probably you," Jagger said, tapping his pen on the paper.

"I'm pretty sure I'd know if something happened to you before a notification could come down, but I get what you're saying."

"Oh." The pen paused. "This is..."

"Yeah," I answered. It was for notification purposes,

determining which doors the army would knock at if we were KIA.

"Who are you putting?" Carter asked from the other side of me.

Shit. "Last time it was Mom, but she was alone when she found out I'd been hurt. I don't want to put her through that again. But Ember..."

Jagger sighed. "That's a tough fucking call."

"Why?" Carter didn't look up, filling his out with quick strokes of his pen.

"She's already answered that knock once, and it nearly destroyed her," I said quietly. His eyes shot up to mine, widening. "Her dad. He was the doc who fixed me up in Kandahar. He's the reason I'm alive."

"Damn. I had no clue." He shook his head. "She's so put together, you know?"

"Yeah. It's been a couple of years, but she's always had that strength. She carries everyone around her, including me some days." My chest tightened, and my fingers tried to rebel, but I scrawled her name for the primary next of kin. She was my life, everything about me began and ended with her. When...*if* something happened to me, she needed to be first to know. I put Mom in second, with the express wishes that she not be alone when they told her.

I closed my eyes, trying to breathe away the images assaulting my overactive imagination. Ember collapsing in the doorway of our house, holding a folded flag at another military funeral, bringing flowers to a cold grave while she cursed the choices I'd made that brought us here.

"What about you, Carter?" Jagger asked.

He didn't answer, just stared at the paper. It dawned on me—for all our time in flight school, I didn't know anything about his family. He'd always been the self-righteous asshole Jagger had gone toe-to-toe with over Paisley. But then Carter had given his Apache slot to Jagger, all in the name of what was on the right side of his moral code, and I couldn't help but put a few more points on his side. When he'd stepped up and helped me during the Blackhawk course because I'd spent way too much time traveling to be with Ember and not enough time studying, I started to genuinely like the ring-knocker.

I glanced down and saw that for all his writing, he'd left that slot blank. "Will?"

He startled, probably because I'd never used his first name before, and shook his head like he was clearing it. "Yeah, I don't know. My parents...well, let's just say there was a reason I needed a school that didn't charge tuition. They're not exactly going to know what to do, if they can pull themselves out of their respective bottles long enough to do it."

Jagger and I threw side-eyes at each other, and he gave a nearly imperceptible shrug. "Grayson would know what to say," Jagger whispered.

"He's not here, smartass."

"Chill the fuck out, we're not having a moment," Carter growled, scrawling a name quickly into the blank.

"Noted, West Point."

"This thing is thicker than the 160th packet," he muttered.

"You thinking of flying for SOAR?" I asked. Part of the 160th Special Operations Aviation Regiment was based here out of Fort Campbell, but it had never occurred to me to put in a packet for an assessment straight out of flight school.

"Yeah," he answered. "They need the best, right?" He shot me a cocky grin and stood to turn in his SRP packet. "But they're not even going to look at me until I have some deployment hours under my belt, so I'll wait until we're back. You should think about it."

"I thought you said they needed the best," Jagger joked.

"Yeah, well I've seen Walker fly." He looked back at me. "You have that edge."

"No, thank you," I said, turning back to my papers. Even though flying for SOAR would be badass, it wasn't the kind of life Ember would sign on for.

I sent up a quick prayer that the army would never have to so much as look at these forms again and gave my packet to the clerk.

One step closer to zero day.

CHAPTER THREE

Ember

J osh's hand on my lower back steadied my nerves as we walked into the hangar Saturday morning. It was the task force deployment kickoff 5K, and since Josh was expected to be there, I figured I may as well go, run, and meet some of the wives in the Family Readiness Group. I'd seen enough deployments with Mom to know I'd need their support.

The floor was open—the aircraft had already been sent to Afghanistan with Josh's unit. I ignored the tightening in my chest that came along with that thought every single time I had it. They were already gone, and he'd be joining them soon.

Too soon.

Today the hangar was filled with family instead of soldiers. I paused at the threshold, ignoring the way the heat of the crockpot handles seeped through the hotpot holders, and simply took in the sight. Children in bright T-shirts raced around a maze of strollers and moms, while a bounce house sat empty to mark the "finish line" near the hangar doors. Tables lined the back wall, buffet-style, where spouses were setting up their dishes in preparation for the potluck breakfast after the run.

It felt like the first day at a new school, except I didn't even have the luxury of an assigned seat.

You have a crockpot, too. You fit in.

"Of course you fit in," Josh said with a little laugh. Guess I'd spoken that thought aloud. He held out his hands to take the crockpot from me.

"No." I clutched the dish tighter.

"It's not going to protect you," he joked, walking with me toward the table.

"You have Kevlar. I have a crockpot."

"You're adorable when you're nervous." He threw me a wink, and I rolled my eyes.

I placed the dish on the table at the nearest empty spot and leaned to plug it into the power strip.

"Well, good morning! What do you have there?" a friendly voice asked.

"Breakfast burritos," I answered with a smile after I got the thing plugged in.

The woman looked to be in her early thirties, with nice brown hair and hazel eyes and a shirt that read "Dustoff Dolls" in sparkly red letters across her boobs. "Oh, well, these are more muffins and things. Maybe you could move it down to where the eggs are?" Smile or not, I knew that wasn't a request.

"Not a problem," I answered.

"Lieutenant Walker, I think Captain Brown was looking for you," the woman said.

"Yes, ma'am. Ember, this is Mrs. Dwyer. She's the FRG leader for our company."

"Lucille," the woman said, thrusting out her hand.

I shook it. "Pleasure to meet you. I'm Ember."

"Lovely! Oh, Lieutenant, I do wish you'd told me about her. I would have made sure she had a Dustoff Dolls shirt to match the rest of us! And we're having a little informational meeting later if you want to find us after the run. I know the girls would love to meet you!"

"I look forward to it," I answered Lucille as Josh unplugged the crockpot.

"Well, there's a spot right down there. Can't miss it!" she

said with a smile way too perky for eight a.m. and went to correct the next misplaced dish.

"I should go find—" Josh started.

"You leave me, you die," I whispered so only he could hear.

He took my face in his hands and smiled, warming me like nothing else could have. "Are you nervous, my December?"

"I'm not a wife." It slipped out before I could stop it.

"So? It's Family Readiness, not No-Non-Wives Allowed." His thumbs brushed over my cheeks.

He was right. "I'm just being silly." My eyes slid shut, and I took a deep breath.

Josh kissed me quickly. "You could never be silly. And like I said, you're adorable when you're nervous."

"Okay. You have a job, so go talk to Captain Brown. I'll find the exact six inches this crockpot should go in and then register us for the race, okay?"

"Sounds good."

He kissed me again and disappeared into the crowd. Well, as much as anyone his height could vanish in a sea of women. The only soldiers here were either on rear detachment for the deployment, or just hadn't left yet, like Josh.

I found the correct spot for my dish and gave a half wave to Lucille when she looked over to see that I had carried out her orders. For someone who'd been brought up in the army, I'd never felt quite so out of place.

Strapping my iPod to my bicep with my armband, I wandered to the registration table and signed us in. "Lieutenant Josh Walker and December Howard," I wrote on the line, adding in his company in the next blank.

Then I tightened my ponytail and waded through the sea of kids and strollers to search for Josh near the starting line.

"Good morning, Ember," Will said, catching up with me.

My stress level dropped about twenty points at the sight of a familiar face. "Hey, Will. You ready for a little run?"

"Most definitely. You making friends?"

I shrugged. "I wish Jagger and Paisley hadn't gone to New York for the weekend. How did he get out of this?"

Will laughed. "Paisley's dad wanted to see him before the deployment started, and there aren't many people who would deny leave when it's requested by one of the top-ranking generals in aviation."

"Good point." Glancing around at all the wives with their friends, I couldn't help but miss Sam, too. Her mom's change of command was coming up, so at least I'd get to spend next weekend with her.

We found Josh near the starting point, and I did a minimal stretch, grateful for my long-sleeve running gear in the slight morning chill, even if I didn't have Dustoff Dolls emblazoned across my breasts.

After a welcome speech by the rear detachment commander, the run started. Will jetted ahead, taking off like this race would determine his next promotion and not just who would buy the first round after. My heart thrummed steadily for the first mile, my feet hitting the pavement to the rhythm of my beats-per-minute playlist, but Josh lagged just behind me. I dropped back a few meters to where he ran and pulled out my earbuds. "Hey, babe, is your leg acting up?"

"No," he answered, his breath steady and even.

"But you're back here?"

The grin he gave me set my heart racing for much different reasons. "I just like the view." His eyes flickered to my rear, and I burst into laughter.

"You're telling me that checking out my butt is more important than beating Will in the task force 5K?"

"December, let's just get one thing straight." He stopped running, pulling me to a jarring stop with him as he wrapped his arms around me. Runners raced on either side of us, like we were a boulder in the middle of a rushing creek. "There's never anything more important to me than a chance to check out your ass."

I pushed his sweaty chest away with a loud laugh and pointed to the finish line. "Beat me, and I'll let you do more than check it out."

He wiggled his eyebrows and shot off at a sprint like he had a sign tacked to him that said WILL RUN FOR SEX.

Josh slowed as I caught up to him, and he kept pace with me, when I knew he could have left me in the dust, but he didn't. As the finish approached, we locked eyes, and with one more glance at my ass and a grin, he pushed ahead and smoked me, crossing the taped line a full ten seconds before I did.

A bottle of water later, Josh walked me to the corner of the hangar where his company FRG was meeting. "They won't bite. Make friends," he whispered into my very sweaty hair.

"Ah, Lieutenant!" Lucille called out with a huge smile in our direction.

Maybe this wouldn't be too bad. They were just wives, nothing I wasn't used to being around.

"Ma'am, I'm needed to tear down the route markers, but I'll leave Ember with you?"

Such a gentleman.

"No problem, we'll take good care of her. Oh, but I didn't get an info sheet on your wife. We'll need that to get her all set up on the roster."

"Oh, I'm not his wife," I spit out, then internally cursed when Josh flinched. "I mean we've been together two years, but yeah...not a wife," I finished slowly, feeling more like an idiot with every word I let past my lips.

Shit. Did he think I didn't want to be? Of course I wanted to be, but I didn't want FRG cop here putting the awkward pressure on.

Lucille's eyes widened and dropped to my very naked left hand. "Oh, I see. Of course. You're welcome to stay today, but deployment information really is for spouses and family only."

No Dustoff Dolls shirt for me.

"Actually, Lieutenant…" A small young woman with a large binder stepped forward, tucking a strand of her blond bob behind her ear. "If you'd just sign an authorization, your girlfriend is more than welcome on our roster."

Josh squeezed my hand, and I looked up at him. "What do you say, Ember? Do you want to stay?"

I knew what he was really saying. *Are you willing to put up with this? Do you want this?* Well, no, I didn't want this, but I could handle the marriage-police if it meant getting information while he was deployed. I nodded my head once, and he kissed my forehead.

"Well then," Lucille said, a sugar-sweet smile on her face. "Welcome to Dustoff."

"Play nice, and I'll go sign their form," Josh whispered in my ear, squeezing my hand before he took off to somewhere far less awkward than here…where all the wives were now blatantly assessing me. *Well, this is pleasant.*

Lucille took up her place at the front of the group and pulled out a clipboard. "Well, shall we get started?"

"Don't worry," the petite blonde with the binder said with a kind smile, sitting in the vacant chair next to me. She handed me a roster and information packet. "It's not just you. She really is a judgmental bitch."

Her tiny, sweet voice only made the statement funnier, and I barely suppressed a snort of laughter. Lucille cocked her head in my direction, and I tossed a smile back at her.

"You're just the newbie. Don't worry," the blonde said. "I came in last year, and let me tell you, when a crew chief marries a pilot and crosses that whole enlisted/officer line? Well, I fed the gossip mill for a good long while. I'm Carol, by the way."

"Ember, and it's really nice to meet you."

"Are you new to the military?"

I shook my head. "No, I'm an army brat."

"Ah, so you get the whole 'you knew what you were getting into' line, huh?" She sighed. "I get that all the time. But let me tell you, it's a lot different going than being left behind to wait."

"Yeah, I bet it is," I answered, looking up to where Lucille was currently lecturing us on keeping our social media safe for Operational Security.

"How long do you have left with him?"

"A little over two weeks." *Ouch.* Not that I didn't always have a countdown playing in my mind, but saying it aloud made it real—made it hurt.

In a couple of weeks, I'd be alone, sitting, waiting...just like Mom had.

She nudged me with her shoulder. "You look strong, capable. You'll do just fine, I can tell. You'll be one of the girls who makes it."

My eyes found Josh like a magnet as he came back through the hangar doors. He laughed at something Will said and gave me a horizontal thumb, asking for my verdict. He'd bail me out if I asked him to. I forced a smile and gave him a thumbs-up. Sitting where I wasn't exactly accepted would be the easiest part of this deployment.

Nine and a half months from now, he'd march through those hangar doors and this would be over. Our life could start, and this sputtering pause in time would be behind us. "What about the girlfriends who aren't strong enough?" I asked Carol.

She followed my eyes to Josh and then looked back at me. "Well, let's just say they're not waving the signs at redeployment."

Because their relationships didn't last *through* the deployment.

But they weren't us. Josh and I didn't know how to fail, and we weren't about to start now.

• • •

"She looked at my hand, Mom," I complained a few days later as I put away another sack full of groceries. "Looked at my hand and basically declared that they didn't want me because I'm not married to him. Like I don't count because I'm a girlfriend."

"Some women see a girlfriend and they think 'temporary,' which we both know you aren't. You know how hard it is to make friends, and if they don't think you're in it for the long haul, well...some judge too quickly. Anyone who spends an hour around you and Josh knows you two are the real deal. I'm sure her attitude isn't shared by all of them."

"No," I agreed, smiling as I popped Josh's strawberry ice cream into the freezer. "I met a lot of nice girls. But she's basically the Regina George of the FRG."

"Regina George?" she asked.

"*Mean Girls*, Mom. The plastics? We wear pink on Wednesday?" Silence came through loud and clear. "Okay, well, we're going to have to do a little movie-watching when I visit in the summer."

"Have you thought about spending the summer here?"

Crap, I knew that hopeful tone in her voice. "I have," I placated her. "But I like it here. This is our home. I want to be where I can still feel him."

"That, I understand, my love. And that dig?"

I paused, and she rushed forward.

"I think it would be great for you, Ember. You can't get experience like that just anywhere. It's really a once-in-a-lifetime chance."

"It's just hard to wrap my head around something like that when he's leaving so soon. I can't seem to get my bearings, or really get a grip on any of it."

"Ah, yes. That stage is awful, baby. I'm so sorry. They're working longer days to get ready, your mind is on overdrive, and you can't stop the clock."

I leaned back against the counter and stared at the island, where a stack of paper had rested ominously for the last two days. "He brought me papers, Mom."

She took a deep breath. "What are they?"

I swallowed, a lump forming in my throat. "The usual. Copies of his next-of-kin. Funeral wishes. Life insurance." Forcing my feet to move, I went to the stack, thumbing through the forms. My mind played a cruel trick, and for just a second, it wasn't Josh's name on the paper, it was Dad's. I dropped it like it was on fire and stepped back, sucking oxygen into my lungs.

"Ember?" Mom asked, her voice soft.

She would understand. Of everyone in my life, Mom would understand more than anyone. "I never wanted this. Any of this. I just wanted Josh."

"I know, baby."

"What do I do? I watched you go through this so many times, but I never really paid attention. I was too focused on soaking up Dad while we had him."

"Good, then I did my job. You gather those papers up; you stick them in a binder and lock it away in your safe. Then you get a grip and you spend the next week and a half with the man you love. Don't you dare let the fear rob you of these last few days, December Howard. They're too precious, so you fight like hell for every second with him."

Because you might not get another one.

CHAPTER FOUR

Josh

Time was moving too quickly, and there wasn't a damn thing I could do to stop it. Somehow the weeks had flown, and we were down to ten fucking days. There wasn't enough time. I hadn't done everything around the house she needed help with. I hadn't made love to her enough, kissed her enough, simply held her enough.

I hadn't found the perfect time to ask the most important question of my life.

I needed it to be perfect. Not Jagger-ish and huge. No, Ember needed something understated and simple...real. But I had to ask, because if this ridiculous, nagging feeling didn't get out of my stomach—well—I wanted my last name attached to her first.

Just in case.

Ember's hands wound around my waist as she pressed against my back. My eyes closed, and I smiled as peace mellowed every tense muscle in my body. Only December could do that to me, soothe the jagged edges I sometimes felt stayed barely stitched together. I needed to bottle this feeling so I could breathe it in on the long nights to come.

Fuck, I hated going to Afghanistan.

"Hey," she whispered, pressing a kiss to my back through the material of my button-up shirt.

I covered her hands with my own. "Hey, yourself."

She peeked around my side, resting her temple against my arm. Her smile was wide and the brightest I'd seen since I'd dropped the deployment bomb on her. "It feels like Rucker," she said softly.

I followed her gaze to where Grayson stood at the grill, lecturing Jagger about his marinade choice while Sam and Paisley roasted marshmallows over the fire pit from a couple of lawn chairs. All of this, even the sounds of Morgan and Carter bickering from the sidelines...it was incredibly precious. So hard-fought. So easily lost.

"It feels like home."

She leaned further into me, simply absorbing it. I loved that about her—how she didn't need to fill every minute with talk. Maybe it was because we'd both suffered loss early, both learned to savor every seemingly ordinary moment.

"Ember, come show Paisley how it's done. She keeps setting hers up like little torches," Sam called.

I kissed her forehead, and she crossed our combined backyard to the girls. I liked that there were no fences between our places. It would be easier for them when we were gone. Ember and Paisley would need to support each other this next year.

"How is Colorado?" I asked Grayson, walking over to where he flipped a shish kebab next to Jagger.

"Exactly what I needed," he replied, his eyes drifting back to Sam. "How are you feeling about heading back?"

"You want to talk about feelings?" I shot him a little side-eye.

"No time like the present."

Because there might not be a tomorrow.

I watched Ember laugh, the firelight playing along the lines of her face. My chest tightened. We were living in a vise, watching the edges come closer, helpless to do anything but wait to be crushed. Fuck, it sucked.

"I don't want to leave her. We're finally together and I'm leaving again. I guess I thought we'd have a minute or two, you know?"

"Embrace it," Grayson said.

Jagger turned slowly, his beer bottle paused just under his gaping mouth. "What?"

"Use this time. Feel every stab of loneliness, relish every second you would rip your very limbs off if it meant you could spend five minutes holding them. Let it push you to be the men you're capable of, the ones they deserve, and let it push you to be even better in the air so you come home to them."

Come home to them.

"Sam turned you into a sap," Jagger said quietly, but there was no teasing as we all stared over the grill at our combined lives.

The small smile on Grayson's face caught me unaware. "No regrets."

Once dinner was off the grill, we took up seats around the fire, the flames warding off the dipping February temperatures. Not that sixty-five had been a bad high for the day.

Ember closed the sliding glass door, four wineglasses clutched precariously in her hands while she managed to keep the bottle of wine under her arm. "Shall we?" she asked Sam once she reached us, pouring the wine like her answer was a foregone conclusion.

"Yes, please," Sam answered, and I didn't miss the glance she sent in Grayson's direction.

"Jagger, can I get a beer?" Grayson asked as Jagger leaned over the cooler. "Don't everyone look so shocked. It's not like we're going anywhere." His eyebrows shot up as he looked at me. "Unless your guest room shares a wall with Jagger. I don't need to hear that shit."

Paisley shot Grayson a death glare while Jagger nearly

choked on his beer with laughter. "No, our guest room does, and that's just Morgan."

"Just me?" Morgan asked Carter so quietly that if she wasn't on the other side of me, I wouldn't have heard her.

That escalated quickly.

"Just you," he said with a curt nod, but his knuckles whitened where he gripped his bottle.

Jagger shot me the that's-none-of-my-business look and passed a beer to Grayson while Ember sent a glass of wine to Morgan.

"Shall we toast?" Jagger asked, a grin damn-near consuming his face as he looked at Paisley.

"Wait, Paisley needs a glass," Ember said, pouring into the second glass.

"Oh, no, I have water." Paisley shook her head with a smile.

"Well, I guess one of us should be sober." Ember laughed, keeping the glass for herself. I pulled her onto my lap, gently squeezing the sweet curves of her hips.

"Behave," she whispered into my ear, but ran her tongue along the edge.

My fingers flexed, teasing under the edges of the black skirt that had slid higher on her thighs as she sat. I couldn't help it—her skin was a magnet for my hands. "You like it better when I don't," I answered.

She locked those blue eyes on mine, and for that second, I wanted everyone to go the fuck away so I could get my remarkable girlfriend out of her clothes. *Not a girlfriend for long.* Not if I found the perfect moment for that little velvet box hidden upstairs.

Mrs. Walker. December-fucking-Walker. Sounded perfect to me.

"Earth to Josh and Ember," Jagger called, waving his hand like he'd been at it a while.

"Yeah, yeah, a toast," Ember said, wiggling against my now-hard lap. I locked her down with my hands, and she threw me a smug grin, well aware of what she'd done.

Jagger raised his beer. "To friends. Hell, that doesn't even cut it. You guys, all of you...I wouldn't be here"—he looked over to Paisley—"or even the man I am, without you. So more than friends...to family."

We glanced around the fire at the family we'd made, and I felt it—one of those moments you can't forget, the kind that stay with you when it's long past, so you try to memorize everything. It was a deep peace, a contentment laced with the silent knowledge that we wouldn't be together again for far too long.

"To family," we all said in scattered rhythm, and I kissed the underside of Ember's jaw.

"Old and new," Jagger said, the firelight reflecting on something on his— *No fucking way.* How had I missed that? How long?

"Holy shit, Jagger, are you..." I couldn't even say it, my throat tightening like a damn woman.

Jagger held out that hand to Paisley, who took it with a smile that could have rivaled the sun for its brightness. "You want to?" she drawled softly as he tucked her under his arm.

"So we went up to West Point last weekend to see the parents—" Jagger started.

"—and got married!" Paisley finished.

Silence reigned for a heartbeat before we all started to call out our congratulations.

"That's amazing!" Ember squealed.

Paisley's face fell a little. "I'm sorry you guys weren't there, but it was just Anna and my parents. We figured with the guys deploying, it just seemed like the right time..." Her hands smoothed along her waist, and I felt Ember suck in her breath.

"It doesn't matter. We're just so happy for you!" Morgan said through a huge smile.

"Good." Jagger laughed, pulling Paisley in for a kiss.

"Because there's more."

Ember's eyes widened and flicked from me, to the wineglass, and back to Paisley. "No way. She's pregnant," she whispered in my ear.

"We're having a baby!" Jagger said, happier than I'd ever seen him.

Holy. Shit. A baby. A tiny Bateman.

The girls all screamed at a shrill pitch, abandoning their seats to envelop Paisley in a huge hug and an unintelligible feminine barrage of questions and coos started.

Jagger made his way around the gaggle of ecstatic girls and took the seat Morgan had vacated. I leaned over and pulled him in, hugging him with a slap on the back. "Congratulations, man."

"Thanks. Some week, right?" He shook his head, his eyes wide with the kind of disbelief he'd had when we'd told him Carter had given up his Apache for him. "I don't know how I got this lucky."

"You deserve every piece of this, brother." I meant every word and made sure he knew it. No one was more deserving of happiness than Jagger. Well, maybe Grayson. I raised my beer. "To family."

"To family." One by one Grayson and Will joined, celebrating.

I swallowed the beer and the tiny stab of envy I couldn't quite keep at bay. Fuck, I wanted that—December with a ring on her left hand and my last name. I wanted to watch her lithe body change with our baby, and hold that tiny, perfect combination of us both. I was done being her boyfriend. I wanted to be her forever.

"How is her heart?" Will asked. As awkward as it could have been, Jagger and Will had made their peace in the last year, turning a bitter rivalry into a close friendship for the sake of Paisley.

"The timing isn't ideal," Jagger admitted, locking his eyes

on his wife. *Holy shit, his wife.* "But she's strong, and her heart isn't giving her any trouble. They'll monitor her more frequently, but the doc isn't too worried."

Will visibly relaxed. "Congratulations, man. Any fool can see how happy you make each other."

"Thanks. I'm sorry it was so fast, but we were there, and I wasn't exactly going to leave her a pregnant fiancée for this deployment. God knows I was just looking for the excuse to marry her. Now she's as protected as I can make her. Make them, I guess." He sighed, nearly splitting his face with a smile. "A baby!"

"God, I hope it's a girl," Grayson said. "I'd love to watch you lose your mind in about nineteen years."

Jagger's eyes widened to a nearly impossible size, and we all burst into laughter. "Don't worry," I said, punching his shoulder. "I'm sure she'll find a guy just like you."

"Fuck my life," Jagger muttered, chugging his beer.

We only laughed harder.

Hours later, the temperature dipped, and everyone started to move inside. I waited until we were the last ones, and then pulled Ember into my arms next to the dying fire.

"How wonderful for Jagger and Paisley," she said, yawning.

"I'm happy for them," I answered. Jagger was right. The marriage protected Paisley in a way that Ember was still vulnerable. She had no legal access to me while I was gone, and she'd aged out of her dependent ID card. She couldn't even get on base without going through the hassle of getting a pass.

She wiggled deeper into my lap, distracting me as she curled so her head lay on my shoulder. I pulled the blanket over us and then kissed the top of her head. "I love you," I said into her hair.

She sat up with a smile and turned, hooking her knee over my lap, straddling me. "Then it's a good thing that I love you, too." She kissed me, opening instantly to leave no doubt in my mind where her thoughts were headed. Her skirt rode up her thighs until there were only my jeans and her panties between us.

Hell. Yes.

One of my hands burrowed through her mass of fire-lit auburn curls to the nape of her neck as the other drifted down her spine until I held her perfect ass. Then I claimed her mouth, sinking into her with deep, swirling strokes of my tongue.

She moaned and slid her fingers under my beanie and into my hair. That one sound was all it took and I was hard, ready to take her in our backyard. I might not have cared if our neighbors could see, but Ember would have, so I tucked the ends of the blanket behind my back, shielding her from anyone who might be looking out their windows at two a.m.

"Josh," she whispered against my lips as my hand skimmed the soft skin of her inner thigh. Her hips rolled over mine, and a wave of lust slammed through me, quickening my pulse. "Touch me."

My fingers dipped under her lace panties, and my dick started throbbing at how wet she was. "Fuck," I muttered, sliding my fingers over her swollen clit. "You want me."

"Always," she gasped, resting her forehead against mine as I rubbed her just where she liked it. Her breath came in short spurts, and I teased her entrance, wishing I could slip into her right here. Hell, a simple zip and I'd— *No, we do not fuck our future wife where people might see her.* Besides, that sound, yes, that one, where her breath caught and stuttered? That was for my ears only. I needed to get her inside so I could get inside *her.*

Her nails raked lightly down my chest, and she raised my shirt to trace the lines of my abs, pausing in the places that had my breath catching this time. But when she reached for my zipper, I stopped her. "Not here," I whispered against her lips.

"No one can see," she urged, rocking her hips against my hand so that my fingers slipped into her with a shallow thrust. "God, Josh. Mmmm. I've been thinking about this all night."

I pressed lightly on her clit with my thumb, unable to keep still while she was moving on my hand like a fucking sex goddess. "All night?" I asked, stroking her inner walls with another measured thrust.

"Mmmm," she moaned, biting my lip softly. "Every night, really."

I circled her with the same movement of my fingers, feeding off every single gasp, the slightest movement of her hips. "Always?"

"There's never a minute that I don't want you inside me, crave your hands on my body, Josh. That's never going to change." Her hand worked its way under my jeans, the angle making it awkward for her to get ahold of me, thank God. The minute this woman touched me, I had all the self-control of a damn high schooler.

Hell, even back then I'd known she was too good for me, but I was going to spend my life proving I was exactly what she needed now. And the timing...well, it sucked, but this could protect her if something happened to me. "Want to gamble on that always?"

Her eyes flew open, locking onto mine, and her hips froze. "What?"

Fuck, the box was still upstairs, and she deserved better than this, but I couldn't keep it in any longer, and the alcohol wasn't helping. "We could make it forever. You and me."

Eyes wide, she leaned back, her hand slipping out of my pants. "What are you saying?"

Shit, just spit it out. "I'm leaving in ten days. I want you to be taken care of, to have the security of my last name, to know you have access to everything while I'm gone."

"Josh?" Her eyes narrowed and not in a good way.

You are fucking this all up—get to the point!

"We could get married!" It flew out of my mouth. Gone was the pretty speech I'd been practicing for the last month, waiting for the perfect, not-too-over-the-top moment. I'd somehow developed verbal stomach flu. "You know, elope, like Jagger and Paisley. Just you and me. Forever."

"Because you're deploying in ten days."

"The timing is shit, I know that. God, I wish it was different and we had all the time in the world. But this would protect you, give you access to my benefits."

"Unbelievable." She pushed off my lap and tugged her skirt down her thighs. "Un-fucking-believable!"

Mayday. Mayday, you're going down, buddy. I leaned forward, reaching for her, but she sidestepped. "December..." I shook my head, wishing I'd had about three fewer beers. "I thought you'd be happy." This was not how I pictured this moment going.

"This...this is a proposal?" If it were anger I saw in her eyes, I could have held my shit together. I could have fired back. But the hurt? Fuck, I was defenseless.

My mouth opened and shut a few times. I couldn't figure out what the hell to say that wasn't going to dig me a deeper hole than the one I was already in. *Fuck. Fuck. Fuck.*

"Because I didn't hear a question, Josh. I heard a business proposal." A single tear slipped down her cheek, crushing my heart in a way her words never could have.

"December..." I stood, but she backed farther away.

"No. My answer is no."

Fuck, I was wrong. One word decimated me.

CHAPTER FIVE

Ember

I swatted the tear away angrily. How did this even qualify as a proposal? I'd fantasized about this exact moment since I was a freshman in high school drawing doodles with his name.

This was more like a nightmare.

"You don't want to marry me?" he whispered.

"What? All I have ever wanted is to marry you, to be your always, to wake up knowing that I'm yours and you're mine." How could he even think that?

He tucked his thumbs in his pockets and rolled his shoulders. "That's what I thought this was about. You and me, forever."

"Really? Because you just proposed like I'm some tag-chaser you picked up in a random bar, and you're offering me free health care so you can make more money on a deployment, and we'd better hurry up and sign those papers before you ship out."

His head snapped back like I'd slapped him. "I guess I didn't think you wanted some over-the-top proposal. Isn't that what you always alluded to? I have the ring upstairs, I can get it—"

"I don't want a fucking ring!" My voice broke. "I just want your heart."

"God, baby. You have it. I love you more than my own life." His eyes squeezed shut. "I probably should have led with that."

"The whole love thing might have helped," I bit out. "Or even something as trite as 'will you marry me?' may have sufficed."

"Then let me start over," he begged, meeting my eyes. "There is nothing more important to me than you, December."

"No." I shook my head. "Not now. Not ten days before you deploy, and not *because* you're deploying."

"I just want to—"

"Protect me?" I finished for him when he couldn't.

"Yeah."

"Josh, if something happens to you, a wedding ring isn't going to save my sanity or salvage my heart. The army has dictated everything about my life since I was born. Where I lived, when I moved, when I lost my friends...when I lost my father. I'll be damned if I give it a say in when I become your wife. Only we get that say." I pulled the blanket around my shoulders, trying to ward off the chill I knew had nothing to do with the temperature and everything to do with the loss of Josh's warmth.

"I don't want to wait another year. I want you to be my wife, and I thought..." He laced his fingers and rested them on the top of his head. "I don't care how I marry you, December. In a huge, crowded church, on a deserted beach, in the fucking janitor closet of city hall. I don't care as long as it makes you my wife, and I guess I thought you felt the same way."

"How I feel? I want you to *want* to marry me. I want you to marry me because I'm the only possible future for you, because I'm the one you can't live without, and not because you think you *have* to. Not because Jagger and Paisley did it."

"Look how happy they are!"

"Happy? For fuck's sake! Did you even ask when their baby is due?"

He blinked. "No."

"October ninth."

He paused midshrug, finally clicking with what I was trying

to tell him. "Yeah. You guys will most likely still be gone. She will go through this entire pregnancy, and probably the birth, on her own. Jagger is about to miss out on almost all of their first year of marriage and watching over Paisley's pregnancy. Do you think that makes him happy? Is that what you want? For our first year of marriage to happen over Skype calls, wondering if we'll ever make it to a first anniversary? Because that's why you're doing this, right? To protect me if you don't come back?"

The muscles in his jaw flexed. "That's not fair."

"No. None of this is." We stood in silence, staring at each other across this giant sinkhole in our relationship.

"I think you're a pompous asshole who wouldn't know love if it was delivered naked to you on a fucking platter!" Morgan's voice carried from the field behind us.

Guess we're not the only ones awake and arguing.

"One, I'm well aware of what love is, and two, what the hell do you expect from me, Morgan? I'm leaving!" Will shouted as Morgan arrived at the nearly dead fire.

"Oh look, a functioning military couple," Morgan said, waving to Josh and me.

"Don't bet on it," I answered.

Josh tilted his head and shot me a look that said he didn't appreciate the comment.

Too fucking bad. He'd just treated one of the most important moments of our life like it was another item to be checked off his pre-deployment checklist.

"Weigh in for me," Morgan drawled, crossing her arms as Will caught up to her.

"Morgan," he warned.

"Oh, come on, Will. My feelings for you are the worst-kept secret since Paisley's for Jagger. I think we can all be honest here."

Josh edged away. "Not sure this is our place."

"Oh, no you don't, Walker." Morgan stared him down. "Tell me, if you had feelings for someone, wouldn't you want to be with them? Even if they only had a couple months before they deployed?"

"Actually—" Josh started.

"Damn it, Morgan! I'll be gone nine months. You want to start a relationship like that?" Apparently Will's drawl was a bit more pronounced when he got mad.

Fascinating.

"It's not like this is World War Two, Will! We can Skype, and write letters, and talk on the phone. Do you think I won't wait for you? Is that it?" Morgan fired back.

Holy shit. Josh couldn't have thought that...or could he?

"Is that the real reason?" I asked Josh, not caring that we'd just turned this into a melee. "Are you scared I won't wait for you? That I don't love you enough, so a ring will keep me around?"

Josh rubbed his hands over his face. "We are not doing this right now."

"Wouldn't you want whatever time you could get?" Morgan yelled at Will.

Enough.

"You know what?" I said, turning toward Morgan and away from Josh. "I'm with Will. If you have feelings for him, then talk during the deployment, be there for him, show him the woman you've grown to be. Don't jump into a relationship because you think you're on some ridiculous timeline."

Her eyebrows shot to the sky.

"Yeah, I think I'm going to head home for the night," Will drawled.

"You should take Josh with you," I called over my shoulder as I stomped into our house, shutting the door with enough force to declare me a tantrum-throwing toddler. My clothes hit the hamper while I muttered to myself about ignorant men.

The bed was cold as I crawled under the covers. *Get used to it. He'll be gone in ten days.*

It hit me. Ten days. We had milk that expired later than that, and it was all I had guaranteed with him. Anything could happen after that. Ten days, and I'd just thrown his proposal in his face and declared it not good enough.

"You're such a bitch," I cried to myself as the tears started to flow. Why couldn't anything be simple? Why couldn't we get engaged and then marry in a year after bickering over wedding details? Why couldn't we have just a tiny piece of normal?

Did it really matter if I said, "I do," in front of a hundred other people? Did it matter if it was now or in a year from now? I wasn't going to somehow stop loving him. He was woven into my soul so deeply that if someone were to pull a single thread of him away, I would unravel.

The door opened softly, light throwing my shadow onto the far wall. Josh was nearly silent as he stripped down for bed, but I couldn't bring myself to move. How could I have done that to him? Sure, his logic was flawed, but wanting to marry me? That wasn't only timing forcing the issue. It couldn't have been.

The bed sank under his weight as he took his spot, the one closest to the door. We laid there in silence, the argument between us so raw that even the softest touch in the wrong way could set us both to bleeding.

But I had to make this right. I turned over and burrowed into his chest, startling him for the barest of seconds before his strong arms closed around me. I pressed a kiss to the fire and ice tattoo above his heart. "I'm so sorry," I said softly into his skin. "Josh, I'm just so sorry."

"Shh," he whispered, kissing the top of my head. "There's nothing to be sorry for. I fucked up something that was supposed to be un-fuck-up-able."

I tilted my head until I caught the moonlight reflected in his eyes. "I was wrong, Josh. It doesn't matter what the timing is. You and I are a foregone conclusion. You're it for me, and I don't need a ring on my finger to remind me of that. But I do want to marry you, I promise. There's nothing I want more in this world than to be your wife." I took a stuttering breath. "Ask me again."

He raised his hand and stroked my cheek with his thumb, an eternity of love pouring from his eyes. "No."

I tried—and failed—not to let that hurt. "Okay."

He pressed his lips to mine in a sweet kiss and traced my bottom lip with the tip of his tongue. "December Howard. You deserve everything I can give you. My body, my heart, my name. They're already yours, we're just missing some paperwork. But you're right. I don't want this deployment to change anything about us, and if I weren't leaving in ten days, we wouldn't even be considering eloping. We'd probably have some huge mountaintop wedding, right?"

I couldn't contain the smile that spread across my face. "We could ride the chairlifts up. And imagine the pictures!"

He laughed, pressing another kiss to my lips but pulling back before I could lean in for more. "I won't let this deployment steal that away from us, too, so I'm not asking you now."

I pushed away the thought that I'd ruined any chance of him asking again, and trusted in him. "But you will ask again."

"On our terms, and no one else's."

I nodded. "You and me against the world," I whispered.

"Always," he finished with a kiss.

"You sure you don't mind snagging notes for me?" I asked Luke before sipping my latte.

"You sure you don't have an Ephesus application to hand me? There is a deadline, even for a shoo-in like you."

"I'm not a shoo-in, and I still haven't decided if I'm going."

He rolled his eyes. "Sure you have. You can't turn this down. You won't. You're not deciding, you're rationalizing it between your head and your heart. But think of it this way—if you go on the dig, you'd actually be physically closer to Flyboy than you are here in Nashville."

"I guess I'd never thought of it that way."

"And as for the notes, what else am I good for as a TA in Senior Seminar?" He shoulder-bumped me as we carried our takeout coffees back to the classroom.

"I know I'll miss class the day he leaves, but I'm not going to mope for longer than twenty-four hours," I said, mostly to promise myself. "Then I'll be back here to kick ass."

"So one more weekend, huh?" He shot me the look...the one that dripped with so much sympathy that it triggered my stop-pitying-me reflex.

"Yep. And I'm going to make it perfect for him."

"Why don't you guys get away? I bet my dad wouldn't mind covering a suite for you guys near the beach somewhere. Atlantic City, maybe?"

"That's so nice of you to offer, Luke, but even all your dad's money can't get the army to cooperate. He has to be able to report within four hours, so that's too far."

"Hmmm." He opened the door for me and we walked inside, taking the stairs toward the room. "Wait. Flyboy was hockey boy first, right?"

"Most definitely," I answered, my stomach immediately fluttering at the thought of watching him play again. God, the way he moved on the ice never failed to turn me on to the point I was ready to rip off that sweaty uniform right there on the ice. And the way he handled that stick with his hands...

"Earth to Ember," Luke sang.

"Oh, sorry." I shook my head.

"Okay, well, if you're done mentally fucking your boyfriend, I think I might have an idea. Remember that little expansion team my dad owns?"

I paused mid step, making Luke back up to fetch me. "I'd hardly call the Louisville Bobcats little. They're an NHL team."

"Yeah, well, I guess he got bored with hotels. Anyway, how about we get you guys phenomenal seats to the Sunday game, and then follow up with a suite at 21C? A little sports for him, a little pampering for you, some hotel sexy-times... What's not to love about that send-off?"

The gears in my mind raced. "He owns the Bobcats."

"I think I just said that. Really, Red, you've never cared about the money before, and this little thing does it for you?" He arched an eyebrow.

"No, it's not the team...it's the ice."

A slow, scheming smile spread across his face. "Oh, I like where you're going with this."

"Yeah," I said with a grin. "Me, too!"

Josh's last weekend stateside was going to be perfect.

CHAPTER SIX

JOSH

Three fucking days.

I tried not to think about it as we drove toward Louisville, but that was like ignoring the countdown on a nuclear bomb. Not going to happen. No matter what I did, the thought was there, tainting everything around me. Even Ember's coffee creamer was a reminder that she'd be drinking it in an empty house in just seventy-two hours.

Because I'd be back in Hell. It would be different this time, right? I'd be medevacing the wounded, saving lives instead of taking them. The rescuer instead of the rescued. I'd be paying back what I owed to the crew that landed under fire to get my sorry ass.

So if everything would be different, why had the nightmares started up again? For the first year or so, they'd been hellish, but I hadn't had them since Ember and I got together senior year in college. Now they were coming damn near every night. I'd never been so thankful that she could sleep through a hurricane.

She didn't need this on her plate, too.

It sure as hell didn't help that we'd had hardly any time together. Getting me progressed for flying in time meant flying odd hours and staying even longer ones at work prepping to leave. When I had managed to be home, she'd been at school.

"So where exactly are we going?" I asked her as we got

closer to the city, threading through the traffic. Her feet were up on the dashboard of my Jeep, newly painted toes wiggling. It wasn't my old Wrangler, but she looked just as good in the front seat of the four-door model as she had in my first one.

"Ummm…" she mumbled, flipping through screens on her cell phone like she did when she needed to distract herself from the speed I was driving.

"You could just put the address in the GPS, babe." Besides, curiosity was killing me. I'd been instructed to pack for an overnight, and that was the only information I'd gotten until she pointed me toward Louisville and said, "Drive."

"What's the fun in that?" she asked. "Okay, in three miles you'll get off."

The corners of my mouth lifted. "Will I?"

She smacked my shoulder. "Seriously."

I caught her hand and brought it to my lips, pressing a kiss against the soft skin. "But, honey, don't you want to give me a good send-off?" I glanced over with fake puppy-dog eyes. "I'm going to war, you know."

A laugh tumbled past her lips. "Did that really work for you the first time?"

My smile slipped. "I didn't leave a woman behind last time."

She stroked the back of my neck. "You didn't have one to come home to, either. This isn't like the last time," she finished quietly.

"I'm not planning on leaving any pieces behind this trip," I tried to joke. It fell flat, and I regretted the words as soon as I saw her turn to stare out the window. "Hey," I said to get her attention. She looked back at me, her eyes holding a depth of sadness I couldn't tease my way out of. "It's going to be okay."

She didn't bother to fake a smile. "This is our exit."

I followed her directions until we pulled into a posh hotel in Downtown Louisville. "Nice choice," I said with an appreciative nod once we hit the art museum-style foyer.

She smiled like a little kid at Christmas. "Wait until you see what else I have planned."

She signed us in while I waited by our bags, checking out the artwork. Hell, she'd barely let me get the luggage when we parked, even insisting on unloading the car herself. She was so hell-bent on making this weekend perfect, and it was adorable, but she had to realize that we could have spent the time marathoning Netflix on the couch and it would have been just as perfect.

I only needed her.

"Let's go!" She waved the room keys, and I followed her lead, taking the elevator up and up until we reached the penthouse.

The doors opened into the kind of hotel room seen in movies, the kind where black-tie parties were the norm, and butter-bar lieutenants didn't belong. "This is amazing," I said, already having mentally kissed half of this paycheck good-bye on what it would cost us. *Entirely worth it.*

She looked into the separate bedroom, and then checked out the view from the window while I checked her out. The afternoon sunlight made her hair a brighter red, the locks heavy where they hung down her back.

I came up behind her slowly, memorizing everything about her, as if the thousands of memories I already had wouldn't be enough. She tilted her head, and I took advantage, sweeping the soft strands away from the delicate arch of her neck. She leaned further, giving me better access, and I set my lips to her skin.

Heaven. She tasted like heaven, and home, and just... December. Her breath caught as I lightly sucked the small patch of skin just under her jaw. That sound was my undoing, like always, and I pulled her back against me. All weekend in this hotel room had never looked so good. No friends. No distractions. Just us.

She moaned when I set my teeth lightly to the junction of

her neck and shoulder, and my body immediately responded.

"You have to stop that," she whispered, her hands digging into the front of my thighs.

"Why?" I asked, running my tongue along the shell of her ear.

"Because it's almost two o'clock and we have plans." Her voice said she regretted making them.

"What if my plans only involve you naked against this window?" I asked, spinning her in my arms.

Her eyes dropped to my lips, and hers parted. *Gotcha.* I wrapped my arm around her lower back and stepped forward, putting her back against the glass. "Josh," she whispered, more a plea than anything.

"December," I answered, loving the feel of her name on my lips. Then I kissed her. She opened for me, and our mouths fused together, a perfect melding of tongues and teeth. I used the hand not pinned between her and the window to tangle through her hair and tilt her head so I could get a better angle.

The only con about driving Ember wild was that she took me along for the ride. It was impossible to kiss her without losing myself in the process, giving myself over to every arch of her back, every gasp from her lips.

"Ugh!" She ripped her mouth from mine. "As much as I would like nothing more than to climb you like a tree, we have to go, or we'll be late."

"I don't care. There's nothing outside this room that could possibly interest me more than getting you out of your clothes." It had been days since I'd been able to get my hands on her, and I was about to spontaneously combust if I didn't remedy that.

"That's only because you don't know what we're doing." Her eyebrow arched, and she had that look—the one that said she was getting her way and there was nothing I could do about it.

I took a steadying breath and begged my dick to soften. She'd gone to a hell of a lot of trouble to plan this weekend, so

I'd have to keep my horny self in check for a few more hours. "I do get you naked at some point today, right?" I asked.

"Oh, most definitely," she promised, and that little sweep of her tongue across her lips almost broke me *and* her damn plans.

I high-fived myself for self-control and stepped away from her. "Then lead the way."

The smile she gifted me with was well worth it.

Ten minutes later, we parked in front of Louisville Arena. I killed the ignition and took note of the nearly empty parking lot. What the hell were we doing?

"We're here?" I said in a light tone that I hoped didn't show my confusion.

"Yep!" she said with a giddy smile. "You ready for some hockey?"

Hopefully she didn't think today was Sunday, because... well, God, I didn't want her feelings hurt. "Babe, you know it's Saturday, right?"

"Yes."

"And you know the Bobcats aren't playing today, right?" I internally cringed, waiting for her to realize we were a day off.

"I know," she said with a slow nod. "They play the Rangers tomorrow. I was honestly hoping for the Avs, but Colorado's not on the schedule until next month..."

"And I'll be gone," I finished for her.

"You'll be gone," she agreed with a watery smile before opening the door and jumping down from the Jeep. I met her at the back, where she was opening the hatch. "Besides"—she heaved my giant bag of gear to the ground—"I never said you were here to watch."

What? "I don't understand."

She surged up on her toes, meeting my mouth in a sweet kiss. "You don't have to. You just have to take your gear inside, and don't forget your stick!"

She headed toward the arena, waving me on as she walked

away. More than a little baffled, I searched the back of the Jeep for my stick, then slipped it into the side straps of my rolling bag. Did she realize that there wasn't exactly an open skate time here? Regardless, I followed her into the arena, hauling my bag behind me.

I crossed the threshold and found her talking to a security guard in low tones. He glanced over her shoulder, furrowing his giant silver eyebrows, and nodded.

"Lieutenant Walker," he said, putting out his hand. "Thank you for your service."

I shook it. "Thank you very much." My eyes flickered between his smile and Ember's Christmas-morning face. God, she was lit up like the tree, except she'd always been my present.

"I'm Earl Singer," the guard said. "If you'll follow me?" He turned and walked off, radioing something in his hand-held.

"You ready?" she asked.

"For what?"

She tugged her lower lip between her teeth with a grin and shrugged, then turned around and walked down the promenade, following the guard. *Where you lead, I follow.*

Down the hallway, a flight of steps, and more than a few twists later, I found myself entering the arena from the ice level. The temperature drop brought me home to the smell of the ice, the feel of the stick in my hands, the quiet roar of adrenaline through my body. As much as I loved flying, the ice would always be my first love.

The glass came into view, and the familiar noise of a practice filled my ears. *Holy shit.* The Louisville Bobcats were on the ice, practicing. "They don't usually practice here," I said to Ember as the guard opened the door in the glass behind the net.

"No, but today isn't usual," she said with a hundred mega-watt smile.

My brain shut down, unable to handle even the possibility

that I was about to get anywhere near that ice, those players. "I don't understand."

"Luke, my friend from school?"

My eyes narrowed. "The guy you grab coffee with?" *The excessively smart one pushing you toward the dig, which makes me like and hate him all in the same breath.*

"Yeah. His dad owns the Bobcats."

I blinked. *Seriously?*

"Ooh, they're calling us." She tugged my hand, and I left my gear outside the glass as I stepped onto the ice.

"Hey," Chase Miles, the Bobcats' captain, skated over to us, taking off his glove. "You must be Lieutenant Walker."

"Just Josh," I answered as I shook his hand. *Don't say anything weird.*

"Well, Josh, we hear you're shipping out in a few days and thought you might want to jump in on a little pick-up game we have going."

No. Fucking. Way. I found myself speechless for the first time since…ever, and gawked up at him.

"Is that a yes?" he asked.

I nodded, almost afraid to blink. Hell yes, it was a yes. Playing in the NHL had been my dream since the first time Mom laced my skates. All those early morning practices, long weekend tournaments, bills that piled up because she wanted me to have the newest helmet.

"Great. Singer will take you back to the locker room. We have a little something for you. See you in a few." He nodded and skated back to the other players who had all gathered here to play…with me.

"You did this?" I asked Ember as Singer closed the boards.

"Luke helped," she answered, that smile still bright enough to compete with the ice.

"And they all agreed?" My eyes darted back to where at least a dozen players waited, goalies included.

"I only asked for a few, but when the rest heard it was for a soldier, they jumped at the chance to come play," she finished. "Do you like it?"

My heart was ready to burst. She'd done this, pulled some magical string to hand me a chance to live out my dream. My throat closed, and words, if I'd had any, were impossible. Instead, I took her in my arms, one hand weaving through her hair and the other lifting her against me. My eyes skimmed her perfect features, from the porcelain texture of her skin to the deep blue of her eyes. "I love you," I whispered just before I kissed the hell out of her.

She broke away after a minute, her breath uneven, and put two fingers against my aching lips. "Go get dressed. I can't wait to watch you out there."

My gaze swung to where they skated, and I couldn't ever remember being happier. "Okay." One more swift kiss, and I met Singer where he waited at the door.

"Quite a girl you have there," he said with a grin as he led me to the locker room.

"She's everything."

He took me to a locker on the end that had been labeled "Walker." Inside was a Bobcat jersey with my name. I was torn between lingering in this moment, taking my time with every piece of gear, and ripping the pads from my bag so I could get out there quickly. The second impulse won out, but I snapped a few pictures of the locker.

I'd unzipped the pocket of my bag and reached in to take out my tape when my fingers brushed against the soft texture of the small box I'd hidden there a month ago, knowing it was the one place Ember wouldn't accidentally stumble onto it. Giving in to my number one dream, I hid it with a smile and took off for the ice, so excited I barely remembered to remove my skate covers.

The hallway opened to the players' bench, and the lights

from the arena shone down, making me feel small and godlike all in one breath.

"Please welcome to the ice, from the University of Colorado, number thirteen, Josh Walker!" The announcement through the PA system rocked me in a way I wasn't prepared for, emotions hitting me as hard as the players slapping my back as I skated onto the ice.

Just before the puck dropped, I looked over to where I knew Ember would be cheering me on from behind the glass. One glimpse of that smile and I was fueled for the entire game. We'd come full circle—me on the ice, showing off for the red-headed girl in the stands, knowing that for just this amount of time, I had her attention, her focus.

The game was fast-paced, even though I knew they'd slowed it down for me. Hell, I wasn't in any shape to be playing against my college team, let alone NHL players, but damn if I wasn't going to give it everything I had. I skated until my legs felt like rubber and my breath came in harsh pants.

We played for over an hour, culminating in the one shot I managed to slip past the goalie. Ember cheered from the stands, and right then everything I'd dreamed about for my life came together in a moment of absolute perfection.

The players smacked my back as they left the ice. I thanked them one by one, and they all acted like I had done them a favor by showing up. Chase shook my hand last.

"Stay safe over there, and we'll do this again when you come back." He looked over his shoulder at Ember. "The ice is empty for an hour or so if you want to spend a few minutes."

"Thank you for everything. This has been a dream come true."

"It's been our pleasure." He nodded once and took off for the locker room.

I opened the door to the player's box as Ember approached with a bag thrown over her shoulder. She stepped inside and swung the bag down. "Huh," she said, sniffing. "It doesn't smell nearly as bad in here as I'd always assumed."

I laughed. "Skates?"

She nodded, unzipping the black bag and taking out her CCMs. "Luke told me I could sneak out there after you were done so I didn't make an ass out of myself in front of those players."

"Please, you'd hardly make an ass out of yourself," I countered as she tied up her skates, pulling them extra tight.

I ditched my helmet and gloves and picked up something entirely more precious. Holding out my hand to December, I opened the door to the ice, and we skated on. "This is amazing!" she said, laughing as she took in the enormity of the arena.

As she spun around to face me, stopping with a precision she hadn't had a couple of years ago, it hit me—right here, under these lights that played with the colors in her hair—this was exactly what I'd been waiting for, the best moment of my life.

It was about to get even better.

CHAPTER SEVEN

EMBER

The ice was a little bumpy under my skates, but that was to be expected after a dozen NHL players had dug it up for the last hour or so. Man, I owed Luke big-time. But the look on Josh's face when he'd realized why we were here, the utter radiance that shined from him as he skated onto the ice when they called his name...they were worth every single second of coordination this week.

Pulling it off had been a miracle, and I couldn't have been more grateful to give him this. After all, he'd already given me so much.

He skated toward me, and I paused, blown away with everything that was Josh. His hair was sweaty, water dripping down his flushed cheeks from dumping his bottle over his head. It was high school and college all jumbled together to make this magnificent man in front of me. I'd never loved him more.

"I've gotten a little better since that first date, huh?" I asked with a flirtatious smile, skating backward just because I could.

"You've always been perfect." That grin was enough to melt me despite the temperature of the ice.

"Did you have fun?"

"Yes. I can't believe you did that for me." His eyes were warm, letting his love for me shine.

"It's your dream."

He shook his head and took my hands in his much warmer ones. "No. It used to be my dream. And as hard as I worked for it, and as difficult as it was to let go when I got wounded, I can't thank you enough for what you did for me. This"—he glanced at the empty seats and bright lights—"has been more than I could have ever imagined."

"I'm glad. You deserve it."

"The jersey, the game, hearing my name, it was amazing. But what made it perfect was seeing you against the glass like we were in high school again. Remembering every time I told myself not to get close to someone as good as you are. Thinking back to that day in college when I told you I was going to chase you. Feeling the warmth of your hand over mine seeping through the glass during the championship. Recalling every time I wanted to kiss you, hold you, tell you how much I love you. I have that now, and you, December, are what made this perfect, because you are all that matters to me now."

My heart caught in my throat, but as I leaned up to kiss him, he sank down—skates and all—onto one knee. My pulse ceased, and then pounded through my veins, tears already stinging my eyes as he held up a ring. "Josh," I whispered.

"You are my dream now, December Howard. You are everything to me. My heart beats for you, my soul is only whole when you're near. You're my home, my shelter, my wildest fantasy, and I cannot imagine a future where you're not mine, because I'm yours in every sense of the word."

He paused, and we both hung suspended in that moment, where it didn't matter that we were at center ice, or that he was deploying in three short days. The entire world stopped, ceased rotating because our love demanded it, and we were the only ones who could command it to start again.

"I love you, December. And I know we said we wouldn't do this because of the deployment, so I'm asking you to do it in spite of it. I'm asking you to *not* marry me right now. Not rush it, not jump because we're scared of what this next year might bring. I'm asking you now because a love like ours transcends any war, any event, any measure of time. The way I feel about you right now, that's never going to fade. It's only going to grow stronger, and I can't wait to feel how much I love you in ten, twenty, fifty years. So please do me the honor of becoming my wife, because you are the gravity in my world, and while I might be the pilot now, I'll do everything in my power to make sure it's your dreams that fly. Will you marry me?"

"Yes," my heart cried out, echoing through the arena. "Yes, Josh, yes." The ring blurred in my vision as tears welled in my eyes, and he had it firmly on my left hand before I could blink them away.

"Thank you, God," he said, his head thrown back in absolute relief. Then he surged to his feet, took my face between his hands, and brought his mouth to mine.

The kiss was perfect, a promise of love that would never wane between us. It was the realization of the dream we'd both fought for, from the moments I'd watched him in high school, through the stolen glances in college, the touches, the way we sent each other up in flames at the first rush of desire.

Then he changed pace, consuming my mouth with the plunge of his tongue, each stroke setting a fire between us. His pads dug into my breasts as he pulled me closer. I relaxed as he lifted me gently, trusting his balance on skates. My fingers dusted over the sweat-soaked strands of his hair, and I didn't mind. Hell, I wouldn't have had it any other way, not when we were right where it all started.

"We'd better get out of here before we melt the ice," I whispered against his lips.

Josh laughed, twirling me so quickly my head spun. No matter what the next year brought, we had this perfect moment to fall back on.

I was going to spend the rest of my life loving Josh Walker, because despite every obstacle that had been thrown in our path, we were making it. I was going to be his wife.

"Turn left here," I mumbled, looking down at the map on my cell phone, more than a little distracted by the way the diamond on my hand reflected the sunlight from the window. *Engaged!* "That should get us to—" I looked up when Josh turned right. "Uhh, babe? Left."

"The hotel is right."

"Indeed it is, but there's a really cute café I thought you might like for dinner."

"I have other plans," he said, his entire focus on the road as he passed the car in front of us.

"Which include?" I asked as he slid between two cars to turn right into our hotel parking lot.

"Room service." He put the Jeep into park and reached for my seat belt in one smooth motion as he unclicked his own. Josh was kissing me before the belt had time to zip back into the door. His mouth demanded my immediate surrender, and I more than gladly gave it as he pulled me toward him.

My fingers bunched the soft material of his shirt as sparks of desire flared, igniting the fire that had been banked while leaving the rink. His grip on my waist tightened as he deepened the kiss, and I leaned across the console, thankful that it kept me from straddling him in the front seat.

I slid my hands under his beanie to feel the gentle scrape of his newly cut hair against my palms as our mouths melded. He groaned when I rubbed my tongue along his, and the sound cued my already fired-up sex drive that it was go-for-launch. His hand slipped under my shirt, stroking the skin along my rib cage until he palmed one of my breasts with a gentle squeeze.

Then I was the one groaning.

His breath caught, and he ripped his mouth from mine. "Upstairs. Now."

I scrambled out of the Jeep, and he met me in front, grasping my hand. He intertwined our fingers, and even the small motions of his thumb against my palm sent pulses of want from my fingers to my stomach.

Josh's face was tight as we walked through the lobby to the elevator. He jabbed the call button and then stared straight ahead at the doors. The only sign I had that he still knew I was here was the constant movement of that thumb against my skin, caressing me with small circles.

With a ding, the elevator doors opened, and we backed up to let the occupants out. Then we walked in, and the doors shut behind us after Josh pushed the button to our floor. He turned, pressing me into the corner of the elevator, the look in his eyes hot enough to take my breath in a rush. His mouth met mine, open and needy, and I forgot that there were probably security cameras, and guards watching them, or hell, that there was even a world outside this elevator.

I had Josh against me from breast to thigh, setting fire to each of my nerve endings as his hands moved to my rear and lifted me into him—what more could exist? *Holy. Shit.* He was hard against me. One of my legs lifted around his waist, and he pressed his hips against mine, rocking subtly against the inseam of my jeans.

The doors dinged behind us. Josh dropped my leg and broke our kiss. I sucked air into my lungs and stepped to the side as a couple of middle-aged women entered, then moved in front of Josh to shield him from their cursory gazes. Their arched eyebrows and quickly shared glance said they clearly knew what we'd been doing.

"We're engaged," Josh said in an all-too-happy voice.

I slowly looked at him, my mouth dropped slightly. We got caught making out in an elevator, and his response was to tell them our marital status?

"Congratulations," one of the ladies said, stifling a laugh before they both turned around and began discussing their plans for the evening.

Yeah, this wasn't mortifying. Not in the least.

They chose their floor and the elevator started to carry us up. Undeterred by our company, Josh took hold of my hips and pulled me back against him, then set his lips to the side of my neck in a soundless, openmouthed kiss. I barely held in a moan when he scraped his teeth over my skin, licking away the sting.

The ladies stood ahead of us, lost in conversation, as his mouth moved up to my ear, only to run his tongue along the shell. "I can't wait to get you naked," he whispered so quietly I barely heard him. A shiver ran down my spine. "Then I'm going to lick a path from your neck to your breasts, down to your stomach, until I reach that perfect, pink—"

The elevator dinged and the women stepped out, the doors closing behind them.

I turned into Josh's kiss, biting his lower lip gently. "You're killing me."

He slowly shook his head. "Not yet."

We reached our floor and stumbled toward our room, kissing our way down the hallway. Josh pinned me against the door while he fumbled with our room key, and I took the opportunity to set my mouth to his neck, breathing in his freshly showered scent and a hint of sandalwood. He cursed at the lock as I ran my hands under his shirt, my fingers playing along the lines of his washboard abs, exploring the ridges as if I didn't know them by heart.

Josh wound his arm around my back so I didn't fall when the door opened, then lifted me off the ground to carry me through. I turned all of my attention to his mouth, his incredibly soft lips and wicked tongue, kissing him as the door shut behind us. We moved through the suite until we reached the bedroom.

The sunset lit the room with a perfect glow as he lowered me to sit on the bed. I immediately raised his shirt and licked the incredibly sexy fuck-me lines that ran along the edges of his abs to disappear into his jeans.

There were times I could still barely believe that he was mine, that I had the right to kiss him, touch him, make love to him. He was an addiction that I was only too happy to have. Even after being together for years, I couldn't keep my hands off him, couldn't get enough.

These next nine months were going to be torture.

The thought made me pause. I looked up at him as his hands wound through my hair. What if something happened to him? What if this was about to be one of the last times I ever had him? I let out a shaky exhale and tried to swallow back the fear that had instantly paralyzed me.

"December?" he asked, his voice low.

"I don't want to lose you," I whispered, my voice breaking.

He sank down in front of me and framed my face with his hands. "You will never lose me. It's impossible. I'm coming home to you. I'm going to marry you."

I couldn't stop my lower lip from trembling. How had this month gone by so fast? How were we down to just a few nights together?

"Say it," he ordered. "Say it out loud."

"You're coming home," I said, willing the words to be true. "We're getting married."

"Damn right we are." He surged up, lifting me by my waist and moving me to the center of the bed before settling his weight over me. He ripped his shirt over his head and threw it to the side, then waited for me to raise my arms so he could do the same for me.

My bra met my shirt on the floor, and then I was skin-to-skin with Josh, letting him warm me even to the depths of my fear.

"I'm going to wipe away every thought from that gorgeous brain of yours. Until we leave this hotel room, your only concern should be about how many orgasms I can wring out of you before we need to order more food. Understand?"

His eyes bored into mine, waiting for my response.

I shoved my fear, my worry, my sadness into a tiny, iron-clad box and then tucked it away in the furthest recesses of my head. There was no way I was letting those emotions cloud my last few days with him.

My hands gripped his ass, and I rolled my hips against his erection. His eyes flared. "Let's see how many you have in you," I challenged.

A cocky grin lit his face, and he ran his tongue over his bottom lip. I arched up and sucked his tongue into my mouth. If he was taking my thoughts, then I was consuming his. It was only fair.

I sent my hand under his jeans and into his boxers, running it over the smooth, warm skin of his hip and thigh, until I palmed his hardness and squeezed gently.

"Fuuuuuck," he growled against my mouth, his breath hitting me in short pants.

As he slid down my body, my hand fell away from him, instantly feeling bereft. Then his lips surrounded the peak of my breast, his tongue laving my hardened nipple, and my hands rose to hold his head instead. He was true to his word in the elevator, licking a path to my other breast, then down the dips and hollow of my stomach.

My jeans came off easily, and Josh breathed through the blue lace of my panties, making my hips buck against him before he drew those down my legs, leaving me bare.

"Yours, too," I ordered, needing him just as naked, just as exposed. Everything about me felt raw, on edge, my emotions so big, so conflicting that I wasn't sure anything besides Josh made any sense.

His tattoos rippled as he removed the rest of his clothes, each line of ink reminding me that under his love-tamed exterior, there was the barely restrained bad boy who always surfaced when unleashed in our bedroom.

He never looked away, letting me see the need behind those gorgeous eyes, his undeniable desire for me. Then he leaned forward, parted me with his fingers, and licked me. My eyes fluttered shut, and a moan tumbled free. "I've wanted to do that all fucking day," he said. He knew every line of my body, exactly where to lick, how hard to suck to bring me to the edge. Josh played my body like an instrument, plucking at my nipples, humming at my clit while my head thrashed on the pillow.

"Josh…"

"December?" He gave me another long lick.

"I want you." My fingers sank into his short hair.

"You have me," he promised, pausing to suck at my clit. My muscles were locking, tension building through my entire body as he continued, the pleasure so deep I swore I could taste it on my tongue. "I need to see you come apart."

He didn't have to wait long. My back bowed as he sucked at me again, my orgasm ripping through me with a searing heat and leaving me limp with tiny aftershocks.

He moved over me, settling between my thighs. I felt him hard at my entrance and lifted my hips. "Josh," I urged.

"I love you," he whispered, melting my heart as he sank into me, my inner muscles quivering. I'd never been happier to be on birth control, that we were secure enough to not use condoms anymore. There was nothing compared to the sensation of him sliding within me, skin-on-skin.

He felt so damn good, like he was made for loving me. I guess that was right, since I knew I was made to love only him. "I love you, too," I said, my breath choppy.

He kissed me, our tastes mingling as he began his steady, powerful thrusts. I felt the muscles of his back start to tremble with the effort to restrain himself. "I'm okay, Josh. Let go," I urged, rocking my hips, swirling against him.

"Not until you do. I love to feel you come around me, the way you tighten. It's incredible." He buried his face in my neck and kept his rhythm, his words stoking the fire in me again, building the spiral.

"Again?" I asked.

"Again, and again," he ordered. "I'm marrying you, December. Do you know what that means?"

How did he have the brain power to talk? My thoughts were consumed with the motion of his hips, on using the bed to push more powerfully against him. Luckily he didn't wait for me to answer.

"It means that every night I'm going to make love to you. Every night I'm going to lick you, suck you, kiss you until you come. Then I'm going to slide inside you so deep"—he followed his words with a powerful thrust, stealing my breath—"that you'll never be able to get me out. Even when I'm not with you, I'll be there, with you, reminding you that you're mine. Every. Delicious. Incredible. Inch. Of. You. Mine." He punctuated each word with a thrust, and I whimpered. That sweet pressure had built again, wiping out every thought, and I wrapped my legs around his hips. I simply hung on as he used his whole body to love me, to tell me again what we both already knew—our souls, our hearts, our bodies, all of us belonged to the other. In giving ourselves over, we gained so much more than we could possibly ever lose.

"Josh," I whimpered, the tension unbearable, hanging on the cusp of release.

His thrusts picked up precisely how I needed, as if he knew exactly what I craved. He slid his hand between us and changed the angle so he could slide deeper. Then he locked eyes with me and used his fingers to push me over the edge, until lights fired in my vision and my body shook with the force of it.

"Yes. God, yes," he moaned, his thrusts finally becoming as uneven as his voice. "You're so beautiful when you come." His face tightened, and I gripped him with my thighs, swiveling my hips in the way I knew would push him past the point of return while my body still shuddered in waves. Then he met me, finishing with my name on his lips, his face buried in my neck.

He was perfectly heavy on top of me as our breathing regulated, the sweat cooling on our skin. As usual, he rolled to his side, pulling me with him, always scared that I couldn't breathe under him no matter how many times I assured him otherwise.

"And that, Mrs. Walker," he said with a kiss on my forehead, "is how we're going to spend every night of the rest of our lives."

Except when you're deployed. The thought intruded, but I shoved it back, unwilling to lose this moment to bitterness.

"You set a pretty high standard," I said with a smile, a scrumptious lethargy settling over me.

"You deserve the best," he said, his voice trailing off in a tone of almost-sadness.

I looked into his eyes, letting all the love I had for him fill my fingertips as I trailed them down the stubble on his cheek. "Then it's a good thing I have you forever, because that's all I want, Josh. Just you."

He pulled me closer, settling his chin on the top of my head, both of us unwilling to say what we were thinking.

There was a chance our forever would only be these next few days.

CHAPTER EIGHT

EMBER

Zero Day. He zipped up his MultiCam-printed backpack, and I sighed with the barest form of relief I could muster under our circumstances. He hadn't found the note I'd tucked inside his headphones. Good. He'd need a pick-me-up once he was in the air.

"You don't have to go with me," he said, his gorgeous brown eyes bloodshot from lack of sleep. "It's three a.m. You could go back to bed."

I zipped his hoodie around me and shook my head. "I'm not ready to let you go."

He ran the backs of his fingers down my cheek. "Yeah. Me, neither."

I swallowed back the panic, the fear that had gradually clawed its way into my throat since last night. *Be strong, but don't hold anything back. You're scared? Tell him. You're proud? Tell him. Leave nothing unspoken.* Mom's words ran through my head as we walked out the front door. Josh closed it behind us and then locked it, the sound way too final for my liking.

He loaded his last bag into the back of the Jeep, and I looked up to Jagger and Paisley's darkened house. Jagger left tomorrow on a different main body flight, and I'd be lying if I didn't envy them this last twenty-four hours.

Time felt so relative right now. Where these few hours might not have meant anything a few weeks ago, right now they were everything and not enough.

The roads were dark as we wound our way to Fort Campbell. Josh held my hand, pressing kisses to my palm every so often as we kept a charged silence. What was there left to say?

Too much for a twenty-five-minute drive.

We pulled into the drop-off line, and as our turn came, Josh hopped out of the Jeep and handed over his massive duffel bags stenciled "Walker, J" on the bottom in spray paint.

"Nothing like curbside check-in," I tried to tease once he'd gotten back in.

"Fly army." He smiled, but it didn't reach his eyes.

He parked the Jeep in front of the hangar and almost pocketed the keys. "Wait. You might need these." He handed them over, the weight heavier than it should have been. Everything about this morning felt heavy, oppressive, like a boulder had parked itself on my chest and was gradually stealing my ability to breathe.

Our eyes met in the dim light of the dashboard. I would have given anything to pause this moment, to keep us here for just a little longer where I could see him, feel his heartbeat. But that wasn't the life I'd signed on for, and I was stronger than this dark feeling creeping along the edges of my heart.

We were stronger than any deployment.

"Are you ready for this?" he asked me.

"Are you?"

"I have to be." He tucked an errant strand of my hair behind my ear.

"Same here."

He nodded. "Shall we?"

"Okay." I took a deep breath and stepped out of the Jeep.

His backpack slung over one shoulder, he held my hand as we filed into the hangar with the hundred or so other families who had gathered to send off their soldiers.

"Wait here. I'll be right back." He kissed my cheek and disappeared into the sea of MultiCam.

I sat on the lowest bleacher, everything in me going blessedly numb as I looked around. Soldiers stood huddled in groups, laughing and talking. They were newbies, the right shoulders of their uniforms lacking the combat badge Josh had on his. They had never been to war, never seen the horrors, or lost friends.

A few fathers held sleepy-eyed children, stroking their hair. I couldn't help but think of the last time Gus had hugged Dad before he left.

No. Don't let that in. Not now. I had to hold myself together for the next hour.

My eyes skimmed the bleachers to the right and locked onto an older soldier. His wife sat stoically next to him, her arm looped through his, her head resting on his shoulder, her eyes a vacant stare. He turned and placed an absentminded kiss on her forehead, his eyes focused anywhere but there. If I had to bet, I would have said they were on their fourth, if not fifth, deployment. She had the same gracefully defeated face Mom had worn when she'd dropped Dad off that last time.

That kind of look only came with years of waiting, strength, and weariness.

"Hey," Josh said as he sat down next to me, jarring me from my people-watching.

"All signed in?" I asked.

"Yeah. Now we wait for them to call formation." He wrapped his arm around me and tucked me into his chest.

"How long do we have?"

"About another half hour."

Thirty minutes. How could I fit all of my love into such a short amount of time? My thumb stroked the platinum band of my engagement ring, and I reminded myself that we had forever. This was just a hurdle. "You have the international cell packed?"

"Yes. I'll pick up minutes once we're in country. I'll never be out of contact for long, I promise."

I nodded. That was one advantage of this being Josh's second deployment. He knew the ropes already. While I'd never be so needy as to call the cell phone, because only God knew what he could be doing, I took huge amounts of comfort knowing that I could text him in an emergency.

"Remember to have the complex come out and look at the water heater. I should have done it before I left. I'm sorry."

"Stop. You did everything you could, and our house is brand-new. I can take care of just about anything that pops up, so stop worrying."

He kissed my forehead, lingering. "Worrying about you is my primary job. I just fly helicopters to pay the bills."

"I'm stronger than you give me credit for." God, I hoped that was true. Josh had seen me at my lowest and watched me rebuild my life, but this would take a strength I had to develop all on my own.

"I know how strong you are, December," he whispered. "Even that won't change how much I worry about you."

Then don't leave me.

We sat there, our arms locked around each other, our heartbeats counting down the moments until he'd be called away. They were the best and worst minutes, flying too quickly. I had never loved him more than I did in that moment. I had never been as scared.

It's when you realize how close you are to losing something that you finally comprehend just how precious it is.

Mom was wiser than I'd ever given her credit for.

A voice came across the PA system. "Ten minutes."

Josh sat up straight. "Let me walk you out."

"What?" I asked, looking up at his stone-set face.

"I don't want to be with all these people. I want it to be just you and me." A muscle in his jaw ticked.

"But I don't want to leave you early, even if it's just for that minute. I'll watch you go."

His face cupped my cheeks. "I don't know if I'll be able to walk away if I know you're watching, December. Please, for me. Let me walk you out."

"Okay." He took my hand and walked me past the desperate embraces of the families around us.

The early morning air cooled my heated cheeks as we walked back to where the Jeep was parked. He unlocked the door for me and opened it. Then he opened his arms.

I walked into them, breathing in his scent until my lungs were full. My fingers clenched his uniform. "I'm not ready," I whispered.

"I know." He settled his chin on the top of my head. "Nine months, babe. Then I'll come home, we'll get married, and our life will start."

I nodded, fear choking the words in my throat.

He leaned back, tilted my chin, and kissed me. Our lips clung as though they couldn't bear the thought of being apart, either. "Nine months," I whispered against his mouth.

"You got it."

"I love you."

He rested his forehead against mine. "I love you. Nothing will ever change that."

I nodded, like his words could keep him here...keep him alive. "Okay." We broke apart, and he turned me to the Jeep door. "Call me from the first step?"

"Of course. Text me whenever you want. I won't get it in the air, but I'll check as soon as we land."

"Okay." *Stop saying okay. None of this is okay.* There was no choice here. I couldn't ask him to stay. I had to be okay, whatever the hell that really meant.

"See you soon," he said with a half smile that was adorable, even if fake.

"See you soon," I echoed.

As he turned to walk back toward the hangar, everything in me slowed, stilled. My heart stuttered; my breath froze in my lungs.

What if this was it? What if that was our last kiss? Our last *I love you's*? What if the next time I held him in my arms, it would be through the cool wood exterior of an unwelcoming box? What if he never came home?

What if this was Dad all over again?

I sucked in air with a desperate gulp, and his name was a cry on my lips. "Josh!"

He turned, his arms already open as I raced into them.

"I love you. I love you so much that it hurts to breathe when you're not here. I know I'm not supposed to say this. I know I'm supposed to be strong, and unbreakable, but I'm so damn scared." My voice broke on the last word, tears clogging my throat and my eyes. They started to fall, soaking tiny wet spots into his uniform.

"I know, baby. I know." His chest shook as he took in a breath.

I pulled back enough to look at his face, gorgeous even in the minimal streetlight. "I don't care *how* you come home. I don't care what parts of you are broken, or bleeding, or... anything, just as long as you come home. As long as your heart is beating, I will want you, do you understand me? I don't care what happens there as long as you come home. Please? You have to, because I've built my world around you, our future, and I don't know if I could survive losing you, Josh. And I know that's selfish, and unfair, but I need you!" My voice rose with every word until I could barely make them out.

"Shh," he whispered before he kissed me. Our mouths met in a final fury of love and fear all mixed with longing and the salt of our tears.

"December, I swear—I *will* come home to you. There's

no force on this earth that could keep me from you, do you understand that?"

"Promise me," I begged, hating myself even as it slipped out of my mouth. I was asking the impossible, for him to tell the future, for him to give his word on something he could never guarantee.

He searched my eyes, time slipping by so quickly I was sure the world was on fast-forward while we stood still. "I promise I will do whatever it takes to come home to you." He sealed his promise with a last kiss and let me go slowly.

My arms fell from around his neck, and he stepped back, the distance between us already more than the twelve physical inches.

"You and me?" he asked softly.

"Against the world," I promised with a smile, my voice shaking.

A nod and a smile later, he left me standing next to his Jeep.

I climbed up into the driver's seat and pulled the door closed. Unable to reach the pedals, I scooted his seat closer. Then I adjusted the mirrors. Just like that, I'd slipped into the driver's seat of our future, and I was responsible for taking care of it until he could make it home.

I held myself together, sniffing back the snot that tried to drip down my nose from unshed tears. This wasn't glamorous, or movie-worthy. There was no waving the handkerchief or kissing through the bus window one last time as I stoically sent him off.

This was unedited pain and gut-wrenching fear in its rawest form. It wasn't even the thought of knowing it would be nine months until I could hold him again. Hell, that was the best-case scenario.

It was the true, paralyzing fear that I'd never get that chance again. Had I said everything right? Kissed him long enough? Showed him how much I loved him?

Music. That would help. I turned on Josh's radio, and
immediately shut if off. Elton John's "Rocket Man" was
definitely not what I needed to hear right now.

I rode home in complete silence, the only noise the hum
of the engine and the tires on the highway. It was almost five-
thirty by the time I pulled into our driveway and set the parking
brake. My hands fumbled with the key, but I got the door open.

I stumbled up the steps to our bedroom, where I saw a
single white sheet of paper on my pillow with a Hershey's Kiss.

Dear December,

*I'm so sorry you'll be sleeping here alone for the next
nine months. I'm so sorry that I can't kiss you when you
need it, or hold you when you sleep. But know that the
miles that separate us are only in distance, never heart.
When I lay my head down, no matter how far away I am,
I'm always there with you. Love like ours can stretch
across the entire universe, so a few thousand miles is the
least of our worries.*

You own my soul,
Josh

I put the Kiss on my nightstand and sat down on the edge of
our bed, which he'd already made up. His clothes were on the
floor near the hamper, and his Av's beanie hung precariously
on the doorknob. It looked like he could walk in at any moment.

But he wouldn't.

Not for another nine long months.

I pulled his hoodie closer and buried my nose in the neckline,
breathing in Josh's scent. Then I laid down on his pillow and let
the tears come.

I cried for love, for the pause our life was going to undergo.
I cried for the choices I'd made that brought me here again,
watching another man I loved going off to war. I cried because I

was deathly afraid—afraid that I wasn't strong enough, capable enough, that all my bravado was just that, and I'd crumble under the strain.

I cried because the deepest, darkest parts of me wondered if that was the last time I'd ever feel his skin under my fingertips or taste his kiss.

I cried until my eyes ached and the sobs stopped shaking my body—until exhaustion lulled me to sleep on a tear-soaked pillow.

I let myself sleep for a few hours, let it take away the misery while my body recovered.

When I woke up, I got into the shower and washed the morning off me. Then I got dressed, went downstairs, and poured a cup of coffee. I'd missed one class, but if I left now, I could catch the last two.

It was what Josh wanted, and it was what I needed.

Deployment or not, the sun still shone, the earth still turned, and I had a life to live.

It just felt a lot emptier without Josh.

CHAPTER NINE

JOSH

The halls of the combat support hospital in Kandahar were unusually quiet as I walked back from my flight physical. Then again, at eight a.m., the day was just getting started.

One month. I'd been in Kandahar one month, and even though it had been years since my first deployment, it somehow felt like I'd never left. In a gross, unexplainable way, it seemed like this was where I lived, and I'd simply been away for a few days.

There were some improvements, of course. Now, I slept in a concrete bunker, spoiled with my own room instead of a giant tent with fifty other guys—on a good night—which meant I had some semblance of privacy when I Skyped Ember.

It was only nine-thirty at home, and if I hurried back, I might be able to get a call in to say good night before I was due on the flight line.

Two hundred and forty more days to go.

I turned the corner, walking past the surgical wing, and managed to glance through the glass of the swinging doors. My body jolted to a stop.

My hands pushed open the door before I knew what I was doing, and my feet followed suit, walking a few steps down the hallway before stopping in front of the picture I'd glimpsed from the window.

Dr. Howard stared back at me, his face as austere as only a government photo could be.

In Memory of LTC Justin Howard.

The picture didn't show the concern that had always radiated from his eyes, or the quick, no-nonsense advice he'd doled out like medication. It didn't show the look on his face when he'd recognized me, or the proud nod of his head when he'd gotten me back on the ice.

It was just a photo. It wasn't him.

But damn if it didn't feel like he was staring back at me. What the hell would he think of everything that had gone down in the last two years? Would he have welcomed that diamond ring on Ember's finger? Or would he have told me to leave her the fuck alone?

"I'm sorry." I whispered so the nearby staff didn't send me to psych. "It was impossible not to love her. Maybe a better man could have walked away and spared her this, but you and I both know I was never the better man. And yeah, you used to joke about me taking her out, but I know if you had known what would happen to you—what she'd have to endure—well, you would never have wanted me with her. I knew it, and I still couldn't help myself. I knew we'd end up here, knew what she'd have to go through, and like a selfish fuck, I kept pushing, kept showing up. She pulled me in with nothing more than one look, and whether or not she'd chosen to be mine, I just knew that I'd always be hers. And I know you're probably pissed, but I swear, I'm doing everything I can to make her happy."

Everything but be there.

I quieted as a soldier came closer.

"Do you know that story?" the young PFC asked, nodding toward LTC Howard.

"Yeah, a little," I answered softly.

"He died in this hallway. Stepped in front of a nurse so she wasn't shot, and he was killed instead."

He wasn't telling me anything I didn't already know. I'd read every report Ember's mom had been given. "Yeah, sounds like him."

The kid's eyes widened. "You knew him? He's kind of a legend."

My eyes drifted to the expanse of floor that ran to the operating bays as if his blood hadn't been washed away...as if it still mingled with mine, spilled in the same hallway. But I was alive and he wasn't for one simple reason—I'd had him.

Life was anything but fair.

"Yeah," I answered. "I knew him. He saved my life."

In every way possible.

Two hundred and twenty-three days to go and I was finally ready to fly missions. Funny how I'd thought that I'd be ready to go as soon as I left flight school. No. Students left Rucker at RL3, and had to make it to RL1 before they could do any flying without an instructor pilot. I'd thought those had stayed in flight school, too. Not so much.

But today I was ready.

Today nothing was happening.

"Is it the slowest day in existence?" I mumbled, tossing a tennis ball against the wall, my boots propped up on the desk.

"Don't curse us. No work is a good day," Captain Trivette said as she took the seat next to me and caught the ball on return. I liked her. She was level-headed, quick, and damn good on the stick. She also didn't take shit as a pilot-in-command.

"Good point," I acquiesced. It wasn't that I was itching for action as much as I was ready to give back, to start paying the debt I owed.

An hour later, I got my chance.

"We've got a call!" Captain Trivette shouted into the

bathroom. "One Bravo, one Charlie. Let's go." *Bravo, urgent. Charlie, priority.* Of course my first call would come while I was taking a leak. I shook it out and tucked it in and then ran for the door, squirting hand-sanitizer on the way out.

I grabbed my gear and sprinted, thankful that I'd kept up on PT since getting here. Seven minutes call-to-air—that was our average. Fastening my vest over my flight suit and moving my weapon from my thigh holster to the vest, I was ready to roll.

A strange mix of anxiety and excitement coursed through me in a way I'd forgotten and yet instantly remembered all too well. Helmet bag in hand, I met Captain Trivette on our way to the aircraft. Sergeant Rizzo climbed into the back as our medic, sliding the door shut after Specialist Frank got in.

I strapped on my helmet and kneeboard, and then we finished the run-up that had already been started. "We get the full nine-line yet?" I asked through the coms, knowing we needed the complete details before we could launch the aircraft.

"No," Captain Trivette answered with a shake of her head. "I'm pretty sure the LZ isn't secure."

Not secure. They're still taking fire, and you're stuck at the fucking FOB. "This is bullshit."

"Roger," she said through gritted teeth.

Every second that passed grated each of my nerves, scraping them raw until I was ready to claw out of my skin to fly. I knew how it felt to be pinned down, under fire, with wounded...or to be the one wounded, praying for medevac. Those soldiers were out there waiting on us, depending on us, and we were still sitting here waiting on the fucking nine-line medevac request.

Just when I thought I was about to lose my shit, the details came in, and we launched. Two definite wounded. One walking. One litter. Unsecured landing zone. The ground fell away as I took us to the sky, heading toward the coordinates we'd been given. The Apaches would meet us there to provide security.

If those pilots were anything like Jagger, we were in good

hands, but he was up at TK. We kept missing each other on the small opportunities we had to meet up.

Thirteen minutes in the air, and we approached the LZ.

"Gunman one-three, this is Dustoff one-two. Three minutes out," I radioed the Apaches.

"Dustoff one-two, this is Gun one-three. LZ is not secure," one of the Apache pilots called over the radio.

"Roger that. Two minutes out, pop smoke," Captain Trivette answered.

Streams of white trailed from the ground, marking the LZ. From the air, I made out several soldiers taking cover behind a small wall, returning fire. This wasn't unsecured, this was still a damn firefight.

"Ma'am?"

"Gunman one-three, how hot are we talking about?" Her head swiveled as she took in every detail of the ground that she could make out.

"Cherry red," came the reply.

"Fuck," I whispered.

She arched an eyebrow at me and took the controls. "Are we all in?"

"Fuck yes!" Rizzo called over coms.

"All in," Frank added in.

I brushed my thumb over the picture of Ember I kept taped to my kneeboard. "I'm in."

Adrenaline rushed into my system, flooding my veins. This feeling...this terrifying rush was only found in one place, and as much as I hated combat, I also craved it with a part of me that was surprisingly outspoken. Hell, it was screaming, *let's do this.*

For a millisecond, my memory flashed to the building we'd cleared when I'd been shot, the wry smile Sgt. Green had given me, and his words flew from my mouth.

"Seems like a good day to die."

Time to pay back what I'd been given.

· · ·

"Mail the application," I told Ember on Skype a few days later.

"Hello to you, too." She laughed, tucking her auburn hair behind her ears as she sat back on our bed at home, unfolding the Hershey's Kiss I'd left for her in the back of my T-shirt drawer. I missed that hair, the way it ran through my fingers like silk, the contrast of its fire against the pale skin of her naked breasts, the way it smelled. Everything. "How many of these did you hide for me, anyway?" She popped the Kiss into her mouth.

"Enough to send you searching on every bad day you could have while I'm gone. Now, I'm serious, December. Spring break is next week, which means the applications are due. Turn it in."

She grimaced, wrinkling her nose in a way that was cuter than she intended. "I haven't decided. You're gone, and Paisley's pregnant, and the timing is just all sorts of off."

"Paisley has a mom and Morgan. This is something you need to do." I unzipped my top and didn't miss the way her eyes widened when my shirt came untucked just enough for her to see my abs. Good to know the extra gym time hadn't gone unnoticed.

"Huh?" she asked, her head cocked to the side and her soft lips parted.

"December. Pay attention," I chastised, and then took my shirt off just for the hell of it. Okay, maybe I wanted to see her drool a little. Besides, the way that little white tank top hugged her perfect breasts, well, I was ready to climb through the screen to get my hands on her.

"You could put on some clothes." She stuck her lower lip out in a pout that my soul echoed. Skype was great because I could see her in real-time, but it made the ache to hold her that much sharper.

"It's hot," I said with a smile.

"Yes, it is," she said with a slow nod of her head.

"You could always join me."

"I'm not nearly desperate enough to start forniskyping with you," she said with her mouth, but her gaze said something very different as she eye-fucked me.

"You will be."

God, how the hell could she do that? Turn me on from eight thousand miles away with nothing but a look?

"It's not exactly private over there," she argued.

"I'd never let anyone see you naked," I promised. "That delectable little body is all mine, and I don't share." I adjusted in my seat as the door burst open.

"Dude!" Rizzo called out in a rush. "If you want in on the— Oh, sorry!"

"Fucking seriously?" I yelled at him.

"Playing through?" she asked with a laugh, reminding me of another time we'd been walked in on.

I swiveled back to her and pointed at her gorgeous face. "Not funny."

"Yet the point is so eloquently made. How's it going, Rizzo?" she asked.

The kid raked his hand over his buzzed head. "Sorry for barging in, Ember. Walker, it can wait until later."

"How's my guy doing over there?" she asked him.

"I'm fine," I answered.

She clucked her tongue at me. "Not asking you. You lie. Rizzo?"

He put his giant head in front of mine and blocked the screen so I couldn't even see her. "You have no need to worry, this guy is already a legend."

"Oh? Tell me about this legend," she said with a giggle. I could imagine the smile that would accompany it and nearly shoved his head out of the way to see.

"He's seriously a badass. Fucking phenomenal pilot, and he's got it, that one percent everyone else is missing." Jesus, Rizzo sounded like I was running for office or something.

"One percent?" she asked.

I swiveled my head to see her, but he still blocked the view. Two more seconds and I was going to boot his ass.

"Yeah. You know, everyone has that last percent of self-preservation, that part that kicks in and pulls you back?"

Fuck. This was not going well. "Rizzo," I warned.

"Yeah?" Ember's voice dropped.

"Walker's missing it. His sense of imminent death kicks in like one percent later than everyone else, so he'll go for it. Hot LZ or not, man, he's in it to get those guys out. It makes him pretty much the most badass pilot we've got here."

I shoved his head out of my way. "Out. Now."

"See ya, Ember!" Rizzo called. "Walker, we'll start without you?"

I nodded and surveyed the damage once Rizzo shut my door behind him. Ember sat crisscross on our bed, her chin held between her hands as she braced her elbows on her bare knees. The smile had vanished from her face, leaving blinking, wide eyes.

"One percent, huh?" she asked, trying to force a smile, which was all the sadder for the attempt. "You might need to tell me where another Kiss is."

"December." I breathed her name like it could soothe her soul as it did mine. "It's not as badass as he makes it sound."

She nodded slowly, her eyes anywhere but on the screen. "I get it. I do."

"I'm perfectly safe," I lied. He was right. I pushed the envelope to where it needed to be, or rather where I felt it needed to be. "I never do anything that I think might get me, or the crew, killed." That part was true. I was well aware that it wasn't only me in that aircraft, that I was responsible for more than just the lives on the ground.

She transformed before my eyes, sucking in a breath and sitting straighter, tucking away the fear into a place that I prayed she wouldn't really examine until she was physically in my arms again.

Seven more months.

"So, I still can't seem to get the office to fix the disposal," she said in a smooth, let's-change-the-subject move.

"What did you stick down it this time?" My memory flashed to the time she set a West Point shirt on fire in the kitchen sink.

"I may have accidentally not seen a fondue stick in there when I started it last week."

Her face was too damn cute, and I burst into laughter. "Of course you did. Was it at least good?"

She nodded. "Paisley wanted it, so of course I hooked her up. She's all southern and sweet, but man, there's a little dragon underneath there, too."

Ember had climbed up to get the fondue pot she had to have. Maybe it was small, but she'd asked me not to put it where she couldn't reach, and I'd done it anyway. I'd made this just a tiny bit harder on her, figuring that I'd be there if she ever needed to get it down. But she'd done it without me.

Everything was stationary here, like our life was on pause, but back there, hers was still turning.

"Call Will," I said, clearing my throat and my asinine thoughts. Like a fondue pot meant anything in the scheme of things.

"I don't want to bug him. He's getting ready to leave."

"Yeah, well, tell him that I said to get his ass over there and fix it. You're still feeding him every Sunday?" My heart sank a millimeter at the thought that Will was having dinner with Ember and Paisley, and while I was immeasurably thankful that he was there, helping, checking on the girls, fixing stuff they broke…well, I kind of hated him a tiny bit for it, too.

"Sunday night family dinners." She gave a sad smile. "Just sans most of the family."

God, I wanted to hold her, to climb through the screen for just long enough to brush my fingers along her cheek. "Soon, babe."

"You on tonight?" she asked.

I nodded. "Yeah, I'm coming on shift in about ten minutes. I'm serious, you need to send in that application. It's only for a couple months, and I'll be home right around the time you are. Win-win."

She sighed. "Yeah, I know. I'll think about it."

"You do that. Meanwhile, I'll think about what you look like under that tank top."

Her laughter bolstered my soul like nothing else could. "You're incorrigible."

"You know it." I stood in my ten-by-ten room, careful not to bash my head on the lofted bed I'd been sitting under. Then I pulled on a clean shirt and grabbed a clean top from my closet. Ember's sigh broke the silence.

"What's up, babe?"

She bit her lower lip in a way that I longed to. "I just miss you," she whispered.

I leaned in close to the camera. "I miss you, too. Every second. Every heartbeat."

"Go save lives and come home to me, Lieutenant Walker." She blew me a kiss.

"Counting down the minutes, future Mrs. Walker."

We hung up without saying good-bye, because those were two words I wouldn't ever use. Not here. I swallowed the ache that threatened to consume everything in me and pushed it to a workable distance. Then I tucked my heart away and went to work.

That day we weren't so lucky, and I did my first Hero Flight, bringing back the body of a fallen soldier. The mission was somber, solemn, and broke my heart in a way that I'd never forget. A way that bolstered my determination to save the next soldier, and the one after that.

A way I knew I never wanted to experience again.

CHAPTER TEN

EMBER

One percent.

It was all I could think about that week. One percent less self-preservation than everyone else had. Not that it was really quantifiable, right? There wasn't actually anyone inside Josh's brain, checking out why the hell he flew like he had a death wish.

The same way he rode that damn motorcycle I hated, that four-wheeler in Alabama last year, or anything else he could push just a little beyond the red line.

He'd been gone seven weeks, and I was okay. Maybe that was the worst part. Yes, I missed him, worried about him, constantly wondered what he was doing, but I was surviving. We'd only lived together for a month before he'd deployed, and in some ways, it just felt like he was at Rucker, and I was...well, here. Other than the deployment sign I had made to hang on the front door that read, KNOCK ONLY IN CASES OF EMERGENCY, it was almost like we'd never moved in together.

Except that I slept in his T-shirts with my laptop perched next to his pillow just in case he Skyped me in the middle of the night.

"Breaker off?" Will asked from under my sink as I walked back into the kitchen.

"Yup. Your hands are safe," I answered, hopping up onto

the island counter.

He reached for another tool and went back to work. "You did a number on it."

"I can't believe he messaged you. It could have waited until Sunday, or I could have called someone."

"I don't mind. I like checking on you two."

My feet swung under the lip of the counter. "I think Paisley fell asleep twenty minutes after dinner. Pregnancy is wiping her out." I cringed. "I mean, in the normal way, not the I-had-a-heart-condition way."

Will slid just far enough to smile at me, his teeth perfectly even. Huh. He was actually a really good-looking guy when Josh wasn't ragging on him. "Don't worry. I knew what you meant. And yeah, I worry, but checking up on you guys every week is about all I can really do, right? I'll be gone in a couple of weeks, and then you two are on your own, broken disposals and all." He slid back under and went to work.

"Are you going home to Alabama before you go? Maybe seeing Morgan?" I tried to keep my tone innocuous, but the pause in his work was enough to let me know I'd pushed a little too much.

"Nope. I think we said everything we could the last time she was here."

"She loves you, you know."

Will sighed. "Flip the breaker? I think I got it."

I went to the breaker box and flipped the kitchen switch. "It's on!" I called. By the time I walked upstairs from the basement, he'd already tested it.

"You're good to go." He ran it another few times to make sure, and then started putting his tools away in the bag.

I took two beers out of the fridge and handed one to him. "Thank you. Seriously."

"Don't mention it. Any of the guys would have done the same."

"Would they have given up every Sunday night to hang out with some boring girls?"

"You're hardly boring. I wanted in on the family dinner nights. Besides, Lee is still one of my best friends, despite our epic efforts to screw that up last year."

He popped the top on the can and leaned against the counter across from me. Josh had hated this guy until the Blackhawk course had made them friends, but here, just the two of us, I saw why Paisley had loved him. He had an uncompromising sense of right and wrong that could be as infuriating as it was endearing. It just depended what side of the line you were standing on.

"So, Morgan?" I pushed again.

He made a face at me. "I have mad respect for you, Ember, I do. But I'm not sure we're close enough to discuss my love life."

"Paisley is one of my best friends."

He lifted his beer in salute. "Correct. Then maybe we're too close."

"You're family," I said with a shrug. "You wanted in on the vacations, the dinners, the whole...well, family, so this is part of it. Now spill."

"You really think she'd want to sign on with someone who wants to fly SOAR? Who wants the no-warning deployments? Impossible schedules? Classified locations?"

"That girl is in love with you." I took a long sip of my beer while he debated opening up.

He took a swallow and sighed. "Yeah, well, I'm not sure Morgan really understands what love is."

"And you do?" I said it softly, so he'd know I wasn't mocking him.

"Yeah. Love is when you'd lay down everything about yourself for the other person's happiness. Be what they need you to be, grow into the best version of yourself because it's what they deserve. Love is knowing when to fight for that person, and when you might not be the best fit. Love is letting go, and the crushing pain that comes with it."

Like when I left Josh back in Colorado. I nodded, understanding more than I wanted to. "Yeah, I get that. You don't think she loves you that way?"

He ran his hand over his close-cropped brown curls. "Morgan is amazing. She's gorgeous, and funny, and reminds me of who I am underneath all the bullshit. I don't doubt that she could love like that. I'm just not sure I could love *her* like that, and if I'm not one hundred percent certain, I have no business asking her to wait for me."

Understanding dawned, and my heart ached on his behalf. "You're still in love with her."

His forehead wrinkled. "Paisley? No, just as friends, I swear."

I shook my head. "Her sister, Peyton."

Will's eyes flew to mine, and I saw it there, the wild, echoed grief that still hollowed Mom's eyes from time to time—the dark, horrible void Dad had left in her that still lingered when she wasn't careful to mask it.

"It's okay, you don't have to talk about it. I'm sorry for pushing. It's absolutely none of my business." I could have kicked myself. After all the insensitive questions I'd had tossed at me the last couple of years, I should have known better.

"No," he said with a sad smile and another sip of his beer. "It's okay. I think maybe you'd understand more than most people." He started to peel the label from the bottle. "I've loved Peyton ever since I knew how to define the emotion. She was like life bottled under pressure, shaken up, and when you took the cap off...God, she flew. Being around her was intoxicating and addictive. She didn't know how to sit still, or how to come in second place." He laughed. "She could be utterly exhausting one moment, and yet feed my very soul in the next. She was my best friend, the only woman I ever wanted, and when she died, I did, too—right there on that field. I physically felt my heart stop the very second hers did, and I just never got the right rhythm back." His face twisted, and my eyes prickled as though I was taking on a piece of his pain.

"Everything I've done since then has been for her. Taking care of Paisley, pushing myself through the Academy, fighting for the top of the Order of Merit List...it's all been because I know she's watching. She knew every limit I had and accepted none, just pushed me past where I thought my barriers were. So I succeed. I choose the right path no matter what. I can't fail. I can't tolerate second, because she never would. And I can't...love. Not in the way someone like Morgan deserves. It's not that I don't want her." He rolled his head back and blew out a long breath. "God, Morgan is...perfect. But I just don't know how to give away a heart I don't own." He set his beer down and crossed his arms over his chest as if the motion would hold him together. "She's like you—she's not the woman who is going to put her career on the back burner for me while I run off and fly for SOAR. She deserves better than someone with no time and half a heart, and I won't make the same mistake with her that I did with Paisley."

We stood there in silence, connected in a way I didn't share with a lot of people, recognizing that grief lasted a lot longer than people had the right words for. So instead of offering him some kind of placating words he didn't need, I simply gave Will a soft smile and the truth. "Maybe you should tell her that. Let her decide if she's willing to battle special ops and Peyton's ghost. She might surprise you."

A slow smile spread across his face, and his eyes focused on something far away that I hoped was his future. "Yeah," he said in a hopeful tone. "Maybe when I get home."

"Maybe when you get home."

He raised his beer to mine, and we toasted second chances.

Later, when I thought about what he'd said, that I would never let my career take a backseat to Josh's, I mailed the application for the Ephesus dig.

• • •

Another month went by, Will deployed, and suddenly I was staring May and graduation in the face.

"Hey, are you ready to go?" Paisley drawled as she popped her head in my front door.

"Am I?" I grabbed my bag that stored my cap and gown. "Yes, I'm ready to go. My sister? Not so much."

"April! I will leave you here if you do not present yourself in the next two minutes!" Mom yelled, straightening Gus's tie. Her hair was swept up in a perfect twist, and her pearls were in place.

"She'll do it, too!" Gus threatened with all the bravado turning nine had given him. His hair hadn't lost any of its strawberry curl, giving him a rather rakish look if Mom didn't keep it cut close.

When Josh had suggested the three-bedroom townhouse, I'd balked, but after having my family here for the week, I was ready to kiss the man for his thoughtfulness. Hell, I was ready to kiss him, period. Or simply skip the kissing and jump him. Ugh. I missed him so much that there was a physical ache constantly present in my chest that felt like I couldn't take a deep breath without crushing something. Next week it would be three months since he'd deployed.

I was going to be a basket case by six.

"How about I drive you down, Ember, and your mom can take your car?" Paisley suggested, checking her watch. "I don't want you to be late."

Mom's eyes lit up. "Yes! Perfect. Go."

"Mom, it's an hour away. I don't want you to get lost or anything."

She shot me the look, and I damn near withered. "December Howard, I'm well aware of where Vanderbilt is, considering you were born while your father was in medical school there. Go with Paisley, and we'll catch up."

"Okay." I kissed Gus's smooth cheek and ran out the door to where Paisley already had her car running, air conditioning on full blast.

After clicking into our seat belts, we took off for the city.

"I saw the roses Josh sent," she said as we pulled onto the highway. "They're gorgeous!"

"Yeah, he hates not being here." I hated it, too. Every single second of it.

"I'm so sorry."

I shrugged. "Next week it's your turn, Mrs. Bateman. We still on for a little Alabama road trip?"

She nodded. "Absolutely." She was quiet for a few moments. "It's okay to be mad, Ember. Mad that they're missing everything. Mad that our world keeps spinning while they're gone."

I swallowed. "Okay, honest moment?"

"Shoot."

"I keep thinking of everything my dad missed. All the plays, and games, and little graduations, and I remember swearing I would never live like that. I was never mad at him, just sad, you know?"

"Yes. The higher up in rank Daddy goes, the less I see him. And I'm proud of him, of everything he's accomplished, but..." She shook her head. "It's not important."

The sun glinted off my ring as the car curved with the road, throwing prisms of color onto the ceiling. "No, it is important. I feel like one of the reasons we get married is because you find your person. The one person you want with you when everything goes to shit, the one person you want when it's all amazingly right. Like you have your own personal witness and cheerleader to your life."

Her hand ran absentmindedly across her emerging baby bump. "And they're missing it," she finished.

"They're missing it, and I can't help but feel like some of the joy is sucked out of everything because they're not here." It was my graduation day, damn it. I didn't want this gaping hole in my chest. I wanted hugs, and kisses, and congratulations. I wanted Josh to be here for me the same way I'd been there for him when I'd pinned him at his commissioning, or when he'd graduated flight school.

I was desperate for an equality that, as a military spouse, I was never going to get. Usually I was okay with it. This was what I signed up for, as Mom loved to remind me. But sometimes, especially on days like this, well, it sucked.

Paisley reached over and clasped my hand. "I'll be your witness, and you'll be mine. We'll fill the holes."

I squeezed her hand gently and thought about what the next months would bring. My graduation, Paisley's, maybe the Ephesus dig, and the birth of the Mini-Bateman. In the face of watching one of my closest friends go through her pregnancy solo, my little cap and gown didn't matter so much.

"We'll fill the holes," I agreed.

With the sun shining on a gorgeous Nashville day, I walked across the stage and received my bachelor's in history.

After the ceremony, Mom rushed me, holding me tightly to her. "Your dad would be so proud, Ember. We're all so proud."

I closed my eyes and felt the sweetest pressure in my chest like Dad was with us, hugging me, too.

"Ember!" Paisley said, shaking my phone toward me. I'd asked her to hold it for me during the ceremony. I took it and gasped at the face on the screen.

"Congrats, baby!" Josh said, his face pixelated on Skype from the less than stellar service I got on campus.

My heart soared, and my nose burned as tears formed in my

eyes. "Hi, love! You made it!"

His smile was enough to bring me to my knees. "I wouldn't miss this for the world. I'm so proud of you." He stayed online while April and Gus hugged me, and he was still there when Luke came over to offer his congratulations.

"Look who made it through Vandy! Congrats, Red!" He pulled me into him with a tight hug.

"I couldn't have done it without you."

"Bullshit. You couldn't have done it without the coffee shop. I just happened to be there."

"Okay, that may be true," I said with a laugh.

He snagged my phone out of my hand. "Well, hello there, Flyboy."

Josh grimaced. "Luke. You done pawing my girlfriend?"

"So jealous, that one," Luke whispered at me. "Shall I make her day even better?" he asked Josh, then looked over at my puckered forehead and handed the phone to Mom. Then he took a white envelope out of his gray blazer pocket and handed it to me. "I asked if I could deliver this one personally."

The envelope was thin in my hands, but heavy in implication. I held it up so Josh could see.

"Well, open it," he said, leaning in to the monitor.

I wet my suddenly dry lips and ripped the envelope carefully. Then I opened the tri-fold letter and began to read. "Dear Ms. Howard, we are pleased to inform you that you have been accepted for the Ephesus Fall Dig program! Ahhh!" I shrieked and jumped, nearly losing my balance in my heels. "I got in!" I waved the envelope at Josh.

"I knew it! God, babe, I'm so happy for you!" His smile was just as big as mine, and in that moment, it didn't matter that he was eight thousand miles away—he was right there with me.

And for that small second, that huge minute...it was enough.

It was everything.

CHAPTER ELEVEN

JOSH

"You want to do my area orientation flight, or what?" Will's voice snapped me out of the study guide I'd had my face in for the last hour.

"Holy shit!" I stood, knocking my chair to the ground, and hugged him. "It's about time you got here, West Point."

"Yeah, yeah." He slapped my back. "I bet you say the same thing when I get home three months after you, too." He grinned and dropped his backpack on the table.

"I think I may have actually missed you, but the verdict isn't in yet."

Will arched an eyebrow but handed me a vacuum-sealed plastic bag. "Well, I know for a fact that you miss her."

"No fucking way." *Ember.* I grabbed a pair of scissors off the desk and cut into the bag, the smell of strawberry-cheesecake cookies wafting through my room. I shoved one in my mouth. "Oh my God," I moaned.

"Would you like me to leave you alone with your baked goods?"

"Want one?" I asked, offering him the bag. *He'd better recognize the sacrifice.*

He shook his head. "It means a ton that you'd offer, but she gave me a few, and I'm not coming between that relationship." He sighed. "She also wanted me to give you a kiss, but I'm going to pretend that never happened."

"Good call," I said, popping another cookie in my mouth. *Slow down and save a few. There's only a dozen here.* They tasted like home, like Ember on rainy days when she baked intricate concoctions. They tasted like kitchen sex and love. I made myself fold the bag over then hid it in the trunk under my bed.

"Have a problem with cookie thieves?" Will asked.

"Jagger has shown up twice in the last month, and I swear, he's devoured the last two batches she's sent. I'm always glad to see him, but he needs to lay off my fucking cookies."

"Noted."

"Where did they get you set up?" I asked, grabbing my flight suit top and slipping my arms through the sleeves.

"Just another building over. I got here a few days ago, but we've been on opposite shifts."

I paused mid-zip. "You've had my cookies over there for three days?"

He didn't blink. "I could have left them in the Op center, but I figured they'd be gone by the time you saw her pretty handwriting on the bag."

I pointed my finger at him. "You know what...fine. Let's get you oriented so you can get on the schedule."

I shot Ember a quick text on the international cell while on our way to the flight line. That thing was worth every penny we spent on it. Fuck, the battery was dying.

Josh: *Hey babe, i'm headed to work.*

We headed to the aircraft, and a few minutes later the phone dinged.

December: *Fly safe. I love you.*

Josh: *Will got here, and the cookies are amazing. I love you, too. Phone is dying. i'll give you a call tomorrow afternoon your time.*

I turned the phone on silent and stuck it in my vest pocket

as we did the run-up on the aircraft. Captain Trivette was flying with me again today, and she tossed a half smile back at Will. "You the new guy?" she called over the coms as the rotors fired up.

"Yes, ma'am," he answered, belting into one of the back seats.

"Welcome to the sand box. We're going to give you a little tour."

"Welcome to the sand box!" Rizzo sang with one hand on his chest, giving his best Elvis impression.

Captain Trivette shook her head. "Take us out, Lieutenant."

"Yes, ma'am." We launched, the ground falling away from us in a series of squares and zigzags. We headed north toward Tarin Kowt, or TK, where Jagger was stationed, while Captain Trivette gave Will a quick course in the area.

Man, it was nice having Will here. It felt like flight school, except for the whole foreign country, hostile enemy thing.

Twenty minutes in, I was enjoying the flight, something I hadn't had much opportunity for in-country. Will asked questions from the back, and either Captain Trivette or Rizzo answered him.

Near the Tor Ghar mountains, the radio crackled. Troops were in contact nearby.

"Do we respond?" Will asked.

"Nothing to do yet, Lieutenant Carter," Captain Trivette answered. She checked the fuel and then took the controls. "It won't hurt to be nearby since we're already out."

My heart jumped in anticipation as she altered our course toward the mountains. Two Apaches came on the frequency, responding.

"Now what?" Will asked.

"Now, we wait," I responded, looking back over my shoulder at him. "You ready to become a man? All buckled in?"

"Yes, Mom."

I tossed him a one-fingered salute with a grin and watched the mountains approach.

"Gun one-one." One of the Apache pilots came on the radio, his voice instantly familiar. Jagger. *Holy shit.* "In pursuit of target. Follow?"

My stomach lurched. "Carter," I called back. "That's Bateman."

He instantly sat straighter, on alert just like I was.

The other helo came on. "Gun one-two, I have your six."

Calls for air support came across the radio, and the Apaches responded. Tense moments passed, but no medevac call was sounded. My shoulders sagged in relief as the ground troops called up their thanks.

"He's all good," I called back.

Will threw a thumbs-up, then lowered his head to his hands for just a second.

"Gun one-one, headed back to FOB," Jagger called out, and I breathed a hell of a lot easier. I'd always known it was a possibility we would cross paths on a mission, but it wasn't something I wanted to— "Fuck!" Jagger called out. My breath froze in my chest. "What was— Fuck, we've been hit! We've lost our tail rotor."

I lunged forward in my seat like I could physically get to him, as my stomach plummeted to the ground hundreds of feet beneath me. The belts held me back. "Go!" I shouted to Captain Trivette. She'd already changed our heading toward the last known location.

"Mayday, mayday," Jagger called over the radio. "We are going down. Repeat, we are going down!"

No. No. No. I was too far away. I couldn't get to him, couldn't save him. Couldn't stop this from happening. *Jagger.* Every moment of our friendship flashed through my misfiring brain— hockey, rooming together, moving to Alabama, graduating flight school, that last barbecue before we left. He was the closest thing I had to a brother.

And I was fucking helpless.

The crumpling blast on the radio broke me into a million pieces, but the silence...it eviscerated me.

"Fallen Angel! I repeat, Fallen Angel!" Gunman one-two called over the radio. "They've gone down!"

Fallen Angel. Helicopter down.

The cry that came from my throat was animalistic, inhuman. "Jagger!"

Will reached through from his seat, putting his hand on my shoulder.

My best friend. My brother. He had to be alive. There was no other option.

"Gunman one-two, this is Dustoff one-two inbound. What is your current position?" Captain Trivette was steady on the stick and in her voice. I input the coordinates we were given, and she nodded. "We are three minutes out."

It was the longest three minutes of my life.

"He's alive, Walker. Even a helicopter crash couldn't take down Jagger Bateman," Will called on the com, but his voice shook.

He's alive. He has to be. He's alive. God. Paisley. The baby.

"Gunman one-two, what's the status of an LZ?" Captain Trivette asked.

"We've got ground troops headed there on foot, but it's cherry red, Dustoff. We've taken a few shots in our direction. I'm not even sure you can land near the site."

Captain Trivette locked eyes with me, her face set and somber. "Are we in?"

"Yes!" Will shouted.

Rizzo hesitated for the smallest of seconds, then called out, "In!"

"Fuck, yes!" I damn near screamed. Every second we wasted was another that he could be bleeding out...if he'd survived the impact. *He survived.*

We flew over the ridgeline and into the valley, the Apache providing cover overhead. Figures darted beneath us, and an unwelcome sense of foreboding lodged in my throat as the walls of the valley rose above us like we were being lowered into a grave.

"Damn it. Could this be a worse location?" Captain Trivette asked as we moved further up the valley.

"There!" I shouted, pointing to the plume of black smoke mixing with the rising dust.

"Shit," Will said.

Jagger's bird lay on its side, a mangled mess, rotors torn off, and looking at the terrain along the hillside he was smashed against, he must have rolled down a fair share of it. *He's alive. That's the only option.*

Gunshots pinged, hitting us in the side. "We're taking fire. We've been hit," Captain Trivette radioed, her voice calm and collected. "Aircraft is stable."

"Everyone okay?" I asked.

"Yeah," Rizzo answered.

"We can see daylight back here," Will added. I turned in my seat to see bullet holes in the sliding doors. *Fuck.*

"Seems like a good day to die," I muttered.

"Roger that, Dustoff one-two, we're trying to cover you," Gunman radioed. They came in closer, laying down fire along the ridgeline.

I scanned the valley floor as my heart threatened to pound out of my chest. "There," I said, pointing to a relatively flat section. "We can put down there."

Captain Trivette nodded, her full concentration on the bird. We passed just over Jagger's crash site on descent, but from its angle, I couldn't see anything but the belly of the aircraft.

Ping! Ping! Glass cracked. My head snapped to the left as Captain Trivette heaved forward, blood streaming from her helmet.

She's dead. Holy shit, she's dead.

Her body slammed into the controls, putting us into a dive.

"Shit! We're hit! Fuck!" I gripped my controls and pulled back, but I couldn't compensate for her body weight on hers. There was no way to recover, not this close to the ground. "We're going down! Brace!" I yelled, but it was too late.

December. Her name was my only prayer.

The ground rushed up to meet us at a terrifying speed.

There was nothing I could do to slow us down, to change the angle, to—

CHAPTER TWELVE

EMBER

I grabbed two bottles of water out of the fridge and met Paisley outside next to the fire pit after our morning hike. "We could have stayed in Alabama another few days. I wouldn't have minded," I said as I took the chair closest to her.

We'd spent most of the weekend at Fort Rucker for her graduation, and even though her parents were stationed in New York, it had been nice to hang out with Morgan for a couple days.

I'd kept the conversation with Will to myself.

"Thanks," she said, taking one of the bottles and twisting the top. "I just wanted to be in our house. I feel him here, you know?" Her hand rubbed over her belly absentmindedly.

"I understand perfectly. We might not have been here long, but it's our home. His clothes are here, his pillow, our life." I took a sip of my water, relishing the coolness in the Tennessee heat. "Remind me why you decided hiking was a good idea?"

She laughed. "It's good for us. You're not getting out of it, either. We're going again in the morning. Besides, school is over, and you have almost three months until you fly to Turkey. We have to fill our time productively."

"I'm still not sure I'm going," I admitted quietly. "I mean, I'm ninety-eight percent sure I am, but there's still this tiny part of me that says not to. You're pregnant, and the guys are deployed, and I'm, what, going off gallivanting in Turkey?"

"We can't always be wrapped up in them. Not if we're supposed to thrive in this life. We can love them—heck, you and I both know that was never a choice, not with men like ours—but we need our own lives. We can't lose ourselves in them."

"It's really the chance of a lifetime."

Paisley leaned across the distance that separated our chairs and took my hands. "Then you go. I'll be fine. Morgan can come for the rest of the summer, and you'll be back at the beginning of October. I'm stronger than you think."

"I know you are. I just don't want you to be alone in this."

She smiled, radiant with a happiness she seemed to carry with her at all times. "One, I'm never alone." She patted her belly. "Two, the guys might not be here, but they're with us. But you and I...we both have amazing adventures coming. You owe it to yourself to go."

"What if something happens?" I whispered.

She squeezed my hands. "That kind of heartache wouldn't care where you are, Ember."

She was right. Where I was had nothing to do with what Josh was doing. If anything, going now would use our time apart to the best advantage.

I checked in with Sam while I gathered up the pile of grad school applications I'd been avoiding, but hearing Grayson in the background made me miss Josh even more, so I made an excuse and got off the phone. Sam was happy, and she deserved to be. She didn't need my issues pulling her down right now.

Settling in with the applications, I cued up the DVR to catch up on what I'd missed while studying for finals.

Maybe it was because it was a Saturday, but I missed him more today than usual. Saturdays had always been our days. Even when we lived far apart, it was the one day of the week I woke up with him and fell asleep in his arms.

What was he doing? I'd texted hours ago, but he was probably still on shift. I grabbed my cell phone and shot off a quick message.

Ember: *I bet you're flying, but I wanted to tell you a quick I love you.*

I hit send and fidgeted on the couch. Without school, and Turkey still three months away, I was sure to go out of my mind.

Paisley knocked and came in without waiting. "Okay," she drawled. "I cannot sit in that house today. Let's go shopping for the nursery?"

I sighed in relief. "I'm so in. Let's get out of here."

CHAPTER THIRTEEN

JOSH

"I'm so glad you're home!" Ember ran from our kitchen and jumped into my arms. She was all sugar and sunlight, her curves filling my hands perfectly.

"Where else would I be?" I asked, and then kissed her.

"I hate when you're gone," she said softly.

"Me, too. God, I've missed you, December." I lifted her by the backs of her thighs, and she wrapped her legs around my waist.

"You don't have to miss me anymore."

"I just want to stay here," I said, a feeling of panic coming over me.

"Then stay," she whispered against my mouth, and then kissed me sweetly, gently sucking on my lower lip.

I deepened the kiss, wishing I could dive inside her and stay forever.

"Walker!" I heard the voice from a distance and looked up, scanning our kitchen.

"Josh!" Ember cradled my face, turning my head with her hands. "Josh, come back to me. Come home."

"I'm home, babe. I'm not leaving you again." I brushed my fingers over her cheekbones, loving the smattering of freckles that summer always brought to her skin.

"Walker!" The voice was closer.

"Come home to me!" she cried, breaking into tears. I wiped them away.

"Stop, December. Stop crying. I'm here." No matter how many tears I cleared, more flowed.

She sobbed, and her tears ran red.

With blood.

"Walker!" she screamed, grabbing my face. "Walker! Wake up!"

Light blazed through my vision, and my thigh buzzed, then burned. Ember vanished, and I jerked my head to the side.

"Thank you, God," the voice said, and its owner dropped his hands from my eyelids.

Pain shot through every inch of my body, and my head rang with a high-pitched buzzing. "Can you hear me?" he asked. "Walker?"

"Carter," I said, recognizing the voice. "I hear you, Will."

"Are you okay? Where are you hurt?"

I blinked steadily until the world came into focus around me. Will lay next to me—wait—above me, shining a light on my face. I tried to block it from my eyes, but my right arm wouldn't cooperate. I swatted it with the left, instead. "I'm fine. My right arm isn't responding, and my left leg is bleeding...or I pissed my pants."

Will snorted and shone the light down. "Damn. I wish it was the latter."

I swallowed, my mouth full of copper. "Rizzo?"

"I'm here, Lieutenant. Pretty sure I broke a few fingers on my left hand, my neck hurts, and my head is ringing like a bell, but I'm okay."

Thank God. "You, Carter?"

"I'm okay. It hurts like a bitch to breathe. I think I popped a couple ribs, but I'm okay."

I couldn't see past Will, but I knew Captain Trivette was still there, strapped in. "She's dead." Somehow I kept my voice level.

Carter nodded slowly. "Yeah. Look, we've been down about ten minutes, and you know we're not going to be alone for long. We have to get out of here."

I nodded and gritted my teeth as Carter ran his hand under my left thigh. "Good news or bad news?"

"Bad then good."

"Well, you have a rather large chunk of metal sticking out of your thigh." He shone the light again, but I couldn't get a look with the angle we were at. "It's pretty substantial."

"Is that seriously the good news?"

"No, the good news is that it didn't go all the way through. You're not pinned to the seat."

"Great. Let's get the hell out of here. How close are we to Jagger's site?"

"About a hundred yards," Rizzo answered from outside the bird.

Will unbuckled me, and my weight dropped to my right arm. I couldn't stop the yell that burst free. "Fuck, that hurts!"

"Sorry," Carter mumbled. Then he grabbed ahold of my vest and pulled. I pushed with my right leg in an awkward scramble out of the cockpit.

"We can't leave her."

"I know." Once we were in the back, I made it out with Rizzo's help. He lowered me to the ground, and then they got Captain Trivette out.

She deserved so much better than this, being laid on the rocky ground of some valley in Afghanistan. Jesus, she had kids. A husband. A life that was now over.

Because I wanted to save Jagger.

Not now. Shove it away.

"Where's the Apache?" I asked, cradling my useless right arm and collapsing against a boulder. Fuck, it had gone dark in the last half hour.

"They've been circling, but they've got to be low on fuel,"

Will answered, drawing his weapon and setting a perimeter, then grabbing his CSEL to radio out. "Gunman one-two, this is Dustoff one-two. Over?"

"Dustoff, this is Gunman. Glad you made it out. We have backup coming your way, ETA seventeen minutes. What is your status?"

"Three Deltas and one KIA." Will looked away from my stare.

"Roger that. You have company coming your way fast. They're armed and don't look friendly. We'll cover you while we can."

I stumbled to my feet and took his CSEL. "Is there movement from the other crash site?"

"Not that we've seen on thermal."

"Fuck." I thrust the radio back at Will and reached for one of the M4s they'd pulled from the bird.

"Sir, I need you to sit down," Rizzo ordered.

"We have to get to the other crash."

"Not until I look at you. As soon as I do, we'll go, so you're just delaying us." He motioned to a boulder.

"Fast."

He did a quick exam while Will got details on our incoming from the Apache pilots. "Get on the ground. Your shoulder is dislocated."

I dropped to the ground without complaint. He braced himself with his feet, gripped my upper arm, and counted to three. Then white-hot pain seared my vision, and lessened as soon as it came. "All better?" I asked with a gasp, blinking through the residual pain that had dulled to a throb.

"Hardly. My guess is your radius and ulna are broken. Can you rotate your forearm?"

Shit. Pain shot up my arm when I tried to do as he showed. "No."

"Can you move your fingers?"

I wiggled my digits. "Yep, so I can fire a weapon. Now let's go."

Rizzo sighed. "Sir, I think you've forgotten that you have a six-inch-long piece of metal imbedded in your thigh."

Holy shit, he was right. As if voicing the injury had given it permission to hurt, it began to scream—pulsing, hot, and insistent. "Damn. Is it near an artery? How did I not feel that?"

"Adrenaline," he answered and ripped a hole in my pants to examine me. "Looks like it's straight into muscle. Painful, but I'm not worried about you bleeding out. To be safe, we'll leave you here with Captain Trivette and check out the other site."

Fuck that. I sat up, grabbed the shard of the slippery, bloody metal, and yanked it out with a guttural yell.

"Damn it, Walker!" Rizzo dressed my oozing leg while he cursed me out. It only took a minute or two, but felt like years.

"Seriously?" Carter asked, glancing at my leg.

"You would do the same to get to him."

He nodded once, and then helped me to my feet. I tested my weight on my leg. It hurt like a bitch, but it would do until we could get to Jagger. With my left hand I took one of the M4s Rizzo had gathered, and checked the clip. My right was weak, and I still couldn't rotate my wrist, but it'd do. "Go figure. I become a pilot, and I'm still on the fucking ground with an M4."

Always keep one bullet. Never let them take you alive. How fast being infantry came back to me.

"Let's go," Will said, with Captain Trivette already over his shoulder.

"Your ribs okay?" I asked as he flinched.

"I'll survive."

I ditched my helmet and ignored every bite of pain and dizziness as we crossed the rocky terrain by flashlight, knowing we were sitting ducks at the bottom of the valley. The Apache flew lower and fired just beyond the crash site. Thank God they were here.

We made it to the site, and I swallowed the paralyzing fear that had made its home in my throat. Carter laid Captain Trivette on the ground carefully and then climbed the fuselage.

"Gunman one-two, we have arrived at the second site," I called over the radio, leaning on a large boulder to keep the pressure off my leg. Mentally, I walled off the pain, willing myself to focus on something else besides the throbbing that kept time with my heartbeat. A quick flashlight shine revealed that I'd already bled through the bandage. *Fuck it.* I climbed the rocks anyway, coming around the wreckage until I got to the cockpit glass, which was almost level with the hillside.

"Roger that. We have a few more minutes of fuel, and then you'll be on your own for about five minutes," the Apache pilot radioed. "We will stay with you as long as possible. ETA of backup is about seven minutes, but these hills are crawling."

Five minutes. It had taken less time to crash. "Roger."

"What can you see?" I asked Will, who'd busted through the cockpit glass. *Just be alive. I cannot take your body home. Just be alive.*

"He's alive!" Will shouted.

Thank you, God.

"What about the copilot?" Rizzo asked, pushing ahead of me to get to Jagger.

Will used a knife to loosen the seal on the glass toward the front of the cockpit and then kicked through it. He leaned in for a few seconds. "Front seater is KIA."

Fuck. The Apache left us to refuel, and I started my stopwatch. Five minutes.

Rizzo cut Jagger loose and dragged him out of his seat. I took the brunt of his weight, gritting my teeth against the pain radiating through my arm. Rizzo jumped down and then helped me lower Jagger to the ground.

His face was a bloody mess, and the rest of him wasn't much better. I put my fingers against his neck and felt his pulse, faint and thready, but there. I leaned over him and lifted his eyelids. His pupils weren't blown. "Jagger, it's Josh. Time to wake the fuck up, man. You have a wife at home, and a baby who needs you."

"Jesus Christ, he's a mess," Rizzo muttered, swinging his bag down from his back.

"He's also my best friend. College through flight school." I bit out each word as I gave him room to work.

Rizzo's eyes flew to mine, understanding dawning. *Keep him alive.* He gave me a curt nod and went back to taking Jagger's vitals, and I helped Will remove the mangled body of the copilot. We got him to the ground, and I checked my watch. Two minutes. The numbers swirled in my vision, and I blinked, trying to focus.

Gunshots popped, then wizzed past us. It was a sound that I thought I'd only hear again in my nightmares. We hit the ground, Rizzo covering Jagger.

A new volley of shots tore up the ground to my left.

"They're up the hill!" Will called out.

"I can't fucking see!" I answered.

We low-crawled to the nearest rocks, hauling Jagger behind us. God only knew the extent of his injuries, but he'd be safer here.

Will and I locked eyes, weapons ready, and with a nod, both rose over the rocks. *Holy shit.* They were coming straight for us, so many that I couldn't count. I fired until my clip ran dry, and then threw my only extra magazine in after Will did.

A gunshot hit the boulder next to me, and I turned to see four more coming around the fuselage. We were surrounded. A battering ram punched into my chest, sending me into the rock behind me. Rizzo fired, crouched next to Jagger.

No blood. Round didn't go through. Now get up or you're dead. You'll never see her again.

I sucked air into my lungs and pushed off the rock, meeting Will to stand back-to-back over Jagger. They kept coming. I dropped the M4 when I expended my ammo and reached for my nine mil off my vest.

"Dustoff one-two, this is Gunman one-four. Two minutes out with Dustoff one-one. Pop illum," the radio called.

I set the device to signal the Apache while Rizzo covered me, then tossed it on top of the fuselage and reached for my radio. "Gunman, we're taking fire. LZ is red hot."

I was firing again before the radio hit the ground. *One bullet. Save one bullet. Never let them take you alive.*

My last magazine loaded, I counted every shot until I reached thirteen. *Two more.*

I will do whatever it takes to come home to you. The last promise I'd made to Ember shot through my mind, and I shouted as I fired the last two shots from my magazine. "I'm out!"

Everything happened at once. The Apaches arrived, their guns splitting the night, but one guy rounded the back of the fuselage and raised his weapon to me.

December, I'm so sorry.

"Josh!" Will spun, shoving me to the ground and firing a round to take out the last of them.

He stood over me, illuminated by the moonlight, and looked down with a relieved sigh and a nod. The Apaches were here, and the radio announced the arrival of the ground troops and medevac.

I glanced at Rizzo, who threw a thumbs-up as he checked Jagger's vitals. *Maybe we've made it. Maybe we'll be okay.*

Will looked at us then offered me a hand to pull me to my feet. As I reached for it, three shots rang out from over the rock.

Will's eyes flew wide, his stunned gaze locked onto mine.

"No!" My scream was so raw that I barely recognized it as my own. "God, no!"

My vision swam in red and pain raced through my body like an electric shock.

We'd been so close.

CHAPTER FOURTEEN

EMBER

This wasn't happening. Not again. Not Josh.

Paisley squeezed my fingers as the officers walked toward us. I fought my lungs to draw air, as if they'd given up the will to do so.

"What do we do? What do we do? What do we do?" Paisley chanted rhythmically in a whisper.

I drew my eyes away from the reapers at our door and turned to her. "We fill the holes."

Her gaze flew to mine, wide and already shimmering with tears. She gave a series of tiny nods, and we stepped forward together to the edge of our porch.

He never called me when he got off mission. He never called. He always calls.

"Officers," I said with a voice much stronger than I thought I was capable of.

The two captains stopped a few feet from us, their eyes darting back and forth between us. Time stopped when the taller of the two opened his mouth to speak.

I blinked, and in that second, I pictured Josh's hands on my skin, his smile when he asked me to marry him. The way his hand had warmed me through the glass when he played hockey. Being held above his head after his game. Everything about him coursed through me, and I held my breath and that feeling as I opened my eyes again.

"Paisley Bateman?"

My breath left in a whimper that was part relief, but more grief. *It's not Josh. He's okay. Not Josh. But Jagger. Oh, God. Jagger.* Her knees buckled, and I caught her against me, holding her upright.

"I'm Paisley," she said in a half whisper.

"I'm Captain Xavier, this is Captain Jones. Would you like to go inside?" The taller one stepped forward onto our front steps.

Paisley shook her head, but we backed up so they could meet us. "Tell me. Just say it."

The shorter one swallowed. "The Secretary of the Army has asked me to express his deep regret that William Carter was killed in action in the Tor Ghar mountains, Afghanistan, late last night, the sixteenth of May. He was killed in a firefight that followed a helicopter crash, which is still under investigation. The Secretary extends his deepest sympathy to you and your family in your tragic loss."

What oxygen I'd managed to suck in left in a gush.

Will. No. No. No. He was just here. Two weeks. It's only been two weeks.

"Will!" Paisley turned into my shoulder, her slight frame shaking in gut-wrenching sobs. I wrapped my arms around her and held on tight, knowing that the ripping my heart felt for the loss of my friend was nothing like what she was enduring.

She loved him.

A thousand words came to mind as tears flooded my eyes— the normal things people said when tragedy struck someone else. But I couldn't lie and tell her it was okay. I couldn't placate her and say that I was sorry. We'd both been here before and knew that the words we needed to hear might not even exist in human language, so I said the only thing I could. "I'm here. You're not alone."

"Will!" His name was an anguished cry, and I felt the first of my tears slip down my face. "Oh, God, not him. His mama—" She sucked in her breath and stood, turning to the officers. "Have you told his mama?"

Their eyes met, and a darker feeling of unease settled over me.

"You're listed as his primary next-of-kin, ma'am. His parents will be notified directly, but everything is in your name."

She wiped her tears away with the back of her hand and nodded, trembling. "Okay."

The officers locked eyes again, and the tall one, Captain Xavier, swallowed.

I was going to be sick. I knew that look. I hated that look.

"They're not done," I whispered. "You're not done." *Helicopter crash. There's never just one casualty from a helicopter crash.*

Captain Jones cleared his throat. "December Howard?"

Every cell in my body stopped functioning. My heart ceased its beat. Paisley took my hand again with a desperate grip. A roaring began in my head that I fought to ignore.

"I'm December." *My mother is June.* Past and present warred for control of my brain.

"Maybe now we could step inside?" Captain Xavier said to Paisley.

"No, you tell us together," I said. "No matter what it is."

The two officers looked at each other. "I've never had this happen," Jones whispered.

"Yeah, me, either," Xavier replied.

"Tell us!" Paisley shouted, her usual sweet demeanor long since forgotten.

Captain Xavier swallowed. "We would normally make a phone call, first. Both Lieutenant Bateman and Lieutenant Walker have been seriously injured in helicopter crashes in the Tor Ghar mountains, Afghanistan. It was a combined incident."

My heart dropped to the porch beneath me. "They're not dead," I whispered to Paisley. To myself. "Injured, not dead." I could handle injured, any kind of injured, as long as Josh was coming home to me.

Paisley nodded.

I straightened my shoulders and tried to shove my grief over Will to the back of my mind. "Officers, if you'd like to come inside, we'd like to hear what you know."

"I'm getting on a plane," Sam said through the phone. As much as I wanted my best friend here, it just wasn't possible.

"No, you're not," I responded, zipping my carry-on. "Where the hell is my passport?"

"Ember…"

"Sam, you have another final to take, and I'll be in Germany anyway. I'm not sure how long they'll keep Josh there." I lifted my suitcase off the bed then pulled it into the guest room so I could sort through the fire safe. "Paisley booked a flight, and we're airborne in two hours."

"I can't do nothing."

I pulled my passport from under a stack of papers in the safe and put it in the back pocket of my capris. "You're not. You're doing exactly what I need you to do, which is take your final."

"There's nothing else?"

My heart sank as I glanced at a framed picture of all of us at flight school graduation. "I need you to check on Morgan, but I'm not sure she knows yet."

"I can do that. Ember, I'm so sorry."

I paused in the doorway and almost let it in, the reality of what had happened. It was like this giant monster screaming at the gates of my sanity, begging to be let in, to be acknowledged.

But I knew the moment I did, I wouldn't be able to function.

I was not my mother. I would not break.

"He's okay," I said. "He's alive, and that's all that matters."

"You're right." A door closed in the background. "Grayson's home from post." She handed over the phone.

"Ember? I'm sorry it took so long to get here. I was…making arrangements. Sam filled me in a little, but how bad is it?"

Grayson's voice buckled my knees, and I sat at the top of our stairs. Thank God he hadn't been with them. "They're alive, and everyone has their limbs. Jagger's legs are pretty torn up, and he has some bad internal bleeding. The last we heard he's still in surgery. It's only been a couple of hours since they notified us."

"Josh?"

I took in two gulping breaths, trying to maintain some semblance of control. "Broken arm, dislocated shoulder, and a ruptured spleen. He's out of surgery but not awake yet. And Will…" The words wouldn't come.

"I know," he said softly. "I've got a call into his unit and already talked to Paisley's dad. I'm leaving tomorrow for Kandahar. I'll bring him home."

Grief welled in my chest, a sorrow that could not be ignored and refused to remain compartmentalized. My throat tightened, and I covered my mouth as if it could keep my internal screams silent. I nodded, like he could see me, my teeth sinking into my lower lip. "What are the odds?" I squeaked. "What are the fucking odds of this happening?"

Grayson sighed. "If Josh knew it was Jagger that went down, you know there was nothing that could have stopped him from going. Any one of us would have done the same. I would have. I should have been—"

"Stop right there." I cut him off. "You are exactly where you need to be right now."

A few moments of silence passed between us before he

finally spoke. "You're headed to Germany?"

"Yeah. Josh won't be there for long, but we don't know about Jagger, and I don't want Paisley to go alone. And honestly, if I can see Josh for even five minutes..."

"You need to feel his heartbeat."

My forehead dropped to my hands. "Yes. Does that make me weak?"

"That makes you human. He's going to need you. I lived with him for almost two years, and he never really talked about what happened his first tour. Someone who carries that around, Ember, they're going to need to lean somewhere."

He hadn't talked to me about it, either, just glossed over details, promised me he was fine, and moved on. But I'd never pushed.

Maybe you should have.

The front door opened, and Paisley popped her head in. "Car's here. You ready?"

"Paisley's here. We have to go. Give my love to Sam, and we'll call you from Landstuhl."

"I'll keep my cell on," he promised then hung up.

"I still can't believe you found us plane tickets so quickly." I hauled my bag down the stairs and grabbed my messenger bag from the couch. There was a knock at the door. "You called a cab?"

"Not exactly." She opened my door to reveal a huge, suited man on our front porch.

"Miss Howard?" he asked from behind dark sunglasses.

"Yes," I answered. He took my bags and walked to the black limousine. I raised my eyebrows at Paisley. "Was there a sale on limos?"

She pursed her lips and shook her head, her face devoid of most color. The back door of the limo opened, revealing a man with Robert Redford looks and a tense version of the smile I knew well. *Holy shit.*

"Shall we go, ladies?" he asked, his voice a perfect balance of concern and efficiency.

"What did you do?" I whispered to Paisley.

"I called Jagger's dad."

My thoughts ran amok once we'd taken off in the private plane Senator Mansfield chartered for the trip. Paisley crashed out on the long couch, sorely needing sleep after today's shit storm, and the Senator handled business at a table toward the back of the jet, aided by a leggy blonde that, I kid-you-not, was named Monica.

Paisley had been right to call Senator Mansfield. It was the only way we could have left this quickly, but what was Jagger going to think about accepting his dad's help? It's not like they were exactly on friendly terms—or even speaking.

I'd called Josh's mom to trade information and love, my mom for moral support, and Grams for a little sanity before we took off.

Now it was just me, my thoughts, and eight hours of flight time from Fort Campbell to Ramstein Air Force Base in Germany.

As thankful as I was that we'd been able to take off ridiculously fast, thanks to super-political dad, I wished that I'd been able to hear Josh's voice when he woke up. At this rate, we'd be getting there right around the same time their medical transport landed.

Was he okay? Was his spleen really the only thing he'd needed surgery on? Did they set his arm there? Or would they do it in Germany? I had way too many questions and not enough answers.

But I'd see him in eight hours. I would hold him, kiss him, simply watch the rise and fall of his chest. I'd know that there hadn't been some mistake—he'd made it.

No book or television show could hold my attention. My thoughts flew as fast as the jet. What did I say to him about the other casualties, the other two pilots who had been killed besides...Will?

Will, who fixed my disposal.

Will, who had given Jagger his Apache slot.

Will, who had pulled Josh through the Blackhawk course academically.

Will, who was coming home draped under a flag.

Like Dad.

I pulled my feet onto the soft leather seat and wrapped my arms around my knees. I was in limbo, stuck between my world falling apart and finding out just how much had been destroyed. Would Josh want me there in Germany? Did he need time? Space? There was nothing I could do besides wait. I felt weak, nauseated, and terrified that everything I was wouldn't be enough for what was coming.

But he made it. He was alive.

And just like he'd taken care of me when Dad died, it was my turn to be Josh's whatever, and that was something I could never fail at.

CHAPTER FIFTEEN

JOSH

The ceiling of the Kandahar surgical center looked different, or maybe I just didn't remember it that well from the last time. I blinked, trying to clear the haze of drugs from my vision, simultaneously wishing for sobriety yet desperate to stay blessedly numb.

I raised my hand to my face but was stopped before my fingers reached the skin.

"You don't want to do that yet." The man's voice was deep, comforting, familiar. "They just cleaned out the wounds. You're not going to scar, but you go around shoving bacteria in there and all bets are off, son." His grip was cool but firm as he lowered my hand.

"How long have I been here?" I asked, realizing I wasn't quite with it enough to turn my head.

"About eighteen hours. Surgery took a little longer than we thought, but you'll have full use of your leg." A wave of déjà vu swept over me.

"Good. And my arm?" The drugs were strong and threatened to pull me back under.

"It'll take some recovery time, but you'll be okay there, too. You were a lucky guy, Josh. I think you'll still be able to play hockey after recovery."

I forced my eyelids open, blinking at the halogen lights

above me. "How did you know I play hockey?" *As if that's even important anymore.*

"I've seen you play."

He didn't have to finish the sentence. I already knew what he was going to say. It was the same conversation I'd had with him four years ago. I forced my head to turn and saw him sitting in the chair next to my bed, leaned back with his hands folded in his lap. His scrub cap sat over a pair of piercing blue eyes I knew well, and his mouth held a kind smile.

This wasn't real. I was still asleep, no doubt drugged from the surgery they'd wheeled me into.

For just this moment, I was okay with that.

"Where?" I asked him, knowing that was the line of the script I was reading.

"My daughter went to high school with you. She was quite the fan. Took me with her to see you play."

"Your daughter?" I asked, my heart burning with the love I hadn't known then.

"December Howard. You probably don't know her. She was a few years your junior."

"I know December," I whispered. "I love her. I'm marrying her. You raised such a flawless woman." But he didn't hear the last lines, because they hadn't been spoken four years ago.

"You do? She's a senior this year, hoping to go to Vanderbilt in the fall, but she has an asshat boyfriend who's pushing her toward CU."

"She'll break up with him," I promised. "He'll hurt her, but she'll heal. She'll go to Vanderbilt, and she'll graduate. She's happy."

"You know how those high school boys are." He laughed, having heard none of what I'd just said, then stood to take my vitals. He looked off in the distance as he listened to my lungs.

"She misses you every day. She doesn't say it—keeps everything pretty close to the vest—but I see it in her eyes," I said as he moved his stethoscope. "I love her with every cell in my body. There's nothing I wouldn't do for her, sir."

"I hope she makes the right decision for her," he said. "She's too good of a girl to get trapped beneath a man's dreams. She deserves her own. He won't give her that, and she's too young to see it."

"I see it," I whispered. "God, I see it." I forced my fifty-pound eyelids open again, but I was losing the battle.

"Don't you worry, PFC, you'll play hockey again. I took really good care of you."

"Thank you, sir." My world faded, leaving only the sensation of his hand on my forehead.

"You're going to be okay, Josh. I swear it. You both will."

"Lieutenant Walker?" A woman called to me from the black. "Can you hear me? Can you open your eyes for me?"

A blood pressure cuff went off on my left arm, squeezing to an unpleasant pressure. It was nothing compared to the overall ache coursing through my body. The left side of my chest felt like I'd been beaten in a bar brawl by at least six professional wrestlers. "Yes," I croaked.

"Here," she said and lifted a straw to my lips. I took in giant sips of cool, crisp water, washing away the taste of dead skunk in my mouth. I blinked, looking up to see a nurse hovering over me.

"Thank you," I said, my voice closer to normal.

She smiled. "Can you tell me your name and birthday?"

I turned my head to the chair next to me, half expecting to see Doc Howard sitting there, but it was empty, of course. Morphine was one hell of a drug.

"Lieutenant?" she prompted.

I took a deep breath and focused on the nurse. "Joshua Walker, September twenty-third."

"Good."

December. Her name rushed through me, soothed me, and then instantly my stomach dropped. God, she had to be losing her mind. Had they told her? They usually waited until we could call, but with helicopter crashes, those were too televised to delay notification until a soldier could call home.

God, had they gone to the house? She must have relived her worst nightmare.

"Ma'am? Can I call my fiancée? She's got to be scared. My mom, too."

"I understand. The transport airplane is here to take you to Landstuhl, so let's get you ready, and see if there's time for those phone calls before we move you." She picked up my chart and gave me a rundown on everything I'd fucked up in the last twenty-four hours.

Dislocated shoulder. Radius and ulna buckle fractured.

I looked down to see the splint covering the lower portion of my right arm, cradled against my chest in a blue sling. *That's not so bad.* But she kept going.

Six-inch gash on my thigh, and I hadn't done them any favors by ripping the metal out in the field and then walking on it. *Yeah, but I lived.* I'd had exploratory surgery on that, with both internal stitches and over thirty external ones. It took all my willpower not to rip back the blanket to see if I'd at least had the luck to bisect the gunshot scar that was already there.

"But the shocker was your spleen. It ruptured, which we didn't catch until you were here."

"I don't remember that."

Her smile was apologetic. "You were pretty heavily drugged. But we took it out, and you're going to be okay. You'll need a couple months to recover, but you will."

"Jagger? I mean, Lieutenant Bateman? Specialist Rizzo?"

"I'll take it from here," Lieutenant Colonel Dolan, our battalion commander, answered, filling the small doorway of my curtained partition. Cover in hand, he ran his hand over his shaved skull, over his eyes, and down to his mustache. "I'm glad to see you're okay, Lieutenant."

"Sir," I answered. "The other guys?"

"Rizzo's okay. A little banged up, but okay." He took Doc Howard's chair.

"Bateman?" I forced out and held my breath. He hadn't been awake, even after they medevac'd us.

"He's pretty mangled, but alive. He'll need some pins to salvage his legs, but they fixed all the internal bleeding in surgery. He's not awake yet."

My breath released on a ragged sigh, and my eyes closed in a silent prayer of thanks to God. Jagger was okay.

"You saved his life, son."

"At the expense of Captain Trivette and"—I took a steadying breath and tried to keep from losing my shit—"Lieutenant Carter." *Will. You got Will killed.*

He nodded slowly. "You were close to Carter?"

"Yes, sir. We went through flight school together, both Primary and Advanced Course. We were friends." *Against all odds.*

"I'm sorry for your loss."

He lives for them. Will's whispered order echoed through me.

I nodded, unable to say anything else about it. There was no opening that Pandora's box. Not here. Not now. "The other Apache pilot?"

He shook his head. "No. CW3 Thorne didn't survive."

I nodded again like a fucking bobble-head doll. "Yeah, that's what we thought, but everything out there went pretty quickly."

The nurse came back in and smiled at us both. "Sir, we

need to ready him for transport."

"Of course." He stood and turned to me in the doorway. "Lieutenant, I know today has been tragic for you, for the entire battalion, but you accomplished your mission. It took a great deal of bravery to do what your crew did. You can be proud. I know I am."

"Thank you, sir." My words were lip service, and we both knew it. I'd killed Will and Captain Trivette because of my single-minded need to save Jagger.

I wasn't even sure I could regret it, which made me ten times worse of a person.

Will had died protecting me. How the fuck was I ever going to repay that? Earn that?

The nurse squeezed my left hand and pushed a drug into my IV. "This dose should get you through to Landstuhl. Transport is here, and you're up next to go."

"My phone?" I asked, my voice raised in panic. I had to call Ember. There was nothing as important, including oxygen.

The nurse handed me a Ziploc bag from the table across my little room. "Here are some of your personal effects. Your uniform was beyond repair. I'm sorry."

"It's okay," I said, digging through the small bag to reach my international cell phone. One new text message.

December: *I bet you're flying, but I wanted to tell you a quick I love you.*

When had she sent it? While I was still in the air? On the ground? In the firefight?

Two soldiers came in, checked my chart, my bracelet, and confirmed my name while my suddenly noncompliant fingers fumbled with the numbers. They popped the brakes on my bed and began wheeling as the phone dialed.

Four rings and voicemail.

They wheeled me out, through the hallway, and the déjà vu hit again, taking me back four years. My eyelids and I resumed our drug-induced battle.

"Hi, you've reached Ember. I'm sorry I can't get to the phone, but leave a message and I'll call you back. If this is Josh, I love you, I miss you, and I wish I could kiss you!"

We came to Doc Howard's picture, taking me over the very same floor he'd taken his last breath on.

Beep.

I locked eyes with him, even though he drifted in and out of focus as the meds took full effect. "Hey, baby. I'm okay. Banged up, but okay." I stayed with him until we wheeled past. *I'll take care of her. I swear, she won't be trapped under my dream.* "December, I love you. Hold tight, I'm coming home to you."

I managed to hit end before falling asleep.

T he drugs started to wear off as we descended into Ramstein Air Force Base. I even felt us touch down. I fought to open my eyes, but the next thing I felt was being lifted into the transport vehicle.

I pried my lids open and turned to the side. I heard nurses talking. The vehicle was lit well enough to see Jagger across from me. He had an IV bag and looked like shit, but I probably wasn't ready for a beauty pageant, either. He made it. No ventilator, so he was breathing on his own. *He'll see his baby born.*

I blinked, the task way more difficult than it should have been, and tried to sober up. I needed to call Ember. Needed to hear her voice and tell her that I was okay, that I wasn't going to die on her.

"We're approaching the gate," one of the nurses said.

"I seem to have misplaced my ID card," I said quietly with a small tilt to my lips.

"Oh, this one has jokes." One of them laughed. He leaned

over me and then checked the drip on my IV. "You'll be just fine, Lieutenant."

As soon as I talked to her, I would be. "What time is it?"

"A little after two a.m. on Monday morning."

Fuck, we'd crashed over twenty-four hours ago. "What the hell have you guys been giving me? Time-suck painkillers?"

He laughed. "Ah, you're on the good stuff, son. But don't get too used to it."

Hell no. I wanted off it as soon as possible.

We parked at the hospital's intake bay, and they started the unload process. I flexed my stomach in preparation to move and groaned, falling back to the bed.

"No, no, don't move. Not yet," the nurse said.

Yeah, that wasn't going to be a fucking problem. Every part of me hurt, from the sharp throbbing in my leg to the ever-present ache in my chest where they'd removed my spleen. I couldn't wait to see what I'd done to myself.

What would Ember think? The scars had never bothered her before, but these?

My thoughts cut short as they lowered me to the ground and began to wheel me through the hospital. "Can you put me next to Lieutenant Bateman?" I asked yet another nurse.

"I'll see what we can do," she said in a sugar-sweet voice. "Are you hungry? It's the middle of the night, but I'll see what I can get together for you."

I shook my head. "The idea of food makes me want to hurl."

Her smile was bright against her skin. "Well, let's not do that, shall we? We can work on that in the morning."

The lights above me passed at measured intervals, feeling more like a strobe-light than the last club I'd been to. An elevator ride and long hallway later, she wheeled me into my room.

There was a window to my left and a bathroom door straight in front of me. I didn't have to pee...great, that could only mean one thing. "When do I get to pee on my own?" I asked her.

She gave me a knowing half smile. "As soon as you're ready."

"Yeah, can we make that happen now?"

She nodded. "Let me get the doctor. We'll finish your intake, make sure you can get yourself to the bathroom on crutches, and solve that problem."

"And my phone? I really need to call my fiancée."

She raised her eyebrows. "Pretty little redhead?"

My mouth dropped. Had she gone through my wallet? Seen the picture on my kneeboard? "Yes."

"Let's get your intake finished, and then get you that call."

The doctor came in, checked my vitals, poked at incisions that I wanted to punch him for, and gave me a general once-over. The trip to the bathroom was successful...and excruciating. My leg throbbed the minute it sank beneath heart-level, and that throb turned into a full-on screaming pressure the minute I stood, even with my weight on the opposite leg. It didn't help that I'd dislocated the opposite shoulder and was basically hobbling with the full use of only one crutch.

I was a fucking mess. I looked briefly in the mirror as I left the bathroom. My face was ashen. There was a laceration above my eye and several scrapes along my right cheek. I'd gotten a glimpse of the white bandage that consumed my upper thigh. But I was alive.

Will wasn't.

Captain Trivette wasn't.

I struggled back to bed, accepting the nurse's help because I was scared I'd end up on the fucking floor and tear something else. She raised my bed so I could sit up slightly, and her eyes sparkled with a grin. She was way too happy for three o'clock in the morning.

"How's your pain level?"

"Four," I answered through gritted teeth.

She arched a single eyebrow at me. "Liars don't get phone calls."

"Fine. Probably a seven."

"Can you manage without pain meds a little longer? I have a feeling you'll want a minute."

"Yeah," I answered quickly. I didn't want to be drug-drunk when I talked to Ember.

"Okay, then give me just a second." She walked to the door and opened it, making a "come here" motion to someone outside. Then she turned to me with a radiant smile. "She beat you here."

My heart stopped as she walked through the door.

"December." *Thank you, God.*

She cried my name and rushed to the right side of the bed. "Josh! You're okay. You're okay!" Her smile was water-logged, and the tears that fell from her eyes broke me in a way nothing else had.

She reached for my face but hesitated, uncertain. I grasped her hand with my left and pulled it to my cheek, leaning into it. "I was so scared," she said, her lower lip trembling.

"I know, but I'm okay. I'm fine." If I repeated it enough times, maybe she'd believe me. Hell, maybe *I'd* believe me.

She leaned down and brushed her lips against mine. I sank into her gentle kiss, savoring her taste, her soft sigh against my mouth—the small things about December I almost didn't get to have again.

I'd almost died.

I'd almost left her alone in the world.

I'd almost been her sad story.

I lifted my left arm. "Come lay with me," I whispered.

She looked up to the nurse, who hovered just outside the door. "I think that might be against the rules."

"I don't give a fuck. Get in this bed."

She walked around to my good side with an awkward laugh,

her eyes darting over my body. "I...I don't know where I can touch you."

I grimaced, pain wracking my entire body as I moved over to the right. "I don't know, either, but we'll figure it out together, okay? But I'll sleep ten times better with you in my arms."

I knew the truth—she needed to be held just as much as I needed to hold her. I needed to feel her heartbeat, her warmth, hear her voice. I needed her to be real.

She nodded, kicked off her shoes, lifted the blanket, and crawled into bed next to me, careful not to touch any part of my chest. She fit perfectly beneath my arm as always, her scent filling me with home, belonging, love. I kissed the top of her head. "I love you. Everything else can be said in the morning, okay?"

She nodded. "I love you. Nothing else matters."

The nurse came back in and clucked her tongue at us while she pushed pain meds through my IV. "If you pop those stitches, Lieutenant..."

Ember's eyes flew wide. "You stay," I ordered her. "She stays," I told the nurse.

She waggled her finger at us. "For now."

I smiled my thanks, and she left. I ran my thumb down Ember's arm as my eyes started to droop again. *For now* was fine. *For now* was better than I had yesterday, or the month before.

For now was my forever.

CHAPTER SIXTEEN

God, I was stiff. I rubbed the back of my neck, willing it to turn even the slightest of inches without screaming. I'd been too scared to hurt Josh to move a single muscle last night.

It was well worth it.

"Hey, want to grab breakfast for the guys?" I asked Paisley as we met in the hall, my yawn distorting nearly all of the question. Jet lag was a bitch.

"Sure, but only for me. They just took Jagger to the OR." Paisley mirrored my yawn. "Ugh, no yawning."

"How is he?" I asked as we made our way to the elevators.

"In and out," she answered, pressing the button to take us down. "He knows I'm here but doesn't stick around for long. He's getting the pins put in his legs now." Her hand swept over her belly. "He's a wreck, but he's my wreck."

I wrapped my arm around her shoulders as the door opened. "How's Josh?"

"Not sure. He was still asleep when I snuck out this morning, and he was too doped up to really talk last night." We made our way down the hallway to the cafeteria and loaded food into to-go boxes. "Want to come eat with us?" I asked her.

She shook her head. "I think I'll go back to my hotel room and try to sleep. He'll need me once he's out of surgery, and Lord knows this baby needs the rest. Tell Josh I'll see him later?"

I gave her an awkward hug, balancing the take-out boxes and lidded cups of orange juice. "Okay. Senator Mansfield?"

She drew back and shrugged. "He's still here but keeping it low key. Jagger's never been too open about his dad. I know the senator wants to see him, but keeping his distance right now might be the nicest thing he's ever done for him."

"I get it. You go get some sleep. Let me know when Jagger is out of surgery?"

"I will, I promise. They said it's going to be hours."

We said our good-byes and split paths, Paisley to the adjoining hotel and me back to Josh's room. Waiting for the elevator, I noticed something...I smelled. When was the last shower I took? The night before the notification? God, it had been twenty-four hours already, but I still wasn't expecting to smell like a sweat factory.

Okay, drop food to Josh, then get a shower.

Noise behind me made me look over my shoulder, where I saw four giant, sweaty guys in PT uniforms. Oh, that made more sense. Thank God, the smell wasn't me. Still, a shower wouldn't hurt.

I got off on Josh's floor. He was half sitting up when I came in, a doctor and new nurse hovering close to his bed. "So we'll get that done this morning and hopefully have you on your way back to the States tomorrow, if you're feeling competent on crutches."

"Thanks, Doc," Josh said. The doctor nodded before heading out.

Josh gave me a relieved smile and patted the bed next to him. He was pale, more so than I'd realized in the lamplight last night. I perched carefully on the edge and placed the breakfast boxes on the rolling table. "What's up?"

"They're going to set my arm today and get me casted," he answered.

"Good. That's good." I nodded like a bobblehead.

"Did you see Jagger?" Josh asked.

I rubbed the muscle of his uninjured thigh. "No. He's in surgery. Not life threatening, but they're setting the pins in his legs. Paisley wanted to see you, but she's exhausted. You okay?" I asked. He'd flinched when I'd said Paisley's name.

"Yeah, yeah. I'm fine." He threw up a mask, like I hadn't loved him for the last couple of years and couldn't tell the difference.

I'd let him have his mask—for now. "Everything else okay?" I addressed the question to the nurse.

"Are you his wife?" she asked, her hair pulled obscenely tight.

"No, ma'am," I answered.

"She's my fiancée," Josh added.

"Does she have access to your medical information?" the nurse asked.

"She has access to my bank accounts, my house, my car, my life, and anything else she wants, so I'd say yes."

Did his eyes just narrow?

"It's okay," I said quietly. "She's just making sure that she's not violating privacy laws by talking to me."

"Exactly," the nurse said with a tight smile. "Everything else is as we expect it. If you'll be the one at home with him, I can teach you how to change the dressing on his leg," she offered.

"I'd really appreciate that."

"After my arm is done?" Josh asked, eyeing the boxes on the table.

The nurse laughed. "Someone has his appetite back. Eat. Do you want another dose of pain meds?"

"Maybe something a little lighter? I'm not too keen on zombie mode."

"Sounds good. We'll come for you in about an hour?"

"Perfect, thank you."

I opened the box as she closed the door behind her, but

turned to see him staring at me. "What's wrong, babe?"

He shook his head and blinked. "When I woke up this morning, you were gone, and I thought maybe I had dreamed you being here."

"Do you dream about me a lot?" I asked with a grin.

"When we crashed, I was knocked unconscious..." His eyes fell away with his voice.

"Josh—"

He glanced at the open box. "Pancakes with strawberries. I love you," he said with false excitement.

Subject not up for discussion yet. Gotcha.

"Me, or the breakfast?"

"Both," he promised and leaned up for a kiss. I kissed him gently, lingering, enjoying every second that I had missed for so long. My heart jumped like I was fifteen again, chills racing down my arms as he cupped my face with his hand.

He was as familiar as my own skin, and yet everything felt new, like I was kissing him for the first time. "God, I missed you," he whispered. His hand tunneled in my hair, pulling it free of the knot I had it tied in. "There are no words for how much."

I pulled back, stroking my thumbs over his cheeks, avoiding the scabbed scrapes. His eyes held me prisoner, drawing me in with a force I'd never understood yet was utterly thankful for. The distance, the time—it hadn't mattered, our connection was still there, still crackling just under the surface. "You scared me. When they came to notify us..." My throat closed.

"I know." His eyes lost their light. "I'm sorry you had to go through that."

I shook my head, my thumb grazing his lower lip. "No. Never be sorry for what you bring to my life, Josh. The good, the bad, the amazing...the tragic. It's all worth it for you. For us."

He placed a kiss in the palm of my hand, his eyes closing like he was in pain.

Because he is, you moron. "I'm so sorry. Let's get you fed." I dropped my hand and turned my attention to his breakfast before he could distract me any further. *Fail.* I cut his pancakes into bite-sized squares while he dipped the neckline of my V-neck T-shirt and my bra strap off my shoulder. My eyes closed with each kiss he laid on my skin, and I dropped the plastic knife when his tongue traced the indent from my strap. "Josh," I tried to lecture, but it came out a little too breathy. "You have to eat."

"Maybe I'd rather have you for breakfast." His voice dropped, the same way my panties practically begged to. We'd never gone a month without jumping each other, let alone three, but for God's sake, he was barely out of surgery. *Down, girl.*

I turned with a forkful of perfectly proportioned pancake/strawberry and syrup/whipped cream and held it to his lips. "I don't even know if that's possible."

He raised one eyebrow, his look so smoldering I was surprised the fire alarms weren't popping off. "Me wanting you? More than possible. More like a certifiable fact." The energy streaming through me vibrated, and my muscles clenched. Josh leaned forward and took the bite. God, he was sex personified, and my body screamed to get reacquainted.

Don't be selfish. He's freaking injured.

"No, I mean possible in the you-just-had-your-spleen-removed-yesterday way." I started to put another bite on the fork, but he caught my wrist and held my gaze as he licked the last of the whipped cream off it. So. Fucking. Hot.

A little whimper escaped before he pulled me toward him and crushed his mouth to mine. This was no gentle kiss like before. There was no sweet savoring, no lingering look. Josh kissed me breathless, all tongue, teeth, and strawberries.

I melted. God, I'd missed him—and this—so much. My fingers ran through his hair, the fork lost somewhere in the bedding, and I kissed him back with every single fiber of my being. I poured everything into it, the nights I'd missed him, the fear that had been my constant companion, the relief of having him in my arms again.

He groaned, and I forgot where we were, what had happened in the last forty-eight hours. It was just Josh, my Josh, and we were doing what we did best. His fingers left a trail of shivers down my neck, and I gasped as he set his lips there next, putting perfect pressure on the spot just beneath my ear that he knew drove me wild.

Josh slid his hand to my waist, and then slid it under my shirt. My stomach muscles tensed as his fingers ghosted over my skin, but it was his breath that caught when he dove under my bra to palm one of my breasts. "Perfect," he whispered against my jawline as he rolled my nipple.

Liquid heat poured through me, but my common sense reared its head when I steadied myself on the back of his raised bed so I didn't bump his shoulder. "Josh, you're hurt."

His hand slipped free, only to take mine under the blankets and press it against his unbelievably hard erection, with nothing blocking me but his boxers. A sound between a sigh and a moan escaped me. "I'll hurt a hell of a lot more if I can't have you. Three fucking months without you, December." My body temp must have spiked another five degrees, because I was on freaking fire.

He took my mouth again, and I gave in to the need screaming at me, squeezing his length through the thin fabric.

Knock. Knock. Click.

I tore myself away from him, hands up like I was under arrest, and nearly fell off the bed. One-armed, Josh managed to lean and catch me, pulling me back in front of him just as the nurse came through the curtained partition.

Her eyebrows raised like she knew what we'd been doing, and my cheeks flamed. "I brought your meds. Name and birthday?" she asked.

Josh answered and swallowed the pills as she wrote in his chart. "Thank you."

"We actually have an opening now, so we'll be taking you to get your cast. Do you want to wheelchair it? If not, we can take the bed."

Josh's eyes darted to the crutches. *Not so fast, rock star.* "I'll push the wheelchair," I offered, tilting my head in a way that let him know I meant business.

His eyes flickered between me and the crutches before he sighed. "Chair it is."

"Good choice," the nurse replied. "I'll go grab one."

"I brought you wind pants," I said when he plucked at his hospital gown. "They snap up the side."

His forehead puckered in adorable lines, but I almost cringed when the gash above his eye strained at the stitches. "You went shopping here?"

I bit my lip and shook my head. "I bought them at home, but thought they'd be easy to get you into...and out of," I finished with a slow nod.

He laughed. "Were you watching *Magic Mike* or something?"

"Hey, I just thought they'd be fun to rip off when you got home, and now look how useful my sexy purchase is." I hopped down from the bed and rummaged through the small bag I'd left in his room, thankful I'd brought it from the hotel.

"Yeah," his tone waxed sarcastic. "Real sexy, here. But hey, I'm alive, right?" his voice dropped to a whisper. "Can't say the same for everyone else."

I snapped up to see him examining the bandage across his thigh absentmindedly. All at once it dawned on me—he was going to have more wounds than the ones I saw...and I had no experience, no idea what I could say or do to help heal them. I'd gone so far into the deep end that this no longer qualified as a pool—it was the ocean, and if I didn't get my bearings, I could end up watching him drown.

You are not your mother.

I stood straight and put the pants on the bed. Then I took his face in my hands and lifted it, leaning in to force him to meet my gaze. He did. I barely controlled my gasp as I caught him unguarded. Misery radiated from his eyes—pain, sorrow, grief…guilt. It was all laid bare for me to see for one precious second before he blinked it away. "You are alive. You are mine, no matter what." I forced a smile. "And scars are sexy."

Carefully, we got him buttoned into the pants and lowered into the wheelchair.

"Shall we go?" the nurse asked.

I moved to take the handles of the wheelchair, but Josh stopped me, gently clasping my hand in his. "Hey, babe, why don't you check on Jagger for me?" he asked. "You won't be missing much."

I did my best to ignore the sting of his dismissal. This wasn't about me. "Yeah, I can do that for you."

"Great. Thanks." He leaned forward, and I met him in a light kiss. Then he was gone, wheeled away to repair another broken part. Somehow it felt like if I'd been allowed to follow, I could have seen how to put him back together, too.

"I thought you were going to sleep?" I asked Paisley as I dropped into the seat next to hers in the waiting room.

She stifled a giant yawn. "I tried, I swear. But I couldn't sleep knowing he was in there."

"How's it going?"

"They came out a little while ago and said it's taking longer than they expected, but okay, I guess. They said he'll have full use, but we're looking at double casts for a while."

"They're alive."

She nodded. "They are alive. I got in touch with Will's

mama. She's not quite...sober yet. She's a little angry that everything is in my name. I couldn't give a fig about the money. It's not like Jagger doesn't have enough of it. But the choices... She wants him buried in Alabama."

I swallowed, my throat instantly tight. "Is that what he wanted?"

"No. He wanted West Point. It was actually a ridiculous argument we had while we were together. He said that was where he became a man, and that's where he'd spend his eternity."

"You didn't go there, so you couldn't be buried there," I guessed.

She nodded, her thumb spinning her wedding ring set. "We never really belonged together. I know that now. I knew it the minute Jagger put his arms around me." Her teeth bit into her lower lip as she struggled for control, taking a shaky breath. "But that doesn't mean that I didn't love Will in a different way."

"I know," I said, wrapping my arm around her as she dropped her head to my shoulder.

"And I'm so relieved that Jagger's alive. He's the other half of me, but I don't know how to reconcile that joy with the gaping hole in my heart—knowing that I'll never see Will again." Tears rolled down her cheeks. "I don't know how to be strong for Jagger and still feel like it's okay to miss Will...like I traded one life for the other."

"You didn't choose," I whispered into her hair. "No one chose."

"I can't be a blubbering mess around Jagger. He'll think... I just can't."

"You can. He'll think that you're pregnant, and as happy as you are to have your husband, you just lost one of your best friends—your first love. You have to feel that, too."

"It hurts," she whispered.

"Yeah," I said, knowing nothing could fill the void. "That part of feeling sucks."

. . .

"Jagger's out of surgery. He's loopy, but he'll be okay," I said as I walked into Josh's room. I'd taken the time to shower, so at least I didn't feel like a '90s grunge star.

"Okay, thank you. Grayson called. He made it to Kandahar. They'll take Carter to Dover tomorrow."

I didn't miss the fact that Josh called him *Carter*, whom he'd hated, as if he had disassociated that guy from Will, our friend. He wiggled the fingers of his right hand, sporting a new black cast that peeked out from the blue sling.

"What time are we leaving tomorrow?" It was already afternoon. It would be good to get him home, settled.

"I'm leaving now, if you'd like a ride," Senator Mansfield said from the doorway. He still wore a button-down, but he'd rolled the sleeves at the elbow. "I've seen my son, and it's not like he's going to let me feed him ice chips, so my work here is done."

"Thank you for the offer, sir, but I'd rather stay with Josh."

"Ember, as much as I'd like you to stay, there's no point," Josh said, taking my hand in his.

My head snapped back like he'd slapped me. "No point?"

He shook his head. "No, babe. I'll leave for Ramstein in the morning, and it's a military-only flight. I'll see you tomorrow night at home."

My heart deflated. "Oh."

"My son won't be leaving for another few days. I pulled strings, made sure Paisley could go with Prescott"—Senator Mansfield shook his head—"Jagger, but couldn't do the same for you. I'm sorry, I tried, but you're not married, and my power ends at that line," he finished with a very political smile.

My eyes flew to Josh. I couldn't leave him. Not now. What if he needed me? What if he wanted to talk about what happened and I wasn't here? What if I missed the only opportunity he might give me to see what was going on behind that mask of his? "Okay, let's get married."

"What?" Josh exclaimed, his eyes huge with what I refused to see as panic.

"Marry me. It's not like we aren't engaged, and come on, they have chaplains. Marry me, and I can stay with you."

"No. Hell no. Not like this." He squeezed my hand. "Ember, we're getting married on the top of a fucking mountain in Colorado, surrounded by our family, not in some hospital chapel with a bunch of strangers and...Jagger's dad. No offense."

"None taken," Senator Mansfield answered.

"We have Jagger and Paisley. That's all the family I need. I could stay with you."

He shook his head, and I saw it—the look of determination he usually saved for the ice. "No. You would regret it. Ember, I don't care about the next twenty-four hours; I care about the rest of our life."

"I won't regret it," I pushed.

"I would."

He would regret marrying me? The same man who had wanted me under any circumstances our entire relationship suddenly had caveats and lines he was unwilling to cross?

Air rushed into my lungs. *This is not about you. Not about you. NOT ABOUT YOU.* I repeated the mantra in my head as I slung my bag over my shoulder. "Okay, Senator. Thank you so much. I would love a ride home."

His eyes volleyed between mine and Josh. "I'll meet you in the hallway."

I waited until the door clicked softly behind him, and then tried to emotionally solder every raw, gaping nerve that was screaming in agony around my heart. I turned to Josh. "Okay, well, I'll see you at home?"

"December," he whispered. "I didn't say that to hurt you. I

would never hurt you intentionally."

I nodded. "Of course. I know that. I'm fine," I lied with a smile. "Where do you fly into?"

"Baltimore," he answered after a pause. "Then straight into Fort Campbell."

"Do you want me to pick you up?" I asked, terrified of the answer.

His shoulders sagged. "Of course."

"Okay. Do you still have the international cell to text me with details?" *Hold yourself together. Just a couple more minutes.*

"Yeah."

"Perfect." I leaned forward and kissed him lightly, unable to stop myself from lingering just a second longer, thankful that he was breathing, speaking, alive—even if he'd just pulverized my heart. "Then I'll see you at home." I forced a smile and backed away.

"I love you, December. Thank you for coming all the way here."

Yesterday I would have told him that of course I came. He was here, where else would I be? But today was different. Today I felt separated from him in a way I never had before, and even if it was an emotional overreaction brought on by jet lag, exhaustion, and fear...well, it still fucking hurt. "Thank you for letting me."

I left Josh's room and met Senator Mansfield in the hallway, who wordlessly led us to the elevator.

Once we were wheels up, gaining altitude out of Germany, the irony struck me—I'd come to Germany twenty-four hours ago to help heal Josh, and instead he'd inadvertently broken me.

CHAPTER SEVENTEEN

Josh

Military transports sucked. They sucked even harder when you spent eight and a half hours trying to figure out how to dig yourself out of the huge hole you'd gotten into with your fiancée.

If she still wants to marry you, jackass.

"What's on your mind, LT?" Rizzo asked, leaning back next to me.

"I'm wondering what color roses say, 'Forgive me, I didn't mean what I said.'"

He gave me the you-fucked-up look. "Pissed off the old lady?"

"I may have told her I didn't want to marry her."

He whistled low. "Not sure about the color, but I'm pretty sure you're going to need to buy out all of Nashville's florists. She give the ring back?"

"What? No." *Not yet.* "That's not what happened. I didn't mean ever, I meant not in the hospital chapel in some rush ceremony so she could be as uncomfortable on this flight as we are."

"Does she know that?"

"I think so. Fucking painkillers."

"Yeah, that's it. You blame the painkillers and she'll forgive you. No sweat."

"Yeah."

He side-eyed me. "Unless you meant it...even subconsciously."

"What?" I snapped.

"Listen, after what's happened, I wouldn't blame you." He shook his head. "I'm not marrying. Not while I'm in. I've got three years left, and then—when I'm out—I'll think about it."

"Why? Afraid you'll change?"

"Nawh. I couldn't bring a woman into this. Waiting at home for us to get back, putting shit on hold, moving where the army says, that's not the life I want for my wife, and that shit's on the good days."

Ember already knew the army life. She'd been born into it. She'd accepted that cost the day she'd pinned my lieutenant bars on me. "Right."

"But it's the bad shit, you know? Look at us, all torn up, stitched together but never really whole. I keep thinking about Captain Trivette's kids, her husband. He's a good guy, a major in the 101st, and now his whole life is just...fucked."

Fresh pain, the kind that couldn't be numbed by the drugs, sliced me open, flayed my soul from my bones. "Yeah."

"More power to you. Marriage is awesome. I'm just not committing myself to a woman until I can give her the life she deserves. Home at five. No deployments."

"No notifications," I added.

"Bingo." He snapped his fingers. "This feeling right here? The shit we're wading through? This is the stuff that changes you. It would be naive to say who I'll be once I'm done."

I nodded, at a loss for words.

"Fuck, I'm an asshole." Rizzo dropped his head to his unbroken hand for a second before looking back up. "I'm not talking about you. You know that, right? You have a girl who put her ass on a plane to be at your bedside. You keep that one. She'll stick through the shit. She's a good one."

"Yeah, she is." Too good for me, for this life, but then again, she always had been.

They'd notified her, pulled her world out from under her feet. I'd sworn to be whatever she needed, and instead I'd brought them to the door...again.

I'd make it up to her.

As soon as I figured out how.

"I didn't know if you'd want me to move an air mattress downstairs," Ember said as she held the front door open so I could crutch myself in.

"Why?" She hadn't shown any kind of anger or hurt since she'd picked me up at the airfield—or any emotion really—but fuck if I wasn't sleeping next to her. I'd hash this shit out with her right now. "Are you kicking me out of our room?"

"What?" She shut the door and twisted the lock. She'd added a deadbolt since I left. Good. I liked her safe. "No, of course not. I just thought you wouldn't want to negotiate the stairs. I was going to sleep on the air mattress, too," she finished quietly.

I hobbled the final foot to the couch and collapsed, gently lifting my leg to the coffee table to keep it elevated. *Home.* We'd only lived here for a month before deployment, but there was no place I more associated with the feeling of home than these eighteen hundred square feet. "I'll make it up the stairs," I promised. "You...might have to help me shower."

Her smile was instant and gorgeous. "Oh, I think I can manage that."

"Good," I said, opening my good arm.

"Do you want anything? I can grab you some water, or—"

"I want you. In my arms. Now."

She nodded and slid into me like a missing puzzle piece, fitting perfectly under my shoulder. "I'm glad you're home," she whispered.

"Me, too."

"What do we do now?" she asked.

"I was thinking of getting you naked—"

She scoffed. "Not what I meant. You? Army stuff? Checkups? Doctors? I mean...can you even actually *get* me naked?"

"Is that a challenge?" I asked, my voice dropping.

She shot me a raised eyebrow. "No."

"I have to check into the Warrior Transition Unit and get with the doctors here. And yes...I can most certainly get you naked, and I'm going to. Repeatedly."

Sure, it was going to be a challenge, since I felt like I'd been put back together by Frankenstein, but getting inside December was my number one priority tonight. Fuck, I was getting hard just thinking about it. I'd willingly pop more than a few stitches if it meant touching her.

"Look." I pointed to the window. "It's already dark. Nine p.m. is a perfectly respectable bedtime. I say we go now."

"Ha!" She laughed, soothing my soul. "I thought you wanted a bath first."

"I said shower. Men take showers."

"Giant, gaping thigh wounds take baths with their legs draped outside the tub, manly or not." She stared me down.

"Get in with me?" I wiggled my eyebrows.

"Oh. My. God. Joshua Walker, you're incorrigible—and a hot mess. No, I will not get in with you." She stood up and offered her hand. "But I will soap you up."

"Deal," I answered, entirely too quickly because my blood was in my dick and my brain had checked out. All I could think was warm water and Ember's hands all slippery. Fuck it, I wasn't waiting. "You know, this is not the hot reunion sex I pictured," I complained.

"Oh no?" She leaned down to help me up. "What did you picture?"

"Something more along the lines of this." I grasped her wrist and pulled her down instead, careful that she landed beside me.

"Josh!"

Her mouth formed that perfect little O, and I pounced. I kissed her, thrusting my tongue against hers and angling to kiss her deeper. She leaned into me instantly, and the twinge of pain I felt in my chest was nothing compared to the heaven of having her breasts pressed against me. Hell, kissing her was the perfect painkiller—all-consuming and addictive as any narcotic. But kissing her wasn't enough.

I tugged on the bottom of her shirt, and she obliged, crossing her arms at the hem and pulling it over her head. My lips trailed across her collarbone and then her neck as my fingers traced her spine until I met the strap of her bra. I snapped my fingers over the closure, and it popped free.

"Josh. Are you sure we should be—" She cut off her own words with a moan as my mouth closed over one perfect nipple. I flicked my tongue over the bud, and she arched, dropping her arms so her bra fell to her lap. I sucked, and her fingernails bit into my scalp.

"Very sure," I said, blowing across it lightly before laving it again.

Her hips rolled, and I would have grinned, but I was too turned on. I gave the same attention to her other breast, and her whimpers grew into outright moans. She came up on her knees and kissed me, her hands firm on the sides of my face. Every muscle in my body tightened in arousal, the kind that sent stabs of need straight to my stomach.

I grasped her ass and kissed her with every ounce of skill I had, willing her to forget why this could be a bad idea—willing her to lose the self-control that had abandoned me the minute we walked in the door. She melted, pressed up against my side. God, she was perfect in my arms, liquid fire as her mouth made love to mine in a way I couldn't wait to do with my entire body.

My hand slipped into the waistband of her shorts, past the string—*fuck, yes*—of her thong, to cup her exquisite ass. A moan tumbled past my lips. "God, baby," I groaned, running my hand around her toned, soft waist, and fumbling with the button. *No time for this shit.* "You're going to have to help me."

She pulled away, her lips swollen, eyes glazed and half open in want. It was my favorite look on her, and my dick jumped in agreement. "Josh..." The battle between what she desperately wanted and what she thought was best for me warred on her face, clear as day.

"I need you," I begged shamelessly. "More than anything, December. Let me love you."

Her breath was shaky as she stood like a goddess between my outstretched legs, all soft curves and lithe limbs. *Holy shit, you actually get to touch her. This perfect specimen of woman is yours.* Mine. Forever. My thoughts ceased when she locked eyes with me and wiggled her hips, bringing her shorts down her thighs with her thumbs. I held her gaze as long as I could, falling into that sea of blue like I did every time she looked at me. But then her hands drifted back up, her thumbs hooking in to the straps of her very small, very pink thong, and my eyes went to them.

My mouth watered, which was going to turn into drool if I didn't shut it. "Off." My voice dropped impossibly low.

A smile ghosted her lips as she teased one strap, then the other, until I was ready to bite her panties off with my fucking teeth. I'd never felt this urgent with her before, this impatient. "December," I growled. "Now."

She raised an eyebrow at my tone. "Where's that famous patience, Walker?"

"On the floor with your fucking shorts." The need raging through me wasn't polite. No, it was primal, and if I'd been capable of carrying her over my shoulder, I would have by now. Damn it, just knowing I couldn't was infuriating. "Baby," I warned.

She dropped her panties, leaving herself gorgeously bare. Then she placed one knee between my thighs, rubbing right against me, and I lost it. Gripping her hip, I sat up on the couch, and urged her backward until the backs of her knees hit the coffee table. "Sit," I ordered.

Ember hesitated just a second before she did as I asked. Her breathing picked up, making her breasts rise and fall at my eye level, but I didn't break her gaze. Ignoring the stab of pain in my thigh, I lowered myself to the floor, sliding my legs under the coffee table until my face was directly between her outstretched thighs. Fuck this sling; I wanted both of my arms around her, filling my hands with every lush curve. I wrapped my good arm around her and pulled her forward until she balanced at the edge of the coffee table.

"Josh," she whispered my name.

She'd be screaming it soon.

I might not have been able to sweep her up the stairs, but I could make her come so hard that she'd forget I was injured, that I'd been gone three months, that I was her living nightmare, because she was my wildest dream.

I held her apart with my fingers and set my mouth on her, tasting, licking, sucking, working her over with my lips and tongue until her hips bucked. The only sounds were her stuttered breaths, gasps, and full-out moans. One of her hands braced her weight against the table while the other held me against her.

She tasted even sweeter than I'd remembered.

I lost myself in her body—her every reaction—from the tightening of her thighs to the slight pitch variances in her whimpers when she threw her head back in surrender. In that moment, I forgot everything and existed for one reason: to please December.

Her breathing quickened, her muscles tensed, and her cries sounded higher and higher as she spiraled closer. With one finger I knew I could make her come. It would be easy, but I let her hover, loving the desperation of her hips rocking against my face, her pleas for more.

"Josh..." She started chanting my name, then screamed it as I pressed on her clit with my thumb, stabbing my tongue inside her. She flew apart. I pressed on her again, lightly, as she came back down, and her body jolted again. She was so fucking beautiful to watch come undone.

She stared down at me, her lips parted, cheeks flushed, and a look of wonder in her eyes that made me fall for her all over again. Then hunger replaced it, and she pushed on my shoulder. "Back."

I shifted my weight, retreating until I leaned against the couch. She licked her lips as her eyes raked over me like I was some buffet and she hadn't decided where to start yet. *Everywhere, December. Everywhere.*

She gently removed my sling, then my shirt just as carefully, pulling it over my cast. "Get rid of it," I said as she ran her fingers over the neoprene shoulder stabilizer. I spoke before she could, knowing what she'd say. "I don't care what it does to me, take the fucking thing off, December."

She undid the Velcro and did as I asked, then sat back on her heels next to me and just...looked. The lust pouring out of those eyes made me so hard I was afraid I wouldn't last. "You're incredible," she whispered, kissing down my chest, careful to avoid the incisions on my ribs. Her tongue left a trail of fire, dipping into the ridges of my abs as I instinctively flexed them. God, it felt amazing.

She unsnapped the sides of my wind pants and took them off. "These don't have snaps," she said, fingering my boxers.

"I think you can figure— Holy shit, babe." She grasped my dick in her tiny, sexy little hands and squeezed gently. I was going to die if I didn't push inside her soon.

I lifted my hips, gritting against the pain in my thigh, and she slid my boxers off, leaving my ass bare against our carpet. "I almost forgot how beautiful you are naked," she whispered, her hands stroking down my sides until she reached my thighs, stopping just before midway, where the white bandage stood out against my skin.

She locked eyes with me and lowered her head. She was going to— No, I'd lose it. I'd be done in two seconds flat. "Up," I begged, far beyond caring that I sounded like I was fifteen. "Please, baby, up. I need to be inside you."

She glanced at my thigh, my chest, my shoulder, and then she shook her head. "No, Josh, I'll hurt you. Let me—"

"Do you trust me?" I asked, my breath choppy. Hell, I was amazed I could still hold a thought.

"With my life," she answered.

"Then trust me with mine," I pled and guided her to straddle me. "Because I don't think I'll survive if I can't bury myself inside you right now."

With a knee on either side of my hips, she kissed me, careful not to press against my chest. I reached between us, reveling in how wet she was, how ready. Then I lined us up and moved my hand to the curve of her ass. We had inches to spare; if we weren't careful, she'd hit the wound on my thigh, but damn, it would be worth it.

"Birth control?" I asked, mentally high-fiving myself.

"Never stopped," she promised and lowered herself inch by flawless inch, taking me inside the perfection of her body until I was completely enveloped by her. "Welcome home," she whispered.

She was everything and everywhere, surrounding me, her soft skin in my hands, her taste still lingering on my tongue. She started to move, gently at first, testing our limits, and it was all I could do not to come, to surrender to the overwhelming need for release that screamed through my body, because I needed this to last.

"I love you," she whispered against my mouth, kissing me deeply. "God, I missed this. I missed you."

"I love you," I promised, then angled for a deeper kiss, needing every part of me tangled in her. Her soul bathed me in love, her kiss intoxicated every sense, and the movement of her hips, the glide of me deep within her began to bury my demons.

Here was my salvation.

December was my saving grace.

Over and over she slid down on me, only to lift just before she took me too deep. But deep was where she loved it, where she lost her head, and I needed her to forget, to be just as lost as I was.

I snapped my hips into her, and she gasped. When she nearly bumped my shoulder, she bit her lip and leaned back instead, bracing her weight on her arms against the coffee table. The angle put every detail of her body on display, from the bounce in her breasts to the tiny, glistening beads of sweat on her skin. Damn. She was...exquisite.

Fuck the burning in my thigh. I pushed it away and instead concentrated on slamming my hips against hers, hitting her inside where I knew she needed it. She responded, clenching around me, our bodies falling into rhythm like we hadn't been apart these last few months.

Her sigh turned to a groan, which grew to that sexy keening sound she made when she got close. Letting go of her ass, I used my fingers to stroke her clit, rubbing in time with my thrusts, barely holding onto the small shred of control I had left. I needed her to come around me, needed to feel her fall apart so she could hold me together.

With a cry, she came, shuddering over me. Uncaring of the damage I might cause, I dropped my arm and pulled her against my chest, taking her gasps as if they were oxygen and I was drowning.

I needed her close. "Closer," I moaned.

She looped her arms around my neck, holding onto the back of my head as she rode me, kissed me, rocked back into every thrust.

The pressure hit at my lower spine, and I knew I was done. "I love you," I swore as I held her against me, calling out her name as my orgasm ripped through me. The release was overwhelming, draining the last of what energy I thought I had, and we laid there for a few minutes, her head tucked under my chin. God, I was never going to move.

Unfortunately she did, kissing me gently before heading to clean up, then helping me out in that department on her return. I grimaced at the rending pain in my thigh as I got my boxers back on.

"Did you tear something?" she asked, dropping to her knees.

"If I did, it was so damn worth it." I grinned, unable to contain how good I felt, or the peace that coursed through me.

She arched an eyebrow. "You're going to be a difficult patient, aren't you?"

"You could climb back on, and I'll show you how difficult," I suggested.

She shook her head and laughed, the sound healing me like another tiny stitch across the gaping canyon that had formed in the last week. "Let's get you in the tub."

We made it to the tub, and finally to bed, exhaustion conquering me. I took the pain pills Ember handed me and put the water back on the nightstand. She propped pillows around my shoulder and then snuggled into my other side, her head fitting exactly where she was meant to.

I was home. I would marry the woman who owned my soul.

I had lived.

Carter and Trivette had died.

My eyes snapped open in the darkness, Ember's breathing already steady and deep next to me. I turned and kissed her forehead. Rizzo's words bounced around my head, unwelcome and unavoidable. "I'll make this life worth it to you, Ember. I swear."

The pills knocked me out, but they couldn't stop the dreams, the nightmares I'd grown accustomed to over the years, which had returned with vehemence since before the deployment.

I wasn't sure anything would ever stop them again.

CHAPTER EIGHTEEN

EMBER

His gasp woke me.

I blinked, begging my eyes to focus on the hazy glare of the alarm clock that read 2:45 a.m. Before I could turn, I heard his arms sweep over the covers between us. I'd moved as soon as his breathing had evened out, scared that I'd accidentally bump the laceration on his thigh or the incision on his chest in my sleep.

"Ember?" he asked, his voice panicked, his breaths quick.

"Here," I said softly, rolling on my side to face him. I caught his hand and set it to my cheek. "I'm here, Josh."

His sigh of relief broke my heart wide open. What had he been dreaming of? The deployment? The crash? How long did I wait before I asked him what happened? Was he going to want to tell me? Should I even ask?

Damn it, I had no idea what to do, how far—if at all—to push.

He tugged gently, and I shifted closer, pressing against his side. "Do you need anything? Water? Meds?"

He shook his head and pressed a kiss to my forehead. "Just you."

"Nightmare?"

He nodded slowly, his chin rubbing the top of my head.

"Do you want to talk about it?" *Please talk about it.*

"No." His answer was whispered but curt.

"Okay." I pressed closer, laying my hand just above his incision to feel his heart beat against his naked skin. Even with everything that had happened, my soul burned with gratitude that he was here. "But when you're ready, I'm here."

He swallowed, then nodded.

After the third time I woke to his panicked, searching hands, I stopped trying to give him space and slept closer.

After lunch the next day, as we were preparing to leave for Fort Campbell, Grayson called from Dover. Josh's eyes had gone dead by the time he hung up the phone.

"Everything okay?" I asked, putting his noon meds in front of him.

"He's got Carter," he answered quietly. "Grayson will stay with him until he's ready, and then he'll take him to West Point for the funeral. Did Paisley get with Carter's mom?"

"Yeah. Funeral is next Friday."

"Morgan?"

"Sam flew to Alabama the day after her last final. She's with her."

His eyes squeezed shut, and my heart clenched. "Okay. Do we fly? Drive? Fuck this leg."

"Jagger's dad is sending a plane—no, don't argue—it's not like Jagger can get around easily in a wheelchair, and you would hate flying commercially with your leg, or being stuck in a car for fourteen hours."

"Hotel?"

"Reservations made."

"Captain Trivette? Do you know anything about her?" His eyes focused on his plate.

"Yeah. Hers is here, a few days before. We can make both."

It had only taken a quick call to Carol, the kind wife from the FRG, to get the details.

He nodded and looked up slowly. "You took care of everything."

"That's my job. I take care of you," I answered with a smile. *In every way that I know how.*

He squeezed my hand and gave me a look that melted me. "Thank you."

"I love you," I answered, as if that were reason enough for anything. Because it was.

His eyes dropped to my ring and lost a little of their life. "Listen, about what happened in Germany."

I tensed. "The whole non-wedding thing?"

"Yeah. I hope you know that I want to marry you. I just didn't want those circumstances. I didn't want that to be our story. Our wedding day should be about you and me and our forever, not some rush job in a foreign country without our family. Not because you felt forced."

"I didn't care. It didn't matter to me." It mattered when he'd said no.

He took my hand, his thumb grazing the diamond on my engagement ring. "It would have, eventually. This...moment— what we're going through—it's just a blip in our lives, something we'll always remember but won't dwell on. I didn't want our wedding memories to be tangled up in that. Please tell me you understand."

I came out of my chair and kissed his forehead, lingering for just a second to breathe him in. I was so lucky, so blessed to have him here. "I understand," I whispered, then cleared our plates.

It wasn't until after the dishes were done that I realized he hadn't taken the pain medication.

"You ready?" he asked from the living room, dressed in a pair of basketball shorts and Under Armour shirt.

"You didn't take your meds?" I asked, holding them in my palm.

He shook his head with a smile I knew he was faking, but I let it slide. "I'm fine. Besides, I've seen what they do to some guys, and I'd rather deal with the pain now than the withdrawals later. I'm fine. Seriously."

I'm fine. It was his damn mantra.

"Okay," I said too quickly and then pocketed the bottle in my purse. If he changed his mind later, I'd have them.

"Ready?" he asked, standing in his PTs, using one crutch to keep the weight off his leg.

"Maybe we should get you a wheelchair," I suggested, grabbing my keys and purse.

"No."

"It would help keep the weight off that leg."

He made his way to the porch. "No. Final answer."

I totally mocked his manliness behind his back as I locked the door. "You're far too stubborn." Turning, I saw him perched at the edge of the steps with a wry smile.

"I know my limits." His eyes shot skyward. "Sometimes."

I became his crutch to get him down the steps.

"Oh man, I want to take my Jeep," he said wistfully, looking at the closed garage where I kept her.

"As soon as you can bear weight, babe. Until then, it's car city."

"Yeah, yeah," he moped, folding himself carefully into the passenger seat of my car. I'd pushed back the seat as far as it would go before getting him the night before.

"Okay, full schedule," I said as we pulled out of the Starbucks drive-through, two white mochas in hand. Caffeine was a biological necessity to get through Josh's afternoon. "Where do we start?"

"Airfield. They want me to meet with ASDAT." His voice went flat.

"In English?"

"Aircraft Shoot Down Assessment Team."

My hands tightened on the steering wheel, and my breath stuttered. "Because you were shot down?" I tried my best to keep my voice even.

The incident is under investigation. That's all they'd told us. "Yes."

My eyes darted from the road to where he stared out the window. "And..." I swallowed and pushed past the boulder in my throat. "...and Will was with you?"

He didn't move a single muscle except the one in his jaw. "Yes."

We pulled up to the gate and I handed the guard our IDs. He scanned both, handed them back, and waved us through. My mind reeled as I drove, questions firing faster than I could even process them, knowing I shouldn't ask. I should wait until he told me. *But what if he never does?* "And Jagger's aircraft?"

We parked in front of the battalion building, but Josh didn't move.

"Josh?"

He looked in my direction, but not at me. "Jagger was shot down. We responded and were shot down, too. Carter survived the crash—" He swallowed, closed his eyes, and took a deep breath as his fist clenched the seat. "I can only go through this once right now. I just...can't."

I reached across the e-brake and squeezed his hand. "Okay." *You pushed too hard.*

Once we entered the building, my Josh disappeared and Lieutenant Walker took over. He gave me a nod and disappeared into a room, the door closing behind him. Soldiers led me to an empty conference room across the hall.

I set my coffee down and pulled out my GRE study booklet and iPad. If I was going to be stuck here for hours, I may as well get some work done.

An hour later, I was bored to tears, my eyes crossing. I hadn't tried to cram this much useless knowledge into my brain since SAT prep, and that had been years ago.

You're the one who wanted a doctorate.

In anthropology. What was I thinking? I could teach while writing. Teaching was mobile, so I could move with Josh's career, but not successfully at the collegiate level. *Are you really going to determine your career, your dreams by Josh's?*

I wanted to flick the devil off my shoulder. Of course I was going to take Josh's career into consideration. That's what marriage was, right? I knew he'd said he'd get out when his obligation was over, but lately he'd been hinting at doing a full twenty, just like when I'd first asked him over two years ago.

You're commissioning. You're going career.

Yes. That's my plan.

But when he'd realized that it would cost him our relationship, he'd sworn that it would just be the obligation from his ROTC scholarship—that he'd get out when it was over.

I'll resign…

I would never be responsible for you turning your back on this. I know what it means to you, what you feel your responsibility is. I won't ever be the one who holds you down.

But what did that all mean now? Now that he was under even more years of obligation from flight school? Now that I'd adjusted to this life? Now that he'd been wounded? Seen his friends killed…again?

My cell phone rang, thankfully saving me from the downward spiral of my thoughts. Sam's face flashed across the screen.

"Hey," I answered.

"You sound exhausted," she said, her voice just as weary.

"You can guess that from one word?"

"I can. How's it going there?"

I stared at the door like I could see through it. "He's in with the assessment team."

"Yeah, Grayson said they'd have questions for him. Is he talking about it yet?"

"Not to me." *Shit, that came out bitchy.*

"Whoa, tell me how you really feel."

I tapped my pencil on the glass topper of the table. "I have no clue what the hell I'm doing. He's not talking, he has nightmares, and his favorite phrase is 'I'm fine.'"

She sighed. "I'm sorry."

"I know it's wrong, but I almost wish I was allowed in that room, like I can't help him if I don't know what happened. I feel like there's this chapter of him I don't get access to, and it stings. I know it shouldn't. I know he'll talk in his own time, but I barely know what happened the first deployment. He never talks about it. And this one... God, Sam, what am I going to do if he shuts me out?"

"I can't imagine, Ember. Just remember that he loves you, and give him some time. It's only been a few days."

"You're right. I know that logically. Emotionally, well, I'm not the most rational over here." A self-deprecating laugh slipped free.

"You have every reason to be upset. For Josh, for Jagger, for Will, and for you. I know he's hurt. I know what he just went through is unspeakable, but this...it happened to you, too. You get to have whatever feelings you're having. I wish I knew how to help you."

"Me, too. I just want him to be okay."

"I know. When do Jagger and Paisley get home?"

"Her email said tomorrow."

"Good. You'll have each other."

"How is Morgan?"

Her sigh told me all I needed to know. "Breathing. Crying one minute, silent the next, mad as hell ten minutes later."

"I'm glad you're there with her."

"Me, too. It almost feels like I never left, but everything is different without you guys here." Her voice cut out for a second. "Oh, that's Grayson. Call me if you need me, okay?"

"I will. Love you, Sam."

"Love you, Ember."

We hung up and I went back to studying. Another hour later the door opened, and Josh stuck his head through. He looked even paler than he had this morning, which was saying something. He was heading into Casper territory. "Hey, babe," I said.

"You ready? We're all finished." His eyes looked flat, like whatever had transpired in that room had sucked the life out of them.

"Yeah." I gathered up my things and dropped them into my messenger bag. "Where to next?" I asked him as we walked out slowly.

"Blanchfield," he responded. The military hospital. Of course—he needed to check in with the doctors.

The hospital was huge. There was no way he was going to one-crutch it and come out the other side with a functioning left arm. It took several minutes of begging and the promise of sexual favors, but he let me put him into a wheelchair to the clinic.

"Besides," I said, flipping through a magazine as we waited in an exam room. "It kept your leg elevated, right?"

He gave me a healthy dose of side-eye from the exam table, his leg stretched out on the paper liner. "It's a good thing I love you."

I blew him a kiss. "You look sexy in PT shorts."

There was a knock at the door and a cursory pause before it opened. "Lieutenant Walker," the flight surgeon said, glancing over his chart.

After introductions, Dr. Ortiz got right down to the exam, keeping it focused on his injuries and not how he'd received them. I did my best to keep my eyes off the sculpted lines of his chest and abs when he removed his shirt. I failed. Miserably.

After the exam, Dr. Ortiz sat on her stool to face us. "Laceration on your thigh looks good. No infection, and not swelling too badly. You need to keep off it for another week."

"Staples?" Josh asked like a kindergartener.

She rolled forward, looking over the wound. "Another four days, and then I'll take them out. How does that sound?"

"Like four days too long," he answered.

She rolled her eyes in my direction. "He always like this?"

"Worse," I answered. "He hasn't asked you about getting on the ice."

"Skating?"

His eyes lit up. "Soon?"

"Maybe once that cast is off your arm, Lieutenant." Man, this woman had the mom look down pat.

"How long will that be?" I asked, putting the notes into my cell phone.

"Another five to six weeks, if I had to guess. We'll get you in for an X-ray with ortho next week and see how it's healing." She jotted more notes in his chart. "Splenectomy incision looks good, too, healing remarkably fast."

"Good nursing care," Josh said with a smile, and gave me a wink.

Dr. Ortiz laughed. "Looks like it. He giving you trouble?" she asked me.

He has nightmares. He won't talk to me. He won't take pain meds. "No, ma'am. Just keeps trying to test his limits."

"That's a pilot for you," she answered. "Okay, that brings us to your shoulder. Are you keeping the stabilizer on?"

"Yes, ma'am," he answered. "How long is that going to be a part of my life?"

"That's going to be up to ortho, but my best guess, seeing your chart...another three weeks in a sling, and then rehab.

We'll see if we can get you into a below-elbow cast for that arm before we yank the sling, eh?"

Josh nodded, his eyes darting back and forth on the floor like they did whenever he was analyzing something, working out a problem. "Okay, so staples out this week, and then how long for full recovery of my leg?"

Dr. Ortiz tilted her head. "Probably six weeks, if it continues healing how it is. Keep it dry for draining, then we'll take out the staples and let you heal."

Josh nodded. "Six weeks total for the arm."

"Yes."

"Stitches over my eye this week, too, right?"

"Yes." Her eyes narrowed at the same time mine did.

He nodded again, calculating, I could tell. What the hell was he trying to figure out?

"Lieutenant, you're in for a little rehab on that shoulder, your arm, the muscle in your leg, and you had major abdominal surgery. Take it easy. I'm putting you on thirty days of convalescent leave to start with, and then we'll see where you're at."

He'd have thirty days of leave. Thirty days that I could take care of him before he'd be put on a desk job with the rear detachment. The relief that rushed through me, relaxing my posture, was almost embarrassing.

"Okay. How long until I have an up-slip?"

All that relief died a swift, painful death, and my stomach turned, nausea rolling through me. He wanted his wings back, the permission to fly. Five days. It had been five days, and he wanted back in a fucking helicopter.

My eyes bored into him, willing him to turn, to see my face.

He kept his eyes locked on Dr. Ortiz.

She turned toward me, but he didn't. Fevered rage mixed with ice-cold fear, and I disengaged, leaning back in my chair as I realized he wasn't asking my opinion. As much as I loved him, in that moment I hated him a little, too.

But maybe he'd need a year, right? Pilots had to be perfectly healthy to fly. Hell, even a sinus infection kept them grounded. If not a year, then maybe six months?

"Let's get you into rehab first, see about range of motion, and then we'll discuss an up-slip. You're at least twelve weeks out."

Now I hated her a little, too.

CHAPTER NINETEEN

JOSH

"Yeah, thirty days of leave," I told Mom over the phone before dinner. I ran my fingers alongside the staples on my thigh. Just a few more days and this shit would be out of my body.

"I don't mean to be all mama-bear, but I'd really like to see you," she said, her voice heavy with emotion.

"Yeah, of course. I have some things to take care of here in the next couple of weeks. Do you want to come here? I'll pay for a ticket if you want." I looked up where Ember was chopping lettuce, and she gave me an approving nod before turning her eyes back to the greens.

It was the closest thing to communication I'd gotten since the doctor's appointment hours ago.

"Oh, a plane? I don't know."

I closed my eyes and rubbed my temples. "Planes are safer than cars, Mom. By about forty-three thousand to thirteen."

"Says the man who just got himself into a helicopter crash," she admonished.

All my speech stuttered on my tongue. "Ehhh, not the same." *No one is shooting at you here, trying to kill you, watching you crash so they can pull your body out and torture you a little more before killing you.* I swallowed, trying to block out the thoughts. I looked up to Ember, her hair pulled into a messy topknot, strands of red framing her face as she rinsed tomatoes in the sink facing me. "Hold up a second," I said to Mom and put her on mute.

"You want to go to Arizona?" I asked Ember. "Mom's afraid to fly."

"At least one of you is," she said under her breath, drying the tomato.

"Ember."

"Yes, I'd love to see your mother." She didn't look up, but I knew she was genuine. Ember and Mom were peas and carrots. I hit the unmute button just as Ember muttered something that sounded like, "You can stay here."

I let out a deep breath. "Mom, how about we come there for a week or so? End of June? We can swing through Colorado after and see Ember's mom at the same time."

Mom burst into an exuberant planning machine, and I let her go with a laugh and a promise to call again soon. Then I turned to the extraordinary, gorgeous, brilliant, angry redhead in our kitchen. "Are you going to speak to me?" I asked as Ember chopped carrots.

She waved the butcher knife at me, her mouth opening and closing like she couldn't decide whether to talk or not. She'd been silent since we left Dr. Ortiz's office, which in Ember-ville meant I was fucked. *Or not fucked, rather.* She turned away from me and attacked the celery.

"It's my job," I told her as she carried a plate over to me. "I just want to do my job," I repeated as she set the plate on my lap. She'd baked my favorite chicken, so she couldn't have been that mad, right?

"Well, your job right now is to heal, so eat that."

Wrong. She was definitely that mad.

She brought over her own plate and sat on the loveseat.

"I had to ask, more for a measure of my downtime than anything. Once I have an up-slip, I'm completely healed."

"Uh-huh," she said between bites.

What did she expect? For me to never set foot in a helo again? *Wouldn't you? What if it had been her?* The fork clicked against the plate as I set it down. "Babe, do you want me to stop flying?"

Her gaze flew to mine. "What? No? I mean, maybe? I don't know. It's not fair to ask me that question right now."

"Are you mad that I asked?"

"I'm not mad that you asked. I just don't understand the timing. It's been five days since the last helicopter almost killed you. I know it's an inevitability, you getting back up there. I know how you feel about flying, the mission, all of it. I get it. But...five days."

"And we probably have another twelve weeks," I said softly, trying to make her see that I wasn't trying to hop in an aircraft and take off right this second.

"Right, but that's where your head is at, getting back in the sky."

Instead of staying safe with me.

She didn't have to say it. Her eyes did, the giant pools of blue wide and shimmering, begging me to see her side.

I set my plate on the coffee table and rose to my feet—or foot, rather.

"Josh, you need to sit."

I hopped the distance to her, took the empty spot on the loveseat, and propped my leg on the coffee table. The pain awoke with a dull throbbing, but it was nothing I couldn't manage.

"Hey," I said, tilting her chin toward me.

She looked at me, and I was a goner, lost like always. Ember held nothing back in her eyes. She laid every piece of her pain bare—her fears, her insecurities. It was one reason I was wildly in love with her. She was confident enough in us to let everything show.

I owed her the same respect, even if it gutted my pride.

"I have to know how long I have, because I don't know if I can do it. I don't know if I can ever get behind the controls again and not hear Jagger's mayday call, or see my death staring at me through the windshield as we went down, or feel the impact. I don't know if I can do it, if I *want* to do it. What does that make me? Because the minute I admit that to anyone in MultiCam, you know my wings are gone. If I can't get back up there, what was it all for? What was Will's death for?"

She put her plate next to mine and turned, tucking her feet under her and taking my face between her soft hands. "I will support whatever you do. I made you that promise, and I'll keep it. Yes, what you do terrifies me. I know that you love it, and it's become just as much a part of you as hockey ever was. But you need to know two things, Joshua Walker. First, you are so much more than a pair of silver wings. I loved you before them, and I'll love you long after you tuck them away, whether that's in twenty years or twenty minutes. Second, your apprehension makes you human, and a better pilot when that time comes. I have no doubt that you will get past this. It's not in your nature to fail, remember?"

I took her mouth, letting my kiss say everything I didn't have words for. My need for her, my awe over her unwavering support, my gratitude for the simple fact that she existed—she was mine.

Then I handed over her dinner and picked up mine, and just hung out with my future wife, reveling in our normal, no matter how odd it was, because it was hard-fought and ours.

"Don't do it! Don't!" Will's voice screamed through the coms, but I ignored him, racing through the rocky valley, the ground speeding by us.

"Walker, was his life worth both of ours?" Captain Trivette asked, just before blood began to drain from her helmet, covering her face in rivers of red.

My heart slammed against my chest as she hit the controls, putting us into the dive I knew I couldn't recover from. We plummeted to the earth, and she reached up with her crushing embrace, welcoming us home as we made impact.

My body jerked, air rushing into my lungs, and my eyes opened to total darkness. My right arm reached for my weapon, only to find my arm trapped, immobile. Panic rose in my throat. We were sitting ducks out here. My left hand flew to my vest to find it missing, my skin bare. *What the fuck?*

There was a pillow behind my head. Wait. Bed. Right.

I turned onto my left side, a jarring pain screaming from my thigh, and swept my hand under my pillow. Gone. My weapon was missing. "Fuck!" I growled. "Where is it?"

"Josh?" Her voice broke through, and I paused.

December. Here? I blinked through the disorientation and saw her form rising next to me in bed.

Our bed.

"Baby?" she asked, slowly reaching across the small distance that separated us, as if I were a wounded animal—as if I would attack her. "You okay?"

Her hand made contact with my cheek, the touch soothing, bringing me into reality. A nightmare. It had been a nightmare. I was home, in our bed, not in Afghanistan. That's why there was no weapon.

"Yeah," I replied, leaning into her touch. "Yeah, I'm okay."

"Another nightmare?" She moved forward, pressing her body against mine as if she'd instinctively known that was exactly what I needed. She was my anchor, holding me to reality, to our life.

I nodded, my chin rubbing against her hair. She smelled like the citrus shampoo she used, bright and alive, and I breathed her in, pushing the nightmare away. Will hadn't blamed me. He'd whole-heartedly agreed to go after Jagger. So had Captain Trivette.

But when I closed my eyes, I still heard their blame, felt it reverberating in every cell of my body.

"Do you want to talk about it?" she asked, her hand tracing a light pattern on the side of my rib cage, just under my sling.

I shook my head. She couldn't get into my thoughts. Not yet. Not until I had my shit straight, or I'd lose her. There was no way a woman like Ember, with her father's morals, would stay with someone who had traded one life for another, not when it cost her a friend. Not until I'd figured out how to pay back Will's sacrifice.

God, I didn't deserve her. Not after what I'd put her through...what I would undoubtedly put her through again. But I was too selfish to let her go.

"What can I do?"

"I..." I couldn't find the words. I just needed her wrapped around me, holding me together. Just her. I needed the haven only she could provide, the moments where nothing existed besides us, where I was lost in her soul, her mind, her body—so deep that I forgot everything else. "Just let me touch you."

She tilted her head up for a kiss, and I took it, an edge of desperation chasing me that I'd never felt before. My hands were too insistent, my kisses a touch beyond passionate, but she met me with the same driving need. Urging her on top of me, I used my mouth and hands to bring her to climax, savored the cry of my name on her lips. Then I sank into her, burying my demons with each thrust, losing myself in everything she was, as if by loving December some of her goodness would wash into me and cleanse the dark away.

Afterward, she fell asleep against me, her body as spent as mine. I contemplated the bottle of pain medication she kept in the nightstand to ease the throbbing in my thigh, the dull ache in my chest, but knew, just like my orgasm, its relief would be only temporary.

So I slept...and waited for the nightmare to claim me.

This time it was Ember's voice in my head, accusing me of killing Will, and her blood on my hands.

"**D**ude, you look like shit," I said, crutching into Jagger and Paisley's townhouse the next day. He was stretched out on their sectional, pillows under his legs to keep them elevated.

"Take a look in the mirror, asshole." Jagger grinned. "At least my complexion doesn't make me look like a ghost. Can you touch your fiancée with those hands, or do they just slip right through?"

I laughed, since his skin was paper-white, still recovering from the massive blood loss. "Oh, yeah, you're Miss Tropicana over here."

He chuckled and smacked the seat next to him. I took it, lifting my leg to the coffee table. Paisley would kill me if she saw, which I had no intention of letting happen...or seeing her in general. "Where did your wife run off to?"

Jagger tossed me an Xbox One controller. "She went to fill the prescription for my meds." He adjusted, grimacing as he shifted his weight back with his arms.

"How are you feeling?"

"Like I crashed my fucking bird and have six pins in my legs. You?"

I nodded. "Yeah, about there."

The home screen flashed on the TV, and Jagger sighed. "I don't remember seeing you in Landstuhl."

"Yeah, well, you were pretty out of it."

"That's what Paisley said. Did she tell you we're having a boy?" Jagger's grin was contagious.

"No! Congrats. Little mini-Jagger, huh?" My mind flashed to a son, to strapping tiny skates on a toddler, handing him a stick for the first time while Ember lectured me on safety from the box.

"God help us." He laughed, but it faded quickly. "Look. I love you like a brother. I just...I just need to know a few things."

My stomach twisted. "Yeah."

"Did you know it was me? Was that all in my head?"

"Yes, I knew. We were on our local area orientation flight for Carter, and we heard you go down. I recognized your voice on the radio."

Our eyes locked for a second, and his slid shut. "You saved me."

"It was never a question, Jag. You are my brother. What do you remember?"

He looked off into the distance. "We lost our tail rotor — RPG—and then everything started to spin. It was like being on that teacup ride at Disney, except you figured it was going to kill you. I knew it. All I could think as the side of the valley came closer was that I'd never kiss Paisley again. I'd never see our son. Then the first impact came." His eyes narrowed. "The sound was..."

"Yeah." I understood, because it was a sound like no other, crumpled metal and death.

"We hit a few times along the valley wall, end over end, I think...and I swore I heard you call my name. That's when I figured I was dead, except you're no angel." He gave me a wry smile.

"Yeah, that was me."

"Did you know the site wasn't secure?"

I swallowed. "Yes. Your wingman was still taking fire."

"And you came anyway?"

"It was you. I mean, I'd like to say that I would have done the same for any downed pilot, and I think I would have, but when push came to shove, it was you, Jagger. I wasn't going to let my best friend die at the bottom of a valley in Afghanistan, not if there was the slightest chance you'd lived through the impact."

He nodded. "Did...did Will know?"

Anguish ripped through me, freezing my lungs, my heartbeat, the very blood in my veins. His face flashed through my mind, seeing him above me right before the shots rang out, his relieved smile that we'd made it.

Except we didn't.

"Yeah," my voice croaked. "Yeah, he knew."

His head hit the back of the couch, a ragged sigh forcing its way through him. "Of course he did."

"He agreed. We all agreed to go in. Carter...he was the one to pull me out, and he was the first to get to you, to tell me that you were alive."

Jagger's eyes were trained somewhere on the ceiling. "Thorne?" His copilot.

"He was gone by the time we got to your crash site."

He nodded. "And then the firefight?"

"That's when we lost Carter."

"Fuck. I didn't wake up, not completely. I thought I heard your voice, but I wasn't strong enough to open my eyes. Where..." He swallowed, and I fought back the misery clawing its way up my throat, the tears I wouldn't let near my eyes. "Where did he die?"

"Right next to you," I answered. "He..." My head dropped into my hands as my heartbeat escalated, and I rubbed at my temples, like it would keep the images at bay so I could just tell Jagger what he needed to know. "Rizzo couldn't get the bleeding stopped. Carter had been hit in an artery and his stomach, just beneath his Kevlar. You guys were less than two feet apart, and he..."

It was too much. My throat closed, nausea rolled through

me, and my brain felt like it might explode if I didn't keep pressing inward with my hands.

"It's okay. I got it." Jagger squeezed my shoulder.

I took deep breaths, picturing Ember's face, her laugh, until the tightness in my chest faded and everything else became manageable.

"Thank you. I'll never be able to say it enough, Josh. Thank you." He squeezed my shoulder harder, and I leaned over, pulling my best friend to me in the hug I'd been terrified I'd never have again.

"Never say it again. You would have done the same. I'm just glad you're alive."

"Yeah, I would have come for your foolish, courageous ass."

"I know." We did the awkward back-pat thing, and I relaxed against the couch.

"So, I'm not really feeling *Call of Duty*," he said, picking up his controller.

I pointed to my shoulder with my controller. "I think the Kinect golf game is out."

He shrugged. "*Lego Jurassic Park*?"

Just like college, except we weren't nursing morning-after hockey game bruises or chasing no-name girls out the door. We weren't healed, weren't close to any standard of what normal might look like from now on for either of us, but we'd both made it out alive. That was more than we could say for our friends.

"Legos."

CHAPTER TWENTY

EMBER

Tomorrow it would be two weeks. I closed the calendar app on my iPhone, which reminded me that we were due at the Cadet Chapel in half an hour. One last pin and my hair was secured, my French twist reminding me so much of Mom that I did a double take.

I patted concealer over the dark circles under my eyes and the small bruise that Josh had sucked into my collarbone last night. I knew what he was doing every time he reached for me, using sex to escape, to hide from the nightmares that still woke him nightly, but I let him.

Maybe that made me a bad fiancée, letting him distract us both with orgasms until we were limp. Maybe I should be saying no, making him talk out the monsters in his head. But I knew he wasn't ready, and pushing him might push him further away from me, which was something I couldn't handle. The other part? I loved when he reached for me, connected us in a way I felt like we were just barely missing when we weren't in bed.

I applied the waterproof mascara and declared myself well-enough done. I'd learned my lesson at Captain Trivette's funeral a few days before. Waterproof-only for days like this.

We'd buried Josh's copilot under giant trees in a cemetery near Fort Campbell. Josh hadn't moved a muscle during the ceremony. He'd barely blinked, his eyes either on the casket or

Captain Trivette's two small children. We'd paid our respects to her husband, Major Trivette, and he'd hugged Josh, asking him to visit sometime, and then we'd left.

Josh hadn't spoken on the way home, other than to answer yes or no questions, but he'd nearly ripped my dress in haste to get to my skin once we'd walked in the door at home.

"I can't get my fucking blues on," Josh growled, but not at me, just in my general direction. In the last couple of weeks, I'd learned the difference.

"Okay, give me a second, and I'll help you." I slipped the sling-backs onto my feet and finished zipping up my black dress.

I crossed our hotel room to where Josh was half dressed. His short-sleeved white shirt was starched and tucked into royal blue pants with a gold stripe down the side. The abrasions on his cheek had healed, and the laceration above his eye had faded to a deep pink line. Everything about him was beautiful, from the carved lines of his torso to the perfection of his ass in those pants. I slid my hands up his shirt and paused at his shoulder. "No stabilizer?" I asked.

"Not today."

"Are you going to hurt it?"

"I don't care. It's too bulky under my jacket, and I'm not fucking with it today. End of story. It's coming off in two days, anyway."

Do not poke the bear. I rolled my eyes.

"Jacket?" I asked, fixing his tie first.

He sighed and handed me the thick blue jacket. I worked it over his new cast first, which ended just beneath his elbow. It was a tight fit, but we made it. Once it was on, I buttoned the front for him. "There you go."

"Thank you," he said.

"I'm still driving." I smiled and took the keys off the desk before he could reach them.

"Baby, if I don't have the stabilizer on—"

"You'll just hurt yourself. You can get in the car, or you can stay here." My chin rose an inch, and I held his gaze, refusing to back down.

"Fine," he said, with a soft kiss against my lips. Over-sexed or not, his kisses were still the sweetest moments in my world.

We drove from the hotel, curving along the stone-walled roads of West Point Military Academy until we reached the parking lot, and then walked the rest of the way, my footsteps feeling heavier as the entrance came closer.

Josh took my hand as we entered the massive chapel. It was beautiful and overwhelming, the giant stone columns stretching skyward to support the panels of stained glass that let in the noon light with prismatic brilliance. The wooden pews were full of gray-uniformed cadets paying respect to one of their own, as we made our way up the center aisle toward the family.

It was such a fitting good-bye for Will.

You cannot cry yet. Hold yourself together.

A few deep breaths later, we moved to sit a couple of rows back, but Paisley waved us up and pointed to the empty pew across from hers in the front row.

Will's casket was closed in front of us, the flag draped across it. Somehow it transformed to Dad's in my warped mind, and I blinked the image away.

"Where is Will's family?" I whispered to Josh as he took the seat closest to the aisle.

"His mom and dad are on the other side of General and Mrs. Donovan," he answered. Jagger sat on the aisle, then Paisley, Morgan, and then the Donovans and Carters.

"That's it? That's all he has?"

Josh nodded. "And they're not much, from what he told me."

"There's Grayson and Sam," I said, waving them forward. They took the seats next to us.

"I can't believe this is how we meet up again," Sam whispered, taking my hand.

Four months. That was all that had passed since we'd sat in front of the fire, celebrating Jagger and Paisley's wedding. Now we were gathered in front of Will's casket.

Life was not fucking fair.

The service began, the minister talking about honor, duty, God, country, everything Will had stood for, and yet not what I'd remember him for. I took Josh's hand with my free one, stroking my thumb over his fingers, which had gone cool to the touch.

General Donovan took the podium, taking a deep breath and bowing his head before he began to speak. "Lieutenant William Carter was a man of uncompromising morals and steadfast loyalty. He was a damn fine officer, but more importantly, Will was an exemplary man. He didn't let many people into his inner circle, but once he did, there was nothing he wouldn't do for you. He would walk into fire for those he loved." He looked at Paisley, who leaned her head on Jagger's shoulder. "He would go to battle for his friends." He looked directly at Josh, then Grayson. "And he would willingly give up his life for his brother." General Donovan's face twisted, his lips pursing and flattening as he battled for control, but he met Jagger's eyes. "Even had he known his fate, Will would have made the same decision."

The first of my tears fell, sliding down my cheeks in hot streams. Josh's fingers tightened around mine, the rough fiberglass of his cast rubbing against my skin. The slight pain grounded me somehow, kept me tethered to reality instead of the wish that this was a dream. A nightmare.

"I've known Will since he was a boy, watched him mature to manhood with pride. I pinned his Lieutenant bars and swore him in as an officer. For you Cadets joining us, this was a man to aspire to, a man to emulate. If even one of you graduates as just a fraction of the man Will Carter was, then this Academy will have done its job. Well, maybe not the cocky, self-righteous butter bar he was for a few months..." A low rumble of laughter rolled throughout the chapel, and Josh nodded. "...but the man he grew to be over the last couple of years. I have heard it said that only the good die young. I call bullshit. He wasn't just good, he was the best of us. He was the first of my sons by choice"—he looked back to Jagger—"and the world will forever be just a little dimmer, a little darker for us without him."

We sang a hymn after General Donovan finished, and then it was Josh's turn as the final speaker. He squeezed my hand one more time and then rose to take the microphone, pulling a tri-folded piece of paper from his jacket and laying it flat. Then he steadied himself and spoke, his voice clear and steady.

"I hated Will when I first met him," he said with an easy smile. Another rumble of laughter echoed against the stone walls of the chapel. "I thought he was a self-righteous prick who wouldn't know loyalty if it bit him, and wouldn't know friendship if it waved a hand in his face. In my defense, I was kind of right." Another wave of laughter. "But I was also wrong. Will didn't just hand out loyalty, you had to earn it. You had to prove that you could live by his code of ethics—which was damn near impossible—or you had to prove that you were worth the inches he was willing to step outside his firmly drawn lines."

His eyes went to the casket and then back to me. I nodded, hoping that I could give him some kind of strength to finish. I swiped away another tear and forced a smile for Josh.

"I went through flight school with Carter. I nearly killed him every day of Primary. But somewhere in there, he stopped being Carter and became Will, as I realized what kind of man he was. He was the kind of guy who gave up the aircraft he wanted, because he'd been honor-bound to select for a member of his platoon." Josh half smiled at Jagger. "He was the kind of man who took notes for me during the Advanced Course when I was exhausted from traveling to see my fiancée on the weekends, and then spent hours quizzing me so I wouldn't fall behind. He was the kind of man who kept that quiet because he knew our friends had enough going on in their lives without worrying about me, too. He was the kind of man who proved to you that he wasn't the second choice," he said with a smile at Grayson, who nodded his head.

"He was the kind of guy who shouted yes, when asked to fly into an unsecured landing zone to save a downed pilot." He looked at Jagger and blinked furiously, which sent another stream of tears down my cheeks. "To save a friend." He looked down momentarily, squeezing the sides of the podium so tightly his knuckles turned white. "I haven't..." He paused while he took a breath, and then another. "I haven't talked a lot about what happened that night, but it was Will who pulled me out of our crash. It was Will who carried out my deceased copilot, who had more valor in her pinky finger than any other aviator I've ever met."

I was caught between the excruciating grief that threatened to tear apart my heart and shock that Josh was talking about this. In front of strangers.

"He took the bullets intended for me, and as he..." He looked at Jagger. "As he died, he reached for you. He took your hand."

The imagery would have brought me to my knees had I been standing. My eyes fluttered shut, hot tears squeezing out between my eyelashes. He hadn't just saved Jagger, but Josh as well. *God, the guilt he must feel. The weight he must carry. Why won't he let me shoulder a little of it?* Sam gripped my hand, steadying me.

"He asked me if you were alive, and I told you were. He then ordered me to keep you that way." Josh's half smile turned into a grimace as two tears chased each other down his face, sending a fresh wave down mine. "He said, 'he lives for them. No matter what, he lives.' Will died completing his mission, and for an officer, a soldier, there is no more honorable death. But as his friend, God, it feels unfair to have lost the best of us."

Josh hung his head, and the entire chapel waited, so silent that even breathing felt like blasphemy. He gathered himself and then faced the rest of the chapel. "The world lost a hero in William Carter, and we are a sadder, less honorable place for his passing. There will not be a day that I don't think about him, don't strive for his level of integrity. I am a better man for having known him, having competed against him, and having been able to call him my friend."

Josh walked uneasily from the podium, having refused to use his crutch today. Then he stopped at Will's casket and laid his hand over the flag, bowing his head. "See you at Fiddler's Green, brother."

My throat tightened at the reference; I knew the army poem well. Josh took his seat next to me and pulled me close, wrapping his arm around me. He held me steady as they performed the roll call, my heart breaking anew when they called for "Lieutenant William Carter."

Hadn't I just done this? Hadn't Josh, Sam, and I just sat in a military chapel with a flag-draped coffin? How the hell did we get here again? Where was the justice in this? Hadn't we both suffered enough already?

The bagpipes lit into "Amazing Grace," the chapel acoustics carrying the sound so well that I felt it in my very bones. Josh stared straight ahead at where Will lay, his face unreadable but his eyes tortured in a way I couldn't understand but desperately wanted to. Even if it ripped me apart, I wanted so badly to climb inside his thoughts and help him heal.

We sang. We prayed.

The honor guard stepped forward, one man short, confusing me until Grayson stepped forward and took his place to carry Will out.

Sam laid her head on my shoulder, her tears falling on my bare arm.

We left, following them out until Will was loaded into a glass hearse pulled by white horses. The drive to the burial was slow, keeping pace behind the horses winding down the hilly path through West Point. I reached over to Josh, rubbing his neck. He leaned into my touch but didn't speak, and I didn't break our solemn silence.

We turned into the cemetery and drove as far back as the paved way allowed. The burial itself was quicker than I remembered from Dad's funeral, but this time I took in the details, where I'd merely existed through Dad's.

The volley of gunfire caught me off guard, and Josh startled, his body jerking in his seat. I held his hand, but he didn't look over at me, still keeping his eyes on Will.

General Donovan handed Will's mom the folded flag, her sobs splitting the relative quiet until "Taps" began to play.

It was too final, too soon for a twenty-four-year-old man to be laid in the ground. It wasn't right, any of it. This war was taking chunks of my soul, of Josh's, piece by piece.

The service ended, and the seven of us stayed until we were the only ones left. Morgan, Paisley, Jagger, Josh, me, Sam, and Grayson all stood sentry as they lowered Will into the ground.

I remembered how cold it had been when we did the same for Dad, and even though the June weather was far mellower in New York, I felt just as frozen, as numb.

"I don't understand," I said to Sam. She turned to me, her eyes red and swollen. "I don't understand how we've gone from burying our parents to burying our friends." I glanced past her to where Morgan stood holding onto Paisley, her head high as tears marked her cheeks. "Burying the men we love. I just don't."

She wrapped her arm around my shoulders.

"I don't, either. I don't think anyone does."

We stayed until he was at rest, and I prayed that he knew more peace in the next life than he had in this one.

CHAPTER TWENTY-ONE

JOSH

The front gate to the cemetery was closed at 0600, so I drove around to the back, where I'd seen a small opening in the gate yesterday. The parking lot was mostly empty, except for the spots closest to the Starbucks on the far side.

I parked our rental next to another white sedan, whose owner had obviously had the same thought, and walked toward the back of the cemetery, cursing the still-tender wound in my leg. Ember was going to be pissed if she woke up and found I'd driven the car, let alone left her without a note. But she'd looked so peaceful, and she'd been getting about as much sleep as I had lately, which meant none. If I wasn't waking her up with nightmares, then I was usually making love to her, taking respite in those small moments where she was all that existed to me. But I'd woken up an hour ago and snuck out like a teenager past curfew and drove around the post, simply elated in the power of being behind the wheel of a car again. I'd gravitated here naturally after a while.

The light morning fog had an eerie effect as I took the small, worn path between the hedges and the gate post. It felt different here this morning than it had yesterday. Yesterday, this place contained all the grief in the world, the voices of those silenced too young. This morning, it felt quiet, peaceful.

I turned to the left and walked among the newer stones,

reading some of the names to myself as I hobbled by. Too young. They were all too damn young. Michael Adams was only twenty-four, just like Will.

I continued the path until I came upon Will's grave and stopped in my tracks. Standing there, a sweater wrapped around her from the morning chill, was Paisley. I started to retreat, but the gravel crunched under my feet and she turned. *Fuck.*

"Josh?" she called out.

I half waved and headed over, the wet grass immediately soaking my running shoes. "Hey, Paisley."

She gave me a small smile, her eyes swollen to nearly unrecognizable proportions. "I didn't want to leave without spending a little more time here."

"Yeah. I wanted to take a couple of minutes, too."

"Did you want to be alone? I can go for a walk."

I shook my head. "No, you don't have to leave. I couldn't sleep and didn't want to wake Ember."

She laughed, pathetic as it sounded. "Jagger's still knocked out. He'll only take the pain meds at night, now."

I'd never wanted to run away from someone so badly, like the joggers who were sporadically making their way through the cemetery as we stood there. Then again, this leg was barely supporting me to stand, let alone run.

"Why are you avoiding me?" she asked, looking up at me with raised eyebrows.

"What? I'm not." I bold-faced lied to my best friend's wife.

She made a *pfft* sound. "Sure you are. You wouldn't see me in Germany. You only come over at home when I'm gone, like you watch the window for my car to pull out—"

"I do not." *You do.*

"—or something, and yes, you do. The first time I saw you face-to-face was at the funeral yesterday. Now you'd better tell me what I did to irk you, Josh. Whatever it is, I preemptively apologize."

I shook my head. "Of course you would think it's your fault."

"It's not?"

More runners crunched their way down the gravel path behind us.

"No." I looked down at the freshly placed grass seeds that would grow over Will from now on. "I killed him." It was the faintest whisper, but she heard it.

"You did not kill him. He died at war. This is not your fault."

"How can you, of all people, say that? You loved him more than any of us. How can you not realize that I basically traded his life for Jagger's, and then again for mine?"

She tilted her head. "You knew it was Jagger when he went down. You went in for him, like any medevac crew would have, friend or not. Will agreed to the extraction, right? He didn't say, 'no,' or, 'hey guys, this isn't a good idea,' right? He went in with both guns blazing because that was his mission. You did not force him into that valley, Josh."

There was no blame in her eyes, only absolution, under-standing—no forgiveness, because she honestly didn't think I'd done anything wrong. "There's more."

"Okay, tell me."

I wavered for a second but pushed ahead.

"After the first deployment, I had this one-bullet policy. I wasn't going to let myself be taken alive. Ever."

"Josh," she whispered, lightly touching my arm.

"During the firefight, Rizzo was working on keeping Jagger alive. It was mostly just Will and I, and when this guy came around the back...I had Ember's voice in my head, begging me to come home. So I made this split-second decision and fired two bullets into his chest. I used all of my ammo, didn't save the last bullet."

She didn't shy away, simply held my gaze in a way that was neither comforting nor threatening. She just listened.

"When the next guy came around, I was out. Will saw him

first and shoved me to the ground, taking him out. He saved my life."

"Sounds like Will," she said.

I nodded and forced myself through the hesitation over the next part. "He was standing over me, reaching for my hand to pull me up when the shots were fired."

Her eyes closed, twin tears tracking her cheeks.

"Damn. I'm sorry, I shouldn't—"

"Finish. Please, Josh. I want to know. I need to know."

"I couldn't even tell Jagger. Will fell on top of me, shielding me as he took two more rounds. I managed to get his weapon as the firefight ended. Reinforcements showed up, but Will...he bled out before they could get him to the medevac."

"That's exactly what he would have wanted, Josh," she said, more tears falling. She swiped them away. "Don't mind me. I'm a pregnant, hormonal mess over here."

"You lost your best friend."

Her eyes squeezed shut, and her breath was ragged for a second. "I did."

"If I had just saved that last bullet, if he hadn't pushed me down to start with..."

"If Jagger hadn't been there," she countered. "If those troops hadn't come in contact. If your copilot hadn't been killed. Josh, there are so many what-if's, and any one of them could have changed the outcome. Maybe Will would be alive. Maybe you'd be dead, and Ember and I would be standing over your grave instead. Would you want to put her through that?"

I shook my head, the image already firmly planted there. "No."

"If you hadn't gone in, if Will hadn't been there to pull you out, to climb the helicopter, and kick in the glass, Jagger would have died. There was no way you were kicking through that glass with your leg, and your medic would have been in too many places at once."

"I'm just so sorry," I said, my voice breaking. "I'm so sorry for what I put you through. I can't even say that if I'd known, I would have chosen differently. It was Jagger."

She took both of my hands in her smaller ones. "Josh. You were exactly where you were meant to be. You saved Jagger. Will saved Jagger, and then he saved you, the overachiever that he is...was. If I had a choice to make, I would have chosen Jagger, too. There's no shame in that, not when he's my husband, the father of our unborn son. I do not blame you for what happened, because you were supposed to be there. Will was supposed to be there, and if you take a second to look around, you'll see that now Will is exactly where *he* is meant to be." She pointed to the row in front of us, to the stone that sat directly in line with where Will's would be. "Do you understand now? He's with Peyton."

I made out Peyton's name carved into the simple, white stone and felt a piece of my soul slide home, making the puzzle one piece closer to whole. "Peyton."

Peyton. Her name played through my mind, spoken in Will's voice as a blood-muffled gurgle.

She nodded, a smile lighting her features. "He never stopped loving her. Not ever. Jagger is my person. Ember is yours. Peyton was his. He could have lived longer, gotten married, had kids, but no love would ever compare to what he felt for Peyton. You didn't get him killed, Josh. He was just called home to the woman who was too stubborn to reciprocate that love in life because she was scared to lose her best friend." She shrugged. "I like to think that now they have a chance to be happy."

She wrapped her slight arms around me. "I love you, and I understand. There is nothing to forgive, Josh. This—" She pointed to the ground where Will laid. "This was never in your hands." She looked toward the sky and then behind us. "Hey, you. Good run?" she asked.

I turned to find Ember standing close behind us, dressed

in running clothes, her eyes bright with unshed tears that she tried to smile away. She failed. "Yeah," she answered, walking to Paisley's other side.

Fuck. How much had she heard? I felt a tearing, a rending of sorts in my heart, but couldn't figure out why.

"This place is perfect for them, isn't it?" Paisley asked.

"Hallowed ground," Ember whispered.

"It is," Paisley agreed. "I should get back to Jagger before he wakes up. See you guys at takeoff?"

"T-minus four hours," Ember answered with a smile. They hugged good-bye and Paisley left, the gravel crunching under her feet as she headed back toward the gate.

"December," I said, reaching for her. She sidestepped me and popped one of her earbuds back in.

"I'm going to finish my run. I'll see you back at the hotel?"

"I have the car. We could grab Starbucks over there," I offered, throwing out the one thing she could never resist—coffee.

"No thanks."

Alarm bells sounded in my head.

She walked past me, just out of my reach. "Ember, what's wrong? What's happening here? Is it because of what you heard?" I was thankful that she knew, as much as I hated it.

"What I heard? No. God, Josh. Weeks. Not once have you..." She shook her head and backed away. "I've been trying so hard to get through to you, for you to open up to me. You know what? I'm glad you found someone to talk to. I guess I just foolishly thought that it would be me. I'll be fine. Just give me...a run." She shrugged, her face crumpling, and darted off before I could say or do anything.

A month ago I would have chased her, swept her into my arms, and fixed my fuck-up. A month ago, I hadn't been broken, physically unable to run or pick up the woman I was soul-wrenchingly in love with, because my body had been whole.

A month ago I hadn't crashed my helicopter and killed more people than I wanted to think about...including two of my friends. A month ago I was a different man.

A month ago, I never would have let her go.

But this me? Yeah, well, maybe she was better off running.

CHAPTER TWENTY-TWO

Ember

I held the steaming white mocha in front of me with both hands, savoring the way it warmed my skin to nearly burning but not quite. It hovered just along the line of comfortable— kind of like how I stood with Josh right now.

We'd been home from New York for three days, tiptoeing around each other. That was one thing about moving in together; when we fought before, we could just hang up, cool off, and talk later. Now, we did this awkward dance around the refrigerator and pretended things were semi-okay.

"Have you looked into plane tickets? They're ridiculously expensive," Luke said, thumbing through his dig packet at the table in front of me.

"No," I answered, my own packet untouched.

Could I even go?

"Well, you'd better start looking. We report in two months." He sipped his latte, looking at me over the brim as I spun my ring with my thumb. "Okay, what the hell is wrong with you, Red?"

"What? Nothing. Shitty few weeks."

He nodded. "How is Flyboy adjusting to being home?"

I took another sip, using the time to construct my answer. "He's okay. Struggling, but that's not really a surprise, right? He was almost killed. His friends were killed. There's going to be some residual damage there."

"Okay, well, how are *you* adjusting?"

My eyes flew to his. "No one's really asked me that."

"Why the hell not? Your fiancée was almost killed. Your friend *was* killed. You're on nurse duty twenty-four seven, and the only reason I even snagged twenty minutes of your time is because I drove all the way up here from Nashville while Flyboy is at physical therapy."

I sat, stunned for a few seconds. "Because Josh is hurt. I'm fine."

"Apparently." He rolled his eyes.

"What? I am. I'm just thankful he's alive. That's all that matters." Wanting more than that made me selfish, self-absorbed. Josh's healing, including when he was ready to talk, was all about him and his timeline. "I stupidly pushed him to talk," I admitted.

"And..."

"And I feel like he talks to everyone but me."

"Your other friends having the same trouble?"

I shook my head and picked at the Starbucks sticker on the cup. "Paisley and Jagger are big on open communication. Grayson and Sam, too. Maybe we're the only dysfunctional ones."

"Therapist, maybe? Couldn't hurt."

"Yeah, because Josh is going to sign up for a therapist. He already shot that idea down. At least he has to go for a psych screening this week, and that's just so it checks the box for his up-slip."

"He wants to get back to flying already?"

"Yep. I guess it's a get-back-on-the-horse thing."

He nudged my packet toward me. "And what about your own horse? Don't think I haven't noticed that you haven't even looked at the information."

"Timing sucks now," I said in a voice that was weak to my

own ears.

"Ember. You chose to go for your PhD. Remember? Studying for the GREs? Applying to the dig? Tell me you're not going to let that all go."

"I... Everything is a jumble right now."

He nodded and leaned back in his chair, crossing his arms over his pale blue polo. "This is the one year they're letting PhD students for anthropology start in the spring, and that's only because the dig is school-sponsored. If you don't go, I'm not sure you'll be able to get in this year. You'll have to wait."

"I can't just leave him. Not when he's hurt."

Luke gave an exaggerated sigh. "Okay, well, at least take the packet and keep thinking on it. Selfishly, I'd love to have you there with me."

"I know. I want to go, Luke." Just the idea made my fingers tingle at the possibility of unearthing new relics, new art, new pieces of history from a civilization long-since dead. But leaving Josh in two months? His body was healing quickly, too quickly for my comfort, really, but his mind? Could I leave him for two months? "But there's nothing I won't give up for Josh. We've been through too much together for me to not put him first right now."

"I respect that, I do. You two have this epic kind of love. Got it. But just remember, it's your future, too."

He was right, but what kind of future had me leaving Josh at a time like this?

"It stopped being just my future a long time ago, Luke. It's us, now. Josh and me against the world—that's what we've always said."

"And does he see it that way?" he asked. My eyes narrowed, and he threw his hands up, palms out like he was under arrest. "Hey, I'm trying to help, I swear."

"Of course he sees it that way. Josh is the least selfish person I know. He's always put me first. He's always been whatever I needed no matter what it costs him. I'm just trying to be the same for him."

His expression softened, as did his voice. "Look, I'm just saying that if he's shutting you out, it's because he's either scared of what he's not telling you..."

"Or?"

"Or maybe he's trying to push you away."

The taste of coffee went sour in my mouth. "He wouldn't."

"Even if he thinks he's not what's best for you?"

Well, shit.

"Trash is out."

Josh walked unsteadily into the kitchen as I popped cinnamon rolls into the oven the next morning. "Thanks, babe," I said, my forehead puckering, "but I could have done that. You need to sit."

He shook his head and smiled at me. "I didn't want us to miss pickup, and besides, PT said I could walk on it yesterday."

I snorted. "She said you could get off crutches but you had to take it easy."

"The kitchen is easy."

"The couch is easier." I motioned to the living room with my head. "Save up your strength for Arizona, since we leave in ten days."

"Only if you come sit with me." He stepped forward, pinning me against the counter.

"You're making it difficult for me to move." A smile crept into my voice as I looked up at him. God I loved him, so much that my heart ached, stretched to max capacity. I'd taken what Luke said to heart yesterday, ignored the sting in my soul that Josh had confided in Jagger and Paisley but not me, and focused on proving to him that I wasn't going anywhere.

Everything else could come in time.

"Maybe I like where I have you." His smile was blinding, his eyes clear of shadows, as if my Josh was shining out from behind his war-ravaged exterior.

"Maybe I like being here," I said, my hands slipping beneath his Under Armour T-shirt. I barely suppressed a groan at the feel of his abs beneath my fingers. Even after everything he'd been through, the man had a body that needed to be molded, sculpted, adored by the public...or maybe just me.

His eyes darkened. "December," he whispered. He hadn't touched me since West Point, and after nearly five days, we both radiated some pretty intense sexual tension.

My lips tingled and parted, my body recognizing its match and becoming hyperaware. His hand left the counter and shifted to my waist, squeezing lightly. I ran my nails down the skin of his stomach, and he sucked in his breath through clenched teeth. I loved that sound. I loved all of this really, the anticipation, reveling in the fact that this man was mine in every sense of the word.

My fingers traced the soft elastic of his board shorts, then dipped past the waistline and tugged, bringing him flush against my stomach. He was already hardening for me. I ran my thumb down his length and was rewarded by a low moan. Standing on my tiptoes, I brushed my lips against the stubble on his jaw. "What's on your mind?"

"You," he answered. "Thinking about the first time I had you pushed up against a kitchen counter."

"Breckenridge," I whispered.

"It's the pajamas," he said, his hand cupping my ass through the flannel.

"Hey, you said movie marathon. I vetoed pants."

"Oh, babe, I am most definitely not complaining." He looked down at me, two little lines appearing between his eyebrows.

"What?"

"There was a little something different," he muttered, then lifted me with one hand and deposited me onto the counter. "That's right."

"Josh! You'll hurt yourself." I fought back a small laugh.

"Worth it to see that smile."

"Now all we need is tequila, and we're good to go. I think that may have eased my way into snagging you."

He shook his head slowly. "The tequila wasn't necessary. I was already intoxicated by you."

Well, if my panties weren't ready to drop before, they were now. "So you wanted to kiss me?" At this height, I had perfect access to his neck, and I took it. He smelled delectable, straight out of the shower, and tasted just as good as my tongue ran along the sensitive patch of skin just beneath his ear.

His hand shifted to my hair, his fingers tunneling through the mass to hold me to him. "Fuck yes. It was the first thing I thought of when I picked you up that night. Kissing you had been on my list of life goals since high school, right up there with the other things I'd never get to do like snorkel in Bora Bora, or race my Ducati again." He tugged gently, pulling me back so he could look into my eyes. "You are a flesh-and-bone wet dream, and you owned me the first fucking moment my mouth touched yours."

"And now?" My eyes dropped to his lips. "How does the reality compare two and a half years later?"

"So much better." He brushed his mouth over my cheek, feathering a kiss to my ear. "If I had known just how sweet you'd taste, how perfectly you'd fit against me with your legs around my hips, how incredible it would be to sink inside you, hear my name on your lips...your dad would have come after me with a shotgun in high school, because I would have chased you, freshman or not."

"I would have let you catch me, especially if I'd known this was where we'd end up." I locked my ankles behind his back, bringing him even closer against me.

A wicked smile flashed across his gorgeous face. "Oh, I knew it. Why do you think I stayed away? I was bad enough news for you then, I'm not sure I would have had the decency to say no if you'd asked me to touch you."

Wrapping my arms around his neck, I looked into his eyes, nearly losing myself in their depth. "Touch me now."

He didn't pause, just launched into a kiss that curled my toes. My thighs tightened around his waist as his tongue consumed my mouth, tangling with mine. It was open, hot, carnal, and by the time he pulled away, his breathing was heavy, and I was ready to wish away my pants, and his.

"You get better every time, and if you keep it up, I'll be dead by the time I'm fifty."

"We wouldn't want that," I teased and pulled him down for another kiss, arching against him. Damn, his kisses were addictive. I took another, and then another, until my hips started rocking against his, and he groaned.

He wrapped his casted arm around my back while his hand caressed the skin of my hip just under the waistline of my pajama pants. A wave of desire hit me, turning my blood to lava as he put his mouth to my breast over my shirt, tugging lightly on my nipple through the material. *Thank God for braless days.* "More," I demanded.

He chuckled, and then sent his hand into my panties. My hips bucked when he grazed my clit.

"Fuck, baby, you're so wet already."

I made some kind of mewing sound in answer as he plunged deeper.

A beep sounded outside, breaking through the haze of lust he had me wrapped in, followed by the sound of rushing air of pistons releasing.

"Down!" Josh yelled, sweeping me from the counter.

We crashed to the floor, my head bouncing against the

fiberglass of his cast as he tried to cradle me, my hip taking the brunt of my fall. He caught my top half, landing on me, and immediately blocking out the daylight.

He'd covered me head to toe, his arms bracketing my head as I lay there underneath him. Our breathing was heavy, coming in short bursts. I couldn't get enough air with his weight on me. My heart crashed against my chest, hammering a rhythm of confusion and fear.

"Josh?" I asked, slowly raising my arms to his back. He sucked in ragged breaths, and I stroked up and down his rib cage. "Baby, it's okay," I whispered.

He picked his head up, his eyes scanning my features in a panic before flinging himself off me. His back crashed against the cabinet, and I sat up slowly as he pulled his knees forward, resting his elbows on them. "Are you okay?" he asked, barely meeting my gaze.

My hip throbbed, but the rest of me seemed no worse for wear. "I'm perfectly fine." I slid over to him, slowly lifting my hands to his arms and moving to his face when he didn't flinch away. "It was the garbage truck."

He nodded. "I know."

"What did it sound like to you?" *Where did you go?*

"An RPG." His eyes squeezed shut. "The pistons..."

The throbbing in my hip moved to my heart, where another piece broke for him. "Okay," I said as I stroked his cheeks.

His eyes shot to mine, wide with incredulousness. "This isn't okay. I basically threw you off the kitchen counter."

"Well, at least I know that if we're ever in danger, you'd shield me." I forced a smile. "You could have just left me up there to fend for myself, and then we'd really have problems."

He huffed, then laughed. *Mission accomplished.* "God, I'm so sorry. That sound... I just reacted."

"I don't blame you." I held my breath and tiptoed across a line I'd never been allowed to before. "After the first deployment, did you talk to anyone? After you were wounded?"

He shook his head. "I did the mandatory psych eval, but no. I was fine in their eyes, so I didn't need to."

I couldn't help but wonder how much more was buried under his surface, left lurking like some forgotten powder keg just waiting to ignite with the right flame. Hell, Josh's whole world was in flames.

Except me.

"I think you should talk to someone," I said quietly.

He shook his head. "If this is about me talking to Paisley..."

"It's not," I promised. "That's a whole different can of worms, and until you're ready to open it, I'll try to be respectful. While we're on that subject, I'm sorry for the way I reacted in New York. That was a lot of shock, and more than a ridiculous level of jealousy. What's going on in your head is your business, and I don't have a right to pry. If talking to Paisley, or Jagger, or the random guy at the gym makes you feel better, then you should take advantage of it. I only want what's best for you."

He cupped my face with both hands, the fiberglass of his cast rough against my cheek. "You are what's best for me." He looked away with pursed lips.

"You have your 'but' face on."

A small smile quirked his lips. "Butt-face, huh?"

"You know what I meant. But, what?"

He looked me over like it was the last time he might see me, his eyes wide and vulnerable with a fear I hadn't seen since we'd broken up in Colorado.

"Josh, you're scaring me."

His face fell, and a soft smile graced his lips. "No. No, don't be. It's just that you're the best thing for me. You're my fucking sanity, the only solace I have, but right now, I know I'm the worst possible thing for you, December. You should run, not walk, the hell away from me. At least for now."

"No," I said, pressing my lips to his clammy forehead.

"Never. There's nothing you could do or say that would make me walk away from you, Joshua Walker. Not now, not ever." I leaned back so I could see the little flecks of gold in his brown eyes. "Once upon a time you promised to be my whatever. Do you remember that?"

"I could never forget."

"Then remember this. I'll be your whatever. Whatever you need, whenever you need it. I'm strong enough to pull us both through this."

"You shouldn't have to be. You shouldn't have to bury your friends, and deal with my nightmares, and get pulled to the ground. This wasn't what you signed up for."

I lifted my left hand. "I signed up for *you*, and everything that comes with you." Reaching onto the counter, I grabbed his cell phone and handed it to him. "But it would sure as hell be a lot easier if you would set an appointment to talk to someone."

He took the phone but didn't dial. "They'll take my wings if I go to a shrink."

A defeated breath escaped my lips. "Okay, then at least schedule your eval. It's supposed to be this week, right? So we'll be clear for leave next week?"

He nodded and started to dial.

It wasn't what he needed, but it was a start...and I'd take it.

CHAPTER TWENTY-THREE

JOSH

"I'm not laying down," I said to the psychologist, Major Henderson, as I shut the door behind me.

"I don't think I asked you to, but that's good to know," he said, looking over his glasses at my file. "I like knowing where we stand, or sit, rather." He motioned to the armchair across from his, and I took it. "Lieutenant Walker, I presume?"

"Yes, sir." We both leaned in to shake hands.

"You all look so much younger in civies," he said, motioning to my cargo shorts and polo shirt.

"I'm on convalescent leave, sir."

"I figured as much. No judgment, just an observation."

I leaned back in the chair and stopped before I crossed my right ankle over my left thigh. The staples were out, but that wound was still angry and pink. "Will there be a lot of those here? Observations?"

"Depends on what you want to tell me. Did you bring the questionnaire?"

"Yes, sir." I pulled the four-page questionnaire from the manila folder I'd brought and handed it to him.

"What will it tell me, Lieutenant?"

"If you're going to evaluate my mental status, you may as well call me Josh."

He nodded with a small smile. "Very well, Josh."

I took a deep breath and settled in. I owed it to Ember to be as truthful as possible, but I knew this system well. There was zero chance I would voluntarily say anything that would end up pulling my wings. No chance in hell.

"Sir, the questionnaire will tell you that this was my second deployment. I was wounded both times, because I guess I'm either the luckiest or unluckiest bastard in the world, depending on how you view it."

"Noted. Continue."

"It will tell you that almost a month ago, I was involved in a helicopter crash that killed my copilot, whom I was very fond of, and then I watched a very close friend die protecting me, all in the name of saving my best friend, who was the pilot of the other downed aircraft."

"That must have been extremely rough on you."

"Yes, sir, it was."

He flipped through my questionnaire, scanning the pages. "How would you classify your mental health?"

Tread carefully if you want to fly again.

"I have a little trouble sleeping, and when I do, I have nightmares once a night." *Three, four, five times. Who's counting?*

"How is that affecting your relationship?"

"I'm engaged to a very understanding woman." *Who you don't deserve.* "I've had no angry outbursts, especially in her direction. I'm not going to, either."

"Anything affecting your daytime hours?"

"Besides this very annoying, itchy cast, the laceration on my thigh, and the incision on my chest from the splenectomy?"

He arched an eyebrow in my direction. "In the mental sense."

"No sir." *Except that one time you tossed Ember off the counter because you thought the garbage man might be packing serious heat.*

He scribbled something in my file. "Crowds?"

"I haven't cared for them much since my first deployment, but things look a lot different from the sky than they do the ground. I've gotten better with it since I'm not kicking in doors on raids anymore."

He nodded. "And what do you generally think about the state of army mental health care?"

"I think we're both checking a block. You want to make sure I don't have a psychotic condition, so you're not to blame if I go on a murderous rampage and blame PTSD, and I want to make sure you'll let me fly again. It's a business relationship."

He leaned forward, instantly intrigued. *Fuck, you need to shut the hell up.*

"Do you want to fly again?"

"Yes."

"Hmm." More jotting down in the file.

"Is that a problem?"

"No." More notes. "Sometimes you see pilots a little more skittish after a crash."

"Yeah, well, back on the horse and everything, right?"

He looked up at me, his eyes seeing things I'd rather they not. "Right. Tell me, Lieutenant, do you think you need ongoing appointments?"

Forgive me, Ember.

"No, sir. I think I've been through this before, and I know how to handle it. The nightmares will stop once I'm done processing what happened. The grief will take a hell of a lot longer, but grief isn't going to keep me from flying."

"No, it's not," he said, tapping his pencil on my file. "What do you plan to use to pull you through this time?"

"If you're asking me if I'm going to turn into an addict, the answer is no. I haven't touched alcohol since before I deployed, and I quit pain meds within the week of the crash. I have a very supportive fiancée"—*aka, your drug of choice*—"and I'm headed to see my mother. Nothing like a few days at home to soothe your soul."

He turned those assessing eyes on me again, narrowing them through his glasses before writing on my chart again. "True. Well, how about we meet one more time when you're back?"

He must have heard my sigh of exasperation because he looked up. "Only to clear you, of course. If you're doing as well as you think you are, I'll have no problem signing off. Until then, a follow-up isn't going to affect your schedule, or go on your record."

He paused, making sure I'd realized what he'd said.

Off the record. He was giving me a way to talk to him that wouldn't affect my wings. "Thank you, sir. I'll make sure to follow up, but only to be signed off, of course."

"Of course."

We shook hands, and I rose to leave, but he stopped me as I reached the door. "Chamomile tea. That always helps me sleep. Melatonin, if you need it. And while you're so certain that it's not affecting the rest of your life, just make sure your fiancée feels the same way. She'll have some adverse reactions to this, too, so take care of yourself."

"Yes, sir. Thank you for seeing me."

"I'll see you back here in two weeks, Lieutenant Walker."

I gave him a nod, scheduled with his secretary, and got the hell away from there before he changed his mind. I knew Ember wanted me to pour my heart out to the guy, but he had control over my career, my wings, my life. I wasn't going to let him take any of those, so I'd given him enough truth to check the important boxes and hid the rest that would check the wrong boxes.

Ember would have to understand…or rather, never know.

. . .

"Pink?" I asked Jagger that Sunday as we sat stretched out, our legs elevated by his coffee table. His new full-leg casts were so bright they were nearly radioactive.

He glanced down and shrugged. "It takes a real man to pull off hot pink." He nodded to the racing game on Xbox. "Besides, I'm still kicking your ass."

"I'm just taking it easy on you and those non-weight-bearing casts."

"My hands aren't broken." He shook the remote with a grin. "Hell, I could probably still beat you if they were."

I flipped my baseball cap backward. "Challenge accepted."

"You looking forward to heading home?" he asked, cutting off my car.

I gunned it and flew by him on the left. "Yeah, it'll be good to see my mom, tune up my Ducati." My lips tilted into a small smile. "I ordered a full set of hot-weather gear for Ember as a surprise. She's never ridden that bike."

His car was back on my rear. "I didn't think Ember was a big fan of motorcycles."

"Everyone likes Ducatis."

He scoffed.

"Okay, maybe I'm hoping she'll like the Ducati." The last time she'd seen it she'd simply shaken her head and walked away. My eyes flicked to the clock. The girls had been gone twenty minutes. "How is Paisley handling all of this?"

He didn't look away from the screen. "She's a little bit of everything. Strong, stubborn, relieved...heartbroken. She refuses to complain, not even about us sleeping on the fold-out down here until I can get up the stairs. She needs to take her beautiful, pregnant ass up to our room and sleep in a decent bed, but she refuses. She takes care of everything. The house, laundry, groceries, getting me to therapy and doc appointments, dealing with the fucking wheelchair... Hell, I almost wish she would complain. It's like she's scared to let me know she's hurting."

"Will?" Guilt slammed into me, ripping apart what little peace I'd gained since the funeral. I shouldn't have taken those last shots. I should have conserved more ammo during the firefight, should have had his back. But a million "shoulds" wouldn't bring him back. *How can Paisley...Ember even look at me?*

Jagger sighed and dropped the remote as the race ended. "Yeah. It's always worse after she calls to check on Morgan. She puts on a brave face, but it's not like I can't see it in her eyes, hear it in the words she's not saying. What about Ember?"

I absently rubbed the skin near the healing, raw, pink line of the laceration on my thigh. "The notification wasn't easy on her. Losing Will, the funeral, all the shit I'm putting her through... Fuck, you should have seen her face when I asked about an up-slip."

Jagger's head snapped toward mine. "You already asked about an up-slip?"

I nodded. "I have to know if I'll be able to do it."

He whistled low. "I'd have kicked your ass if I was Ember. You just get home after nearly dying, and you're asking to get right back in the death machine?"

"You don't want to get up there?"

"Hell yeah, I do. When my legs are ready, when I'm ready, but also when Paisley is ready. But I'm looking at six months before that's even a remote possibility, and I know she needs this time just as much as I do. This has been pretty damn rough on her."

Images of Ember played through my head. Burying her father, burning the West Point shirt, pinning my bars...my wings. The look on her face when I'd told her I was deploying, her tears that morning, the desperate way she'd clung to me, knowing almost better than anyone what could happen over there. Her soft sighs when she curled up next to me in Landstuhl, the slight way she trembled at Will's funeral. But it was the look of shock when I'd thrown us to the floor last week that stuck with me.

She deserved so much better.

"Do you ever think that they'd have been better off if we'd just stayed away from them? Ember would have been. I know that." The words slipped from my mouth before I could stop them.

"What. The. Actual. Fuck. Where the hell is your head at? Don't even think things like that."

"This life—what we do—it's going to destroy her. I knew it back in college, and I should have stayed away, but I was too selfish. I wanted her too badly, and look what that's brought—"

The door opened, and my mouth shut.

"We're here!" Ember sang as she danced through the door, three boxes of pizza in her hands.

"Hey, babe." I forced a smile for her, and she winked as she passed.

"Don't get up, I'll grab you a couple slices," she ordered, taking the boxes to the dining room with Paisley following after she bent to kiss Jagger's forehead.

Jagger looked at me, narrowing his eyes.

I shook my head and ran my hands over my face as the Skype app rang on Jagger's television and he answered it. *Stop voicing thoughts you shouldn't even have.*

"Sunday night dinner?" Sam asked from their dining room table in Colorado.

"You bet!" Jagger answered, saluting with the plate of pizza Paisley handed him.

"Pizza? Really? I thought we agreed on chicken cacciatore?" Grayson glared. "Italian, remember?"

"Pizza is Italian," Jagger answered, his mouth full.

"There are no words for you," Grayson said, shaking his head. We caught up on the week, as close as we could be with the eleven hundred miles that separated us.

Ember sat next to me and handed over two pieces of perfection with a beautiful smile. She was so damn happy lately that I'd gone to see Dr. Henderson. "Thank you," I whispered and kissed her lightly. *Thank you for loving me. Thank you for staying when you could so easily walk away.*

I shoved my earlier thoughts to the back of my head, the dark corners where monsters, regret, and truth lurked, and coped how I did best—I locked it away.

But not before I realized how crowded it was getting back there.

CHAPTER TWENTY-FOUR

"Oh my God," I said in disbelief as he walked through the door at the orthopedist's office. Had it already been four weeks?

"Do you like it?" he asked, waving his arm in the middle of the waiting room.

"What is it?" I slipped my Kindle into my purse and stood.

"It's an air cast. Sexy, right?"

I gingerly took hold of it, turning his arm over and inspecting the device. "And you'll still heal?"

"Faster, at least that's what they said. They were minor fractures, really, in good locations, or as good as you can get when you break your arm, right?"

"And you can take it off?" I fingered the Velcro.

"Yeah, but only to wash my arm." He ran his tongue across his lower lip and gave me a look that screamed pure sex. "Or maybe other things..."

I fake-punched the good side of his chest. "Ha-ha. You have jokes. It comes off in the shower and that's it, mister."

"There are no rules against getting you in the shower," he whispered in my ear, throwing his arm around my shoulders as we walked out of the orthopedist's.

The image of him naked against me, water dripping over the lines of his muscles, hitched my breath. "After your arm is one hundred percent," I promised, leaning up to kiss him on the cheek. "As for now, we're due at the airport in two hours."

"I'm driving," he said with a wicked grin, snatching the keys out of my hand.

"Josh, you have a cast on!"

"Ember, your car is an automatic!" he teasingly mocked me, even nailing my eyebrow arch. "I'm good, I swear. I asked."

He opened my door and winked when I glowered at him and settled into my seat, then clicked the belt in place. "I don't like this," I said as he slid in behind the wheel.

He sported a sexy-as-hell grin as he waited for the power seat to scoot back. "It'll be fine, relax." His hand crept up my thigh, and I plopped it back on the gear shift.

"Nuh-uh. You need both hands, buddy."

"Okay, but be patient with me. I might be a little rusty."

I bit my tongue. He shouldn't have been driving *period*. I ran through Mom's advice from volunteering with PTSD soldiers in my head. Be patient. He might drive a little more slowly than normal. He might drive between lanes. He might be a lot more defensive.

He pulled out of the parking space without incident, and I breathed a sigh of relief, then another one once we'd made it off post.

Then he gunned it.

The force of his acceleration threw me back in my seat. My gaze snapped to his face, the small smile that grew as the speedometer climbed. I found the door handle in my hand before I even thought about gripping.

"You know we're not late or anything, right?" I asked, hoping my voice stayed neutral.

He shot me an amused look. "God, I missed this."

He darted between cars, switching lanes to weave in and out of the building traffic...and that was before we got on the highway.

Once we hit the on-ramp, I mentally steeled myself. Josh had always driven fast, that was never in question. So why was I so nervous now?

Because whatever that was in his eyes at this moment, that slight edge—it hadn't been there before. My breath froze in my lungs when he passed the car in front of us, narrowly shooting the gap before darting back into the lane. I snuck a look at the speedometer. Ninety-five.

Don't nag. Do. Not. Nag.

"Babe, if we get pulled over, I'm pretty sure we'll actually be late for the flight."

He looked at me, and I wanted to turn his face back to the damn road. "You're scared," he remarked.

"I'm nervous," I answered, trying to keep the middle ground.

"Did you forget how I like to drive?" he joked.

"Did you forget that my VW doesn't have rotors? This isn't"—my sentence faltered as we threaded another needle to pass—"a helicopter."

"Okay, okay," he said, his shoulders sagging as he pulled into the right-hand lane.

As our speed dropped, so did the light in his eyes. Doubt gnawed its way into my head with each passing mile that Josh stayed within five mph of the speed limit. Should I have asked him to slow down? I mean, was there really a danger? Sure, he'd always driven like he was a lost member of the crew from *The Fast and the Furious*, but I'd never been worried enough to actually ask him to slow down.

Had I overreacted?

Wait, was I overthinking this now? I shook my head like the unwelcome line of thought would tumble loose. "I'm sorry. I didn't mean to take your fun away." Okay, that was the lamest apology ever.

He took my hand in his and lifted it to his lips, kissing the back gently. The air cast did give his fingers way more mobility. I'd definitely wigged over nothing.

"Babe, if you're ever scared, just tell me. I'd rather slow down than make you think I don't care how you're feeling. Besides, like you said, we have plenty of time to get to the airport."

That was why I loved this man so deeply. No matter what he wanted, he always took my feelings into account first.

Right. That's why he won't let you in about what happened to him over there.

I flicked the thought-devil off my shoulder and tried to enjoy the remainder of the drive to the airport.

We checked in at the skycap after parking the car and headed inside the terminal. The line for security wound down the small hallway, and we found ourselves packed in like little sardines.

"This is taking forever," Josh muttered, shifting his weight from foot to foot, his eyes scanning the crowd around us.

"You okay?" I asked.

"Never better," he said, still checking out the lines.

It clicked. "Is the crowd bothering you?" I asked gently.

He shook his head, then caught my eyes and slowly nodded. "A little."

I took his hand, stroking my thumb into his palm and pressed lightly.

"Mmmmm." He closed his eyes, and I began to massage the muscles. I kept it up until it was time to slip off our shoes and walk through the scanner. Josh rolled his eyes but sat through the advanced screening for his air cast, mumbling something about what he did for a living. Then we took up residence in an empty gate across from ours, which was packed, and waited it out.

He wrapped his arm around my shoulders and tugged me into his hard frame. "Thank you," he whispered against my forehead and then placed a tender kiss there that melted my heart into a puddle of warm goo.

"There's nothing to thank me for," I responded truthfully.

"You shouldn't have to deal with...all of this."

I snuggled in further and turned to kiss his jaw. "All of this is all of you, and it's nothing. You don't like crowds right now? We'll avoid them. You want to drive fast? I'll find you a racetrack like one of those NASCAR things. We got this."

"NASCAR, huh?"

"How did I know that's what you'd pick up on out of all that?" I laughed. "Besides, maybe they'll teach you how to use a brake."

"Oh, you've got jokes?" He tickled me, and I lost it, flailing my arms.

"Ahh! Stop!" As soon as I asked him to, he did, but not before I sent my bag sprawling at our feet, dumping my Kindle, wallet, and papers from the biggest pocket to the floor.

"Here, babe," he said, scooping up most of it. His hands paused on the paperwork, but he put it back into the manila envelope. "Is this..."

My cheeks heated, like I'd been caught doing something I shouldn't have. Like I'd been sneaking it. "Dig paperwork," I answered.

"Oh," he answered, his voice fading as he slid the envelope into the bag.

"I basically just need to look at it so I know where to send the papers to cancel," I said in a rush. "I'm not going."

His gaze swung to meet mine. "You're what?"

"Not...going?" *Why are you asking him? Isn't that your choice?*

"Yes, you are."

They called our flight to board. "Looks like that's us," I said.

"You're going. You're not turning down this dig because I got hurt." His lips flattened into that determined I'm-not-giving-up line, and I sighed.

"It's not just you getting hurt. I'm not leaving you for a week, let alone two months. Not when I almost lost you." My voice dropped to a whisper.

He cupped my face in his hands as they called our flight again. "You are going."

"It's too soon."

"For who? I'm the one who crashed, and yet you're the one afraid to spread your wings. December, I've been responsible for a lot lately, but I'm not going to stand by while you give up this dig, and your entrance into the doctorate program, because you're scared to leave me. Nothing's going to happen to me."

"They're calling our flight."

"We'll sit here until you agree to go."

"You'd hold your mother hostage against my dig?" I arched an eyebrow.

"Fuck. You had to bring my mother into this?" His eyes closed, and he took a deep breath. "My one weak spot."

I shrugged, unapologetic. "She hasn't seen you in months, and she's been so worried…"

His mouth dropped. "Cruel."

"Effective."

He stood, pulling me with him, and swung my bag over his shoulder. "This conversation is continuing on that plane."

"I brought noise-canceling headphones."

"The sass-mouth on you, I swear. No more talking to Sam on Skype. You're cut off."

I laughed as the attendant scanned our tickets, and we walked the Jetway. The line shuffled forward until we stood at the threshold of the plane.

Josh paused just behind me, and I looked over my shoulder to where he held up the rest of the line. "Babe?"

He swallowed, and it was as if he'd pulled the color out of his face in the same motion. "Yeah. I'm okay."

What was going on? He'd never freaked out when we traveled before. I was usually the one who had to have my hand held while we were...oh, shit...flying.

"Babe, we don't have to go. Or we can drive," I said with a smile, ready to walk off that plane at his signal.

He shook his head and stepped forward. "Nope, I'm good. Let's just get to our seats."

We found our seats, and I took the window while Josh took the aisle. He put my bag under the seat ahead of me, knowing I tended to freak if I couldn't reach my laptop, but pulled the folder out before sliding it home.

"I told you we weren't done." He waved the papers.

Shit. "Okay, give me one good reason I should go, and then I'll tell you why I'm not. We'll see who's left standing at the end." I arched an eyebrow. "Because I'm not going, and you can't make me."

His eyes skimmed my face, a slow, easy smile tilting his lips. Then he leaned forward and kissed me. Uncaring that we were on a plane in full view of anyone who wanted to see, Josh launched an assault on my senses. He tugged on my lower lip with his teeth, and I acquiesced, opening to him. He quickly pounced, devouring my mouth in a way that was highly inappropriate and sexy as hell.

My hands tangled in his hair, and I'd quit caring where we were by the time he lifted his head. "You're cute when you're mad."

An unladylike snort erupted from me. "I'm not mad, I'm determined."

He dragged his tongue across his lip, and the cabin was suddenly very hot. I reached up, quickly turning the dial for air, shifting my weight to ease the ache he'd woken with just a freaking kiss. Damn it, now I was turned on, too? This was going to be a long trip.

"This dig will make it so you can apply to start your PhD in the spring term."

"So?" I asked, still fighting with the freaking air.

He reached up and turned it, and cool sanity hit my face. Now if only it would douse my thighs in ice. That'd be great.

"So, you couldn't apply in time for normal term because we didn't know where I'd be stationed until December."

"Right." Yeah, I'd been pissed. Of course my future would revolve around where Josh was stationed, but that was the life I'd chosen. So I'd bitten my tongue and waited for his assignment, knowing that it would cost me a year.

"So now you'll get to go on an amazing dig and be on track with your peers for your PhD."

The plane pulled away from the gate. Josh gripped the armrest but showed no other sign of nervousness.

"I'll be gone for two months."

He shrugged. "I was gone for three. It's your turn."

"And look what happened during those three!" I hissed and immediately regretted it.

"Okay, well, as long as you're not flying helicopters in enemy territory, I think we can safely assume the same won't happen to you." He winked.

Winked. How could he look like everything was okay when I knew the truth?

I barely held myself back from sputtering. "Not funny. What if you need me?"

"I'll adapt, just like we do during deployments."

A shudder racked me. "Okay, don't say that in plural. One is enough."

"You need this," he argued, brushing a strand of hair off my shoulder and lingering on my exposed bra strap.

I pulled up the boatneck of my T-shirt. "I need *you*," I argued.

"No, you don't. You stood on your own while I was gone, and I was proud of you, December. I'm not going anywhere, our relationship, our marriage…" He paused, as we both smiled like idiots for that second, but his faded. "It's two months, and you're going."

We taxied out to the runway, both ignoring the monotone explanation of the jet's safety features.

"I don't think you understand, Josh. I don't know if I can walk away and leave you here. You coming home alive is this giant gift, and I can't just ignore that and go spend two months in Turkey. If Dad had come home, Mom wouldn't have left his side."

He swallowed. "You're not your mother. I love her, Ember, I do, but you've never been the woman to let your dreams take a backseat to mine. It's one of the reasons that I love you. You know who you are and what you want. I'm not going to be responsible for you losing that."

"Me not going on one dig while you're recovering is not going to alter the course of my life, our life," I argued.

He rubbed his hands over his face. "Stop. Just stop. This fucking mess I'm in the middle of, I'm not dragging you into it. Captain Trivette is dead. Will is dead. Jagger's legs are pulverized, and I'm…" He shook his head. "I'm responsible for enough tragedy without adding your future to it, so you're going. End. Of. Story."

"We," I whispered as the jet whirred to life, sending us hurling down the runway.

"What?" he barked, his knuckles white against the armrest.

I covered his hand with mine. "*We* are in this mess, not just you. When are you going to see that?"

His eyes swirled with emotions I couldn't name, they flickered by too fast, but the anger, the determination—that stayed front and center.

"You're going to fucking Turkey," he snapped as we went airborne.

He leaned his head back against the seat and closed his eyes, effectively shutting me out. My hand fell away from his, and I looked out the window as the ground dropped away from us.

I'd felt closer to him when he was in Afghanistan than I did with him sitting right next to me.

CHAPTER TWENTY-FIVE

Ember

The Arizona heat hit as soon as our feet touched the oven that was aptly called a Jetway. I was sweating by the time we made our way into the air conditioning of the terminal.

I took Josh's offered hand as we made our way to the baggage claim. As close as he was, even with his skin against mine, he was a million miles away. He'd white-knuckled the flight, pretending to watch the movie, and hadn't said more than a handful of words to me.

I'd shoved all the Turkey papers back into my bag, sorry that I'd even brought them to look over. It was in another six weeks anyway, what did it matter right now?

As we passed through the security doors, Josh's mom ran to him through the crowd. She was a small woman, even shorter than me, with close-cropped brown hair and brown eyes that laughed easily. He leaned down to hug her, and I briefly wondered how old he'd been when he'd passed her in height.

"Oh, thank you, God," she said as she embraced him. Her relief was palpable, bringing a quick sting of tears to my eyes.

"Hey, Mom," he answered, hugging her just as tightly.

She pulled back, wiping at her eyes. "I'm so glad you're here." She smiled, then yanked me in for a tight hug. "Both of you."

"I'm glad we could make it." I loved her hugs. They felt like macaroni and cheese on a cold day—just the perfect amount of comfort.

She looked me over with a critical eye. "Yes, I do believe engagement looks good on you. I approve." Her grin was instant, and mine quickly followed.

A small wait at the baggage claim, then we piled into her Durango, heading for their house in Winslow. Josh slid into the driver's seat, and I cringed.

"Only if you agree not to drive like a bat out of hell, Joshua," she lectured as she fastened her seat belt.

"I'll obey all speed limits, Mom."

He arched an eyebrow at me in the rearview mirror, and I couldn't help but smile, fight or no fight. I relaxed after he pulled onto the highway and stayed true to his word.

I checked my emails while Josh and his mom caught up in the front seat. She didn't mention the crash, and he didn't bring it up.

It was like we'd entered this tiny alternate universe where it had never happened.

"The drive seems so much shorter now." Josh laughed around the half-hour mark.

"Than the last time we came in?" I asked.

"No, since Mom used to drive me every day. There's no ice in Winslow, so she brought me to Flagstaff almost every day for practice."

"'Play football,' I begged him." She laughed. "'No, Mom, hockey. It's my passion.'" Her Josh impression was spot-on, and I couldn't contain my giggle. "Like an eight-year-old knows what passion is."

"Hey, I was good," he argued.

"Keep telling yourself that." His mom side-eyed him. "Now at nine, nine you were good. Eight...you were like a puppy with huge paws."

"You have to embarrass me in front of my fiancée?" he joked.

She threw me a grin and a wink. "Your fiancée should know what kind of genes she's giving my grandchildren. I'm sorry, Ember, they're all going to have huge feet."

"Seriously with the kids already?" Josh sputtered.

"I can wait...two years. I think two years is sufficient."

"Mom!"

"You know what they say about guys with big feet," I added, and the car went silent. Josh's eyes flew to mine in the mirror, almost as big. "Really big shoes."

His snort was drowned out by his mom's laughter. She'd never pressure us, not really, but God, it was funny to watch Josh squirm.

Two years? Kids? Maybe not two. I'd be in the middle of my PhD program, and that wasn't the best set of circumstances for a new mom. But maybe three years... Josh would be back at Rucker for the Captain's Career Course, and we'd have him for a year, guaranteed no deployments.

And if we timed it just right, we could make the most of that year.

Wait. Are you planning a baby around his military career?

Yes, I was. Like everything else. Like where I was going to get my PhD. Like whether or not I was going to Turkey. As much as Josh wanted me to determine my own future, he had to understand that his was definitely setting my parameters.

It wasn't like a marriage between us could exist any other way.

A buzzing sound woke me up from an unintentional nap the next afternoon. I lifted my head and brushed off a flashcard from where it had stuck to my cheek, and smacked my tongue against the roof of my mouth. Ugh, that after-nap mouth feeling was anything but clean. Untangling myself from the maze of books and papers on Josh's bed, I reached for my phone on the nightstand. Four thirty p.m. I'd been asleep over two hours.

Mom: *Hey, I just wanted to check on you.*

I blinked some semblance of awareness into my brain and rubbed some circulation into my eyes.

Ember: *Day 2 in Arizona. Everything is good here. CO?*

Mom: *Just missing you. How is Josh?*

I knew she didn't mean it as a loaded question, but it was. How was Josh? Fine, if you asked him. Everything was fine. He slept fine, ate fine, felt fine, and we were fine. Liar.

Ember: *He's fine.*

Now I was just as bad as he was.

Ember: *I actually need to go find him, I'll check in later?*

Mom: *Sounds good. Love you, honey.*

Ember: *Love you.*

I stacked my study materials neatly on the little corner desk, checked to make sure my mascara hadn't made a run for it while I was passed out, and brushed my teeth in the adjoined bathroom, smiling at the Colorado Avalanche shower curtain.

I shut the door softly behind me and walked down the short hallway. The house was a homey two-bedroom, one level with tile floors and high ceilings. Josh's hockey pictures decorated the hall to the living room, but there was no grown-up Josh waiting there. His mom looked up from folding a pile of laundry. "Hey, how are you feeling?"

"Great," I said, pulling my hair into a knot on the top of my head. "I must have passed out. I'm so sorry. Can I help you?"

She smiled, pulling a shirt out to fold. "Nothing to be sorry about, and no, you're on vacation. I peeked in on you earlier when Josh went out, but you looked peaceful. What are you studying so hard at?"

"GRE's, the test to get into grad school. It's next week."

"Smart girl." She smiled at me. "I've always loved that about you."

"I'm trying," I answered. "Now that Josh is at Fort Campbell, I can eek out my PhD there. We might have another few months in lag time apart while I finish up, but it's my best chance of getting it done between PCS moves."

She sighed, shaking her head. "I don't know how you do that."

"Do what?" I said, sneaking a shirt out of the pile to fold.

She tilted her head at me but let it slide. "Plan everything out so far in advance around Josh's moves. I hated moving from here when we went to Colorado. We're lucky my brother kept the place up for us, rented it out while we were there."

I shrugged. "This is the only life I've ever known. I moved as a kid, as a teenager, and now as an adult. I'd like to stop, that's no secret, but I'll follow Josh anywhere."

She paused, looking at me way too deeply with those Josh-like brown eyes. "You should go to Turkey. Have something of your own."

"Josh told you."

"Just enough. He's right. This is about you, and looking at the way he lives, the way you're already maneuvering around his choices, well, this would be for you."

"I can't leave him, not now. There will be other digs, other schools, other deadlines. If I can't get into Vanderbilt's program, there will be another."

She put the last folded shirt onto the pile. "Ember, I raised Josh on my own. I worked two jobs to afford hockey. I moved us to Colorado to keep him from ending up a criminal with that stupid bike—or worse, in a body bag. I know what it is to sacrifice for someone you love, to put their needs first. I get it, and I admire and love you all the more for it. You are, in every way, Josh's perfect match because you both do whatever the other needs. But you have to understand—loving yourself, honoring your intelligence, your ambitions, that doesn't mean you love Josh less. It means you're staying true to the woman he fell in love with in the first place."

"Do you regret it? Putting him first?"

Her eyebrows rose. "No, but he is my child. Children always come first. In a relationship, there's got to be some give and take so you don't end up looking like a parent and child." She smiled. "Want to know a secret?"

"Sure." I added my last shirt to the pile.

"I'm going on a date tonight."

Her joy was contagious, and suddenly the woman in front of me wasn't Josh's forty-five-year-old mother. She was just a girl excited to see a boy. "With who?"

She shrugged but couldn't fade her smile. "A very handsome police officer. It will be our third date this month."

"That's great!"

She nodded. "Well, I have to go get ready. You two are on your own tonight, so you know…just don't do anything that gets the cops called to the house. That could put a damper on our evening." She tilted her head toward the kitchen. "He's in the garage."

"Thank you, and have fun tonight. You more than deserve it."

"I think I will." She walked off with a little spring in her step.

I crossed the living room to the kitchen and opened the door to the garage. The sound of "Paint it Black" blasted me along with the heat, and I shut the door quickly behind me so they didn't lose the cool air in the house.

Holy shit…he did *not*.

Josh's mom's car had been backed into the driveway, and in its place was the bane of my fucking existence. Josh's silver Ducati Superbike.

His Harley, the cruiser? Yeah, I was okay with that. It was a laid-back form of biking in my mind, more about the ride, enjoying the moment. This thing? It was death, shined up and sexy. He'd won it when he was seventeen, in the race that eventually got him kicked out of Winslow, and unable to break her son's heart, his mom had put it into storage.

I just wished it had stayed there.

My eyes didn't linger on the two-wheeled death machine once Josh stood up on the other side of it, putting his tools on the workbench behind him. One glimpse and I wasn't just hot because of the temperature.

My future husband was incredible.

His shirt was off, little beads of sweat glistening on his skin. Every line of his abs was carved, dipping down toward his low-slung board shorts, where the very fuckable V-shaped lines from his stomach disappeared. His tattoos rippled as he lifted his hands above his head, resting them on his backward Avs baseball cap.

You get to marry him. Sleep with him the rest of your life, laugh with him, kiss him, make—

"Earth to Ember," he called out, turning off the music, and my eyes snapped from his abs to the grin that told me he knew exactly where my head was.

"Yeah, hi," I said, blinking excessively.

"Good nap?"

I stepped down onto the concrete floor and walked around the bike until I was toe to toe with him. "It would have been better with you." My fingers had a mind of their own and pinched his waistband, running just inside, against his skin. It was damp with sweat, and I had the most incredible, overpowering urge to lick it off.

"You need your sleep," he said, his voice dropping.

I ran my hands over his abs, and his grin faded, his eyes darkening. I leaned forward and placed a kiss over the pink line from his splenectomy, then lightly traced the scar with my tongue.

Josh's fingers tangled in my hair, then gently pulled me back. His attention darted between my eyes and my lips. "What's on your mind?"

"You," I answered, my voice more than a little breathless. "I mean, you weren't, but then I came out here looking for you, and you have no shirt on."

"It's hot."

"I've noticed."

I knew I was supposed to be mad at him for shutting me out. I knew I was supposed to keep up the awkward, private stalemate we'd had since the flight yesterday, but in that moment, I just didn't care. I needed his mouth on mine more than oxygen—and he knew it.

He kissed me, lightly at first, as though asking me permission. I opened for him as he licked the seam of my lips, and sucked his tongue into my mouth. He groaned, his grip shifting from my hair to my ass, and walked backward until he landed on a stool near the workbench.

He gripped and lifted me onto his lap with a smooth motion until I straddled him, my feet braced on the supports of the stool. "Your shoulder," I mumbled against his mouth.

"Shh, it's fine."

Even that word didn't fire off my temper. I was too consumed by his skin against mine as my tank top rode up over my stomach. "Josh," I whispered as he ran his tongue down my neck, stopping at the spot he knew triggered my instant need for sex. It may as well have been labeled with a bull's-eye for how well he knew my body.

"You're so fucking sexy," he whispered.

"Have you looked in the mirror?" I asked.

"No, but we could try it," he answered, his mouth gliding over the neckline of my top. "Could you get into that? Me behind you, watching you, watching us."

I groaned, his words bringing images into my mind that definitely weren't safe for a garage with the door wide open. "That was not what I meant."

"Oh, I know," he replied, peeling my top down over one of

my breasts and lifting it from my lacy bra cup. "Damn, I've missed this. How many days has it even been?"

"Too many." I gasped when he flicked his tongue over my nipple. The heat of my body, the air around us, his skin, all blended together until I felt like I was a living fire.

"I need you," he whispered.

I knew what this would do. He was using sex to bandage the gaping wound that festered between us. I needed to care, to stop and make him talk this out, not give in to the primal need to feel him moving inside me, to let our bodies connect us. "Josh…"

"Fuck," he growled, popping my breast back into my shirt when the door handle turned. To his credit, he didn't throw me off his lap, but when his mom came down the steps, I wished he had.

My head hit his shoulder, and all the blood that had centered between my thighs a moment ago rushed to my cheeks.

"Mom," Josh said with a nod.

"Uh-huh," she said, a laugh finishing it off.

"Mom," I mumbled, tossing up my hand as a wave but leaving my face firmly hidden.

"Well, my date should be here any minute," she said sweetly, "so you two kids play nice, and I'll see you later?"

"No lecture?" Josh asked, his arms wrapping around me to keep me from moving.

"Well, I did say that I wanted grandbabies," she joked.

I groaned my mortification into Josh's neck as a car pulled into the driveway. "No way," he muttered, and I turned to see a nicely dressed man climb down out of the truck. "Sherriff Lane?"

Okay, that was it. I pushed back off Josh's chest and slid until my feet touched the floor, pulling down my tank top along the way. "Hi," I said with as much dignity as I could muster.

"I'm Dwayne." He introduced himself with a firm handshake.

"I'm Ember."

"Josh's fiancée," Mrs. Walker clarified.

"Nice to meet you," he said with a nod, then looked past me to Josh. "Good to see you, Josh. I've heard you've grown into quite a man."

Josh stood behind me. "Still working on that one, Sheriff."

Dwayne's eyes narrowed at the bike. "Well, it's been a few years since I've seen that."

"Well, you kids play nice, and have a good evening," Josh said, using his mother's own words, then took my hand, firmly pulling me into the house and shutting the door behind us.

"What was that about?" I asked, basking in the sweet rush of cold air.

"I cannot believe she's dating him."

"The sheriff? He seems nice enough."

"He's the one who kicked me out of Winslow. He was the deputy who caught me."

My mouth hung slightly open for a second. "Oh." The Josh I knew was more than a little bit of a daredevil. Hell, I even remembered the playboy from high school. But I'd never really met the Arizona version of Josh who had wound up in the back of cop cars, even when we'd been back on previous trips.

He shook his head. "You know what? Never mind. I want to take you somewhere."

"Okay."

He walked back to his bedroom, and I followed, backing up while he pulled a giant box out of the bottom of his closet. "I ordered everything you could possibly want."

I peered into the box and took in the protective pants, jacket, and helmet. "No way am I getting on that organ-donation-mobile."

"You ride the Harley at home," he cajoled.

"Josh..."

"I'll be careful."

"You can't even drive it," I said, pointing to his air cast.

"Speaking of which, how did it even get here from the storage unit?"

He wiggled his unencumbered fingers. "I can drive it just fine; that's how I got it here. If anything, it'll keep me from going too fast, right?"

"This is wild."

He took my hands and kissed my fingers. "Please? December, I want to show you this place like I remember it, not just let my mom tour-guide you like the last time. I will literally give you anything you want if you ride with me."

My teeth worried my lower lip while I debated. "It doesn't even have a sissy bar. I'll fall off."

His smile was instant, and gorgeous, damn him. "First, I'd never let that happen, and second, it's just an excuse to hold on tighter."

"Anything I want?" Maybe this could be good. Maybe we could use this time together to recharge, not forget what had happened in the last month, but to see past it to where it was just us again.

"Anything you want," he promised.

Tonight was going to suck.

"Fine. I want you to get off my butt about Turkey. For the remainder of the trip, don't bring it up or try to change my mind."

The muscle in his jaw ticked, but he nodded. "Deal. Anything else?"

"As long as I'm on the back of that bike, you do the speed limit."

A wicked grin caressed his lips. "Deal."

"And shower first."

"Now you're getting picky," he called, already on his way to the bathroom.

I picked up the white and pink helmet that matched everything he'd ordered. "When in Rome, right?" I asked it. "Or Arizona."

CHAPTER TWENTY-SIX

EMBER

I kept my body plastered to Josh's back as the highway flew beneath us at a dizzying speed. It wasn't that I hated motorcycles really, or that I didn't trust Josh. He was one of those guys with a gift for driving, flying...anything where he became part of the machine.

My dislike of motorcycles was that I felt like we hovered just an instant away from death. One miscalculation, one shift of weight, one car not paying attention, and we'd be hurled from the bike, our bodies still going seventy-five miles an hour.

Riding a motorcycle reminded me constantly how delicate my life was, how easy it was to die, which made me nervous, anxious for safety. But for Josh, it did the opposite, feeding his need to walk that delicate line, to push just a little further over the line... *One percent over.*

Our disagreement over this bike stemmed from the simple fact that I saw it as a way to die, and Josh needed it as a way to live. And maybe I hated the bike even more for it, like it was this dirty little mistress lurking in a corner of his mind, ready to steal him away from me at the first opportunity.

We rode for entirely too long until Josh pulled off onto a smaller road, reaching a giant sign that read BARRINGER CRATER.

A small ridgeline loomed before us as we parked the Ducati. I took off my jacket and protective pants, revealing shorts and a pink, halter-neck tank. The gear was meant for hot-weather riding, but there was zero chance I was hiking around in pants and long sleeves, not in a hundred degrees. Josh did the same, packing it all into my backpack before carrying it himself.

"Ready?" he asked, holding out his hand.

"Sure," I said, intertwining our fingers perfectly. We hiked the short distance to the top of the ridge, the heat dry but still oppressive. The sun was setting as we crested the incline, casting the desert sky in gorgeous swirls of orange and pink.

"Wow." The crater was huge—maybe "vast" was a better word. "It makes me feel so..."

"Small?" Josh supplied.

"Yeah," I answered, trying to get some kind of perspective on the sheer size. Even the little astronaut cutout far at the bottom wasn't helping me get a grasp. It was hard to keep my eyes on the steps as we descended a little ways into the crater.

"Hey, we're closing soon," one of the attendants told us as we passed by the red brick museum. By the looks of the empty path, we were the last ones there.

"We don't need much time," Josh promised.

The guy nodded with a reluctant sigh and let us pass. At least running had kept me in fairly good shape—I wasn't too badly winded by the hike. I was, however, a sweaty mess. I forgot all about the heat, even the damn motorcycle ride, with every step onto the metal observation deck.

"I used to come here when I was having a bad day," Josh said, "or if I needed a little jolt to remind me just how small everything is when you step back and really look at the big picture."

"And now?" I asked.

"Now it speaks to a different part of me." He stared into the distance with a look I knew all too well, and I couldn't help but wonder if he was really here with me, or thinking about the crash.

"It's huge," I said, hoping to bring him back.

"About three-quarters of a mile across and over five hundred feet deep." He leaned on his elbows, looking over the metal railing.

"And the meteor that caused it all?"

He gave me that deer-in-the-headlights expression that told me I'd be better off Googling. I laughed and pulled out my cell phone. "No problem." A few swipes later and I had all the information I'd ever want on the crater. I scanned through it quickly. "They think it was one hundred and sixty feet across."

"So little compared to all of this."

I scanned through the rest of the article. "Sometimes the littlest catalysts cause the biggest impacts."

He pulled me in front of him and wrapped his arms around me, my back pressed to his chest. "Like you."

I tilted my head back to look up at him, and his small smile lit my heart with the same colors as the sunset. My love for Josh never ceased; it grew steadily every day, but it never failed to surprise me how quickly he could make me slip right back into teenage-infatuation mode. That giddy feeling kept me hooked on him like the most addictive drug. "How like me? Because I came crashing into your life?" I joked.

"Yes and no," he answered. "You were this tiny girl in high school. I'm not oblivious—I didn't love you then, but I sure loved the idea of you. Someone smart, brave, gorgeous in a way that didn't need an hour in front of the mirror to go to a game. I'd seen plenty of hot girls by then, but you were the first really beautiful one, inside and out."

I pressed a kiss to his bicep. "Not sure I made the impact back then."

"No, you did. Enough that when your dad said your name that day...the first time...in Kandahar, my heart leaped. Because of you, he knew who I was. Because of you, he pushed me to get back onto the ice. Because of you, I went back to college hockey. Before I knew you well enough to honestly love you, you'd already altered my world in ways you couldn't have known. So small, but such a huge impact."

I took in the crusted lines of earth around the crater, the sparse vegetation that persevered in the desert heat, the way the earth hadn't softened to heal its wound. "A pretty long-lasting impact, by the look of it."

He turned me in his arms, bracing me against the railing, and tilted my chin up. "A permanent impact, December. But you change me every day, make me want to be a better man for you."

He kissed me lightly, sweetly, tasting like promise and mint from his gum. "I love you," I whispered.

"I'm not sure love is strong enough to describe how I feel about you, but I guess it will have to do."

I leaned on my tiptoes and kissed him. For that one moment, there was no helicopter crash, no deployment, no fights, no nightmares. In the breath of that kiss, it was just us, and the love that would see us through the worst of this storm. I wanted it to last forever, but the park closed, and a picture later, we were speeding back toward Winslow.

"No, seriously, they have the best strawberry malts here, ever," Josh said, pointing to the picture on the menu. I turned back and forth on the bar stool at the fifties-themed diner as I debated dinner. As date-nights went, Josh was rocking it.

"They look really good," I said as I scoped out the huge milkshake handed across the bar to a customer a few seats down.

I gave in as we ordered, already drooling over the thought of that ice cream. "So you used to hang out here?"

Josh casually pointed to the corner booth. "I did my

homework there every day after school."

"You did homework?" I teased.

"Hey, you made the grades or you didn't get on the ice. B average or better or you got cut."

"Thank God for hockey."

He gave me a smacking kiss. "Hey, it got you to notice me."

I laughed as he headed off to the bathroom. Our malts arrived a few minutes later, with a wink and a smile from the older waitress. "Thank you," I told her, and then lost myself in strawberry bliss.

Heaven, I thought as I sucked the concoction through the long straw, holding on to the stemmed glass like my life depended on it. *I bet this is why he loves strawberry ice cream.*

The bell rang to my right, announcing new customers as I happily ruined my dinner. I glanced over to see three guys walk in. The one standing in the center searched the diner for something, rubbing his hand over a shaved head.

"I'd know that fucking bike anywhere," he said.

"Evan, I highly doubt—" the guy on the right started.

"Walker!" The center one shouted in excitement, his eyes still scanning the seats.

I let the straw fall from my lips, looking to see if Josh was back yet. *Nope.* Well, maybe they meant a different—

"Josh Walker!" Evan called again, walking past me.

Nope, they definitely were looking for Josh. "He's in the bathroom," I answered.

Evan looked me over in a way that made me want to shower. Alone. Then he leaned in way too close, bracing his hand right next to my malt. "And who might you be, princess?" Logically, I knew I wasn't in danger, but this asshat might be if he got any closer.

"My fiancée," Josh called, and I wanted to fist-pump. "Now get the fuck away from her, E."

"Holy shit, he lives!" Evan called, turning from me to launch at Josh with a hug.

Josh hugged him back with a laugh. The two were nearly comparable in height and build, Josh having only a couple inches on him. Josh shook the other guys' hands, and then cut through them to take his seat next to me.

They flanked us at the counter, the shortest one taking the stool next to mine. "Tom." He introduced himself by shaking my hand. "And you are?"

"Ember," I said with a smile.

"Nice to meet the girl who nailed him down." He motioned toward Josh, and then leaned across the counter. "Hey, Mrs. White! Give me a Coke and a piece of apple pie?"

She waved at him with a nod.

"Yeah, me, too," the other one with the dark hair said from the other side of Evan.

"Use your manners, Samuel!" the woman called back.

"Yes, Mom."

Josh laughed, the sound clear and honest. "Good to see some things don't change."

"Yeah," Evan said, "but some sure as hell do. What have you been up to? I see your mom from time to time, but she's not exactly in a talkative mood."

"That's because she still hates you," Josh answered. "Thanks, Mrs. White," he said as she put our dinners in front of us.

"Hey, I never made you do any of that shit. Fuck, you were talking me into it most of the time."

"What shit is this?" I asked, leaning around Josh.

"Oh no." Josh leaned forward to block Evan. "No, no, no. There's a reason I haven't told you any of that."

It should have been funny, and I faked the appropriate smile, but it stung something deeper. *You're so good at not telling me the inconvenient things.*

"You don't talk about us? Now I'm hurt. Where's the love?"

"Plenty of love," Josh said between bites. "I just have a

different life."

"Doing what?" Samuel asked, stealing a fry from Josh's plate. I bit into my own, savoring the salt.

Josh looked my way and then back to Samuel. "I fly helicopters for the army, now."

"No shit?" Evan remarked. "What? Not getting enough thrills from the bike, you gotta take it to the sky?"

You have no idea. I kept my thoughts to myself as I devoured my burger, hungrier than I'd initially thought. Besides, I wasn't giving Josh an excuse to shut them up. I'd learn way more about this part of his life by being quiet than I would by asking questions.

"Something like that," he answered as their pies were delivered.

"Is that where you got the hardware?" Tom pointed to Josh's air cast, and I paused, my French fry suspended an inch from my lips.

"Something like that," he repeated.

"Yeah, okay. Well, do you want to something-like-that with us for a little ride?"

Josh's eyebrows shot sky-high. "Tonight?"

"No, next week when you inevitably disappear under whatever rock you've been hiding under for the last eight years. Yes, tonight."

I polished off my burger and waited for Josh's answer.

"I'm kind of on a date, here, guys." Josh's answer was weak, even to my ears.

"She gets you the rest of your life. We're just asking for a couple hours. Besides, you should see the bike the Klemensky brothers put together. It's fucking fast."

"They're like twelve, what the hell are they doing working on bikes?"

Evan laughed. "They were twelve eight years ago, man."

"Right. Of course."

"Well, what do you say? You want to see it?" Tom pushed.

Josh asked me with raised eyebrows.

"Just a ride?" I asked, trying not to sound like a nagging fiancée.

"Just a ride," he promised. "I'll even have you home by curfew. Besides, now you'll get to see what you keep asking about." The naked pleading in his voice was my undoing. Weren't we here for him? To give him a little respite from the hell we'd been living in for the last month?

I scoffed. "Asking once a year is hardly always."

"Is that a yes?" Excitement lit his eyes in a way I hadn't seen since before he left on the deployment.

"Okay. Just a ride."

"Just a ride." His smile was breathtaking.

"Just a ride!" the other three said in unison, saluting me.

I laughed, unable to keep a serious face. Josh paid the bill, and we headed out to the bike. I put on all my protective gear, thankful that it was designed so I didn't sweat to death.

"What are you thinking?" Josh asked, strapping my helmet. I was more than capable of doing it myself, but I loved how protective the gesture was.

"Oh, there's a lot going on in here," I answered.

He sat sideways on the bike and tugged me between his legs. "Enlighten me."

I made sure the other guys couldn't hear from where they were parked. "You have never once mentioned these guys."

His smile faded. "There's good reason for it. Good reason that I don't search them out when we're here, and I don't keep in touch."

"But you're friends?"

"They were some of my best friends. They also sat in the back of cop cars with me so often that by sixteen we were court-ordered not to be within fifty feet of each other until we turned eighteen." Josh shrugged. "Small town."

"You trust them?"

"With everything but you," he answered.

"Why is that?"

His arms wound around my back. "I don't trust anyone with you. Hell, it killed me to ask Will to come over and…" The light in his eyes died swiftly as he realized what he'd said.

"Fix the disposal?" I finished for him. He nodded. "You can talk about him. It's okay."

"No. I can't. That's one of our problems, right?"

"We have more than one?" I whispered.

His mouth snapped shut. "Nothing we can't get past once I'm back to normal."

It was a roundabout way of admitting that he wasn't okay, so I'd take it. "Okay. When you're ready."

He swallowed, looking over at his friends and then back to me. "What else are you thinking?"

I glanced at the guys who were currently throwing raunchy remarks at each other. "That Jagger has more common sense in his pinky, but he'd like them."

"And Grayson?"

I scrunched my nose.

Josh let out a half laugh. "Yeah, he'd have no tolerance for these guys."

"Are you coming? Or am I going to have to drag your ass?" Evan called out.

Josh flipped him the middle finger, then snapped his helmet and swung his leg over the Ducati. "Want to snuggle?"

"Very cute," I said, climbing on behind him and then doing just that.

We followed the other three on their motorcycles through the quiet streets of Winslow, more than a few heads turning as we sped by. Josh pushed the speedometer to keep up with the others, and I didn't give him flack, just held on tighter and tucked my head beside his.

Ten minutes or so after passing the town's limits, we turned off the highway for a series of smaller roads. Why didn't these things have coms? I had no way of asking Josh if he knew where we were headed.

We slowed as we passed through the gate of a chain fence, coming upon a crowd of a couple dozen people our age or younger.

Josh pulled to a stop and killed the engine. I removed my helmet. "Okay, where are we?" I asked as he helped me off the bike. His friends had already headed over to the crowd.

"Saturday night in a small town," he answered with a grin, taking off his own helmet.

"And you know everyone?" I took off my jacket but kept my protective pants on.

Josh looked over the crowd. "More or less. Same crowd different year." He cupped my chin. "You're not going to want to know what I think they're doing."

My conscience warred with my need to know every little part of him, especially the darkest parts he kept hidden. If I couldn't handle this, would he trust me enough to tell me about what happened to him in Afghanistan? "I'll be fine."

"You sure?"

"I go where you go."

"Okay." He took my hand and walked through the bikes and the crowd as Evan climbed up onto a wooden box everyone had gathered around.

"You made it!" he called over to Josh. "Thought we were going to lose you back there for a while, but we slowed it down for you, Walker."

Every head turned in our direction. I looked up to Josh, and my breath stuttered in my chest.

His expression had turned hard and more determined than it ever had even while playing hockey. This...this was not my Josh. "Just letting you feel overconfident," he called back.

Evan laughed, and the group joined. My hand tightened reflexively on Josh's when more than a few girls raked their eyes up and down his body. "That's right," Evan pointed to Josh. "I've brought Walker home. Shall we show him what we've built since he's been off flying helicopters?"

The group cheered and then split down the middle, revealing two bikes standing side by side and a long concrete road lit by road flares.

"What is this?" Josh asked.

"A failed attempt at a new airport from about six years ago," Samuel answered.

"And what are we doing here?" I asked. Not that I didn't already know. There was only one reason to light a path like that. They'd moved their street racing out of Winslow to this little strip.

Evan pointed to Josh with a sly grin. "He's going to let me win back my Ducati."

CHAPTER TWENTY-SEVEN

"You've got to be fucking kidding me," I said under my breath, wishing my heart would start beating again. "He's joking, right?"

The muscle in Josh's jaw flexed, but he didn't take his eyes off Evan. "I don't think he is."

"You're not seriously considering this, are you?"

He didn't answer. *Holy shit. He actually is.*

Words failed me.

Evan hopped off the box and made his way to us. "Come on, Walker. You up for it?"

"I don't do this anymore," Josh said. The tiniest bit of relief leaked into me.

"You too good for us now?" Evan asked, crossing his arms in front of his chest.

"Fuck, Evan. You know it's not like that," Josh answered, ripping his hand over his hair.

"I'm not so sure. You don't call, you don't write, don't even say hi when you're in town." His tone was kidding, but his eyes were anything but. "Least you can do is give me a shot at winning her back."

"Not happening."

Evan turned his attention to me and let his eyes openly wander. "Come on, it's not like you ride her."

I barely suppressed a shudder.

Josh pulled me under his arm and glared at Evan, his expression more than a little scary. "Don't go there," he said in almost a whisper.

Evan shrugged. "One ride. You win, you walk. You lose, and I'll pick my bike up from your house in the morning."

"I don't see any reason to," Josh answered. I wound my arm around his waist, the muscles so tense he felt like stone.

"Because you owe me. You got a fresh start and left the rest of us here to rot." Any trace of joking bled from Evan's voice until there was only thinly veiled hatred.

Josh shook his head. "I had no choice. It was leave or they'd press charges."

"Yeah, well, what do you think the rest of us went through? Not everyone's mom was cool with picking up and moving."

Josh's arm around me tightened. "I didn't know."

"You didn't look back. So do this one thing, and we'll be even. Show me how many layers of the new and improved Josh Walker I have to strip off to see who you really are, because you can fool your pretty little red-headed fiancée, here, but you can't fool me. I know who you are in the marrow of your bones."

"Things change."

Evan scoffed. "People don't."

They stared each other down in what was probably the most uncomfortable silence I'd ever witnessed.

"One race." Evan broke it. "Come on. No cops, no danger of getting caught, just you and me like we're sixteen."

"Except we're not kids, and we have a hell of a lot more to lose," Josh argued.

"Ha. Speak for yourself."

"Josh," I whispered. He couldn't do this. He wouldn't. Not something he'd left behind eight years ago. There was no chance, right? I knew him better than Evan did.

Josh's eyes narrowed, but his concentration stayed on Evan.

"One race," he agreed.

Or maybe you don't know him as well as you think. My blood turned to ice, freezing everything in its path to my heart.

"For the bike?" Evan asked.

"For the bike," Josh agreed.

Josh dropped his arm from around me to shake on their ridiculous deal, and then Evan walked away, announcing that they'd race.

Josh turned his back on the group, taking a deep breath and putting his hands on his head. I willed my limbs to move, my mouth to speak, but nothing functioned.

"Ember?" he asked, then touched my shoulder. When I didn't turn, he took my hand and guided me back to the Ducati, far enough to have some space from the crowd. "Babe, it's just a quick race. It'll take maybe five minutes."

My frozen blood flash-boiled. "Five minutes. That's not so bad. I mean, what, that's about the time it takes to crash a helicopter, right?"

He stepped back like I'd slapped him. "Not fair."

"Not fair? What's not fair is you almost dying a month ago. What's not fair is burying our friend. You choosing to hurl your body down a concrete strip for the sheer fun of it? What the fuck is wrong with you?"

His jaw flexed. "I don't expect you to understand."

"Good, because there's no way that's going to happen. Damn it, Josh! You're twenty-five, not seventeen!" My fingers bit into my palms.

He put on his jacket and zipped it up before taking my face in his hands. "This is who I am. Hockey, motorcycles, flying. You've always known it. Please don't act like you didn't."

Wasn't he right? Josh, at his core, was always going to push the envelope, always going to seek the thrill that lay just past the safe zone. It was what had drawn me to him in the first place.

"Please don't do this," I begged shamelessly.

He flinched. "December."

"I will do anything you want if you just walk away from this right now."

An engine revved in the background, and he looked over my shoulder. "I have to go."

"No, you're choosing to go. Make no mistake about that."

He sighed, and then brushed a quick kiss on my lips. "You know me better than that. I love you."

"I'll take care of her," a leggy brunette said, rubbing her hand on Josh's shoulder.

Josh startled. "Simone."

She flashed him a smile. "Just like old times, huh?"

That look on her face said their version of "old times" hadn't just been street-racing. My stomach turned over. God, this was college all over.

No, it's not. Don't give in to that kind of drama.

"If you mean Evan pulling me into shit I have no business being in, then yeah, kind of." He looked back to me, his gaze softening. "Ember, Simone will take you to watch."

"I don't want to watch," I said through my teeth.

"Five minutes," he pled.

I shook my head, stepping out of his hands. "Ridiculous."

"I love you." He buckled his helmet and drove the Ducati over to the starting line, where Evan was already waiting.

"Let's go, princess," Simone said, leading me to a tall dais. I climbed the ladder, cursing Josh with every rung until I stood on the top, at least six feet off the ground. A few bikes took off to watch the finish line, while others lined up along the route.

I had half a mind to leave, but what the hell was I going to do, call an Uber driver to the middle-of-nowhere, illegal racing strip? I didn't know a single soul other than Josh, or even have the slightest idea of how to get back to Winslow.

"Uncomfortable?" Simone asked, leaning on the metal railing so far that her ass nearly hung out of her short leather skirt.

"Just a little out of my element," I admitted, resting my elbows on the rounded metal. Josh and Evan waited about fifteen feet ahead, both talking to Samuel and nodding at intervals.

"Yeah, well, I never thought he'd end up with someone like you," she muttered.

Hell no. "Josh left here eight years ago. Please don't act like you still know him."

She straightened, looking down on me. "I know you'll never keep him happy. Josh has always needed the rush, and seeing as he's here right now, that's still true."

My muscles locked one by one, as if my body was trying to forcibly contain the anger that was rolling in my stomach. I concentrated on Josh's helmet and sent up a little prayer that he not do anything that would get him hurt even more. "That may be true, but you don't know me, or us."

She laughed, the sound grating on my last nerve. "He'll never stay tucked away in some safe little desk job, and I know that's what someone like you would want."

Start the damn race already, before I throw her off this thing. "And what makes you think that?" Crap, I'd taken her bait, and her Cheshire-cat smile told me she was all too happy about it.

"Because he didn't give in when you asked him not to race. I heard you."

Okay, that hurt, but I breathed through the crippling pressure in my chest. She didn't know us. Didn't know what we'd been through in the last two and a half years. Didn't know the strength of our love, our determination, our commitment. I ran my thumb over the band of my engagement ring.

Josh swung his leg over the bike, and my heart stuttered. Maybe he was going to listen. Maybe he wouldn't race. Hope lit my smile as he jogged over to me, and I crouched down. My happiness that he'd decided to see reason squashed the near-rebuke at running on his leg. "Thank you," I said as he looked up at me.

His forehead puckered as he took off his jacket. "No, I just… I wasn't getting enough mobility."

The sound of Velcro unfastening nearly paralyzed me. "What the hell are you doing?"

He handed me his air cast. "I'll put it back on as soon as we're done."

My hands took it, despite my brain ordering them not to, my mouth hanging slightly open as he put his jacket back on and zipped it. "I love you. You and me against the world, right?"

"Right," I whispered. *But what if it's just me against you and the world?*

He flashed me a smile and ran back to the bike, sliding on in one smooth motion. I stood slowly, clutching his cast like it was a link to the only piece of him that I recognized.

Simone didn't say anything. She didn't have to. Her point had been made loud and clear by the one person I'd needed on my side of an argument he didn't realize we were in.

"Here we go, princess. You ready to console him? Evan hasn't taken the eight-year break Josh has."

"I won't need to console him." My chin lifted and my shoulders straightened.

They revved their engines, and Samuel backed up a few feet, raising his arms.

"Why is that?" Simone asked, lifting her eyebrow at me.

"Because I know him better than you do."

She might have said something, but I tuned her out, my brain focusing 100 percent on Josh as Samuel dropped his arms.

The noise was deafening as the bikes sprang forward. Nausea tore through me as the engines whirred to a high pitch and then back down as they coursed through the gears. *Just let him be safe. Please, let him be safe.*

They sped down the runway lit only by the red road flares and their own headlights. I gasped, my fingernails biting into his cast as Evan swerved to the right, knocking Josh off-course. *Asshole.*

Josh corrected and then drove even faster. The speed sucked my heart straight out of my body. He'd never survive if he crashed going this fast. I'd lose him.

What if that was what he wanted? Was that what this was? Did he feel so guilty about what had happened to Trivette, to Will, that he was testing his own fate? Or was he so numb to it all that he truly couldn't understand what the hell he was doing to me? To himself?

Did I even have the right to push the subject?

His taillight got smaller the farther he went from me, and I couldn't help but feel like it was more than physical distance growing between us on that strip of concrete. My breath stuttered in my lungs as the lights swerved again, but then stayed steady.

The engines died down as they passed the finish line, but the cheers were almost as loud. "I can't tell who won from here," Simone said.

"Josh did."

"What makes you so sure?"

I kept my eyes locked on Josh as he sped back toward us, Evan on his heels. He came to a sudden halt at the start line and ripped his helmet off before dismounting. The smile he gave me was blinding. The race had invigorated him, forced life back into his veins. Or maybe he had simply siphoned it from me.

I gave Simone a smile that Paisley would have been proud of. "You might have doubted the Josh that you knew, but my Josh, the one I'm marrying? He doesn't know how to fail. It's not in his vocabulary." *Go to hell.*

He walked toward us, his eyes never straying from me despite the girls who pushed into his path. The sight took the edge off my razor-sharp anger. He was a flaming, hot mess of a man, but he was mine, and he knew it.

He reached up for me, and I handed him his cast. *Put it on.* I said it all with one arched eyebrow, and his grin only widened as he did. Using the railing, I swung to sit on the edge of the platform, and he pulled me through the opening, holding me tight as I slid down the length of his body.

"I won." His face looked like a five-year-old's at Christmas.

"Yes."

"What did you think? Pretty badass, right? There's nothing like it."

"I think there are quicker ways to kill yourself that don't include making me watch. Now take me home."

"Ember..."

"Your five minutes are up. You can put me on the back of that bike right now and take me home, or I will start walking, and if that happens, good luck ever getting me on that thing again."

We locked eyes, a battle of wills that Josh never had a prayer of winning, not when I was this pissed off.

"Congrats, Walker," Simone said, leaning up to kiss Josh's cheek. "What's the matter? Little lady calling in your curfew?"

He didn't look away from me, but the muscle in his jaw flexed.

"That offer is about to expire," I warned softly.

He stepped back from me but held my hand, gently leading me toward the Ducati.

"Leaving so soon?" Evan asked, his helmet off and his arm around Simone's waist. "We just got you back."

"Nawh, man, I was just visiting. But thanks for having us." Josh got on the bike and offered his arm for balance as I took my helmet and jacket from Tom and put them on. Then I climbed on behind him and scooted forward until I was flush with his body, my arms wrapping around his rock-hard midsection.

I couldn't help but sag a little in relief. We were leaving. He wasn't hurt...well, any more than he'd been when we'd come here.

"Look me up if you're ever in Tennessee," Josh said.

"Yeah, well, you always know where to find us."

Josh nodded and made sure we were clear of the crowd before he opened the Ducati up. The force tried to pull me away from him, but I held tight, refusing to fall off the bike. A hysterical giggle bubbled up. Wasn't that my life right now? Trying to hold on to Josh while he put the pedal to the metal in every aspect of his life?

God, what was I doing? Was this who he was, or had the crash brought something out in him that had lain dormant? Was it PTSD? Was it just his nature? Was he grieving Will, or scared of the permanency of marriage? Was it all of the above? Was I trying to force him into being someone he wasn't?

My eyes fluttered shut as the wind roared past us, tears slipping down my cheeks nearly unnoticed. I was so tired. Tired of the fear that hadn't left me since the moment he'd told me of the deployment. Weary to my bones of the eggshells we'd surrounded ourselves with since he'd been back. Exhausted from lack of sleep, lack of understanding, lack of knowledge. I was holding on to Josh so tightly that every inch of me had been scraped raw.

We pulled into the driveway, and I slid from the bike before he turned it off, already headed inside with my helmet in hand before he called my name. "December."

I shook my head, all the fight simply...gone.

The air-conditioning hit my face, chilling the tear tracks, and I wiped them away with the back of my sleeve on my way to the bedroom. I stripped quickly, wanting every piece of that motorcycle gone. What a beautiful start of a night. I'd finally felt like we were connecting again on the level we needed, only to end it worlds apart.

"Talk to me," Josh said, shutting the bedroom door behind him.

"No point."

He took my face in his hands, tilting it to his. "There is always a point."

"Why? You won't listen. Maybe I'm not enough of a rush for you, or whatever it is you're seeking—whatever it is you need."

His eyes, deep brown in the dim lighting, searched my face, widening in a panic. "You're everything I need." His mouth crashed to mine, hard and insistent. My cry was muffled against his lips, but he jerked back. "Babe?"

"No," I said, shaking my head free of his hands and backing away. "No. You're not going to sex your way out of this."

"It was just a race."

"It wasn't just a fucking race!" I yelled. "It's everything! It's the bike, and the speeding, and the sex, and the nightmares. But most of all, it's the 'I'm fine' and the silence. God, Josh, that's the killer. You act like I don't know you well enough to see that you're not fine. None of this is fine, and you won't let me in. You won't let me help, and that's not a partnership. That's not a marriage."

"What do you want me to say?" he asked, raking his hands through his hair.

"Something! Anything that's real. You can talk to Paisley? To Jagger? But I'm left wondering what's going on in your head...in your heart."

"I have always loved you. I will always love you. That will never change." He stepped toward me, and I retreated.

"Then give me something to hang on to."

"You don't want inside my head." He moved back until he leaned against the closed door.

"Yes, I do! I'm not some weak little girl, Josh. Don't treat me like one. The distant look in your eyes, the way you drive, even the way you make love to me...you're not fine. We both know it. And I'm trying. I swear, I'm trying to figure out what I'm supposed to do—where I'm supposed to push, where I'm supposed to give you space—but I can't because you won't even tell me if I'm in the ballpark. Am I supposed to just stand here while you self-destruct?"

"I am doing the best I can." Every line in his body was tense, like he was ready for the fight...or to flee.

"Then talk to me. Let me help you."

"You can't," he said softly, his eyes dark with a sadness I couldn't seem to touch, to heal.

"Let me try. Please. Don't shut me out." I reached for him, and he stepped to the side, avoiding my touch. "Josh, please!"

"Damn it! Has it ever dawned on you that I don't want you to know? That you are the last person I want in my fucking head? It's with me every second, every day. No matter what I do, it's there, waiting...festering. The only time I can escape the thoughts, the memories, the nightmares is when I'm with you. When I'm kissing you, holding you, inside you. You are the last safe place I have in this world, and you're going to have to forgive me if I'm not ready to give that up and trade it for the look in your eyes when you realize what an ugly mess it is in here." He tapped his heart. "Forgive me if I'm not ready for you, of all people, to see me as broken."

"You're breaking me."

He sucked in his breath.

"Every time you keep me in the dark, every story I hear secondhand, every reckless act you pull, every time you reach for me out of need instead of desire...you break off another piece."

Pain contorted his face for a second before he swallowed and looked away. "I'm sorry for that. You deserve better."

"Josh." I whispered his name as I moved forward, cupping his cheek in my hand. "I deserve you. But I deserve all of you, and not just what you're willing to let me see." He stared at me so long that I finally realized he still wasn't going to say anything. "You really can't let me in, can you?" I whispered.

"Let's go to bed." His voice dropped.

Just when I thought my heart couldn't hurt any more, another slice opened me up, bleeding and raw. We readied for bed in a tense silence that didn't dissipate once we'd climbed beneath the sheets.

"I love you," he whispered to my back.

I turned over to face him, the contours of his face lit by moonlight through the window. "Then let me in, Josh."

His eyes closed as if he was in pain. "I can't."

I closed the distance between us, putting my palm to his cheek. "You know the thing about the crater today? That giant impact?"

"That tiny, red-haired meteorite," he added, looking at me as the memory softened both of us. But in my case, it was more like a slow breakdown of everything I'd used to hold myself together the last month.

"That meteorite wasn't so small to start with. Half of it burned up in the atmosphere, just trying to get to Earth. The rest of it... It almost all vaporized upon impact. It made that impact, for good or bad, but all that's left of it are tiny, scattered pieces."

His lips parted, little lines forming between his eyebrows. "December." He said my name like a prayer, a plea, but when nothing else followed, I rolled onto my side away from him.

I slept like crap, and when Mom texted in the morning, I took it as a sign and packed my bag in silence.

I was in a cab for the airport before he'd even realized I was gone.

CHAPTER TWENTY-EIGHT

JOSH

The sunlight streamed through the window, hitting me in the face as I opened my eyes. No matter how late I slept, I was still exhausted. Always exhausted.

Ember must have beaten me out of bed, because her side was empty. I rested my forearm over my eyes after I saw the time on my cell phone. Ten o'clock. Damn, that fight had been brutal. I should have gotten up early, gotten her coffee. I should have done a lot of things. Instead I'd given in to my pride, my need for that thirty-second thrill, my craving for the speed, and I'd let Evan push me into a race. *Like he even had to push hard.*

Her eyes, God, they'd killed me, but how could she understand?

She can't when you won't tell her, you asshat.

I groaned, wishing I could crush the tiny conscience that hammered away at me. My feet hit the floor, and I pulled on shorts and a Pearl Jam T-shirt before going in search of my fiancée. Mom only looked the other way on the tattoos as long as they weren't thrown in her face.

The house was quiet in an uncomfortable way. Something was off. The tiles were cold under my feet as I walked into the kitchen, where Mom sat at the small table. She gave me a sad smile. "Good, you're up. I poured you some coffee."

"Where's Ember?" I asked as I took the seat across from her, where a still-steaming cup of coffee waited.

"She's gone," Mom said softly, her eyes nearly dripping sympathy.

I sat up straight. "What do you mean, she's gone?"

Mom shrugged. "I caught her on the way out. She said her brother broke his nose at hockey camp, and she was headed home for a couple of days to see him."

"Gus, what? Why wouldn't she tell me? I would have gone with her." The chair squeaked as I pushed back from the table and stood. I needed to pack and find a flight.

"Sit down, Josh."

Her tone didn't allow for argument, and I did as ordered. She gave me "the look." The one that my five-foot-three mother used to send me running for the hills. "Mom?"

"We haven't really talked about what happened to you... over there."

Fuck my life. Her, too? "Mom..."

"Stop. We didn't talk the first time, and I thought maybe that was for the best, to let you deal with it in your own way. I figured as long as I didn't get calls from the police department that you'd been racing, you were fine."

"I don't race the Harley."

"Well, then I should have set that Ducati on fire," she said with a smile.

I tapped my fingers on the table, knowing that anything I could have said would have only earned me another foot deeper in the hole I'd apparently dug. "I was fine."

"If you're so fine, then how did you send your fiancée fleeing first thing in the morning? She didn't even pause for coffee."

"She..." I shook my head. "I raced the bike last night."

"Joshua Walker."

"It was reckless, but Evan—"

"Evan? We moved away from here for a reason. I know you

were hurt in Afghanistan, but I don't think it knocked you back eight years."

I dropped my head to my hands. "She wants things I can't give. I'm not capable."

Mom reached across the table until her hands covered mine. "Then figure out how to give them to her."

"Maybe she's better off without me. Did you ever think of that? Twice she's had notification teams at her door, Mom. Twice. She's buried her dad. We buried Will, and she almost buried me. How much more do I have a right to ask of her? At what point does me pushing her away become a mercy? She told me I'm breaking her, so how long until I destroy the one thing I love most?"

"What you two have is something I've never seen, never been lucky enough to have. You don't let that just walk out. I'm incredibly proud of the man you are, Josh, never more so than the way you love December. But I'll kick your ass from here to the Colorado border if you don't pull your shit together."

Our eyes locked and I knew she'd do it. "What's inside me, it's ugly."

"You let her decide what's ugly. You owe her that much."

Let her go, my conscience screamed at me, but my heart couldn't contemplate a life without her in it, not when she was the reason it beat in the first place. "Okay, let me find a flight."

She tilted her head. "You have fifteen minutes to pack. You're on the one p.m. flight into Eagle County."

"What?"

"She'll be in Breckenridge, at their cabin. That's where her mother is sending her."

"You talked to her mother and already booked a flight?"

She peered at me over her coffee. "Not all of us sleep in like seventeen-year-old boys."

I let the jibe slip. "You're not mad that I'm leaving? I've only been here a few days."

She smiled at me. "I just needed to see you, Josh. Every time you're hurt I can't seem to breathe until I lay eyes on you. I've done that now, and don't need to hover, or tend you like a nurse. I need you to go be the man I raised, so you don't lose me my daughter...or my future grandbabies."

"Yes, ma'am." I stood from the table.

"And Josh?"

I turned at the doorway.

"Make arrangements for that damn Ducati or it becomes my bonfire."

I gave a single nod. "Done."

Everything was ready. Or, at least, I hoped it was. I'd gotten to the cabin two hours ago, parked my rental in the driveway, located the hide-a-key, and stocked the place with groceries for the next three days. That was all the time we had, but damned if I wasn't going to use every minute of it.

The sound of tires crunching the gravel of the driveway sent my pulse racing. What if she was pissed that I was here? What if she refused to talk to me? What if I'd already blown it?

While my heart was telling me to get a grip, that this was Ember, my head had spun off into the twilight zone of insecurity and was in no hurry to bring its ass back to reality.

What if she really was better off, and I was just prolonging the inevitable? As hard as I tried, I couldn't get Rizzo's whole stance out of my head. Maybe he was right, and I'd done Ember the biggest injustice simply by falling in love with her.

Shut the fuck up. Open the door and fight for your woman.

My hand turned the knob before my head was ready, and then I stepped out onto the porch. The dying afternoon light caught in her hair, illuminating the strands of red like a flame as her mouth hung open just a fraction, her eyes wide. "Josh?"

I leaned on the heavy porch railing, my arms aching to hold her but knowing I needed her to come the rest of the way on her own. "Hi." *That's the best you have?*

"How did you know where I'd be?" Her footsteps were light as she came up the wooden steps.

"My mom called your mom and the rest is..." I gestured between us with my hands.

"Ahh." She nodded, biting her lip. Her eyes dropped to her toes, and those four feet that separated us felt like a giant canyon.

Not for long.

"I'm an asshole," I said, very matter-of-fact, and her head snapped up.

"Josh, no...well, maybe a little."

"How's Gus?"

"He's already given us a list of A-list actors who have broken their noses. He says it gives him character." She smiled but still held herself away from me. The distance between us, physical and emotional, was killing me.

I moved toward her and cradled her face in my hands. Her skin was unbelievably soft as I stroked my thumbs up her cheekbones. "Are you mad that I'm here?"

"No," she whispered. "Embarrassed, a little, but never mad."

"What reason do you have to be embarrassed?"

She rolled her eyes, instantly inflaming my need to kiss her. Ember was too damn cute. "I snuck out this morning because I just needed some space. Needed to breathe. I ran away like some drama-filled teenager instead of staying to fight things out with you."

"We all need a little time to think sometimes," I said, moving my hands through her loose, gorgeous hair to the back of her head.

"I literally ran home to my mother, Josh. She then told me that she wasn't going to watch my mope fest and to come up here if I wanted to breathe."

"And now?"

"This is the first full breath I've taken since I left you this morning." She sighed, a look passing between us that said everything words couldn't.

"Yeah, I get that. You're my oxygen," I admitted. "I woke up without you this morning, and realizing I'd driven you to that—to leave me—I never want to feel that again. And yet, there's still this part of me that says you'd be better off if I just let you go."

"Josh." Her face fell.

"No, if you want in, and I mean all the way in, that's where this leads. There are ugly parts of me, December. Parts that think I should have spared you all this pain and walked away years ago. Parts that hate myself for loving my job, loving my mission. Parts of me that won't stop screaming that my choice killed Trivette. That I killed Will, and he should be alive. Not me. That I'll never live up to earning that sacrifice."

"That's not true," she whispered.

"What's true is a very clouded concept in my head. On one hand, I'm shoving you away from this nightmare because you're not a part of it. You are the one place that isn't shadowed to me. On the other hand, I'm holding on to you as tight as possible, because the moments I'm kissing you, holding you, it all evaporates and I'm whole."

"And you think you'd lose that?" she asked.

"Like I said last night, I've never been willing to risk it. The way you look at me, the way you see me, Ember—I'm not sure that guy exists in me anymore. You said that I'm breaking you, but if you see those broken pieces of me..." I shook my head, words failing.

She brought her hands up slowly to my arms. "Josh, it's all just you. Every tiny piece, whether you like it or not, it all combines to make you who you are, and I am wildly and desperately in love with you. Nothing is ever going to change that. There is nothing you could do or say that could make me stop loving you, so it would be a lot easier if you stopped trying to push me away. I don't need you to lay bare every detail. I'm not pushing you for that, but if you can't lean on me for support, then what are we doing? Why are we getting married?"

"Because even the pieces of me that know I'm in no shape to love you, can't stop loving you. I don't exist without you. You're in every fucking beat of my heart. You are my first thought when I open my eyes. You were my last thought as we crashed. I almost ruined you. I...I could still ruin you."

Her eyes didn't leave mine—they were open, honest, and bluer than the Colorado sky above us. "I made my choice years ago. I knew all of this was a possibility, and I chose you. I still choose every part of you, every day."

"And when you realize that those parts of me might be too broken to fix?"

She smiled, so beautiful and accepting. "Then I'll fall in love with the broken pieces. You just have to trust me."

"Okay." My throat closed, emotion welling in my chest so powerfully that I was afraid of exploding from the pressure. I closed my arms around her as she tucked her head under my chin. Holding her was so easy when the world around us got too complicated. Everything else slipped away until I was left with the simple, incorruptible truth that I would always love December Howard.

I just prayed my love wouldn't destroy her.

The next morning, I had coffee waiting when she stumbled out of the bedroom, her hair a riotous mess that made me want to take her right back to bed. But we weren't doing that, not yet.

She'd accused me of sexing out of conversations, and she'd been right, and maybe last night we'd both been too raw to really talk, too emotionally exhausted to do more than curl around each other and sleep, but today I was coming out with all guns blazing.

"Good morning, sleepyhead," I said, passing her a fresh cup of coffee, already creamed and sugared.

"Hmmm," she mumbled, sipping at the cup.

"Sleep okay?"

She looked over the cup at me. "Yeah. You only woke up once, right?"

Don't lie. Lay it bare. "Once that you woke for. I got up again around three a.m. but fell right back to sleep."

"Are the nightmares getting worse?" She hopped onto the counter, and déjà vu hit me. It was the same exact place I'd kissed her for the first time.

"No. They're actually less frequent, less violent. If they weren't, I'd be worried." I leaned back against the counter, keeping a respectable distance between us, or I'd have those pajama pants around her ankles in two seconds.

"Good. That's good."

"I want to take you somewhere."

She gave me a wan smile. "Last time that didn't work out too well for you."

"Yeah, well, no bike here. Just us."

"Can I shower first?"

The image of water dripping down her tight little body took over every brain cell.

"Josh?"

I blinked. "Yeah, shower. All good." A week without touching December and I was ready to combust. How the hell had I survived three months of deployment?

She hadn't been standing in front of you.

I waited forty-five minutes while she showered, dried her

hair, and dressed. I didn't go after her, touch her, hell, even so much as peek. It was an incredibly long forty-five minutes.

"Ready," she said, coming from the hallway in a baby blue sundress. Her hair was up in some kind of messy knot, with soft tendrils that caressed her cheeks. I clenched the arm of the couch to keep from sending my hands up her skirt. If sex had been my drug of choice, I was sure as hell going through withdrawals.

"You look...edible," I said, getting to my feet.

"As do you," she said with a smile, gesturing to my khaki shorts and short-sleeve button-down. Luckily it was green, so we weren't too matchy-matchy.

"Shall we?" I offered my hand, and she took it. A ten-minute drive in my rental car, and we pulled up to the ski lifts in Breckenridge.

"What are we doing?"

I simply smiled and held open her door. "Trust me."

She arched her eyebrow, knowing full well that I'd just used her own words against her. We walked, hand in hand, to the gondola station, waited our turn, and after I slipped the attendant a fifty, had a private ride to Peak Eight.

"This is beautiful," she said, her nose pressed against the glass as we took to the sky over Breckenridge.

"Yeah, it is," I said softly.

She smiled at me over her shoulder. "I love it here."

"Me, too. This whole town makes me think of possibilities, reminds me that the things you want most, sometimes you can actually have."

She turned to me and curled up on the seat just under my arm. "Like us."

"Like us," I said, then kissed her lightly, lingering just a moment to savor the way her soft lips clung to mine.

"I miss you when you're gone."

"You're never far from my thoughts. I keep a picture of you

on my kneeboard." *Which currently is spattered with my blood.*

"Really?" Her eyes lit up. Had I never told her? Never let her know that she was with me on every mission?

"When we go into a situation where the landing zone isn't clear, where it's hot, there's a moment when we all make sure that we're in. Everyone agrees, and then we go to extract the wounded."

"Because you know what could happen." She didn't flinch, just spoke as a matter of fact, and it gave me the courage to keep going.

"Yes. I always say yes."

"I would expect nothing less of you."

"Even if it means I don't come home to you?"

She took a deep breath and then laid her legs across mine. "I have faith that you'll come home. It's all that gets me through each day that you're gone. I can't live thinking you won't. That kind of fear suffocates me. So I choose to believe that every choice you make will bring you home to me, and save others."

"I always look at your picture before I say yes. I know what I'm choosing in that moment—the possibility of you holding a folded flag—and I do it anyway. I chose to go after Jagger, and I could have left you holding a folded flag. I chose the possibility of saving him over the certainty of coming home to you. How can you love someone who doesn't choose you?"

"How could I not love someone who risks his own life to save others? Josh, you didn't choose Jagger over me. I wasn't lying wounded and bleeding on the ground in Afghanistan. I was hanging out with Paisley in our home. I was never in danger. Stop blaming yourself. You made the right choice. I know the debt you feel you have to pay. I see the war raging just under your skin."

"What else do you see?"

"Besides the man I love?"

"Yes."

She sat up enough to look at me comfortably. "I see the struggle, the way you watch the news, the look you get when you're trolling the internet for what's happening over there. Mostly..." She searched my eyes for a long moment and let out a stuttered breath. "Mostly, I see the moments when you're not here. Your body is here, but your mind...it's there. And those moments scare me the most, because I'm terrified that I won't ever truly have you home again. Not one hundred percent. Does that make sense?"

"More than you know." I grazed my thumb over the diamond on her hand as we passed through the first station on our way up. "Do you want the ugliest truth?"

"Yes. I want everything." She forced a half smile. "And maybe if you tell me the worst, the rest will be easier."

"I feel like I left pieces of myself there, and I don't just mean the physical ones." I looped my arm over her thighs, resting my palm on her bare skin, trying to ground myself in her warmth, her light. "Our unit is still there, filling in the gaps from me, Trivette...Carter. I'm not sure I'll really be myself until they're all home, everyone we left there. I feel like I'm split between home and Afghanistan, like I don't really belong here."

"Okay," she said in simple acceptance that meant more than she could ever know.

"And when I'm with you, that all fades away. You ground me in a different reality, where there's just you and me. I haven't used alcohol or drugs, because I've used you."

"I knew that," she whispered. "It's never bothered me. It only got under my skin when you wouldn't talk to me, like sleeping with me would answer all my questions, explain everything I needed to know. Sometimes it felt like you were distracting me from asking. That, I despised."

"No, I was distracting myself. Answering your questions meant examining them, because I've never been able to hold back with you. It's always been full measures or nothing. No halfway bullshit."

She ran her fingers through my hair, and I groaned when she scratched her nails lightly over my scalp. God, it felt so damn good.

"I've always loved that about us. We're all in. Always."

"Yes."

"But that's not ugly. Nothing you've told me is ugly."

My stomach dropped, and we passed through the station on route to Peak Eight. I looked up to the green mountains, their beauty overwhelming, their sheer size distorted because we were too close to accurately gauge their mass.

"Even knowing everything we have, this incredible love that we share, our beautiful life that we're building..." I shook my head and looked down at her knees.

"Josh." She tipped my chin. "I'm here. No matter what you're about to say."

"Having done that mission, medevaced the wounded... Ember, I've found my purpose. I'll always go when they call. How many deployments can you wait through? How many times can I leave you?"

Fear streaked through her eyes, but she masked it before I could question her. "As many as it takes. I would rather sit home and wait for you, than spend a lifetime with anyone else. By the time the next deployment comes along, you'll be healed, and I'll be stronger."

"That's not the life you wanted. We said I'd get out after my contract, remember?"

She nodded. "Yeah. I know, and I still want that. And this is the life I wanted, because I have you. Everything else will fall in place."

The gondola stopped, and I helped Ember to her feet. We came out at the base of Peak Eight, and I walked us toward the superlift.

"Okay, now you have me confused," she said, her hand

tightly in mine. "Everything there is to do is over there." She pointed toward the alpine slide.

"Oh, you think I'd sign up to hurl myself down a mountain with nothing but a sled and a tube slide?"

She scoffed. "Yeah, it's probably not nearly enough of a rush for you."

"You wound me." I slapped my hand over my chest as we made our way to the base of the superlift.

"Mr. Walker?" the attendant asked.

"That's me, well, us," I said, gesturing to a very confused Ember.

"Ms. Patricks will meet you at the top."

"Thank you," I told him as we sat in the middle of the four-person lift chair. It accelerated at the very edge of the platform, and we were airborne, our feet kicking without ground beneath us.

"Oh my God," Ember muttered, trying to tuck her dress under her thighs.

I laughed. "No one can see you, babe. Let it fly free."

"No way in hell," she muttered. "There's got to be cameras."

"Then they can catch this." I captured her face and turned it toward mine, then kissed the breath out of her. She melted into me, her dress long forgotten. I kept the kiss slow, lazy, savoring every gasp from her lips, every time her breath stuttered. There was no distraction here, no phone ringing, no one in the background. The absolute quiet was perfection.

She giggled when my hand grazed her thigh. "One-track mind?"

"When it comes to you? Always."

The lift reached the top of the hill and slowed. I helped her dismount and swung her into my arms when she tripped. She looped her arms around my neck, and I couldn't ever remember feeling as happy as I did in that moment, carrying the woman I loved.

We made our way through the longer strands of grass, the tiny wildflowers that dotted the terrain, until we reached a large, wooden platform. "Are you going to put me down?" she asked.

"No," I answered, climbing the few steps it took to come out onto the stagelike surface. "There's room for about seventy people up here. At least, that's what they're telling me."

"Oh?" she asked, not really looking at the platform. Her eyes focused on the view. "Josh, it's gorgeous."

The mountains rose before us in stark contrast to the blue of the sky. They were covered in green to the treeline, the town of Breckenridge appearing tiny beneath us. "It's perfect."

"I've never seen a more beautiful view."

I set her down, her little sandals plunking against the wood, and then I stood opposite her, taking her hands in mine. "I think this view is as good as my life will get. Except maybe in about a year. This is perfect."

"Perfect for what?" she asked, tilting her head.

"For marrying me." I watched closely as her eyes widened and her lips parted. Her gaze swept over the platform behind us to the view in front of us and then back to my eyes.

"We can get married here?"

"We can. They don't have an opening until early next summer, so we'd have to wait until June and pray there's no snow, but yeah. You said a mountaintop in Colorado, and I thought, what better place than where this all started for us—Breckenridge. We can have the ceremony up here, and the reception in the lodge, which I've been told is very sought-after. Repeatedly."

"We can ride the chairlift?" Her eyes lit up, and I wanted to fist-pump, to shout to the world that I was this woman's man.

"We can, dress and all."

She laughed, her smile wide and bright, clear of the shadows that had dragged us both down lately.

"Mr. Walker?" a woman asked, walking over to us with a clipboard. "I'm Mrs. Patricks, the wedding coordinator. What do you two think? Is it what you're looking for?"

"Well, Miss Howard, what do you say?" I lifted her hand and kissed her palm.

She spun, taking everything in one last time while she deliberated. Then she turned back to me, radiating happiness from every line in her body. "I think it's absolutely perfect."

"Yes!" I shouted, scooping her into my arms and lifting her above my head. She braced her hands on my shoulders, and her laugh healed another broken line in me, stitched it together with love and the promise of our future.

I slowly lowered her until I could kiss her, and then I didn't give a hot damn if the wedding coordinator was there or not. She tasted like summer and felt like home.

We broke apart, and I turned to the open Colorado sky and shouted at the top of my lungs. "I'm marrying December Howard!"

She laughed, and damned if it didn't put a little more life into my soul. "Louder, babe. I don't think they heard you in Kansas."

I took a deeper breath and yelled even louder, pretty certain the whole world got the message that time.

CHAPTER TWENTY-NINE

EMBER

The next month passed in what was my idea of working perfection. We talked, laid everything bare, and accepted each other's fears, doubts, ugly little truths. The nightmares were down to a couple of times a week, and he managed to sit through an entire movie at the theater without leaving because of the crowds.

But no matter how much progress we made, I still saw the moments where he wasn't with me. That vacant look came over his face, his eyes focused in the distance, and I knew he was... there.

The scars faded to a light pink, his air cast came off after one week longer than he'd originally been told, and he'd even admitted that he'd screwed up by taking it off for the race. He was getting stronger in physical therapy and, two and a half months after the crash, had almost full mobility.

I took my GRE's and was waiting on my scores. Waiting to decide if I was really going to Ephesus in a few weeks. I still leaned toward no. After all, we were finally in a great place after surviving a shit storm, and these last couple of months had been the longest we'd ever lived together. I wasn't exactly in a rush to run off to Turkey, not when it could jeopardize what we'd worked so hard for. But we talked, we loved, we touched. We did easy, simple things like cooking dinner.

We lived.

We planned our wedding, which may end up being the single biggest reason we'd never divorce. Hell if I was ever going to go through this crap again. "Ugh. Who seriously needs that much time to book out?" I groaned, nearly throwing my iPad onto the couch as Josh did shirtless pushups on the living room floor. Good God, that man was a marvel of creation.

"Who now?"

"Photographer. We need to find a different one. If we want the one that's recommended on the wedding site, he needs ten months."

"Well. We're. At. Ten. Months." He spoke between reps, just breathless enough to make me want to slide under his body, sweat and all.

"And he's like...two thousand dollars."

He paused. "Damn."

"For a deposit."

He hit the floor. "Okay, well, I don't plan on getting married more than once, so give the man what he wants and book him."

"Between this and the reception..."

"Yeah, well, I married a girl with good taste. It will be fine."

"Mom offered."

"No," he answered, coming to his feet. He stretched his arms above his head, the lines of his abs rippling, and I damn near fell off the couch. "Your mom is still paying for April's school and supporting Gus. The answer is no."

"Maybe I should think twice about grad school," I muttered. "The money Dad left me for college is dwindling."

"You'll get a scholarship. I'm not stressed." He headed for our kitchen, grabbing water from the fridge. "And if you don't, we'll pay for it."

He came over, kissed my forehead, and walked toward the stairs. Even the man's back was sexy. "Want some company in the shower?"

"That's something I could most definitely agree to."

There was a knock at the door. *Crap.* I hopped up and checked the window. "Paisley's here." *With awful timing.*

"Well, have fun, and don't forget we have that barbecue tonight." He disappeared up the stairs.

"Hey," I said, opening the door.

"Morning," she answered, a small gift bag in her hand. Her eyes were slightly puffy, and her smile forced.

"Why don't you come in?"

She nodded. "Just for a second."

I shut the door behind her and turned to see her pacing my living room. "Is everything okay? Jagger? The baby?"

She paused, startled. "Oh, yes, they're okay." Paisley ran her hand over her belly like she could actually caress their son. "Everyone is fine. I just got a box from Will's mom. I'd taken all his things down to Alabama for her to sort through, but I must have missed this." She handed over the bag. "It's for Josh."

I took it by the handle, its weight far heavier than the ounces it felt. "Oh."

"I don't know what's on it—the USB drive—but mine was a video."

My heart sank. The videos I'd seen of my father since he died were such a double-edged sword. "Oh, Paisley."

She shook her head quickly and blinked back tears. "No, no. It was…good. Good to see him. I watched it before Jagger got up," she whispered the last.

"Why?"

"I didn't want him to see me cry. I'm better most days, really, I am. And I don't want him to think that my tears mean I love him less. I just…I miss Will. Even after we broke up, and he was such an ass…" She laughed. "He's always been a part of my life, and that hole he left, that's not something that can be filled, you know?"

My fingers tightened on the small paper handles of the bag.

"Yeah, I understand that perfectly."

Her lips quirked upward. "It's funny how they're the ones that die, but we're the ones who are changed."

"Irrevocably."

A look passed between us, just as it had the first time we met and understood each other on a level not many people could. "We on for Sunday night dinner?"

"Always," I replied.

"I'd better get back before he tries walking on his own again. Two months in those casts did a number on him, but he'll get it back."

"Well, if he starts growling, you're welcome to hide out here and throw food through the window so he's fed."

She laughed and hugged me before she left. As soon as the door shut, I took out my laptop and set it up on the coffee table, then put the bag next to it. Josh jogged down the stairs a few minutes later in MultiCam pants and a T-shirt.

"What did Paisley need? I can hop over before I go to my appointment."

"No, she's good. But she brought you something." I picked up the bag. "It's from Will."

He paused mid step, then took a breath and walked over to me, gently taking the bag from my hand. He brought out the USB drive first and raised his eyebrows at me.

"Paisley said it was a video. Do you want to see it?"

"Yeah," he said quietly and sat next to me on the couch as I booted it up on my computer.

"Ready?" I asked, my finger on the mousepad.

He nodded, and I tapped the play button.

Will's face illuminated the screen, and I sucked in my breath. "He looks so—"

"Alive," Josh answered.

I took his hand as Will sat in front of the camera and gave us an awkward wave from his old apartment.

"Hey. So I guess I should start with: if you're watching this, then things did not go the way I planned, which definitely...well, sucks. I hope that I went doing something meaningful, and if not...well, let's just pretend I did, okay?" He smiled, and my chest tightened like a vise on my heart. "But listen. There's something I want you to have."

Josh pulled a ring box out of the bag. "Oh, shit," he whispered, and then popped the case open. Will's West Point ring stared back at him and tears instantly welled in my eyes.

"I know you called me a ring-knocker on more than one occasion."

"You were," Josh muttered.

"And I was," Will agreed as if he could hear Josh. "There was this one time we were on the flight line, remember? When you told me that I knew nothing about loyalty. That I wouldn't last a day—"

"In a real platoon," Josh finished in time with Will, then hung his head.

"Stop kicking yourself, because you were right. I wouldn't have, not back then. But all those times we were studying, when you were catching up on my notes in the Advanced Course, I don't think you realized that you were really the one teaching me." Will sighed. "Once I knew what you'd been through on your first deployment, I watched you. Watched how you took on the world like you'd never been scarred by it. I watched how you loved Ember, how you're protecting her even right now while you're in Afghanistan and I'm just getting home from fixing her disposal."

I whimpered, my hand flying to cover my mouth. I'd seen him right before he filmed this. He'd stood in my kitchen, helping me, talking to me, and died a few short weeks later. The unfairness of it was devastating.

"Being around you taught me the value of friendship, and I know you guys didn't want to let me into your little club, but you did. And I'm thankful. I learned more about loyalty in the last two years from being with you guys than I did in four years at the Academy." He paused and took a deep breath. "Okay, so tell Ember to take care of Paisley. I know that's Jagger's job, but I also know that what we do means we're not around as often as we'd like to be. And you should probably marry her, because I'm telling you that you're not going to find a better woman."

My teeth sank into my lower lip as tears spilled down my cheeks.

"So, I guess, thank you for teaching me the things I needed to learn. Thank you for being an asshole and showing me my own...assholishness...I guess. You've taught me perseverance, and brotherhood, and from the reports we're getting back here of those missions you're flying over there, the rescues you're making, well, I have a lot more to learn from you once I get there. Maybe I can talk you into going SOAR with me." He grinned.

"But just in case, live well. Love hard. Try to follow a goddamn rule every once in a while, just to throw people for a loop, okay?"

He stood, and I wanted to yell at him not to turn off the video, just to give us another second, but he reached for the camera—and paused, coming back into eyesight. "For the record, I should have moved that fucking polar bear with you. Bye, brother."

A click later, and the screen was black.

Josh snapped the ring box shut and dropped his head over his hands, sucking in long, deep breaths. "I killed him."

I wrapped my arm around his shoulders and leaned into his arm. "You gave him what he desperately needed. Friends. A family. Everything else was out of your hands."

"Logically, I know that, but I close my eyes and see his face above me, taking those shots."

"I'm so sorry." I pressed a kiss into the fabric of his shirt.

"Me, too," he said quietly. His lips brushed my forehead, then he stood. "I'll be back after my appointment, okay?"

He was gone a few moments later, and I pressed play again, pausing when Will grinned. I wanted to remember him just like that. "It mattered, Will," I told him. "Your death. It mattered. It will always matter to me."

I was going to fucking kill him. "Dead, dead, dead," I muttered as I stood in the garage doorway. What the hell had he been thinking?

Jagger whistled low, leaning against the doorframe, crutches braced under his arms and giant boots on his lower legs. "So this is how death-by-fiancée begins..."

"Shut up," I snapped. "And are you even supposed to be walking around?"

"It's part of my physical therapy," he flat-out lied. "Seriously. I'm cleared for weight-bearing casts."

"Paisley's going to kill you if you overdo it."

"What she doesn't know isn't going to hurt her." His eyes shifted to the Ducati.

Well, I sure as hell knew about the motorcycle now. "I can't believe he did this."

Jagger sucked his breath in through his teeth and shook his head. "You know, Josh is my best friend, but on this...yeah, I've got nothing."

"Speak of the devil," I muttered as Josh pulled into the driveway behind me. He hopped out of the Jeep, the doors long since removed in the hot weather.

"Hey, babe." He walked over and kissed my neck. "Oh! She made it! Damn, I thought she was being delivered tomorrow."

"Yeah, well, I hope that bike looks good wearing an engagement ring." Jagger laughed and left us, walking with tiny, excruciating steps back to his own house.

"What?" Josh asked. "Do you need me to carry you, old man?"

"It's going to be hard for you to walk once she kicks you in the balls, man." He flipped Josh the bird and kept going.

"Why would you do that?" Josh asked, but then caught the look of hell in my eyes. "Whoa."

"You brought that fucking Ducati here?" I spat the words at him.

His mouth opened and closed a few times. "My mom said it couldn't stay there."

"So you thought it should come here?" *And invade my sanity?* Next to Josh's Harley, it looked like the brother no one in the family wanted to talk about...because he was still in jail, and somehow knocking up nuns.

"Bad idea?" he asked honestly.

"Only if you wanted to ever have sex again because your fiancée is still hugely pissed about the death machine in her garage."

We stood there, side by side in relative silence for a moment while he digested the news that his pretty little baby wasn't welcome. *Because it's the spawn of Satan.*

"Okay, well, I love that bike, so we're going to have to come to a compromise. I swear on my life that I will never race it again."

I side-eyed him. "A compromise like it not being here?"

He cringed. "Like a storage unit nearby?" His tone was pleading.

I wanted to kick the damn thing over, but that was about as mature a move as the one I'd pulled running away from him in Arizona. "How about we go to this barbecue and we'll talk about it later?" *After I find an appropriate junkyard.*

His entire posture relaxed. "Thank God. I mean, yes, that sounds like a plan."

"Nice. Go get changed. I'll meet you in the car."

The barbecue was in full swing by the time we made it to the Trivette's house on the outskirts of Clarksville. It was a beautiful two-story with a wraparound porch and a giant backyard that was currently full of families.

"Walker!" Rizzo called out, waving us over.

"Hey, how are you feeling?" Josh asked, taking the offered beer. I declined, since someone would have to drive home so we could fight over the silver speedster in our garage.

Rizzo lifted his hand, squeezing his fingers. "I'm healed up. Got the all-clear and everything. How about you?"

Josh lifted the leg of his cargo shorts to expose the long, pink scar. "Good to go. I actually got my up-slip today."

My stomach hit the floor. "You did?"

"Yeah," he said with a huge grin. "I'm ready to get back up there. I meant to tell you, but we got distracted."

That's a word for it. I shouldn't be worried, right? He needed to get back in the seat for his own well-being. Besides, it wasn't like people were going to shoot at him on Fort Campbell. This was for the best.

Then why does it hurt like a bitch?

Was I ever going to be able to watch him fly again without remembering the notification? Will's funeral? The scars on his body?

"What about you, Mrs. Walker?" Rizzo asked, checking out my ring.

I snapped out of my thoughts. "Oh, well, that's not until next year. I'm still Miss Howard."

"Well, then how are you, Miss Howard?"

"I am still a work in progress, but I'll let you know."

He gave me a knowing nod. "I like a truthful woman."

Josh pulled me under his arm. "Well, this one is mine, so find your own."

He laughed. "Hey, you know my policy on that one."

"Gentlemen, I'm so glad I found you," a deep voice came from behind us. We turned to see Major Trivette walking toward us, his cute five-year-old daughter on his hip. She had her father's blond hair and solemn eyes. Way too solemn for a five-year-old. "Can I steal a few minutes?"

"I can take her," I offered.

"No, you should stay. Abigail, why don't you run and play with your friends?" he said, lowering her gently to the ground with a kiss. She gave him a small nod and raced off, her sundress bouncing as she ran for the swing set.

Major Trivette turned back to us. "I'm sorry I haven't had the chance to check on you guys. I meant to so many times, but just..." He sighed. "Alice would never forgive me for that oversight."

"Sir, you've been otherwise occupied, and we would never expect that of you," Josh interjected.

"Well, nonetheless. How are you?"

"We're both cleared for duty, sir," Rizzo answered.

Hearing Rizzo say it felt like someone cocked a loaded shotgun and pointed it at my heart.

"Good, that's good." He looked to Josh. "She liked you. She said that you showed a great deal of promise. Courageous. I believe that was the word she used."

Josh paled. "Rash, impetuous, foolish. I think those words might better suit."

Major Trivette's eyes narrowed. "You still blame yourself."

"Well, sir, that falls squarely on my shoulders. You've read the report." Josh tensed, and I wanted to reach out and hold him, to assure him again that it wasn't his fault. I just wished I knew how many times I'd have to say it before he believed me.

"Yes. She gave the order to fly into that valley."

"Because it was my best friend."

"No," Major Trivette snapped. "Don't you dare take that from her. She would have made the call for any soldier. She was the pilot in command, not you, Walker. She knew what was at stake, and she chose to take her crew into battle. She chose to medevac those pilots. I miss her every time I take a breath, but I'm also incredibly proud of her. You can't take that away by acting like she was guilted into going in. You and I both know Alice didn't do a damn thing she didn't want to."

Josh picked at the label on his beer. "I am so sorry we lost her," he said once he looked up.

Major Trivette reached across us and clasped Josh on the shoulder. "I am, too. God knows it. But she'd be proud of how she died. She'd be prouder that you two carried on and saved that other pilot. And I can tell you that she lived for the mission. She'd be the first in the saddle and back on the front line. Don't ever think anything less. She died the way she lived, and it was her honor, not your fault. There's a difference."

Josh nodded, his jaw working. He was tightly strung, clinging to the strands of his control with slipping fingers. I added my hand to his, offering a quiet support that he took with a gentle squeeze. "She was a hell of a woman, sir."

He looked over to where his children played. "She was."

We left the barbecue early, both more than a little raw from the day's events. As Josh sat in our living room that night, turning Will's ring over in his hand, I couldn't help but wonder if we'd just paved the way for closure, or ripped the scabs off anew.

One thing I'd learned about grief—it was almost impossible to tell the difference between the two.

They both hurt like hell.

CHAPTER THIRTY

JOSH

"Are you certain you want to do this?" Captain Brown asked me from behind his desk.

The gravity of my decision made it hard to breathe, to force out the words that I knew needed to be spoken. It wasn't a question of what I wanted. It was a matter of what was right. Of what Will would do. What Captain Trivette would do. A matter of being the kind of man Ember deserved, even if she'd hate me for this. "Are you certain there's not another date?"

He grimaced. "I am. This is the last one."

Damn it. "Then, yes, I am."

"And you've thought this through?"

"Every day since I realized it was a possibility, sir."

He fumbled through my file. "You've been cleared medically, flights have been good, psych released you."

As long as I keep Dr. Henderson's deal. "Yes."

He leaned back in his chair, tapping his fingers on the glass topper of his desk. "I'm not going to pretend to know what it was you went through over there, or what kind of mark that leaves on you. But I'd be a shit commander if I didn't ask you one more time. So, are you absolutely certain this is what you want?"

Ember's face flashed through my mind. She'd understand. She had to. *And if she doesn't?* Fuck. At least she'd be better off. She deserved to love a whole man, and if I didn't do this, I wouldn't be. Ever. "I'm sure."

He nodded and signed the top paper. "Okay. We'll see you tomorrow. If you change your mind, Walker, just call me."

I stood. My heart tore, suddenly at odds with what I'd been contemplating the last two weeks. *Stop.* "Thank you, sir."

"For the record, I think what you're doing is incredible."

"It's nothing more than what any other soldier would do, sir." Before he could say anything else about how damn brave or selfless he thought it was, I got the hell out of his office. It was the last thing I wanted to hear, and it sure as hell wasn't true.

"You tell her yet?" Rizzo asked, standing in the hallway as I closed Captain Brown's door.

"No."

He whistled low.

"Yeah, I know. She's had a ton on her plate, deciding about going on this dig next week. I've even caught her trying to get out of it, and I'll be damned if I let that happen."

"You can't tell me this is about her going on a dig."

I shook my head. "No, it's about us both doing what we need to. Ember and I have always been amazing together, but it's because we're both strong enough to stand on our own when we need to. It's a hell of a foundation."

"Pretty harsh timeline, though," he muttered as we walked into the sunlight.

"Yeah, well, we had no control over that, either."

Rizzo laughed. "Yeah, let me know when the US Army starts asking when things are convenient for us."

"Maybe it's when we stop making things so much harder on ourselves."

"Yeah, like you dropping a SOAR packet?"

My steps faltered. "It's just a thought. One discussion with one of their recruiters."

"Yeah, well, thoughts become actions. For what it's worth,

you're exactly the kind of pilot they're looking for."

"Still just a thought."

We said good-bye in the parking lot, and I drove home, stopping along the way to pick up the last of the things on my list.

It had been two weeks since I'd been cleared to fly, and they'd gotten me up nearly every day. The first time had been the worst, but I hadn't panicked. I'd pushed past it just like the pain.

Maybe I'd vomited once we'd landed, but I'd gotten through it.

I was back at it the next day. I focused all of myself on the controls, the flight, the technical aspects of flying, and did my best to forget that I'd almost been killed in that crash. Not so easy, yet I found that if I compartmentalized, it worked out.

I wasn't going to let a little fear fuck over the soldiers who needed help. If they were bleeding, dying on the ground, I could risk bleeding, dying in the air. It was only right.

But driving home now, knowing what was about to happen... God, dying and bleeding sounded preferable.

"That smells so good," Ember said as she walked into the house a few hours later.

"Don't give me the credit. I cheated." I waved the two bags from the local Italian restaurant and savored her laugh.

Takeout was all I'd had time to do, considering how I'd spent the hours after telling Brown my decision.

She dropped her bag and walked over to me in the kitchen, her legs three miles long in those shorts. "Hiya, babe." She grinned and looped her arms around my neck.

"Hey, yourself." I wrapped my arms around her waist and tried to take in everything about her in that moment. Ember's hair trailed down her back, brushing my arms, the shorter layers framing her lightly freckled cheeks. Her eyes sparkled with happiness, drawing me in like always. Her mouth, those perfect lips, formed a contagious smile. She felt like a piece of heaven in my arms, the realization of every dream I'd been too scared to even think possible. And she was mine.

For now.

"What?" she asked, her trouble-radar working perfectly.

"I just really love you." I swept my hands down her back to her tiny waist. "There's nothing about you that I don't love."

"I love you, too," she promised, but the suspicion was still there.

I kissed her, melding our mouths together in the sweetest way possible, taking my time. She leaned into me, her grip tightening on my neck as she kissed me back. I let her go just as her breath hitched, memorizing the sound.

She pulled back, quirking her head to the side. "Okay, I know something's off. What is it?"

"Tell me how your day was first." I dished food onto our plates, my appetite suddenly gone. She grabbed a bottle of wine from the fridge. "Whoa. That bad?"

"Ha," she said, no amusement in her tone. "I told Luke I couldn't go on the dig."

I nearly dropped the damn plate. "You what?"

She avoided my eyes, instead concentrating on opening the bottle. "I told him it just wasn't the right time."

My stomach churned, and it took every ounce of self control in my body to keep my voice level. *No. Not for me. Not because of me.* "What did he say?"

She popped the cork. "That I was making a mistake, and he'd hold off until tomorrow to tell Dr. Trimble so I could change my mind overnight."

Overnight. You can fix this. "You need to go."

She poured the wine into two glasses. "Seriously, we're not

having this conversation again. This isn't the time. You're still healing—"

"I'm fine!" I lied. Her eyes flew toward mine, widening. *Fuck.* "I'm sorry. I'm fine," I said softer. "I need you to stop assuming that I'm not. I've flown, I sleep, I eat, the nightmares have stopped. I need you to know that I'm okay."

"I do know," she replied in a near-whisper. "Maybe I'm not."

"Maybe I need you to go."

She flinched. "Why?"

"Because I need to know that I didn't cost you the future you've worked your ass off for. I can't let your dreams get crushed under mine. Now more than ever."

Her eyes narrowed, her head tilting slightly. "Josh. What are you talking about? What did you do?"

I carried our plates past her to the table, setting them in our places. "Let's have dinner, then we'll talk."

"Let's talk now."

"December—"

"What is it?" she pushed. "Why especially now?"

I hated everything about this, the way her voice pitched higher with worry, the frantic darting of her eyes, as if she could find something different about me. "I just think you might get pretty pissed at me soon." *Pissed enough to run, like you should.*

Was I really about to do this to her? She'd been through so much, and I just kept heaping it on. She didn't deserve it.

I didn't deserve her.

"Did you bring that bike back? Is the Ducati in there?" She stormed past me.

"Ember, no!" I called, but she'd already thrown open the garage door. I leaned over the kitchen counter, my hands gripping the granite so hard I was surprised I didn't bleed.

"I swear, Josh, if you took that thing out of storage again, I'm—" She halted midsentence, and in that exact moment, I hated myself. I hated the life I'd chosen, the risks I took, the bags that she'd just found packed in our garage. I hated myself for loving her, for going after her in the first place, for putting her through this. Again.

"Why are your duffels packed?" she asked so quietly I barely heard her. I pulled air through my lungs, forcing my heart to beat.

"Because I'm leaving."

She stood across from me, the island separating us, her stare burning a hole through my very soul. "Where are you going?"

I squeezed my eyes shut, wishing I could block it all out, skip this, make everything perfect. But nothing was perfect in the world we lived in. It was all broken puzzle pieces slammed together, the edges jagged and tearing while we pretended it clicked, pretended that if we loved each other enough, the rest would fall in line. "You know where."

"You're going to have to say it."

I sucked in a breath and looked up. My resolve nearly cracked there, with her eyes begging me not to confirm her worst fears. "December..."

"Say it."

"Afghanistan."

Her whimper damn near broke me. She looked away, her face showing so many emotions at once that I wasn't sure even she knew how she felt. God, we were twin souls in that. "When?"

"Please don't hate me."

"Josh, when?" she snapped.

"Tomorrow."

Her head whipped toward me, her every muscle going rigid. "What? You're going to have to say that again, because I think you just told me that one, you're going back to war, and two, you're leaving tomorrow."

"Yes."

She shook her head. "That's just not possible. I refuse to believe that's possible."

"I wasn't officially cleared to deploy until this morning. Tomorrow is the last flight out to bring personnel. We only have two and a half months left in the rotation. Any later and there's really no point in going."

"Then don't fucking go!" She slammed her hands onto the counter, and I cringed.

"I have to."

"Were you ordered? Because I can't believe that someone would order you to go back this soon after you almost died in that crash."

Here it was, the line I knew she'd never understand me crossing, the wedge I wasn't sure she could get past, or if she even should. This would be her reason to walk away. But she'd go to Turkey. She'd live her dream. "I volunteered. Rizzo and I both did."

"You volunteered." She drew out each syllable, looking for meaning I knew she couldn't find.

"They're short pilots—"

"It's the army. They're never short pilots. They can take them from whatever other unit has them. Don't use that bullshit excuse on me. You're going because you want to go."

"That's not it." I stepped toward her, and she skirted around the island, keeping it between us. "You've seen it—the times I'm not here. It's because parts of me are still there, Ember. My guys are there, my unit. What the hell kind of man heals up and then stays behind while his unit is at war?"

"The kind who lives! The kind who doesn't promise his fiancée a wedding she might not get to have, because he'll die this time around." She choked on the last few words.

I wanted to tell her that I wouldn't die, that her worry was unfounded, dramatic even. But how the hell could I do that when I knew what she said was the truth? When part of me felt like coming full circle would end with her holding my flag? "Would you want that man? The one who knows he's capable of helping, of being where he's needed, but does nothing? Who stays at home while others die in his place?"

Her chest heaved as her head hung low. Finally she looked up at me. "When it comes to you, to how much I love you, Josh, I have no morals. No honor. I would lie, cheat, murder, steal, dishonor everything I hold dear if it meant spending my life with you. No measure of duty, or God, or country could ever make up for losing you."

"I can't sit home while others risk their lives. This is the right thing to do, and you and I both know that what's right and what's easy are never the same thing. We've always chosen the hard road, but, baby, we've always come out on top."

"Until we don't. You're playing Russian roulette every time you go, putting a gun to your head and pulling the trigger. You've nearly died twice. Lightning has struck you twice. What the hell happens when you go and this time you don't come back?"

Words failed me. "I don't know."

"I don't know, either. But this... How could you just spring this on me? How long have you known it was a possibility?"

"At the barbecue, Major Trivette said something that triggered me, about how Alice would have been the first back on the line, and I knew he was right. And that was the honorable thing to do. So Rizzo and I both asked the next day, and Captain Brown told us about the last flight out, but I swear, I didn't know for certain I would even be capable of going until they'd gotten me back in the air. I'm current, ready for missions as of this morning."

"And there was no point in this process where you thought you might want to tell me?"

"I didn't know it was a definite possibility. There was nothing to tell."

"Don't you dare start lying to me now." She grabbed the glass of wine on the counter and downed it like we were still in college. "You made this giant decision without so much as asking my opinion."

"I already knew what it would be, and if there had been time to discuss it, we would have. They cleared me and needed the manifest all within the same hour."

"Then get to a phone, Josh!" She leaned on her elbows, resting her forehead in her hands, and let out a primal cry. "How could you do this?"

The tears I saw hitting the granite fractured pieces of what was left of my soul and cracked my resolve. God, how *could* I do this to her? Leave again? After what she'd just been through? But how could she love the guy who didn't go?

"Because it's what we do." *Do not yell.* I looked past her, to where Will's West Point ring box still sat on the fireplace mantel. "It's what Will would have done."

"Yeah, well, we can't ask Will, because he's dead."

"Because of me! Because of my choices. I have to make up for that somehow."

"Were you going to use that same argument with my dad? Because I'm not sure if you noticed, but he's dead, too, and you had nothing to do with it. That's just what happens. War kills the people we love, either in body or soul, but they're both equally devastating. So please don't stand there and talk about what they would have done, because they didn't get to make the choice. You are making the choice."

"How many more people die if I don't go? Trivette, Will... how many more bodies should I add to my tally?"

She looked away.

"I know the timing is shit. I know I should have asked you, talked to you. But what if that had changed my mind? What if while trying to keep your love, I became something you loathed? God, please, December. Forgive me. I'm so sorry, but there was no other way."

She turned her back on me but straightened her spine. "Two

and a half months?"

"That's it." Was there a possibility that she'd accept this? God knows I wouldn't have. Had it been Ember, I'd have tied her to a fucking chair to keep her safe, and I was the worst kind of hypocrite for expecting her to let me go.

I could risk my life in a heartbeat, lay everything on the line, but I could never chance her life. In that regard, she was so much stronger than I could ever dream of being. Where I'd give my blood, she gambled something so much more precious—her love. And I was the ungrateful bastard taking it half the way around the world.

"That's ten weeks. You typically flew five days a week, so that's fifty days of flying. Countless lives you could save."

"Yes."

"Countless chances for you to be killed." Her head started to shake. "No. I can't. It's too soon."

"December—"

"Don't do this."

Fuck. My. Life. "Please, don't ask that."

She turned toward me, and the sight of her tear-streaked cheeks and reddened eyes destroyed another chink in my armor. "Don't say good-bye again. I'm begging you." Her face twisted, and she drew her lower lip between her teeth. "I can survive almost anything, but not another good-bye. Not now."

"I wouldn't be the man you loved if I stayed."

She crumpled, her shoulders sagging as sobs wrecked her. "I don't care. I don't care about any of it as long as you're not dead. I know it's wrong, and I'm supposed to stand by all proud that you're such an incredible man, and you are. God, you really are. You have more integrity than anyone I've ever known. You're strong, courageous, selfless, everything an amazing officer should be." She walked around the island until we stood toe to toe. "And maybe this makes me a wretched person, or even a coward, but Josh, I'm begging you. Choose me. Choose my love over your integrity, just this once. I promise I'll be ready when the next deployment comes, just...not this one. This one already tried to kill you. I don't know how to hand you over to it again."

She shredded my soul with her words, and I reached for her, tunneling my hands through her hair. "I can't—"

A knock at the door interrupted us, Paisley's knock. "Come in," Ember called out, wiping her tears away furiously. "It could be the baby or something," she whispered, and I nodded.

"Hey, we were just wondering if y'all wanted to..." She stopped mid step in our living room, seeing us over the half wall. "Oh. I didn't mean to interrupt. Jagger was feeling well enough to stand at the grill for a while and burn some burgers, but why don't we do it tomorrow night, instead?"

Ember laughed, the sound nearly hysterical. "Oh, that could prove problematic."

"Everything okay?" she asked.

Ember's eyes dropped to the swell of Paisley's stomach, and she forced a sad smile. "Yeah, we're okay. Just maybe tell Jagger another time?"

Jagger. Shit. I had to tell him, too. "Yeah. Another time. And I need to steal a couple of minutes from him in the morning."

Her gaze darted between us, but she nodded. "Of course. You two have a lovely evening."

"Thank you for inviting us," Ember told her just before Paisley shut the door.

The silence was deafening, as though we had expended every word we had, and now all that hung between us was the poison they'd left behind, killing us both. Ember turned to me and tucked her hair behind her ears. "Okay."

"What?" I asked.

"I said okay," she snapped, then squeezed her eyes shut. Her lips pursed, and her hands fisted in front of her on the counter. "Seeing Paisley..." She shook her head and drew a choppy breath. "Jagger. He'd be dead if you hadn't been there. Paisley would be raising their baby alone, and I can't imagine…I get it." Anger vibrated from every line of her body, like she was at war with her words, but she still got them out.

My breath stuttered and my heart split, one side elated that she understood, that I'd fallen in love with a woman so supportive that she was willing to shove her feelings aside for mine. The other part of me hated that I'd brought this incredible woman so low that she was sacrificing her very nature for what she thought was my best interest.

What the fuck had I done to her?

"What time do you need to report in the morning?" she asked, still focused on the counter in front of her.

"Early," I whispered, walking toward her.

She nodded. "Okay. Okay…okay." Each repetition got softer, until it was barely a murmur. Her hands opened and closed, like she was trying to grasp something she couldn't catch, couldn't hold on to, until her fingers started to shake.

"December…" I whispered her name like the prayer it was and took her face in my hands, overwhelmed by her, by everything she was willing to sacrifice in the name of our love. I was the ultimate selfish asshat, demanding things I had no right to. She was my everything, my reason for existence, and I was her number one source of misery. "God, I love you."

"Don't. Don't talk about loving me in the same breath you want to say good-bye. I may understand why you're doing this, but it doesn't mean that I agree, or that I'm happy about it."

"It doesn't change how much I love you," I promised.

"Love has never been the issue between us, Josh. Loving you is second nature to me. But as proud as I am that you're the kind of man to do this, to be the hero and volunteer to go back…" Something rare and precious died in her eyes. I saw the change happen, the moment my choice changed her. "A part of me hates…" Her eyes drifted shut. "Hates what you're doing to me, to us."

Hates me. That's what she meant. Her words reverberated in my head as if she'd shot me with them. She had every right to. She'd never wanted this life, but I'd forced my way into hers, past her defenses, her protests. My chest tightened with an unbelievable pressure, like my heart took her side and was ready to claw its way out of my chest, abandon me, to be with her. Of course a part of her hated me. Hell, I hated myself. "Is your hate deeper than your love?"

Her eyes narrowed. "I hate that you made this choice without me. I hate that this is what you need, like I'm not enough to make you whole. I hate that I change everything about my life to accommodate yours, because there's not a lot of room for an 'ours' right now. I hate that the minute you walk out that door, I'll just be waiting for someone to knock on it again, and I hate how much I love you. But never in a million years could I hate *you.* And I almost wish I could!"

She didn't pause, didn't really end the argument. One minute she was yelling at me, and the next second she was in my arms, her fingers in my hair, her mouth pressed against mine. *What the hell?* She caught me completely off guard for maybe two seconds, but the feel of her lips was all I needed, and we were on the same page.

She's using this to vent, hiding behind it just like you used to.

Fuck, but I didn't care. I swept one arm under her ass and lifted her into my arms where she belonged. If I only had one last night with her before I ripped our hearts apart, I was going to make every second count. Every kiss. Every touch. Every time she cried out my name.

I was going to love her like I'd never get the chance to again.

CHAPTER THIRTY-ONE

EMBER

I quelled the rage rolling through my veins with a different kind of fire that burned hot enough to incinerate anything in its path.

I was done thinking. Crying. Begging. If this was our last night, then I just wanted to feel. I'd be angry tomorrow.

Josh lifted me as our mouths fed off each other in a kiss so carnal I thought we might combust. My back hit the refrigerator, magnets crashing to the floor. I wound my legs around his waist, locking my ankles at his back, and arched into him, craving the friction of his chest against my breasts.

When I reached for the buttons on his shirt, he grasped both of my hands by the wrists and pinned them to the cool, stainless steel above my head. "December." My name was rough on his lips, fought for. Just like every inch of this relationship. "Is this what you—"

I cut him off midsentence, setting my mouth to his and rocking my hips against his. At the touch of our tongues, he groaned and stopped trying to make sense of what was happening. "I want your hands on my body. Is that something you can give me?" *Because I'm losing in every other department.*

His breaths were sweet on my face, coming in erratic bursts as he focused on me, his eyes darkening. Damn, that stare was hot. Everything about him was an aphrodisiac to me, from the sensuous curve of his lips to the incredible way he smelled, like he'd been dipped in pheromones specifically designed to get me wet.

"What's the verdict?" I asked.

"Like there was ever a question," he answered, his gaze dropping to my lips a second before he kissed me deeply. He let go of my hands, trailing his fingers down my upstretched arms until he reached my shoulders. Then he tilted my head and assaulted my neck with his lips, teeth, and tongue. White-hot desire drummed through me in a steady beat.

He shifted his hands to under my thighs and held me tight, backing us up through the kitchen. I buried my hands in his hair, putting my entire focus into kissing him, pulling his lower lip with a gentle bite. He hissed, and I found a wall at my back, my ass sliding over something—the railing on the staircase.

He devoured my mouth with small nips, slow kisses, and deep, rhythmic slides of his tongue. I was going to be a puddle on the floor if he kept it up much longer. My hands found the material of his shirt and yanked it free from where my thighs held it prisoner. He took it from there, unbuttoning the first few holes and then pulling it over his head in one smooth motion that I never tired of seeing, not when it revealed the cut lines of what lay beneath.

I placed my hand over the tattoo above his heart, the one he'd gotten for me, *fire and ice*. "You're incredible. I never get tired of touching you."

A cocky grin appeared on his face. "Feeling's mutual." He took my mouth again and finished carrying me up the stairs, not bothering to shut our bedroom door behind him.

I landed in the middle of our bed, and he turned on our bedside lamp. The pure want screaming from his eyes had my thighs restless as he took off my shoes. He ran his hands up my legs, pulling them apart, and rose above me, stealing my breath. Josh settled between my thighs, then stripped my top off with a fluid move. "God, December. Every line of you is fucking perfect."

"To you." I smiled as his fingers traced the lacy cups of my pink bra.

"For me. You're mine. Don't you dare forget it."

His kiss was as hot as a branding iron, and just as effective. He made quick work of my shorts and thong, tossing them haphazardly across the room. My bra was next, leaving me naked. I leaned up on my elbows as his shorts and boxers hit the floor, and then he was as gloriously bare as I was. My core clenched and my breath quickened as he lowered himself over me, skin against delicious skin. "Are you mine?" I asked as he skimmed kisses over my collarbone.

"In every way. You own me, December."

Except where the army does. The thought snuck into my head, and a tidal wave of anger swept over me, wiping everything else away for that second. My fingers gripped his hair as he covered my nipple with his lips, transforming the anger back into lust in a way only Josh was capable of. The mix was overwhelming, both emotions raw, passionate, all-encompassing.

I pushed on his shoulder and he complied, rolling so he sat with me straddling him. I knew I only had as much control in bed as he was willing to let go, which made these moments all the sweeter. But sweet wasn't exactly what I wanted. I poured every emotion I couldn't contain into my kiss—my love, frustration, desire, and red-hot fury. He palmed my breasts as I rolled my hips against his erection, and I caught his moan in my mouth. "Baby, you're killing me."

"Good," I whispered, rising up on my knees to let him slide between my folds.

He sucked in his breath, resting his forehead on my collarbone, and then had me gasping as he swirled his thumbs over my nipples. "Oh no, not yet," he said as he ran his mouth along my jawline, the stubble from his cheek leaving a slight burn in his wake.

"Josh," I begged, but he caught my hips before I could sink down over him.

"Not yet," he repeated. One hand slid between us, and my hips bucked as he brushed over my clit, a shock of need radiating through my limbs to my toes and bringing a gasp to my lips. "I'll never get enough of this," he said as his fingers slid along me, and he slipped one inside.

I groaned his name, my head crashing to his shoulder as all my thoughts centered on the magic his hands created. He added another finger and pressed his palm against my clit as I rocked against him. Damn, that felt amazing. He knew exactly how fast to move, where to press, where to stroke. My body was as familiar to him as his own, and he played it expertly. "There," he whispered, as his fingers curled with each withdrawal.

I whimpered, riding his hand as tension built in my muscles, need spiraling tighter and tighter with each movement of his hands, each kiss he placed to the nape of my neck. "Josh." His name was a plea, a prayer, a lamentation. I wanted him inside me. Now. I needed the blissful surrender I only had with him, the moments when we were both lost to the other, where nothing else could intrude.

"Not yet." His voice was gravelly, his breath uneven, but his hands steady as he worked me with one and led my hips with the other.

"Don't make me beg." Anger bled into my tone, and he heard it, lifting his face to mine.

"Why would you ever beg?" he whispered against my lips as his fingers thrust faster, deeper. My core tightened, my moves becoming erratic, frantic. "You're the one with all the power."

He pressed harder on my clit and rubbed in just the right spot. Every muscle in my body locked, the tension at the point where I thought I might break. "You're so close, I can feel you squeeze my fingers. So damn tight. Now, come," he ordered.

God help me, I did, crying his name as he pressed where I needed him. An orgasm took me, so powerful that I saw lights behind my eyelids. He held on to me as I shuddered over him, my body rippling with the small aftershocks he brought with simple motions of his hand.

We locked eyes as his fingers slipped free, dragging my wetness up my stomach until he gripped my waist. I rose to my knees until we were lined up, and then sank down without waiting, so wet that he slid in with little resistance and the perfect amount of friction.

"December," he hissed my name as I paused, letting my body adjust for a moment.

His eyes were wild as I began to ride him, watching every nuance of his reaction to the motion of my hips, the angle and roll. I concentrated for as long as possible, until the pleasure became all-encompassing. Then I simply obeyed my body and enjoyed.

It wasn't long before he flipped us with a groan, settling me under him. I almost pushed him back, but he raised one of my knees and lifted my leg over his arm so he could slide deeper. *Holy shit.* Josh started a pounding rhythm, pulling out slowly only to slam home so perfectly that I couldn't stop the small, keening cries that escaped. He kissed me in time with his thrusts, our breath mingling. My hands reached for his back, my nails scoring lines down his skin, desperate to hold him, keep him closer to me.

He stayed in perfect rhythm until sweat beaded on both of us and that same tension built again within me, demanding release. "Josh," I cried as I spiraled.

He adjusted my leg, changed the angle so he rubbed against my clit with every thrust, and sent me straight over the edge into an orgasm even more powerful than the first. He met me a few moments later, looking at me as if I was some kind of miracle to him and calling out my name.

I would never tire of this.

My hunger for him, the need that made my body sing the minute he walked into the room, only grew.

I stroked his hair as our breathing slowed, our heart rates calmed, until he rolled onto his side, kissing my shoulder. Then he sat up, resting his forehead in his hands.

Red, angry lines crossed his skin. *Shit.* "Josh, your back," I whispered.

He stood, looking over his shoulder in the mirror. "Well worth it. It's actually hot as hell."

"I'm sorry," I apologized anyway.

He slid next to me, bringing me onto my side to face him. My body was limp, still vibrating with residual energy. "It's not like you were trying to," he said with a little smirk.

"Maybe I was," I answered honestly, knowing that hadn't been all about love. There had been too much anger in me for that.

He took my hands and pressed kisses to my fingers. "You don't need your nails for that. One of your tears draws far more blood."

The air shifted between us, everything spoken downstairs having finally caught up with us. "What are we going to do? I don't know how to say good-bye to you again."

He closed his eyes and took a deep breath before refocusing on me. "I think we have two options for right now. The first, is we go downstairs and finish this talk over a dinner that is way cold by now."

"And the second?" I asked, in no hurry to get back to the angry discussion that wouldn't change a damn thing.

He shrugged. "We get in the bathtub and start this all over again." His tongue swirled over my index finger.

I had no idea what tomorrow was going to bring. Would he change his mind?

No, you know better than that.

Would I have to take him to the hangar again? Relive that good-bye? Panic rose in my chest until it crept up my throat. *Shut it down. Now.* If I had one night to spend with him, what would I rather do?

"I have been wanting to try out that tub."

His grin was enough to know I'd chosen the right option.

Morning light filtered in through our window.

I blinked the sleep out of my eyes and reached across the sheets for Josh, but he wasn't there. Come to think, the sun was really bright. We'd been up until at least three a.m., barely breaking away from making love for food, and even that had been hand-fed between kisses. No wonder I was still exhausted.

I rolled over, grabbing my cell from the nightstand.

9:30 a.m.

"Josh?" I called out, then flew from the bed. "What time do you have to be there?" I asked again, this time louder.

I threw on clothes and grabbed a pair of flip-flops, racing down the stairs as I pulled my hair into a makeshift knot. "Josh?"

The living room was empty, and he wasn't in the kitchen, either.

A sick feeling settled in my stomach, and my mouth watered like I was about to vomit. He wouldn't. There was no way.

The dishes had been done, the dining room table was bare but for a few papers. I raced past them and flung open the door to the garage. His bags were gone.

He'd left.

A buzzing sound filled my head, and the world seemed to slow as I spun, looking for any sign that I was wrong, that he might still be here. I dialed his phone number, but the voicemail picked up on the first ring.

Jagger. Jagger would know.

I ran back into the house, through the kitchen and into the dining room, but stopped when I saw the papers again. My legs felt like they were dragging concrete as I took the last few steps.

Oh God, there was an envelope with my name on it.

"Josh, what did you do?"

I cracked the seal and pulled out the lined paper with shaking hands.

My December,

I couldn't make you say good-bye again. This one's on me, on my own cowardice. I'm not sure I would have had the strength to leave you. You are everything that is good and right in my world, and the only woman I have ever or will ever love. You've been right about so many things, especially that it's my career that's dominating our life, our future. So go to Turkey. Live your dream. I called Luke, and he'll be waiting at the airport for you next week. Maybe we both need these next couple of months. You to prepare your future, me to heal my past. So take this time. Figure out what your life can look like if you're not limited by my career...by me. You deserve everything this world has to offer, and the chance to make a choice once you actually see that your only option isn't just the next-door neighbor you fell in love with at twenty. The whole world is open to you, just as my heart always will be.

Just don't forget that you own me.

All my love,
Josh

I stifled a sob with my fist and sank into a chair. There,

underneath the letter, was a plane ticket to Turkey with the printed itinerary, and underneath, our lease.

But it wasn't our lease anymore. It showed that our rent had been paid through the end of this year, but it was only in my name.

I glanced around the room. His things were still here, everything but Will's ring. He hadn't moved out, but he sure as hell had made it easier to walk out if he needed to.

Or maybe just easier for me if something happened to him over there.

"Damn you, Joshua Walker," I whispered as a new fear gripped me.

He'd left, deployed, and hadn't even given me the chance to kiss him one last time, or tell him how much I loved him. But maybe that's what last night had been. Instead of a tearful mess at the hangar, he'd made love to me until we were both too exhausted to keep our eyes open any longer.

Maybe that was his good-bye.

A knock sounded, and I dropped the lease onto the table and sprinted for the door. I flung it open, stupidly hoping, even though I logically knew he wouldn't knock at his own house.

Paisley stood in front of me, her eyebrows drawn together, biting her lower lip. "Oh, Ember."

"He's gone," I whispered.

She nodded. "Jagger took him about a half hour ago, while I was out. I didn't know, I swear. I would have gotten you. I can't believe he did that."

"He's gone," I said again, unable to say anything else. My vision blurred, and my throat clogged until a sob tore through, hot tears spilling down my cheeks. "He's gone!"

Paisley caught me as I collapsed to the floor, a puddle of tears and anger.

"I know," she whispered. "It's going to be okay. You're going to be okay."

But it didn't feel okay. No, this was an excruciating ache that threatened to separate my heart from my body. Hell, I almost wished it would. My breaths came in heaping spurts that bordered hyperventilation, my entire being focused on the simple, unchangeable fact that he'd left, gone back to Afghanistan.

I wanted to hold him, kiss him, and promise that as angry as I was, this didn't change a thing. I was his, and he was mine, just as it always would be. There wasn't any other way for us to exist. I didn't need two months away from him to know that he was the only future for me.

Paisley's arms tightened and held me against her shoulder until I cried myself out and my sobs quieted. "What are you going to do?" she asked, stroking my hair back from my forehead like I was a child.

I thought about the lease, the house, the plane ticket.

"Pack."

CHAPTER THIRTY-TWO

JOSH

"For the record, I think this may, in fact, be the most foolish fucking thing I've ever seen you do," Jagger said as I took my duffel out of the back of my Jeep.

"Volunteering?" I clarified as I shifted it over my shoulder painlessly. Part of me wished it hurt, wished I hadn't been cleared, that this had never been an option.

"No. Going back is the definition of badass, heroic, courageous. We're talking movie-worthy shit. I only wish I was healed enough to go with you. But sneaking out on Ember? That's bullshit."

The parts of my heart that still functioned ceased for a few beats as I thought of her sleeping next to me, her hair spilled around her like flames, her lips swollen from my kisses. "She knew. I didn't sneak out. She told me she couldn't do another good-bye, and she shouldn't have to."

"And that shit with the lease? Are you just burning your relationship to the ground, or what?"

I swallowed, my throat tight. "She deserves a choice, and I keep taking them. This, leaving? It's what I'll always do, and it's not fair to her. I love her too much to destroy her. So, if over these next couple of months that we're apart, she discovers that she's"—my shoulders dropped—"that she's worth more than this, then it's easier. She should be home from Turkey just before I redeploy, and she has options. I fucking owe her that much."

"You want her to leave you."

My eyes slid shut as I thought about a life without her. "She deserves so much more than this. She deserves everything she's ever dreamed of, and..." I took a breath to steady my next words, but it didn't help. "She deserves a man who can put her first. Who isn't obligated to anything else in this world besides her." Blood boiled in my veins when I thought of another man touching her, kissing her lips, holding her love. "God knows I don't deserve her. I never did. And we both know I'll never be able to leave her. She's the only woman I'll ever love."

"You're being an ass." He leaned against the Jeep, his walking casts almost reaching the bottom of his cargo shorts, and crossed his arms. "That girl loves you more than anything. She chooses you every day, and I bet if you went home right now, she'd forgive this jerk move you're making, but I can't say the same in two months."

God, I wanted to see her, to wrap my arms around her and promise that I'd be home soon. I wanted to tell her to have a good time in Turkey, to soak up every second that she could— she'd worked so hard for it. "If I go back there now, she won't go to Turkey. Everything she worked for will be flushed down the drain because of me. There's zero fucking chance I'm going to let that happen. If it takes me...losing her"—agony ripped through me, making me almost physically ill—"for her to have her dream, then I'm going to have to risk it."

"I love you like a brother, Josh. But I want to smack some sense into you. Ember will always choose you. She's proven that time and again, but you have to be an option."

"We'll see what happens in a couple of months."

"You're Josh and Ember. If you guys don't make it, there's zero hope for the human race." He pushed off the Jeep and grabbed me into a hug. "Be safe. Save lives. Don't fucking die."

I hugged him and let him go. "Take care of her for me, and hopefully I'll see you before Mini-Bateman is here."

Jagger grinned. "You'd better, since you'll be the godfather."

"Really?" *Godfather. Kick-ass.* "That's amazing. I'm kind of speechless."

"Just get your ass home, because something tells me you're going to have a mess to clean up."

"Yeah, I know it. If she's even still interested. Chances are she'll realize that I'm holding her back and our futures aren't exactly compatible."

"Love makes everything compatible. You'll find a way, but if you're so hell-bent on this weird fucking...break—"

"We're not on a break," I snapped. She was mine and I was hers...until she decided otherwise. No bullshit breaks. Wait. Were we? Had I inadvertently implied that we were? And I'd just shoved her straight at Luke. *Shit. Fuck. Damn it.* I rubbed my hand over my eyes and shifted my bag. It was time to go.

"Right, well, whatever. Just use this time to figure out how the hell you can compromise, too, because it seems to me like Ember's the one doing the majority of the bending. Figure out where the hell you can bend, too, or you just might lose her."

"Walker!" Rizzo called from the hangar door.

"Gotta go," I said to Jagger. "You sure you can get my Jeep home?"

"Yeah, I'll have Private Newbie and his friend over there drive me."

"Take care. Don't do anything wild while I'm gone," I tried to joke.

"You've cornered the market on stupidity for both of us, Walker." He pulled me into a hug. "Godspeed, brother."

. . .

"Welcome back," Lieutenant Colonel Dolan greeted me as I hauled my bag into the barracks. *How the hell did I get here? What the fuck am I doing?*

"Thank you, sir," I answered.

"I was pretty surprised to hear you were coming."

"I'm healed, and we have a mission, sir."

He assessed me with knowing eyes. "That we do. Well, get settled and let me know if you need anything."

"Thank you, sir."

I lifted my bag over my shoulder and walked down the hall until I reached my room, where I knocked. "Come in," I heard a voice say.

The door opened—to a brand-new kid, straight out of flight school who'd been on the flight before ours. I'd seen him a few times at Campbell. "Can I help you?"

"You can get the hell out of my room," I answered.

The kid's eyes widened. "Uh, this is mine? I've been here two weeks."

There were only eight months between our graduation dates at Fort Rucker, but somehow I felt older, weathered. "This is my room. I got my ass blown up, and now I'm back. Once you do the same, you can have it, but for now, the room on the end is empty, now move."

The kid scurried, packing up his few belongings. "Uh, I packed up some stuff when I got here, it's in tough boxes in the storage locker."

"Thanks," I muttered. At least I knew where my shit was.

Fifteen minutes later, he'd vacated, and I stared at the room I'd spent three months in. I had an instant, overwhelming need to burn it to the ground. *Why not, you just fucked your entire life.*

After I retrieved my footlocker of stuff and unpacked, I crawled up onto my bunk and lay down. I needed to catch a couple of hours of sleep and try to get myself on the right time schedule. I stared up at the ceiling.

Three days of traveling had left me exhausted, but sleep wouldn't come. I ran my hand above my head, into the small opening construction had left in the wall, and sighed. They were still there. I pulled out the two worn pictures of Ember and shone my small flashlight on them.

Her smile warmed me in one, her eyes bright with love. The other, she hadn't known that I'd taken while we were in Breckenridge a year or so ago, but the wistful look on her face as she'd looked out over the mountains was too breathtaking not to capture.

"I'm so sorry," I told her. My thumb stroked her printed cheek, and I wished I was still close enough to really touch her, to pull us from the brink of disaster I'd brought us to. To undo the last three years and make all the right choices from the start, the ones that would protect her instead of putting her through another hell.

I had nightmares that night, but they weren't about the crash, or even Will's death. No, they were of the look on her face when she realized I was leaving, and my brain's prediction that she wouldn't be there when I returned.

I would have rather had the other ones.

My alarm went off after a shit-filled, five-hour attempt at sleep, and I climbed off the bed. I got dressed as Skype fired up, wishing there would be a certain redhead on the other end.

Instead, a middle-aged psychiatrist with glasses answered. "Ah, Josh! Good to see you."

"Hey, Dr. Henderson."

"Well, how does it feel to be back?"

I glanced around at the walls, my pinned pictures of Ember, and the smell of deployment. "Like I never left."

• • •

My fingers traced over the map on my iPad. There were forty-five hundred miles between Kandahar and Ephesus. Hell, I could even drive, if I wanted to see the inside of an Iranian prison.

Ember had been in Turkey for a week now. I'd checked in with Jagger, made sure she'd gotten on the plane. He'd assured me that she had and reminded me yet again that I was a fucking jackass. Maybe, but she was in Turkey. That's what mattered. She was the closest she'd ever be during a deployment, but I'd never felt farther away from her. Was she set up there okay? Did she have everything she needed? I knew her internet was limited, so it wasn't like I could even really check, but the worry was killer.

Was there someone there she'd rather be with? Someone who didn't go to war or leave her alone for a year at a time? Someone who came home at five p.m. and didn't force her to choose between the career she wanted and the one he already had? Someone who deserved her a hell of a lot more than I did?

I logged onto Facebook in a moment of supreme weakness and clicked her profile. Hell, at least it said we were still engaged. Her latest picture filled my screen, her hair in a knot on her head, her tank top and shorts dust-covered, and her smile wider than I'd seen in way too long, glowing.

She was happy in Turkey.

Happier than she'd been with me since the deployment started.

I flipped to the next picture and saw her standing in front of a huge ruin, another man's arm wrapped protectively around her waist, and my pulse pounded.

Luke.

"They're just friends. Shut the fuck up, or you'll drive yourself mad," I whispered to myself, shutting off the iPad.

She'd looked so damned…ecstatic. I wanted that for her—to live her dream, that kind of happiness filling every day of her life. She'd never have that if she stayed with me. Marriage for us would have way too many days with good-byes and tears that tasted like fear and missed holidays. Life with me meant struggling to get her PhD at one duty station, years of time we'd miss together, and burying our friends along the way.

The friends I'd killed.

Every tear she'd cried when Will had been killed was there because of my choice, my decision. Because I'd played God, and inadvertently chosen Jagger's life over his.

It should have been me...but then Ember would have been alone.

Where the hell was the right choice?

God, she deserved that life she'd dreamed of, and I could never give it to her. But I could give her the freedom to choose it, if I could only kill my heart and give her up.

The threads of my soul were pulling apart under the strain, one half wanting to give Ember the freedom she deserved—the life she deserved with someone a hell of a lot better for her than I was. But the selfish half of me was screaming to hold on to her—to the love that had carried me through—because the thought of living without her was unimaginable.

But if I didn't find a way to let her go, I'd end up breaking my promise to her father and crushing her dreams under my obligations.

I slipped Will's ring from its home in my pocket and rolled it between my fingers like I could somehow channel him.

"You're on today, too?" Rizzo asked, interrupting my thoughts as he kicked his heels up onto the table next to me in the office.

"Yep," I answered, trying to shut off my brain.

"Well, I guess it's only fitting. I mean, you were my last flight, too." He cracked a smile, and I couldn't help but give a little laugh.

"Yeah, let's just keep it in the sky this time, shall we?"

"Nervous?" he asked.

"A little," I admitted. We'd been here almost two weeks and had finally come up on the actual flight rotation. I'd been okay with the break. It wasn't even the fear of flying—I'd gotten over that back at Campbell—but I was a little anxious to see how I'd react in the field.

"Good. It keeps you humble." He punched my shoulder. "You submit that SOAR packet yet?"

"Yeah," I said quietly.

"Is that what you really want?"

I shrugged. "It isn't really for me."

"It's a hell of a life to live for someone else."

"It's a hell of a debt to pay." Whether or not I wanted to, it was the most I could do to earn the life Will had given me. It wasn't fair to Ember, and she would never understand what I'd done. Hell, I barely understood. Besides, if they invited me, it's not like I had to assess. I'd see where Ember stood on the subject and go from there.

"And how is Mrs. Walker? I've missed cookie days."

Like he'd ripped a scab off my heart, I weakened, emotionally bleeding out. At least it was internal and no one could see. "Not sure. She's working in Turkey for a couple months."

"Ah, international traveler. She's a good woman. You should definitely lock that down."

Unfortunately, I'd done the fucking opposite. "What happened to no women until you're out?"

He scoffed. "Ah, man. That was my personal philosophy. I'm not hunting them down. You already found the right one, and given the level of shit you've put her through, and she's still standing? Yeah, keeper."

Any response I might have made was cut off by the radio call. It was go time.

Adrenaline flooded my system as we ran for the bird. The gravel flew under my feet, and my leg held steady, just as it had over the miles I'd been running the last month.

My copilot started the run-up, and I did a double take. Logically, I'd known Trivette wouldn't be sitting there, but CW3 Stiver's bulky frame still caught me off guard. He was efficient as we finished the checklist and waited for the official request to come in.

Six minutes after the initial call, we were airborne. The sky was crystal clear and perfect for flying as we headed toward the coordinates. I handled the controls while CW3 Stiver took the radio, coordinating the extraction.

"How's our LZ?" he asked.

"We're red," the voice answered.

Fuck. There were two Alphas down there who needed immediate surgery.

"What do you say, boys?" Stiver asked over the coms.

"Let's do it," one of the medics answered.

I glanced over my shoulder at Rizzo. He gave a sardonic headshake and then sighed. "I'm in."

Stiver took the controls and looked at me. For the first time in my career, I hesitated. I brushed my hand over the picture of Ember on my kneeboard—I'd replaced the blood-stained one. This wasn't about the rush, it was about those lives on the ground that I could save...or die trying. "Let's go."

It's a good day to die. I couldn't say it, couldn't bring myself to form the words, but that didn't mean they didn't race through my brain. Everything but the mission fell away, and my focus sharpened on exactly what mattered at the moment—saving those soldiers. I didn't flinch or hesitate again.

We completed our mission, and in the process of rescuing those soldiers, I saved a little bit of myself as well. Maybe if I did this enough times, I'd be almost whole, almost enough to fight for Ember.

Or maybe she was right, and each mission was an amped-up game of Russian roulette. Maybe I was ushering in my own demise.

At least it wouldn't be hers.

CHAPTER THIRTY-THREE

EMBER

I zipped up my Vanderbilt hoodie and headed out into the morning chill, my coffee hot in my travel mug. I took a sip and cringed. The only creamer Luke had been able to find had been all the way in Izmir, powdered and unflavored. I'd hoped I'd get used to it after a month, but apparently my taste buds were more homesick than I was.

I didn't miss the States yet, or even the internet, but every molecule in my body screamed with missing Josh. I looked to the east, where I knew, forty-five hundred miles away, he was probably on shift. *Please be safe. Just be okay.*

A deep breath later, I forced him to the back of my mind. Well, tried to, at least.

The sun was already bright, the temperature mild for September. I skipped down the steps of our little setup of rowed trailers and crossed the cypress-tree-lined dirt road into the ruins. At seven thirty a.m., I had about a half hour before the busloads of tourists began arriving.

Morning was my favorite time in Ephesus. Except for the few other dig members who got up early, the ruins were vacant, hauntingly beautiful. I made my way down the rough cobblestone street, keeping to the left so I could look at the uncovered mosaic tile walkway that the ancient Romans had used in front of their shops. It was hard to believe that something so beautiful, so intricate, was made to be walked on, or that it had survived thousands of years before being uncovered.

Maybe that was the trick—keeping the valued things covered, tucked away. It seemed that when we exposed what we treasured to the elements, that's when things got pretty fucked up.

"Hey, Red," Luke said, catching up to me, jumping over a broken cobblestone.

"Morning, sleepy," I answered and took another god-awful sip.

"You moving into the terrace houses today?" he asked, motioning to the newly constructed cover that housed the latest dig site.

"Yep, I get the pleasure of working with Reed." My voice dripped sarcasm.

"It's all in the name of discovery!" He lunged forward dramatically, and I laughed. We paused as the library came into view, its tall, massive pillars standing in defiance of the passage of time. "There are moments I realize how lucky we are to be here," he said quietly.

"Yeah, it's been surreal. Did you hear Charlotte found an entire antechamber at her site yesterday?"

"No way! I want to be on that team."

"Finish your doctorate," I teased him. "Until then, we get the honor of sweeping dirt away with toothbrushes."

"While supervised," he joked. He sighed as we reached the fork in the path. "Amazing, isn't it, that we could reconstruct something that fell so long ago?"

I looked toward the library. "It's gorgeous."

"Let's hope we got it right," Reed said, coming up from behind us and passing on the left. "Let's get going, Howard," he ordered, pulling his cap down over his short blond hair. "Those mosaics aren't going to uncover themselves."

"I somehow doubt they're in danger of going anywhere!" Luke shouted back. "I wonder if he's right. Maybe we fucked it up." He tilted his head as he looked back at the ruins.

I shrugged. "It's better to have tried, right? How can we ever know just how beautiful something was, how important, how epic, if we don't at least try to put it back together when it breaks? Even if some of the pieces are in the wrong place, at least it's standing."

He shot me a little side-eye. "And how exactly is Flyboy?"

My grip tightened on my coffee mug. "Don't."

"You could come with me to Izmir tomorrow. Internet's shitty in places and shittier in others, but you could at least try an email. Or at least upload pictures to your own Facebook instead of having me log in for you."

"My mom wanted to see them."

"Then give her some more to see. Reach out to Flyboy. Come on."

I'd said no the previous four times he'd asked, knowing there was nothing I could say that would erase the way we'd left things—the way he'd left things, since I hadn't had much to do with it. But just the thought of being able to reach out and connect with him had me tempted. "I'll think about it."

He fist-pumped, and I rolled my eyes. "You guys will pull through."

"Howard!" Reed yelled, the sound echoing down the stone steps.

"Coming," I answered. "Napoleon needs me."

"All in the name of conquest," he joked, and we split at the path, Luke to his dig site, and me to mine. I passed the already unearthed terrace houses and continued to climb, wondering, as always, what women had climbed here before me. Who had they been? What had they wanted for their lives? Which of our assumptions about their way of life were completely wrong?

I opened the door to the enclosed dig site and started the

climb over the see-through walkways above the uncovered rooms. "Where do you want me today?" I asked Reed, who was waiting midway.

"This way." He led me down the next set of steps into a room where a Turkish boy, maybe seventeen, waited with a smile.

"This is Ilyas. He'll be assisting you. Ilyas, this is Miss Howard."

I waved. "Hi, Ilyas. And it's just Ember."

He grinned. "Hi, just Ember."

Reed rolled his eyes and pointed to the tools. "We're uncovering this one. You've been trained in all these tools?"

"I've been with Dr. Trimble for the last month, so yeah, I've got this."

He blinked. "Of course. I'm sorry, I didn't mean to insult you."

I smiled, surprised that he'd actually apologized. "No problem." I waved it off.

His eyes widened. "You're going to take off that rock, right?"

I glanced at my engagement ring. "Yeah, of course." I needed to stop taking it off the chain around my neck, but I loved seeing it on my hand when I woke in the morning.

"Good. Okay, it's almost eight."

I nodded. *Nine-thirty in Kandahar.* That half hour in the time difference always got me, like time itself was either trying to lean forward to connect us sooner, or lean farther away to make it harder.

"Well, let's try to get a few good hours in. Call me if you need me. I'll be a couple of rooms over." He climbed out, leaving me in what would be my workspace for the next month. I took off my ring and hung it on the chain around my neck.

A cynical laugh bubbled up. Talk about metaphors for my life. I had to tuck everything I loved about Josh away so

I could work, and he had to do the same. So where was the happy compromise? Was there such a thing?

Who had to give more?

I grabbed my tools and got to work. At least this was a mess I could clean up. Everything else would simply have to wait another month.

Izmir was ridiculously hectic, especially when there were two cruise ships in port. Luke led me to the hotel he'd found that charged for internet and hooked me up. I half expected to hear a dial-up tone.

My email booted up, and I answered a note from Mom with a few, quick lines, then a joint one to Sam and Paisley, letting them know I'd call when I could. I answered two questions from the wedding coordinator in Breckenridge like nothing had changed.

Then I opened a blank email and addressed it to Josh. What the hell was I going to say? I love you? Why did you do that to me? Are you safe? Should I lie, hide everything about my feelings until we saw each other again? The last thing I wanted to do was stress him out during a deployment. He had enough on his mind already, and God knew how he was flying missions.

Were his nightmares back?

I hated not knowing the answers.

Hey, Josh,

I've settled in here. It's gorgeous and surpassing every expectation I've ever had. So far I've helped uncover one room, and catalogue its contents, and now I've moved on to uncovering and preserving a beautiful mosaic.

Holy shit, you'll bore him to death if you continue like this.

Anyway, I hope you're doing well, staying safe when you can. Everything here reminds me of you.

Delete that.

I took out the last sentence with slightly aggressive key-strokes. Since when had I started censoring myself with Josh? *Since he decided to give you a couple of months.*

I miss you.

Yeah, that's safer.

All my love,
December

I hit send before I could talk myself out of it, and for that tiny second, felt connected to him. It was like the second you accidentally touched scalding water, how there was always the tiniest breath before it hurt like hell.

I stared at the screen for a couple of minutes and hit refresh, hoping that maybe he was online right now. That I'd hear back. Then I opened my Facebook and uploaded a few more pictures for Mom.

"Hey, van's leaving," Luke said, tapping me on the shoulder.

"Yeah." I nodded. I closed out my email, a pang of longing sucking the breath from my chest. The first three months of the deployment had hurt, no doubt, but this disconnect was excruciating. What if it became permanent? If he didn't pull his head out of his ass?

God, is this how he'd felt those months after Dad died? When I hadn't known what to do with myself?

It would take a hell of a lot more than his nonsense last month to stop me from loving him, but if he didn't love me anymore, what was I supposed to do with that?

"We can come back in a few days," Luke offered.

"It's a forty-five-minute drive," I muttered.

"Yeah, well, we'll grab some supplies while we're here. Make it a legitimate run." He leaned against the computer table.

"I miss him," I whispered, like those three words could even slightly define the gut-wrenching sensation of having my heart ripped from my body.

He stood and looped his arm around my shoulders. "I know. What you guys have is the real thing, the legendary stuff they write songs about. Just hold on to that."

Right, but what kinds of songs? The ones with the happy endings and sappy melodies? Or the morose country ones that ended with sobbing into a bottle of liquor? I held myself together as we filed into the van, Luke and I taking the back row when four other dig students grabbed the middle ones.

My mind wandered as we left the city limits and headed back to the ruins.

I loved Josh. That was never going to change.

What we had couldn't be diminished by a couple of months apart. We'd made it through just about everything, and we'd come through this, even if I had to pull him kicking and screaming. I wasn't giving up, wasn't backing down.

He'd waited months for me to get my shit together when Dad died. He hadn't given up; he hadn't lost faith. And even when all hope had been stripped from him, from both of us, he'd held on to the love we could never deny, no matter what the consequences.

It was simply my turn to grit my teeth and hold on tight.

I'd never taken pleasure in soaping up a floor before. Then again, I'd never been uncovering something as beautiful or unique. Each inch I uncovered revealed something new yet ancient, the faces in the mosaic knowing secrets I could only guess at. It was incredible to think I was the first person to see it since the city had been evacuated thousands of years ago.

I'd spent the last four weeks discovering the floor of this room, and I'd never felt so in awe of something.

Except the first time Josh kissed you.

And every kiss after that, if I was being honest.

"Knock knock," Luke said from the top of the ladder. "Feel like a break? You've been down here for hours."

I pulled a sweaty strand of hair from my face and tucked it back under my bandana. "Sounds good. Ilyas, break time?"

"Absolutely. I'll take one, too, and see you in a bit."

Ilyas had been fun to be around, and he taught me bits and pieces of Turkish while we'd uncovered the mosaic.

Luke took the bucket of dirty water I handed to him, and then I ascended the ladder onto the walkway. "We're tourist heavy at the front. Do you want to sneak out the back?"

"Heck yes."

We dumped the water, left the bucket at the filling station, and then walked out at the top of the enclosure to sit on the hill where we'd stashed a couple of lawn chairs.

The October breeze cooled my skin, and I lifted my face to the sunshine. "Gorgeous day." I peeked at the crowd below. "I think they agree."

"Why do you think they all come?" Luke motioned to the flocks of tourists hiking on the pathways.

"The same reason we do. To touch history, to try to understand what we have in common with people who lived thousands of years ago."

"How's Flyboy?"

I cut my gaze toward him. "Real subtle, Luke."

He shrugged. "You went into town without me yesterday. I have to live vicariously."

"He's good, I guess. His emails are short and mostly just updates on what he's doing, but he signs them 'Love, Josh,' so that's got to be good." I pulled my engagement ring from between my breasts and slid it along the chain absentmindedly, as had become my worst habit of late.

Luke sighed. "You'll be home next week. And he should be home soon after?"

Next week. It was hard to believe time had gone so fast here, but it seemed like forever since I'd seen Josh, or heard his voice. "Right. I'm not exactly sure when he's due home, actually."

Luke reached over and squeezed my hand. "It's going to be okay. You know that, right? No matter which way things go, you will be okay."

"There's only one way it can go," I said, my voice stronger than my heart felt. "I know why he did it. Logically, I know that he never would have really healed if he hadn't gone back. It was the final stage for him, and God help me, the right thing to do. He'll eventually reconcile himself with what happened, and I hope that's what he's doing there, but he never could have forgiven himself if he hadn't finished his mission. It's not in his nature to sit on the sidelines. It never has been."

"You're a damn fine woman, Ember. I hope he realizes it."

The corners of my mouth lifted. "I have the love of a damn fine man. I hope he realizes *that*."

A safari hat peeked above the hill to our left as Dr. Trimble sidestepped down the path toward us. "Miss Howard?" he called. "If I could have a word?"

Luke gave a low whistle. "Good luck with that one," he said with a little hand pat. "Catch me up later?"

"You bet," I agreed, and then started up the path toward Dr. Trimble. He waved me on, and I followed just over the ridge, where his trailer sat out of the sight of tourists.

"Have a seat," he said with a smile and pulled a bottle of

water out of his cooler. "You've been working very hard."

I took the bottle and opened it. "Thank you. I love the work I'm doing."

"Well, it shows." He leaned back in his chair, studying me as I sipped the water. "You applied to the doctoral program for anthropology?"

I swallowed carefully, immediately nauseous. "Yes, sir, I did."

"You were accepted." He handed over a sealed envelope.

A shaky laugh stuttered my breath as I opened the envelope. *Dear Ms. Howard, we are delighted to inform you...*

I'd gotten in. I closed my eyes and clutched the letter to my chest. *I made it, Josh. I'll be a PhD. Dr. Walker.* A small shred of my happiness flew away. The only person I wanted to tell was anything but accessible. "Thank you," I said to Dr. Trimble, knowing full well it was his letter of recommendation and this program that had secured my acceptance.

"You did the work, Ms. Howard. I've never been happier to recommend a student. Your efforts here have been excellent, and I think you'll make a fantastic anthropologist."

"This trip has been a dream, and I can't thank you enough for inviting me."

"Are you ready to go home?" He leaned forward, bracing his elbows on the desk.

"Yes and no. I'll miss everything about this place, especially the work, but I'm happy to get home to see my fiancé. He should be redeploying right about when I get there."

He sighed. "Did you know that we were able to secure permission to continue the dig on a smaller scale for another two months?"

My eyes widened. "No. I thought the setup was on pause until next year."

"It was until a couple of days ago. I've also been given permission to keep a percentage of my staff."

Luke would be thrilled if he got to stay. "Good. That will give you time to finish the terrace house excavation."

"Yes. Of course it would go faster if you were the one to head that part of the dig."

I swallowed. "Sir?"

"Reed has to go home. You're young, and it's not like I'd let you just run roughshod. I'd officially be the lead, but you'd be leading point. No one knows that excavation site better than you, and I'm not just talking about the room you've been uncovering."

"I know it exceptionally well," I admitted. While the other dig members had taken their free time in Izmir, or visited the leather markets, I'd spent every second exploring, making sure this trip was etched into every crevice of my memory.

"Yes. So I understand that you probably need to go home next week…"

I nodded, my eyes focused out his window—toward Josh. "Yes." What would he say? He'd probably tell me to take it, and then, for an extra rush, volunteer to go join some special ops team while I was gone. *You know he needs a few more years under his belt for that. Chill out.* "I do need to go home and see him. And my friend's baby is due tomorrow."

"Why don't you see if you can take off a few days early? Really think it over? Since you'd be listed as a team head, we can compensate you not only for the job itself, but for the return flight as well. I'd love to have you back, but of course it wouldn't affect your position in the program come January. There's always next summer, right?"

I blinked. Next summer. This could be what my future looked like—spending the school year teaching, writing, and the summers on archeological digs. *It's everything you've wanted.*

But Josh. What was it worth without Josh?

Nothing.

I at least needed to see him before I said yes, to make sure we'd be okay for another couple of months. Because saying no was ridiculous, right? It was a hell of a line for my resume, and I'd be home before Christmas.

"I'll think about it," I promised.

I cringed over the change fee to my airline ticket, but made it. One packed bag and two days later, Luke took me to the airport, already having agreed to stay for the remainder of the dig. "You sure you only want to take one bag?" he asked as we walked toward the terminal.

I nodded. "I'll be back for the rest."

His grin was instant. "I knew this place would get into your blood. I'm glad you're staying with me!"

"Yeah, yeah. I'll see you in a few weeks?"

He hugged me tight. "Please, for the love of all that is holy and good, bring real coffee creamer."

I laughed and promised to do so, then boarded my flight. Frankfurt, Philadelphia, and finally Nashville...fourteen hours later, I was stateside. Exhausted, but stateside. I fired up my cell phone as soon as we taxied. "It's nice to be home," I whispered as my signal picked up.

I skipped the thousand Facebook notifications, the Twitter updates, and the Instagram feed, going straight for Paisley's number.

"Ember?" she answered, out of breath. "Do you have service over there now?"

"I'm actually in Nashville!" I exclaimed, something in my soul righting at the sound of her voice. We'd docked the plane, and now people were milling about the cabin, waiting their turn to disembark.

"You are? Jagger! She's in Nashville!"

"What?" his voice was muffled in the background.

"How?" she asked.

"I came home a few days early. I was offered the chance to

run my portion of the dig site for the next couple of months, but I wanted to come home first and think it over."

"That's amazing! I can't wait to see you. Do you think you can get here pretty soon?" she asked.

"As soon as I get off the plane, I'll rent a car and head home." Finally my turn, I grabbed my backpack from the overhead bin and walked toward the front of the plane. Excitement lit my nerve endings. I'd get to sleep in my own bed tonight. Make dinner in a full kitchen. *Yes! You can get Starbucks!*

"I meant the hospital. If you're not too busy, I'm kind of in labor."

My jaw dropped. "Oh my God. Yes! Yes! I'll be there as soon as I can!" I broke into a run as soon as my feet hit the Jetway.

I heard Jagger mutter something in the background. "I absolutely will not ask her that, Jagger Bateman."

Another muffled response.

"What's up?" I asked.

"There's something else," she said before I heard the phone change hands.

"Ember?" Jagger's voice filled the line.

"Congrats, Daddy," I said, my voice uneven as I sprinted through the terminal.

"Yeah, this is amazing. But listen, I need a favor."

"Anything." I bypassed the Starbucks by the security entrance and headed for the rental car desk.

"Yeah, I was kind of supposed to be somewhere in about an hour and forty-five minutes, and I need you to fill in."

"Done. Where am I going?" I asked as I slid past people on the escalator.

"Josh is coming home today. I need you to pick him up."

My feet failed me, and I tripped over the end of the escalator, sprawling on the floor in a graceless heap that was more metaphor than painful.

"Ember?"

I stumbled, maintaining my hold on the phone. "Yeah. Yeah, I got this."

"You sure?"

"Absolutely."

Hell no. Not even close.

CHAPTER THIRTY-FOUR

EMBER

My hands shook as I killed the car engine in the hangar parking lot. 8:25 p.m. *Thank you God, I made it in time.* Twenty minutes until the ceremony was scheduled to start, and I was a hot mess. I shoved a few bobby pins in my hair, trying to put it into some kind of style that didn't immediately say I'd been traveling for sixteen hours.

Of course this is the way it would happen. I lifted my neckline to my nose and sniffed. Oh. My. God.

I twisted and pulled my bag through the gap in the front seats. I looked around to make sure no one was watching, and then risked an indecent exposure, changing into a clean tank top and semi-wrinkled button-down. The shorts would have to stay. There was zero chance of me stripping down to that level in the parking lot.

Unless Josh wants—

Nope. Not going there.

I gave myself a once-over in the mirror, popped on a coat of mascara and some lip gloss, and declared myself done. Without a shower and a straight-iron, this was as good as I was getting.

The stands were full as I walked into the hangar. I passed the little girls in red-white-and-blue tutus, and the little boys in camo outfits as they danced to the band, making my way up the bleachers until I found an empty seat near the top.

My phone buzzed in my back pocket, and I swiped it to answer when I saw Mom's picture. "Mom?"

"Hey, honey! I'm so sorry I didn't answer earlier. I was in my yoga class. Where are you?"

There was something about hearing her voice that crumbled my composure. "I'm at Fort Campbell. I came home a couple of days early, and now Paisley is in labor, and I'm here picking up Josh."

"Well, that sounds like quite the homecoming for both of you," she said. I plugged my other ear, trying to hear her better.

I looked around at all the other women in their carefully chosen outfits, their glittery signs, and perfectly done hair. "Mom, I don't have anything for him."

"What do you mean?"

"I came straight from the airport. I don't have a sign, or my hair done, and I've been in the same panties since Turkey!"

A few heads snapped in my direction, and I glared them down.

"Ember."

"This isn't how it was supposed to be. I was going to have the house perfect, and his Jeep detailed, and a big sparkly, funny sign. My makeup was going to be done, and my legs definitely shaved, and a cute outfit, too. Instead I've been traveling for almost sixteen hours, I don't really know where our relationship stands, and I don't have anything!" Oh God, I was going to be sick.

"Do you have arms?"

"What?" I damn near shouted. "Yes, I have arms."

"Then open them. That's all he needs."

"Mom. It's so much more complicated than that."

"It's not. December, nothing in the army is perfect. No amount of planning can make a homecoming perfect, and nothing will go as planned. He's not going to care about any of those details you're stressed over. He's only going to care that you're sitting in those bleachers ready to welcome him home. You are his perfect homecoming."

"What if he doesn't want me here?" Giving voice to my worst fear zapped some of my last caffeine-generated energy, and my shoulders drooped.

"He does."

"How can you be sure?"

"Because that boy—that man—he loves you in a way that a deployment doesn't kill. I know you have a lot to discuss, and I'm not suggesting you forget the way he left, but don't give up, either, Ember. You and I have the same taste in hardheaded men, so you hold on tight with both hands and fight like hell. And Ember..."

"Yeah?"

"Remember every single thing about this moment. There's nothing like it."

The crowd came to their feet with a deafening roar as the hangar doors opened. "I love you, Mom," I yelled into the phone above the noise.

"I love you, baby. Go get your man."

We hung up as more than two hundred soldiers marched in through both open hangar doors. The air electrified. My heart slammed against my ribs, and my head started to spin. There were too many emotions fighting for supremacy—my excitement at seeing him, my anger over the way he'd left, my confusion over where we stood—but they were all eclipsed by the stark relief of knowing he'd made it home alive. Tears stung my eyes, as if my body simply couldn't contain my feelings and needed the outlet.

They came to a stop, and my eyes raked over the lines of soldiers as the Commanding General welcomed the troops home. I didn't have to look far.

Josh stood at attention in the first row, faced forward.

Butterflies attacked my stomach, and everything lower clenched. He was gorgeous. My soul screamed out for his as if it were an actual physical being, desperate to fly forward and get him into my arms. He looked tired and worn but accomplished—haggard but whole, yet empty all at the same time.

I kept locked on to him as the general dismissed the troops and the stands emptied in a rush to the hangar floor. Then I carefully walked down, telling my rebellious body that I couldn't simply fling myself into his arms. He looked side to side as he walked forward, no doubt searching for Jagger, until he'd reached the bottom of the stands just before I did.

"Josh." His name came out in a breathless whisper.

His eyes met mine, his jaw dropping slightly. "Ember?"

I took the final step, until I was on the first bleacher, just at his eye-height. "Hi."

"How...? You're not supposed to be back for a few more days."

There was no regret in that tone, right? Damn it, I wanted to throw my arms around his neck. I wanted to kiss him until he couldn't think, and then smack him hard for what he'd done to me. I wanted *us*, complicated futures and all. "I came home early, like you, I guess." *Jackass, he knows that.* "Are you mad?"

"Hell no," he said, his gaze darting to my lips.

He still wants you.

Unable to control my hand, I cupped the side of his cheek, thrilling at the scratch of his stubble against my palm. A giant sigh of relief escaped me, and my eyes slid shut. When I opened them, he was staring at me with a cross between want and trepidation. "Can I hug you? I mean, I don't know what we're—"

My words were muffled into his shoulder as he pulled me off the bleachers and into his arms. One of his hands wrapped around my back while the other tangled into my hair, pulling my pins loose. His scent enveloped me, and I tilted my head to nudge my nose against his neck, breathing in home. Nothing ever felt as good, as right as when he held me.

"I'm glad you're here," he muttered against my hair.

That reminded me... "Jagger—" I shook my head and pulled back from the safety of Josh's warmth, trying to remember the important stuff. "Paisley is in labor. He sent me."

Josh straightened immediately. "I'll get my bag, and let's go."

He took my hand and led me through the crowd to where their bags had been lined up. Two heavy bags later, we were marching to the car. I clicked the unlock button, and the taillights on the SUV I'd rented flashed.

"Uh. New car?" he asked, loading his bags into the back after the hatch raised.

"No," I said. "I rented it at the airport."

"When?"

"Oh, a couple of hours ago when I landed." I scrunched my nose. "I'm sorry I'm not more dressed up. I kind of traveled halfway around the world today."

He laughed. "Yeah, I'd be a hypocrite if I minded, since we're in the same situation."

"Right," I said with an awkward head nod. We stared at each other for a few seconds, our eyes speaking volumes that our lips couldn't yet say. Then I thrust the keys in his direction. "Think you can keep it at the speed limit?"

He gave me a cocky grin that sent heat spiraling through me. As if my body had sensed his nearness, my sex-drive clicked on, more than ready to make up for lost time and pretty damn uncaring that our relationship was in a gray area. *Down girl.*

"Let's go meet Mini-Bateman," he said and walked me around to my side. He opened the door for me and I climbed in, but before I could pull on the seat belt, he reached across and clicked it in himself like I was twenty again. "I like you safe," he murmured against my forehead as he slid out of the car to get behind the wheel. My chest tightened and fought my need to kiss the hell out of him.

He was true to his word and kept it at the speed limit as we made our way to the hospital. My hand felt naked without being able to take his, so I gripped the edge of my seat instead. We exchanged sideways glances, until the heavy awkwardness was too much for me. Since when did we ever act like this around each other?

"How are you?" I asked.

His grip shifted on the wheel, his knuckles whitening. "Okay. Better, I guess, in some areas." His eyes cut toward me. "Worse in others. What about you?"

"You hit the nail on the head," I said softly.

We pulled into the hospital parking lot, and Josh parked the car. Neither of us said a word as we walked inside the massive building and headed for the maternity ward. The magnetic pull between us was almost too much for me to take as we rode the elevator. Each floor that lit on the display seemed to metaphor my level of need for him. *We're at a four. Nope, make that a five, edging toward six, seven…* God, I was about to become a movie cliché and jump him against the wall.

Would that be so bad?

The doors dinged open, saving me from the potential embarrassment of a rejection. This was definitely new territory. Even when we'd started dating, I'd never really been afraid of Josh rejecting me. He'd always been so open, honest with his feelings and his intent when it came to me.

"Paisley Bateman?" I asked the desk nurse.

"Room 804," she said after checking the board behind her. "But she's pushing, so there's a waiting room at the end of the hall, there."

Holy cow. Any minute now they would be parents. Josh and I walked, nearly touching but not quite, our steps evenly matched. "I still can't believe they're having a baby," I said.

"Yeah. Most days I feel like we're still in college, arguing over who's ordering the keg, and now he's a dad."

I couldn't help but smile at the grin on Josh's face. His smile lit him up in a way that had always drawn me to him. "True," I said. "And I honestly never thought Jagger would be first, you know?"

He looked over at me, radiating an intensity that stole my breath. "I always figured we would be."

"Me, too," I confessed in a whisper as we came to a standstill in the middle of the hallway. The moment we stood there, held together by nothing more than our eyes, seemed like an eternity. The long nights I'd spent in Ephesus, staring up at the brilliant stars, wondering if he was looking, too, or if he was safe, all came rushing back with a feeling of such longing that my heart leaped into my throat.

"December?" he asked softly, concern softening his face.

"This is hard," I admitted.

"What is?" His voice dropped as he stepped forward slightly, until I had to crane my neck to keep eye contact.

"Standing here, within inches of you, aching to kiss you, and not knowing if I'm even allowed to. Not knowing what we are."

His jaw flexed and he looked away, fighting a battle I couldn't see. Then he glanced over my shoulder, sidestepped, and walked right past me, grabbing my hand to pull me behind him. He opened the door to the stairwell, and I stumbled through after him. "Josh, what are we doing?"

He pushed my back against the brick wall, cradling my head in his hand, and then took my mouth. *Yes, yes, YES*. He felt like heaven and tasted like...Josh. Home. I rose up on my toes, kissing him back with two months of pent-up want, anger, and love. His lips moved perfectly against mine, our tongues intertwined, my body arching naturally toward his.

This was Josh, the man I loved, the only person I wanted to spend my life kissing. His hand moved from my waist to my ass, lifting me against the wall. I wrapped my legs around his waist, locking my ankles behind him, and rolled my hips into him.

"God, I fucking missed you. Every second of every day." His voice was low, gravelly, and so incredibly sexy. He trailed kisses down my neck until I gasped. Then I lifted his head back to mine so I could kiss him again. I sucked on his lower lip, gently tugging it between my teeth, and he groaned.

I didn't care that we were in the stairwell of a hospital, my body was screaming for him, need vibrating through every one of my nerve endings. "Josh," I moaned softly when his hand rose to cup my breast over my shirt.

The door beside us opened.

He dropped his hand and rested his forehead against my shoulder, sucking in deep breaths as two nurses walked past, the door shielding us from their vision as they headed down the stairs.

I tried to calm my racing pulse, but Josh slowly lowered my feet to the floor, rubbing that delicious body against mine, and my breath hitched again. He stepped back, running a hand over his hair, his eyes darting back to my mouth.

My tongue skimmed my lower lip, and he closed his eyes with a low rumble from his throat. "We should go sit in the waiting room, and...you know."

"Wait?" I supplied.

He nodded and took my hand in his without another word, walking us back into the hall and down to the waiting room. We were the only ones there, and he took the loveseat, tugging me down next to him. He wrapped his arm around me, and my head settled in the pocket of his shoulder, where it fit perfectly because we fit perfectly. We always had.

I nearly dislocated my jaw with a yawn. "I'm sorry. I'm just so tired."

"Sleep," he ordered, pressing a kiss to my forehead. "And December?"

"Hmm?" I asked, his heartbeat already lulling me to give in to the bone-deep exhaustion that traveling and jetlag was wreaking on me.

"You can always kiss me. I don't care if we're in the middle of an intense fight, or in a house full of priests. There is never a moment I don't want you."

With another kiss on my forehead, I drifted off, only to be awoken what felt like moments later.

"Wake up, welcome home, and come meet my son!" Jagger beamed, standing above us with the biggest grin I'd ever seen.

I blinked the sleep from my eyes and willed my brain to focus. "He's here?"

Jagger nodded. "He is. Seven pounds, nine ounces, and utterly perfect."

"Congratulations," Josh said, his voice husky from sleep.

We untangled from each other and stood, Jagger hugging both of us. "I'm so glad you guys made it. Seriously." He turned to Josh. "And look at you! Not dead, or blown up, or anything!"

"Nice," Josh said with a sarcastic smile. "Take us to this son of yours, who no doubt inherited his perfection from his mother."

Jagger's grin didn't diminish. "Damn straight."

I glanced down at my phone and noted that I'd slept a little over an hour. Josh was still stretching his neck as we walked.

We opened the door gently to see Paisley, her hair in a messy bun, holding a tiny bundle, and my heart flew. "Oh. My. Perfect!" I squealed softly as I tiptoed to the bed where she sat.

"He took his sweet time," she drawled, her smile radiant. She looked up at me, her eyes bright despite the ungodly hour. "It's so good to see you."

"I'm glad I made it. How are you feeling?"

She winced. "Like I just had a baby." She laughed. "Do you want to hold him?"

"Oh, no. You enjoy him," I said, trying to be sensitive. Hell yes, I wanted to hold him. And snuggle him, and bask in everything that was new and glorious about the world.

She lifted the tiny baby to me, his face peeking out of the blankets. "Oh, we've had about an hour. And now might be the only time you get. My mother arrives tomorrow."

"Well, in that case!" I ran to wash my hands and then held them out. His weight was slight as he slid into my arms, his tiny head cushioned at my elbow. I moved over to the rocking chair and sat carefully. I heard them talking in the background, but they faded into a blur of noise as I studied the tiny life I held.

He was just as Jagger had said, utterly perfect. Paisley's button nose and Jagger's eyes looked back at me. I lifted his exposed hand, marveling at the tiny fingers, his exquisite little nails. "What's his name?" I asked without looking up.

"Peyton," she answered, her voice catching.

I looked over to where she sat, her eyes sparkling. "That's beautiful."

"Peyton Carter Bateman," Jagger finished for her, sitting on the edge of her bed.

Tears pricked at my eyes as I looked at Peyton. "It's a big name to live up to, little man, but I think you'll be up to the task. You're a good one, I can tell." I brushed my thumb gently over his soft little cheek. He was the culmination of everything Jagger and Paisley had fought for—a family.

"Can I?" Josh asked, wiping his hands dry.

"Of course," I said, and transferred Peyton over.

He cradled the baby tenderly, tucking the blanket to cover

any rough parts of his uniform. His face was rapt with wonder as he took in everything about Peyton. A low ache settled in my stomach. This was what I wanted.

I wanted to see Josh holding our baby, marveling over what our love had created, what our family would become. I wanted our children to have his protection, his love, his sense of duty and honor, and just enough of his recklessness to be fierce. My hands covered my mouth as I tried to contain the tears of absolute joy that threatened to spill.

"Yeah, I was right. He's gorgeous like his mom," Josh said with a grin toward Paisley.

"No arguments here," Jagger answered, wrapping his arms around his very exhausted wife.

Josh looked up at me, and time stood still. I saw it there in his eyes—our future, our possibilities, our family. I saw little boys at hockey practice and little girls with their noses in books. Then I pictured pink skates and brainy boys. Every which way I imagined our life, it was perfect, because we had a love that was rare, precious, and worth fighting for. Worth sacrificing for.

There was no way I was going back to Turkey, not when we were so close to having everything we wanted together. I needed to be here, at least until we had our issues worked out. There would be other opportunities, other digs. There was only one Josh.

He echoed my smile, but as he glanced down where my fingers traced Peyton's arm under the blanket, his expression fell, first hurt, then hardened the longer he looked at my hand. When he looked back up at me, there was a distance I couldn't explain and instantly feared. What the hell had just happened?

Paisley cleared her throat. "So have you decided if you're going to take the job running the dig?" she asked.

Josh's eyes widened. "They offered you a job?"

"Yeah. It's only two months, and I'd be home in time to

start the semester."

"That's amazing," he said, his voice full of pride but laced with that same hurt in his eyes. "And it explains a lot," he murmured.

Before I could ask him what he meant, he leaned away from me, stood slowly, and walked over to Jagger, going around the bassinet to avoid me, and handed over the baby like he was deathly afraid of dropping him. "Congratulations, he's beautiful. I think we're going to head back and get some sleep. Are you staying here?"

"Yeah," Jagger answered, pointing toward the little couch. "That's where I await diaper-changing time."

"Sweet. Then do you mind if I crash in your guest room?"

Every sweet feeling I'd had crumbled, burned, and then left acidic ashes, scorching me from the inside out. He didn't even want to sleep in our house, let alone in the bed next to me. Fuck, the pain was unbearable.

Paisley's eyes flickered to me, but Jagger didn't miss a beat, God bless him. "Sure, if that's what you want," he said slowly.

"It is." Josh's tone was final, the same timbre as when he'd told me he was going back to Afghanistan. He'd made his decision, and there was no way to sway him.

Jagger handed Peyton to Paisley and then retrieved his keys from his pocket. *Breathe in. Breathe out. Focus on that.* Sucking oxygen through my lungs became my only thought. Everything else was too horrible to manage.

Josh thanked Jagger, took the house key, and we headed for the parking lot in silence. There was none of the confusion or anticipation of the drive here. Now there was simply a lingering sadness between us. But hadn't he just said there would never be a time he didn't want me? What was this bullshit? What set him off? The job offer? At least I hadn't snuck off in the middle of the night to take it without telling him.

Anger blossomed, and I welcomed the way it masked the hurt.

Maybe I needed to change my flight, get back to Turkey tomorrow, and take the damn job. Maybe he'd screw his head on straight while I was gone...or maybe it would kill off whatever was left of us. Why was there never a right answer lately?

Twenty minutes of pregnant silence later, we pulled into the driveway. I opened the hatch before he could and brought my bag to the ground.

"Do you want me to carry it in for you?" he offered.

"No," I snapped. "I want you to pull your head out of your ass."

"December."

I tossed my backpack over my shoulder and tugged on my suitcase, pulling it behind me up the stairs. I shoved the key in our door and let out a relieved sigh when it turned without sticking. The door opened soundlessly, and I walked through.

"December!" he nearly shouted as he followed me in.

"Oh, is this what it takes to get you in our house?" I asked, dropping my purse on the couch.

"It's for the best."

We squared off a coffee table apart. "Please, do explain how you know what's best for us."

"You have a job in Turkey waiting for you."

I shrugged. "So? I never said I was taking it. I said it had been offered. I don't make those kinds of decisions—the kind that alter our life—without talking to you. I wish I could say the same for you."

"Are we still having this argument?" He rubbed his hands over his hair.

"You leaving in the middle of the night didn't void the fight, Josh. It just pressed pause. You made that decision, and now you get to reap the consequences."

"I had to go back!"

"I know that!" The shout took some of the fight out of me, and my shoulders sagged. "Don't you think I figured it out? I get it. You came home a different person, and you told me you felt like you'd left bits of yourself there. I listened. So yes, I get it. You went to put yourself back together, to finish your mission, but you didn't discuss it with me, you just chose and left."

"I'm sorry that I hurt you. It was never my intention." His eyes were soft with regret, but everything else about his posture, from his crossed arms to how far he was away from me, screamed his resolution.

"I wish apologizing was enough. Do you feel like you succeeded? Are you all whole now?"

"Yes. It was exactly what I needed. I could have never looked at myself in the mirror knowing I stayed home when I should have been there. I couldn't be the man you deserve unless I did it."

"What I deserve? What I deserve is you, and I'll take you in any way you come to me. Whole, damaged, ripped the fuck apart—you're still mine."

"Oh, is that so?" he spat back, his tone utterly ironic.

"What is that supposed to mean?"

"It means that I'm not the only one making choices by myself, am I?" He gestured at me with a tight jerk of his hand before momentarily covering his eyes with it. "Maybe this is what I deserve. I left you when you asked me not to. I put you through hell constantly, and I hate myself for it. But I can honestly tell you that every single minute I was gone, you were in my head, in my heart. I may have doubted myself, maybe even our future, but I never once doubted *you*."

My mouth dropped. "Me? Our future? All I've done is fight for us, Josh. Since the moment you deployed, I've been holding on to you by my fingernails. But I don't let go. I don't run away. I have faith!"

"Is that why you took your ring off? Because you still have all this faith in us?"

What? My gaze flicked to my bare left hand. "Is that why you got pissed at the hospital? Why you're sleeping at Jagger's?" I yanked the chain around my neck until my ring popped free of my neckline. "I never took it off. I wear it on a chain when I'm on the dig so I don't hurt it or the artwork, but I never changed my mind. I never changed the vision of our future. Unlike you, apparently."

He doubted us. That admission shook my foundation and suddenly, that crack dividing us felt like the Grand Canyon, with him standing on one side in that uniform while I wore myself thin trying to stretch across it to him.

His whole frame sagged, and his gaze dropped to the floor before coming back to meet mine. I saw the relief I needed, but also a lingering sadness in those brown eyes that cut through my anger. "You didn't take it off."

I shook my head.

"I'm an asshole."

"It appears that way," I answered. "You...you doubt us?"

"Not us," he said, "but maybe where we're headed. Do you want to take it? Do you want to run that dig?" He searched my eyes as if his very future hung on my next words.

"Yes. Of course I do. It would be absolutely amazing. But nothing is more important to me than you. I don't want to leave you."

His eyes slid shut momentarily. "You need to take it. It would be huge for you."

"Yeah, it would, but our relationship is more important. I'm putting us first, because that's what you do in a relationship. You compromise for the sake of the person you love. You put aside your selfish goals so you can build one future."

"You're staying because of me." His head hung as if there

was some kind of blame to be placed here...like being together was a bad thing.

"Not because of you, for you. For us."

"It's the same difference!"

Why was he so angry? "So what? You'd wanted to be stationed in Texas, right? Closer to your mom?"

"What does that have to do with it?"

He still wouldn't meet my eyes, so I stepped around the table. "You chose Fort Campbell instead, so I could finish college. So we'd be together."

"This isn't the same."

"You're right. You moved your entire life. I'm only giving up two months. There will be other digs. I'm choosing you this one time."

"That's just where it starts," he muttered. "God, he'd kill me." His whisper was so soft that I barely heard it.

"What? Who are you—"

He didn't let me finish. "This is just the beginning."

"It's one time. We need it."

"And nothing I say is going to change your mind?" he asked, his mouth tightening.

"Nothing will ever change my mind about you. About us," I said softly, hoping to soothe him. "This dig would be great, but we are extraordinary. It's a tiny sacrifice—"

"I'm fucking sick of you sacrificing!" he shouted. Before I could respond, his head snapped up, the panic in his eyes quickly masked by aloof, untouchable ice. "I'm assessing for SOAR next week."

A bomb detonated somewhere in the vicinity of my heart, and the fallout decimated everything in me. "Special Ops? But..." I didn't have words. He'd never even hinted at wanting to fly for SOAR, and now he was assessing? For the first time, I felt like our relationship wasn't even on the radar of his concerns.

Fuck, that hurt. This wasn't the snap decision he'd had to make about deploying. No, this was a well thought out choice. Here I was, putting our relationship, our love, first, while he treated it like a side piece of baggage. The Josh I fell in love with, my rock, my whatever, never would have done that. Had he changed so much in the nine months since he'd deployed that we were no longer his priority? Red-hot rage tensed every muscle in my body. "Who *are* you, lately?"

He winced but didn't pause. "This is the right thing to do. Just like you taking the job in Turkey is right for you."

I scoffed. "Yeah, a temp job that I delayed while I came home so I could see you. Because that's what I do, right? I put my career second while you make the decisions—while you apply for SOAR behind my back and volunteer for Afghanistan like it doesn't affect me." I ran over any attempt he made to speak, my fury overtaking my usual level-headedness when it came to Josh. "You are the one with the changes. Three years ago it was, 'I'll just do my required four years, and then I'll get out.' Then you went aviation, and I get it. You didn't know that I'd be a part of your life, so I sucked up the fact that it would be another six years after you finished flight school. But this? SOAR? That's not temporary, and it's changing what our future looks like without so much as asking me, and that's not fair."

"This is what I have to do," he pled, stepping toward me.

I retreated. "No. It's not. You've never wanted to do it. Is this like that stupid Ducati? Do you need the adrenaline rush to feel alive? Is that it?"

His jaw tensed. "I don't know."

"I don't, either, but you're asking me for things I don't know that I can give, things you never would have asked me to do nine months ago. Do you not want to be with me? Is that it?"

His mouth dropped in shock. "No. There has never been a moment since I met you that I didn't want you—want to be with you. But you need to go run that dig. I'll assess for SOAR. We'll both live our...dreams." He ended on a whisper, as if he could barely speak the lie, because he and I both knew SOAR had never been his dream.

"Separately." My heart rebelled at the idea of building separate lives.

"Yes. This...this is what I want my future to be. Our future." The flat tone of his voice sounded more like defeat than determination.

"What kind of future is that? The one where we see each other in passing between your deployments and my digs? Or maybe we can manage a hookup halfway between. Is that what I am now?" We stood on the edge of something I couldn't fathom, and I had no clue how to bring us back. Not without him fighting for us equally as hard. "This isn't how I want our life to be. How can this be the future you want?"

"I know it's not fair of me to ask you to live like this, or how I can make you understand." His eyes met mine, and the anguish, the honesty I saw there stole my breath. "I know that this choice—this moment—might cost me you, and it's fucking killing me."

"Then stop making these asinine decisions. Stop ripping me apart. Stop making these choices pretending like they're all about me when they're really about you! That's why you want me to go on the dig, right? So I resent you a little less? So you feel righteous that I'm not sitting at home waiting for you to die? Because let me tell you, I had the same damn fear every day on that dig that I did while I waited at home. Maybe it was easier on you—" My mouth dropped. "Is that it? Did you figure out that it was easier for you to be gone while I was away?"

"No," he whispered, apology streaming from his eyes. "Don't you see that this is what's best for you?" His head shook. "For...everyone."

I ripped the necklace over my head and put it on the coffee table, the ring making an obscene sound of abandonment against the glass. "How do we build a future if we don't agree on one? What? We just sleep together when we're in the same state? Send emails?" He couldn't mean it. There was something else there, but I couldn't put my finger on it. Was he looking for an out? "Josh, do you even still want to marry me?" The question ripped through my soul like razor blades, and the bleeding was instant, excruciating.

"I want that more than my own life. But you're right. Living like this isn't fair to you. The waiting. The worrying. The sacrifices. Not after what you've been through. Not after what I've promised you...all the promises I'm breaking right now."

"Why do you have to do this? What we have...what we've fought for, it's like you're just throwing away everything we've wanted."

"Sometimes the things we want aren't the same as what we need."

"I don't believe that for a second. Need and want have always mixed into one when it comes to us." There had to be an explanation, some reason that he would put us through this, jeopardize us. It had to be a sense of duty...

Or guilt.

Will.

Another shard of my heart broke, crumbled like tiny pieces of sand sifting through my fingers. Was he ever going to get past what had happened? Really and truly?

"It's just something I feel like I have to do," he whispered.

"No." I shook my head. "No, it's something *Will* had to do."

His head snapped, his gaze widening. "December," he warned.

"That ring?" I pointed to where it lay on the table. "I accepted it from Josh Walker. The boy I fell into lust with on the ice, and the man I fell in love with when he held me together. I don't want to marry Will, or his dreams, as great as they were. You want it back on my finger? Then you act like the man I love, and not the man we lost."

"That's not fair."

"None of this has been fair! We didn't ask for any of this. We lost Will. We almost lost Jagger. We almost lost *you*. Hell, some days it feels like I did. But you have to stop punishing yourself for what happened. Joining SOAR isn't going to bring him back."

"Nothing I've done is enough. This is the only way I know to make his sacrifice matter!"

"It already does!" My throat tightened as tears bit into my eyes, the sting the only feeling I recognized. "You are an amazing man. A wonderful friend. He knew that. Stop thinking that you need to be more, because you're already more than enough."

"I can't. I'm not."

"Then see yourself through my eyes. See the man that I love. The one who promised to be my whatever. I'm holding on to you with everything I have, until my fingers—hell, my very soul—are raw and bleeding. You're trying to live for Will, but you're killing me."

He sucked in his breath, his eyes closing slowly. "You're right."

A small sliver of hope spiked through the fog of my misery.

"You're right," he continued. "You should go back to Turkey. You should take the job—follow your dream. There have already been enough casualties, and I refuse to watch you wither away. Go."

My chest tightened, every nerve ending screaming to latch on to him and hold tight. Not to let him nail shut the coffin he'd built to put our relationship in. Desperation took hold and squeezed my lungs. "Stop. I...I can figure it out. If this is what you need, then I can do it." Deployments without warning.

Never knowing where he was. Never ending. "I can do it for you, for us. Josh, I love you, and nothing is ever going to change that. Whether we're on different continents, different beds, or different wavelengths, you're my everything."

He walked forward slowly and pressed a lingering kiss to my forehead that felt too much like a good-bye. "Go run your dig. We'll—" He glanced at where my ring sat on the coffee table, echoing the same defeat that radiated from him. "We'll figure this out when you get back. Two months isn't going to change how much I love you. A lifetime couldn't."

Then he turned and walked out, pausing in the doorway. "But if this changes your love, if you realize that all I'm doing is holding you back..." He swallowed. "I won't blame you. I'm not really sure I could love me, either. Not under these circumstances."

"Josh," I whispered. "Stay." *Don't give up. Don't abandon what we have.*

His knuckles turned white on the handle, but he walked through, shutting the door behind him.

I took in a gulping breath. Fear, pain, heartbreak, it all coursed through my veins, but anger trumped it all. He'd made another fucking decision for us. I stomped up the stairs like a petulant toddler. Fuck it. If he didn't want to sleep next to me, then I didn't want to sleep next to him.

I knew that was a lie about twenty minutes later when I crept back down the stairs, put my ring around my neck, and then crawled into our guest bed, simply because I knew Josh was on the other side of the wall. I let my hand rest on the smooth paint as a tear slipped down my cheek.

Two and a half years, and we were back here, our headboards separated by a wall and our hearts separated by something a little less tangible.

How could he have changed so much that we were no longer his priority? Unless he hadn't. Unless this was about something different altogether. But what? *I'm not really sure I could love me, either.* His words gutted me more than his SOAR declaration.

His walls had grown so thick, and he shut me out until I was freezing, my heart barely able to endure the cold.

But that heart still beat for him in a way I knew it never would for anyone else.

Some damned homecoming. My eyes blurred with tears as I pulled out my cell phone and opened my flight app. One hundred and ninety-nine dollars later, I changed my departure date.

Then I emailed our wedding coordinator.

CHAPTER THIRTY-FIVE

JOSH

"**I** swear this is the second time in two months that I've told you that you're being a fucking jackass," Jagger said as he grabbed clean clothes out of his dresser.

"What the hell do you want me to do, Jag? She took her fucking ring off. I'm pretty sure that says it all right there." I flexed my hands to keep from punching a hole in his wall. When I'd finally realized that her left hand was as naked as I'd wanted to get her, my heart had been crushed. She may as well have driven a construction truck over it. Then to realize I made assumptions and it was hanging around her neck, only to have her actually take it off? That tiny action rocked the foundation of my very being.

In that instant I realized that letting her go wasn't just going to break my heart, it was going to obliterate it.

What the hell was I going to do? My most basic instinct was to march over to our house, throw open the door, strip her naked, and keep her screaming my name until she agreed to put that fucking ring back on her hand. But she'd already accused me of trying to sex my way out of things, and she'd been right.

"So you told her to go? Pushed her even further away?"

"Yeah, well, it's what she needs."

Jagger stopped shoving his clothes in a bag and flat-out

glared at me. "Get a fucking grip."

"I have one!" I shouted. Okay, well that sounded childish. "I'm fine," I said softer. "No nightmares, found my purpose, you name it, I've done it. I corresponded with my therapist overseas with Skype sessions, I flew missions, I got my head back. My heart just seems to have left."

"You left her, Josh. You walked out in the middle of the night after she asked you to stay. Paisley put her back together and then put her on a plane."

"You don't think I know that? This is for the best. I've put her through hell the last few months, and she didn't deserve it. Not any of this. If she's done with me, I can't blame her. She can go back to Turkey, and I can..." Move out? Walk away? Fuck, the thought hurt more than a fucking bullet.

He shook his head. "Damn, Josh. I know you're used to being her rock. You're used to swooping in and saving her like you did when her dad died. But Ember is a hell of a lot stronger now. She doesn't need you to save her—she needs you to save yourself. Sort your fucking head out before you lose her. You'll never find another woman that loves you like she does."

"I don't want another woman." Ever. She was it for me, and if I lost her, everyone else would pale in comparison.

He zipped up the bag. "Then what the hell are you doing?"

I threaded my hands through my hair and closed my eyes. "What she needs." I repeated it in my head, my personal mantra to get me through this shit.

He scoffed. "Do you even want to fly SOAR?"

My eyes opened. "No. It just seemed like the right thing to do. Will never got to."

"For fuck's sake. Didn't you learn anything watching Paisley struggle with Peyton? You can't live for someone who's dead."

"It's not the same," I snapped.

"Oh? How?" He folded his arms over his chest.

"Paisley didn't get Peyton killed."

Jagger's posture softened, and he rubbed his hands over his face. "I'm too sleep-deprived for this shit. You did not get Will killed. If anyone shoulders that blame it's me, and if I can function, you can, too. Because Carter would kick your ass for what you're doing right now. If you don't want to fly SOAR why would you put Ember through that?"

I didn't answer, but I didn't have to. Jagger had been my best friend for years and knew me entirely too well.

He paused, then swore under his breath. "You did it so she'd take the job."

I nodded.

"Because she was going to stay here for you."

I swallowed back the growing boulder in my throat and nodded again.

"I can't decide if you're the most unselfish asshole on the planet or the most manipulative."

"She said she wanted the job. The only reason she wasn't taking it was for me. Do you have any idea what she's given up to be with me? What she risks?"

"They all do. Every woman who marries a military guy takes that same risk. They might not have the same scars Ember does, but they all know the same fear. Morgan, Sam, Paisley, Ember...they all knew what they were doing. They were all willing to change their lives for love."

"So, I'm supposed to watch her give up everything she worked her ass off for, and then leave her with what? A kiss and a prayer that she won't hold a folded flag? She deserves better. A hell of a lot better than me."

Jagger shook his head and clasped my shoulder. "Trust her to make her own choices."

"I won't be the reason. I won't hold her back. If it means taking myself out of the equation, then I'll do it. She's already given up too much for me."

"You still love her?"

My soul burned with the thought of her smile, her tenacity, her incredible level of courage. "With everything I am. Hell, she *is* everything I am."

"Then you need to make it clear that she can have both— you and her dig."

"And the SOAR stuff?"

"That's between you and that heavy-ass guilt you're carrying. I'm not going to tell you not to do it if it's what you think you have to do. We all owe our debts to Will, and we all pay differently. You just have to decide if your guilt is worth losing Ember."

"I don't know how to live without her."

"Then stop standing here like a whiny bitch, get out the kneepads, and hit your knees. Beg. Plead. You, of all people, taught me the value of laying our shit bare, of fighting for the women we love."

"She took the ring off, and I basically told her it was okay. I gave her the out. How the hell do I fight that?" It was all I could say, because it was all I could think. How could she walk away when I couldn't so much as contemplate a life without her?

Because you made her, you jackass.

"Then put it back on her hand. Don't accept the invitation to assess for SOAR. Fix your mess, Josh. She's stood by you through a hell of a lot." He put his hand on my shoulder. "I get it. You've walked through Hell these last six months, and I love you like a brother. You saved my life, and I will never be able to repay you for that."

"Jagger, don't." I couldn't take one more thank-you.

"But because I love you, I will kick your fucking ass if you don't loosen your sphincter to let your head out."

My head snapped toward his. "You know I can physically

take you, right?"

"Yeah, well, it's worth the risk. You two have always been what I've looked up to, and I'm not really thrilled that Paisley and I are beating you out in the 'stable couple' department. Hell, Grayson and Sam are beating you, even with all their drama. Get. A. Fucking. Grip. Or you'll be right, and she'll be gone. You can be the badass SOAR pilot, and you can fly the covert missions, but it's going to cost you Ember. Even if she stays with you, that mission will eat a hole in her soul, and you know it."

Trying to envision a future without December—her laugh, the way her arms wrapped around me, the feel of her body underneath me as I made love to her... My eyes squeezed shut, like they couldn't bear to see it. "What am I going to do? She doesn't even realize that this is equally about giving her the future she's worked for. She thinks I'm only living for Will. To make his sacrifice mean something. She doesn't see that by doing one, I give her the other."

Jagger slung the bag over his shoulder. "Yeah, well, maybe Carter would want you to fly SOAR. Maybe he would have wanted you to carry out that legacy, but I can tell you for sure that he never would have wanted you to lose Ember over it."

He pushed past me and headed downstairs.

"So that's your advice? Pull my head out of my ass?" I called over the railing.

"That about sums it up!"

"And what if I'm right? What if she's done?"

He paused midway down and looked up at me. "You've never been a coward, Josh, so don't start now. You'll fly into a hot LZ to save a soldier, so take the fucking risk and save your relationship."

. . .

I stood in our living room later that afternoon, but it didn't feel the same. She'd left an hour ago for the airport, taking the out I'd foolishly given her—forced on her. I'd watched from Jagger's window as she pulled out of our driveway, taking my heart with her. I was pretty sure I'd left fingernail marks in his windowsill to keep from going after her.

Who the hell was I to keep her from her dream? Then I'd be the epitome of what her dad had hated about Riley. *I swear, she won't be trapped under my dream.* My promise to him twisted the knife I'd cut myself open with.

"I set her free," I called out, my voice morbidly loud in the empty house. "I didn't keep her caged." My voice dropped to a whisper. "But if it was the right thing to do, why does it feel so wrong?"

Without Ember, this house was just a shell, an echo of something beautiful. The warmth, the welcome, the feeling of home, it was gone, because she was gone. Our pictures, our furniture...everything we'd started building together was here, but without her, none of this meant anything. It felt as empty as I was without her.

Without her love holding me together, I started to unravel. Every fuck-up I'd put her through the last few months replayed in my head. Every time I couldn't talk to her, couldn't let her in. The motorcycle race, the nightmares, returning to the deployment. The short emails we'd exchanged during the last couple of months, which did nothing to bridge the monumental canyon I'd created.

She deserved this job without me fucking it up for her, or feeling like she had to choose. Hell, she deserved a fuck-up free life. Maybe taking off her ring was her way of saying she knew it, too. I stared at the empty portion of the coffee table where she'd laid it last night. Maybe she'd taken it with her? Maybe she had put it back on?

Or maybe she'd left it in her jewelry box.

My steps felt leaden as I climbed the stairs. Everything felt heavy, my heart, my limbs, my choices. What if I found the ring in her jewelry box? What if she'd really given up on us... given up on me?

What the hell was I supposed to do? If I didn't join SOAR, would Ember come home? Give up on the dig? If I did join, would that be even worse for her? What would Carter say? That they needed the best? That it was our obligation to step up? What would Doc Howard have said? Would the father in him demand that I take a desk job and protect his daughter? Or would the soldier he was understand the debt I had to pay?

He'd kick your ass for the way you've hurt her.

The sun came in through the window, and my face reflected in the glass frame of the print at the head of the stairs. I looked as shitty as I felt. I focused past my pale face and sunken eyes to the words beneath the glass. The Gettysburg Address. My eyes skimmed the words, my mind filling with memories of sitting next to Ember in history class, trying my damnedest to keep my focus on our professor instead of her.

I'd failed.

What's your full measure? she'd asked me. Where was my resolve? I pulled Carter's ring from my pocket and turned it over in my fingers as I read through the address.

"'But, in a larger sense, we cannot dedicate—we can not consecrate—we can not hallow—this ground. The brave men, living and dead, who struggled here, have consecrated it, far above our poor power to add or detract. The world will little note, nor long remember what we say here, but it can never forget what they did here.'" My voice carried through our empty house, reverberating off the walls like I lived in a tomb.

*We cannot hallow this ground...*because they'd already made the greatest of sacrifices. There was no higher elevation to ascend to, no better way to consecrate that ground because those soldiers had already done so with their own blood. To have tried would have been arrogant, as if there was anything the living could have done to compare with the price that had already been paid.

My forehead rested against the cool glass, and my eyes slid shut.

"This is the only way I know to make his sacrifice matter!"

"It already does!"

Our words from last night's fight slammed through me, shattering the last of my grief, my guilt, into manageable pieces. I was doing the same, trying to make Will's sacrifice mean more, trying to earn it. He'd offered up his very life for mine, and there was no way to make that sacrifice mean more than it already did.

Now I was the arrogant bastard.

My fist closed around his ring, and I concentrated on the edges cutting into my palm, letting the pain ground me. SOAR was his dream, not mine. And yeah, he'd think it was kick-ass if I flew with the 160th…but he'd be pissed if he could see what I'd done to my relationship.

He lives for them.

He'd needed Jagger to live for Paisley. That love, their future family had been his last thought. His last word had been garbled through his blood, but I'd heard when he'd whispered Peyton's name.

Love.

His last moments weren't a lament of never flying with SOAR. They weren't spent talking about how honorable it had been to save our lives. Because in those final, gasping breaths, that hadn't mattered. He'd only needed to know that his friends would live, that Paisley would be okay, that he'd be with Peyton soon. If Will left a legacy, it was love. And I let mine slip through my fingers because I was an arrogant bastard with my head up my ass.

Of course she'd left, given up, taken the out I damn-near

shoved down her throat. I had taken the last of her hope and crushed it when I walked out that door last night.

God, I'd wanted to stay, ached to, but I knew I would have given in if I'd lingered one second longer. I would have put my hands on her, forgotten every reason she needed to go, and I would have let her stay.

Maybe I could live with the guilt of what happened to Will, but watching that fire inside Ember die slowly? That would kill me.

My cell phone buzzed in the pocket of my shorts, and I fumbled it before I swiped it to answer the Colorado number. "Hello?"

"Mr. Walker?" a sweet voice asked.

I glanced at the phone again, trying to place the number with the slightly familiar voice. "Yes?"

"Hi! This is Mrs. Patricks, your wedding coordinator?"

Well if this wasn't the most fucked-up moment for this call. *Fuck, what if she already canceled our wedding?* Or maybe it was the deposit. Yeah, that had to be it. "Hi, Mrs. Patricks." I rubbed the skin between my eyes. I'd been making payments from Afghanistan, but there was still a thousand due before next week. "I know the balance for the deposit is due."

"Oh, no. That's not why I'm calling. With yesterday's payment, your balance is paid in full. I was actually letting you know that the photographer you wanted has signed his contract."

Great, now we'd have to cancel that, too, if I'd lost her. *Wait—* "Did you say the balance was paid in full?"

"Yes." Clicking sounds resonated in the background. "Miss Howard emailed me last night and made the final payment."

I nearly hit my knees. "She did?"

"Yes. Late last night, actually. Five hundred dollars. The other payments had been spread out between the ones you've sent me directly and the ones posted online."

Ember. She'd been making payments. She'd made one after we fought last night. Somehow, even after everything I'd put her through, she still wanted to marry me.

She still had hope.

"Mr. Walker?" Mrs. Patricks asked.

"Yeah, thank you for letting me know, but I have to go. I'll tell Ember about the photographer, thank you." I hung up and raced down the stairs, jumping the last four.

My feet damn near flew as I raced through our living room, grabbing my keys off the coffee table and leaving Will's ring in their place.

What about her ring? Don't you need it? I skidded to a halt in the kitchen. Nope. Fuck the ring. If she'd left it here, I'd buy her a new one. I'd buy her five new ones.

We'd work it out. We had to. I'd crawl on my fucking knees if I had to, but I wasn't losing her. I'd find a way for her to have everything—our love and her career— without choosing. I dialed her number as the garage door opened painfully slow, and the call went to voicemail as I climbed behind the wheel.

When the third call went to voicemail, and I was halfway out of our neighborhood, I broke down and called Sam.

"What the hell do you want, Walker?" she snapped.

"Her phone is going to voicemail."

"Maybe she doesn't want to talk to you. Hell, I don't even want to talk to you, and I'm not the one you crushed."

"Sam!" I shouted, coming to a screeching halt at the stop sign. "I fucked up, okay? I put...everything before her, and I know she's hurt. But I have never, not for one second, ever *not* loved Ember. She's my entire reason for existing. I just need to talk to her, Sam. I have to clear this up. I'll do whatever the fuck she wants, but I can't lose her. So if you wouldn't mind just maybe giving me her damned flight information, I would be very appreciative!"

"You're losing your shit."

"I have nothing to lose, Sam. Come on. She's everything."

"Give him the flight information, Samantha," Grayson said in the background.

"Do you have me on speaker?" I nearly gagged.

"It seemed like a family kind of moment."

I could practically see her shrug from here.

"Sam—" Grayson hissed.

"Fine. But you hurt her again, Josh, and I'll add more scars to that body of yours."

"Deal."

"She's on TransAtlantic Flight 3305 out of Nashville in... one hour."

I was fifty minutes from the airport. "Thank you, Sam."

"You know, she has her cell phone off. She's not avoiding you," she admitted softly.

A giant sigh of relief tore through me as I hit seventy-five on the highway. "There's hope."

"That girl loves you more than an ancient city full of relics."

A grin tilted my mouth. "That's really saying something."

"Yeah, well, love like that doesn't come along every day."

"No, it doesn't. I'm going after her, Sam."

"Good, and for once...screw the speed limit, Josh."

I pressed the pedal to the floor as we hung up and drove like a bat out of hell to the Nashville airport. This was our moment, and it was fucking movie worthy. I made it in forty-three minutes.

The car was barely in park before I jumped from my seat and ran into the terminal, cueing up the flight-tracker app on my phone. I just had to buy a ticket, and I could get through security. The shortest line was for StatesAir, so I headed that way as my phone pulled up the departure info.

I could get through security in about two seconds thanks to being TSA pre-checked, so that wouldn't take me—

Fuck.

My fist clenched around my cell phone, and I sucked in air through my teeth to keep from exploding.

No. No. No...

Her plane had already left the gate. I'd missed my chance.

I stuttered through one breath, and then another, trying to relieve the god-awful pressure in my chest. I refused to lose her. Not like this, not ever.

Now I just had to prove that to her.

CHAPTER THIRTY-SIX

EMBER

The room was coming together nicely, each newly revealed tile joining in a gorgeous mosaic. I hummed, enjoying the soft echo as I used a small brush to remove the smaller debris from the new section we were working on.

"Are you sure you don't want to break?" Ilyas asked. "I'm going to run to town while Dr. Trimble brings through his investors."

I lowered my handkerchief from my hairline and caught the sweat off my forehead, then pushed it back up. How could I have forgotten that Luke's father was coming through today to see how we were doing? "No, I'll stay and work."

"Alone?" he asked, concerned.

"I'm fine," I assured him.

"You're alone a lot, Miss Ember. You're here alone, in your room alone, walking in the evenings alone. If you get much more alone, you're going to be a certifiable recluse."

"I know," I said over my shoulder with a small smile. "I'm okay. I promise. I just want to say hi to Luke's dad." I turned back around, letting the tiles consume my vision, and I focused on the beautiful colors.

"Do you need anything? I'll pick it up for you."

"Oh." I nodded, sweeping a small bit of debris off a darkish red tile. "Powdered creamer."

He laughed. "Have you not learned to drink your coffee the real way yet?"

"I'd rather milk a camel." I fake gagged, and he laughed harder.

"Let's make sure that doesn't happen." He rinsed off his hands in the corner by the archway that connected us to the next room.

I'd never develop a taste for the dark, sugar-brewed roasts they preferred over here. I missed smooth, silky cream too much.

I missed the States, really. Okay, mostly Josh.

Always Josh.

His smile, his eyes, the way his arms wrapped around me at the perfect moment, simply knowing what I needed.

A familiar ache settled into my chest, constricting my breaths for a few painful seconds. How had we gotten here? We'd made it through more than a couple should have to over the last three years, and now we were teetering on what...all-out collapse? Why? Because we couldn't see eye to eye on his job?

Because you don't see the same future.

"Miss Ember, are you okay?" Ilyas asked, now in front of me, snapping me out of my depressing thoughts. He'd done too much of that lately.

"Yeah," I nodded with a forced smile. "Let me grab you some money."

I reached into my back pocket and felt only soft fabric. *Shit. You did not...* A quick check of the other pocket, then the small, skinny ones in front, and I swore under my breath. It was a half mile walk back to my room...and my wallet.

"Ugh, it's in my room."

"No problem," Ilyas said with a shrug.

"I've got it."

That voice sent shivers racing down my limbs, and the ache

in my heart morphed into butterflies of disbelief. Forty Turkish lira appeared in front of me in a hand I knew all too well.

I turned slowly, my breath catching in my throat as I looked up and met his eyes. *Josh.* His name was my only coherent thought, my every heartbeat screaming it. My first instinct was to throw my arms around him and forget every reason we were ripping each other apart. A myriad of emotions crossed his face as we stood there, eyes locked on each other. Joy quickly flickered to worry until he tilted his head, sighed, and gave me a half smile. "December," he whispered.

"What are you doing here?" I shook my head. "Not that I'm not glad to see you. Crap, that came out wrong," I verbally vomited. Fuck me, but he looked good in that Henley and vest. And he was in Turkey. Turkey!

"I came for you."

So simple. So very complicated.

"How about I get your creamer?" Ilyas said and backed out of the room, a giant, goofy grin on his face.

I brushed the dust from my hands onto my already too dirty cargo capris, well aware that I looked like I'd been on the dig site all day. "God, I'm a mess," I said, trying to think of something to say that wasn't *I'm sorry, I'll do whatever you want, move wherever you want to, lose myself to support your absurd need for special ops stuff, just love me.* It was so tempting to say, to heal the rift between us, but it would be shoving a Band-Aid on an arterial bleed.

"You're perfect," he said softly, tucking a sweat-curled strand of hair behind my ear. "Perfect and exquisitely beautiful."

I barely stopped myself from kissing his hand as it skimmed down my face, his thumb dangerously close to my lips. "I can't believe you're really here."

He smiled, and my heart skipped. "I'm sorry it took so long. I got to the airport about ten minutes too late. You'd already taken off, and then I had to go through all the redeployment stuff, and we just now got leave."

And I think I might have melted. "You came after me at the airport?"

He nodded. "Yeah, well, I realized that everything we're fighting about...none of it matters if I lose you."

"But aren't you supposed to be at SOAR assessment?"

He shook his head. "I declined. I'm not assessing."

My chest felt like every rainbow in the world had crammed itself in there. "You did? You're not?"

"I never really wanted it. I applied because it was what Will wanted, and I was going to talk about it with you when I got home. But then you said you were giving up all this"—he gestured to the ruins around us—"for me, and I couldn't let you do it. I couldn't let your career, your dream, get run over, not even for our relationship. You've already given up so much for me. So when you felt like you had to choose, I did the only thing I could think of—I took myself out of that equation. I'm so sorry. You deserved to make the choice."

"I would always choose you."

"I know." He cupped my face in his hand and stepped closer, bringing our bodies to a near-touch. The small distance was sanity and ache all in one. "We've always said it's you and me against the world, and these last few months, we've been letting the world win because we've been divided. You were right. I've been making decisions about my future based on guilt, while your future widened into this world you've worked so hard for. I got caught up in this idea that I had to be your foundation, and I was...cracked. Then in trying to fix myself, I forgot that what we're built on isn't just you and isn't just me. It's both of us. We're strong because we carry each other. We build our relationship on equal ground, and I'm so sorry that I lost sight of that. It's unforgivable."

"Nothing is unforgivable. You weren't trying to hurt me. I know you never would. You were trying to be a better man *for* me, but you have to know that you're already the best. Even when you were wounded, and bleeding, and a little broken, you were...you *are* mine. There's no one else for me."

His eyebrows lowered with his voice. "I'm sorry I ever made you doubt it. Can I fix this? Did..." He sucked in a shaky breath. "Am I too late?"

"I'd wait forever for you," I answered, slipping my ring out of my shirt on its chain to show him. "I love you. I have always loved you, and I *will* always love you. These last few months have sucked, but that's what marriage is, right? For better, for worse? So maybe we get the worse out of the way now. There's nothing you can say or do that could push me far enough away that I would stop loving you. I was...I am willing to wait as long as you need, but I'll never give up on us, Josh. Whether I'm in Turkey, or you're in Afghanistan, or we're both at home, my heart is always with you."

He glanced down at the ring and back to my face. My breath caught at the love that poured out of his eyes.

"I'll put it back on, if you want. I never emotionally took it off. I'm sorry I even threatened it. It was childish, and untrue."

Josh looked over my shoulder at the mosaic I was uncovering. "That's lasted thousands of years under all this dirt?"

A smile tugged at my lips. "Yes. It's beautiful, isn't it?"

His eyes dropped to my lips. "Yes. And there's no way I'm letting you ruin it with a piece of jewelry. Besides, I don't need a ring on your hand to know that you're mine."

Josh brushed my mouth in a sweet kiss. Our lips lingered as our breaths mingled, restoring gravity to our world in the space of a heartbeat. I leaned into him and brought my hand to his neck, savoring the warmth of his skin. He deepened the kiss, and I moaned my approval, the sound echoing off the stone walls.

There was nothing in the world that compared to kissing Josh. Except maybe being kissed by Josh. He used his lips to tell me he loved me, the strokes of his tongue against mine to say how much he'd missed me, missed us.

I answered in kind, forgetting everything around me and abandoning all logical thought. There in his arms, standing in the middle of a room that was thousands of years old, in a foreign country thousands of miles from the States, I was home.

This was all that mattered.

Need spiraled through my nerves, tightening in my stomach as Josh's grip turned more possessive, more demanding. It had been so long, and I was starved for his touch.

"Whoa...Red?" Luke's voice barely broke through the haze of desire Josh wrapped me in.

Josh released me, and I peeked around his rather massive frame. "Hey, Luke."

"What are you..."

Josh turned, and recognition lit in Luke's eyes. "Ah, so the Flyboy has come to make amends?"

I stepped to the side and nodded. "It's all good."

"Good, because you've been the most pathetic, love-sick puppy I've ever seen these last few months. By the way, you left your wallet on my bed last night." He waved it above his head, and I skipped over to retrieve it.

"Thanks," I said with a smacking kiss on his cheek.

"Movie nights are my favorite, and next time the ice cream is on me, but I really wish you'd branch out from just strawberry." He glanced over me to Josh, then back. "Call me if you need me."

"She won't," Josh answered, his voice gruff.

Holy shit, he's jealous. Of Luke?

Luke snorted back a laugh. "Relax." His eyes drifted down Josh's impeccable body, and I choked back a laugh when Josh caught on. "You're far more my taste than your fiancée." He gave Josh's chest an appreciative pat and walked out, calling back, "Oh, and Dad is walking through in a half hour, so...you know. I'll lock the door on my way out."

"He's gay," Josh said.

I bit into my lower lip until my smile tore it free. "I never told you that?"

Josh shook his head.

"I guess it never seemed important."

He wrapped his arms around me, and I laid my head against his chest, setting my breaths to the steady rhythm of his heart. "I love you," he whispered into my hair. "Tell me I didn't lose you. I need to hear it one more time."

I tilted my head enough to press a kiss to his stubbled jaw. "You couldn't lose me if you tried, Josh Walker. Though you've made me wonder lately if that was your motive."

"Never. I just want what's best for you."

"You're what's best for me, and not just because I love you. You make me a better person. Stronger. You push me to achieve things I'd only ever dreamed of, and never hold me back. You're my perfect match in every way."

"No more bullshit," he promised. "I even sold the Ducati."

I jerked back in his arms to get a better look at his face. "You what?"

He nodded. "I've been in counseling this whole time, too."

I blinked. "Okay, the counseling I applaud, but the Ducati?"

His grin was enough to seriously drop my panties. "You hated the Ducati."

"I didn't…" I shook my head. "I hated the Ducati. I hated what it represented—a giant, flashy death wish."

"I know, and you were right, so I turned it into something you'd love. I paid off our wedding."

My jaw dropped. "You paid off our wedding?"

"Including the photographer."

A stab of guilt went through me. "But you loved that thing."

"No, I loved being a seventeen-year-old on that thing. Now, I love you. I will always love you, December."

My eyes flew wide. "But the Harley? Oh, God. Please tell me you didn't sell the Harley. I know I hate how dangerous they are, but you love it, and I have to admit, you're sexy as hell on it—"

He cut me off with a kiss and then laughed. "I kept the Harley, but I'd sell it in a heartbeat if it made you happy."

"No! No. You make me happy. Keep it. Just...you know... helmet."

He kissed me softly. "Anything for you, future Mrs. Walker."

"Say it again," I whispered against his lips.

"Mrs. Walker. December Walker. Dr. Walker."

This time his kiss was blatantly erotic. I melted into him, and he took complete advantage, kissing me deeper, with hotter swirls of his tongue until I whimpered, ready to give these tile mosaics a show they wouldn't forget for another few thousand years.

"A half hour, huh?" he asked, worshipping my neck with kisses that sent chills rocketing down my arm.

"Yeah," I answered.

"I can do a lot with a half hour."

A giggle burst free. "And then what?"

"Then I'm yours for the next two weeks, if you want me. You can work, and I'll watch, or I'll help, or I'll just study 5&9s in your room until you're done at night. I don't want you to choose between the dig and me, so you get both."

This...this was heaven. Uncovering ancient relics by day and making love with Josh at night. The picture was exquisite. "You don't mind? You're using up all of your leave, and I won't have time to vacation or anything."

"I don't need a vacation. I just need you. Your career is just as important as mine, and maybe selfishly, I want to understand what you do. This place"—he glanced around at the stone walls and back to me—"it's part of you. Usually, you have to live where the army tells us to, handle deployments, and wounds, and…funerals, because you're forced to live in my world."

"Because I love you, Josh."

"I know, and I love you," he said, pressing a kiss to my forehead. "Now show me around, December, because I'd like to live in your world for a little while."

My smile radiated the joy that reached through my limbs to my fingers and toes. "The army, Colorado, Alabama, Tennessee, Turkey… It's all our world."

"Our world," he agreed and sealed the promise with a kiss.

The world had never felt smaller because my heart had never felt so big.

CHAPTER THIRTY-SEVEN

EMBER

Under the cloudless Colorado sky, during a sunset in June, I kicked my feet on the ski lift like an over-excited five-year-old.

"You're going to lose a shoe," April chastised.

"Ease up, April," Gus said from the other side of me. He stretched his neck, trying to shove his fingers between his collar and light blue tie that perfectly matched the ribbons around my bouquet of white calla lilies. "I love you, Ember. I do. But this thing sucks."

"Don't say sucks," I chastised, handing my bouquet to April so I could loosen Gus's tie enough for him to breathe.

"Does it at least match Josh's?" he asked as I finished.

"It does," I promised. "Just think. In a few minutes, you'll have a brother."

A grin lit up his face, and he leaned into the slight breeze ruffling his strawberry-blond curls. I sent a silent thank-you to my hairdresser for shellacking my up-do to my head. "I like that idea."

"Good." April laughed, bringing my bouquet to her nose. "Everything is perfect, Ember. I couldn't be happier for you."

I squeezed her hand as she handed me back the flowers. "I think we turned out okay."

"Yeah." She smiled. "You don't mind that Mom brought

that new guy?"

I looked at the chair in front of us, where Mom currently wore a smile that could light the world. "No, I'm just glad to see her happy."

"Me, too," Gus agreed. "I like Paul. Plus, he said his intentions are honorable."

April leaned forward, her mouth dropping open. "You asked him that?"

"You can never be too sure," he said with a straight face.

April and I burst into snorting fits of laughter that lasted just about until the chair stopped at the top of the mountain. Gus hopped down, and then April waited, offering her arm to keep me steady as my feet reached the step. Then she cleared the lace train of my gown and lifted it as we walked down to the path.

Butterflies took flight in my stomach as she adjusted the thick lace straps of my sweetheart neckline and then made sure the jeweled belt was secure. "One moment..." She bit her lip in concentration and pushed something into my hair. "One of the crystals had come loose."

"What?" I asked as she blinked.

"You're just...beautiful."

"I'm proud of you, April. Everything you've fought through, and going to CU, getting great grades... I couldn't be prouder to have you as a sister." Our hug was short, since I saw Mom approaching us over her shoulder, and then Paisley and Sam came off the next chair.

They all sniffled, dabbing at their eyes, but I was too excited to cry. Too ready to be Josh's wife. *Wife!* I used to think "fiancée" was the prettiest word until I became one, then I realized that "wife" was quite possibly the best word in the English language next to "husband."

"Okay, ladies, the clock is a-tickin'," Gus called out.

"Never rush a lady, August." Grams clucked. "You have

never looked lovelier, December," she said with a kiss on my cheek.

"December, you are radiant," Mrs. Patricks said, earpiece in and clipboard in hand. "Are you ready to become Mrs. Walker?"

"I've always been ready," I answered with an effortless smile.

We walked to the area just before the aisle, hidden by the large trellis. Mom kissed me on the cheek. "Your father would be so proud of you. So happy with the love you've found." Her eyes glistened as she pulled back. "I love you. This marriage only means that we gain Josh. You'll always be my baby girl."

"I know, Mom," I answered. "I love you, too."

She walked down the aisle with Grams as the music played, followed by Josh's mom, who blew me a kiss as she walked by. Morgan sat next to Mom, Peyton happily chewing on part of her dress as he sat in her lap. Paisley and Sam readied themselves to walk, and Gus gently tugged my hand.

"What's up, little man?"

"I wish Dad was here. Is that okay?"

Tears pricked at my eyes. "I wish he was, too, Gus. But I know that he's really happy that you're walking me down the aisle."

April fixed his hair, leaning down in her pale blue dress. "He's here, Gus. Trust me, he's watching, because he wouldn't miss this for the world. Not after all the work he did to get these two together."

I squeezed her hand, and our eyes locked, so similar yet so different. "Thank you."

"You're up, April," Mrs. Patricks said, and April nodded, then walked down the aisle.

"Shall we?" Gus said, tilting his chin and offering his arm.

I took it, marveling that he was already approaching my jaw in height. "We shall."

The music changed, and we stepped into the arch.

Josh came into view, and it was all I could do not to race

toward him when his mouth dropped slightly. I kept my eyes locked on his and my steps measured, but my heart flew higher than the mountains around us.

Josh in a hockey uniform, hell, Josh in MultiCam didn't quite compare to Josh in a tux, waiting for me at the end of the large deck.

Gus nodded to Josh as we approached, and Josh leaned down as my little brother whispered in his ear. With raised eyebrows, he nodded then shook Gus's hand. Only then did Gus give my hand over to Josh.

"I think Dad's happy," he whispered to me.

"I do, too," I said, kissing his cheek before he walked to stand between Jagger and Grayson.

Then the world faded away as Josh looked into my eyes and said, "You...you're perfection."

I saw forever in those brown eyes. "You, too. What did Gus whisper?"

Josh's eyes danced. "That if I ever hurt you, he has a BB-gun and knows where I sleep."

I leaned around Josh and widened my eyes at Gus. He had the nerve to smile and throw me a thumbs-up.

Josh and I were both laughing as we turned to the minister.

In front of seventy-five of our closest friends and family, we pledged our love, verbalizing everything we'd known from the start—we were meant for each other.

Josh vowed to love me forever, cherish me above all, and always come home to me,

I vowed to love him for eternity, adore him when he was wrinkled, and to always be waiting for him...unless I was digging up something really old. Then he'd have to do the waiting.

"I now pronounce you man and wife," the minister said. "You may kiss your bride."

My heart sang, feeling as if it was made entirely of joy.

Josh paused, his eyes alight with wonder and love as they

skimmed over my face, as if he was trying to remember every detail of this moment. Then he stepped forward, cupping one hand behind my neck and the other at my waist. My free hand came around his neck, and as he dipped me backward, my bouquet almost brushed the floor in the other.

He kissed me, filling me with promise, and hope, and so much love that I thought my heart might burst from the sheer volume of emotion pouring through me. I was vaguely aware of an uproar of applause as he deepened the kiss for the smallest of seconds before pulling me back to a standing position, my lips still clinging to his.

The claps became even louder as we drew apart, and I saw his arm lifted above us, his fist clenched in victory.

"You and me?" he whispered against my lips.

"Against the world," I promised.

And what a beautiful world it was. Our world.

EPILOGUE

Five years later

Damn it, I was going to be late. I shouldn't have taken that last call, but the new shift wasn't on for another twenty minutes, and they'd requested Flight For Life, so we'd gone. I'd call later and check to make sure the little boy had made it.

I parked my Jeep in the closest spot available and grabbed my bag from the back, sprinting into the practice rink at the World Arena. She'd never forgive me if I was late.

I threw open the glass doors and raced toward the locker room to see Ember coming out with Noah on her hip, her cheeks pink from the cool air in the rink. "Josh! You made it!"

Our lips met, and that same lightning ran through me, bringing every one of my nerves to attention. I kissed her again just because I could, until Noah pulled on my bag strap.

"Hey, Hulk," I said, lifting our seven-month-old son into my arms. He had his mother's eyes and disposition, and after the hell-raiser Quinn had been, and still was, Noah was the perfect second baby. I kissed his soft cheeks and caught his giggles while Ember adjusted the baby carrier, and then I helped her get him situated, running my hand over his little bald head before pulling his Colorado Tigers hat over it. "How was work?" I asked.

"Good! I edited that article for *Archaeology Magazine*, graded a stack of papers, and put in the grant paperwork for the new dig site."

"You put me to shame, December Walker."

"Save any lives today?"

"A few, I hope. How is our little hockey player?"

"Annoyed that Coach Dad isn't here on time." She smiled. "Seriously. I'm not even allowed to tie skates. Apparently I'm not cool enough, because Daddy does it better. You've created a monster, Josh, and you must now tame the beast. And seriously, with the fight over the number?"

"Hey, there's nothing wrong with wanting your old man's number."

"Uh huh." She smirked. "Because Quinn was definitely the one fighting, right? Or wait...that was you and Mr. Parkins."

"Hey, Quinn was just as entitled to that number as the Parkins kid was."

"Uh huh, you'd better get in there before the beast shreds you."

"I will don my armor."

"Game starts in fifteen minutes." She smacked my ass and wiggled her eyebrows. "Looking good today, Walker."

I shot her a look that told her this wasn't over. "You just wait until we get home. Noah may sleep through the night, but you won't."

"Promises, promises," she said with a laugh and headed toward the stands.

I came through the locker room doors and searched the benches full of squirming kids for mine.

"Thank God you're here, because I got shot down when I offered to help Quinn," Gus said, shaking his head, which was almost level with mine.

I'd never known anyone as particular about hockey equipment, and who put it on, as Quinn was.

"No worries, I got caught up at work, but I'm here. Thanks, Gus."

"No problem." He bent down to help one of the dozens of boys who took up the benches. Quinn's arms were waving, and I picked my way to the back of the locker room.

"You're late!"

"I know," I said, crouching down to grab one tiny skate. "But Daddy had to help save lives. I'm here now. You wouldn't let Mommy tie your skates?"

There was a tiny headshake under a massive helmet. "She doesn't do it tight enough. She's scared of hurting me, but I'm tough."

"I know you are," I assured our firstborn, finishing up the other skate. "Are you ready for your first game?"

"I'm ready."

"What do we do?" I asked, careful as those tiny skates met the padded surface of the locker room so we could walk to the ice.

"Skate fast, shoot steady, and don't hog the puck."

"Good job." We fist-bumped before we stepped into the bench.

"Daddy? My helmet feels weird." Quinn plopped onto the bench with as much grace as a four-year-old decked out in gear could.

"Okay, let me peek." I unhooked the snaps and then pulled it off.

A tumult of red curls fell from the helmet, and I stared into eyes that mirrored my own with the attitude to match. "That's better," she said.

"You didn't let Mommy braid your hair?" I asked, pulling an extra hair tie out of my coaching jacket.

"None of the boys have to," she argued.

"None of the boys have Princess Merida hair. Now turn." I straddled the bench behind her, divided her hair into three sections, and braided it with practiced fingers. "Done."

She ran her hand down the seam. "Mommy does it smoother."

"Then you should have let Mommy do it, you imp."

She burst into laughter and grinned up at me. "I'm not an imp, I'm Quinn!"

I kissed her on the forehead, and then secured her helmet. "Yes, you sure are. Now get on the ice, and we'll go out for hot chocolate if you score."

"Daddy," she whispered.

"Quinny?"

"What if I don't score?"

I grinned at her perfect little face, so like her mother's, and thanked God again for this life I'd been given. "Then we'll go out for hot chocolate."

"Okay." She nodded, then turned to where Ember sat in the stands. "Hi, Mommy! Noah!"

Ember waved, and then lifted Noah's hand from her hair to do the same as Quinn took the half-ice that was set up for the Mites-level game. How was she already four? How was this already her first game? How...had my daughter just stolen the puck from that massive six-year-old?

Quick on her feet, she skated past the lone defenseman and scored on the goalie-less net, throwing up her arms in victory as if Lundqvist himself had been in goal.

I clapped for her, and then turned to Ember, who had covered Noah's ears and was cheering loudly against the glass for our daughter.

I had never loved December more than at that moment—though I thought that just about every day.

All these years, and we were back here, at the same rink, cheering on the jersey with number thirteen and the name Walker emblazoned across the back.

And now it was our daughter who was terrifying every boy on the ice.

Ember raised her hand to the glass and smiled at me with a slow nod that let me know her thoughts were along the same line.

We weren't in high school, or even college, but one thing remained the same—I was head over heels in love with December Walker.

And I always would be.

ACKNOWLEDGMENTS

Thank you, first and foremost, to my Heavenly Father, who has blessed me beyond reason, and without whose mercy I could not exist.

Thank you to my husband, Jason. For being my strength, my safe place, my inspiration, and for always accepting me for exactly who I am and not only loving me in spite of my flaws, but because of them. Thank you to my children, who give me a reason to put my feet on the floor before the sun rises, and fill my heart and my arms with warm, squishy hugs. Thank you to my sons for standing tall and strong while we lived eighteen hundred miles apart from your dad these last seven months—while I wrote this book, edited another, wrote another, took too many phone calls, snapped one too many times—all in the name of adopting your little sister. Thank you for loving her with the ferocity of the fire-breathing dragons you are. To my sister—I'm coming home, so tune up your guitar. Love you, mean it. To my brothers—thank you for the unique perspectives you bring to my life and your ability to simultaneously make me yell that I'm now an adult while making me wish I was not. To my parents, who never doubted for a second, and learned how to live again with five kids underfoot while we transitioned. To Grace, for always seeing the best in me and loaning your name to our daughter. She will wear it well.

Thank you to my amazing editor, Karen. I can't believe we're here, not just at the end of our fourth book together, but the end of this series. These Flyboys are just as much yours as they are mine. Thank you for teaching me, laughing with me, and being incredibly patient with me. To Jamie, for believing in Josh and Ember, and me. To the insanely talented team at Entangled: Liz, Debbie, Heather R., Heather H., Ellie, Jessica, Brittany, and Curtis. You're all rock stars. Thank you to my incredible, sassy publicity team, Melissa, Linda, Sharon, Jesey, and Kristi, for eleven p.m. messages, cocktails in NYC, strawberry whiskey in Nashville, and love in Philadelphia. I couldn't do this without you ladies. To Ashley, I'm so praying that I haven't scared you off yet. To my agent, Louise, for every time you've stepped in when you didn't have to and for your unwavering faith in me.

Thank you, Molly, for three a.m. critiques and swift kicks in my ass when I'm ready to torch a manuscript. It's you, my dear, who is the golden goddess. To Emily—nearly twenty years, and you're still my best friend. Either you're incredibly brilliant, or your pain tolerance is wicked high. Linda, thank you for taking a chance and sending a newbie author an email. My life has been irrevocably changed for the better because of you. Katrina, I have no words for the way you are able to answer every question with a smile. Rose, because Oliver Queen always trumps RT. To Lizzy, for your steadfast friendship and inspiring heart. The rest of the BBA crew, Rachel, Cindi, and Melissa, you guys keep me on my toes and constantly striving to better not just my writing but myself. To my Backspace Survivors, what a road this has been. My Epics, you guys blow me away. To the incredibly talented group of writers I find myself lucky enough to call friends: Jen, Fiona, Megan, Tessa, Mindy, Brenda, Amy... and now I'm going to kick myself because you know I'm leaving someone out. To the women I couldn't make it without, Claire, Corinne, Whitney, Pepper, Alessandre, Christine, Laurelin, Lauren, Mandi, Kyla, Rose, Kristy, Aleatha, the whole crew. You give me a safe place, incredible insight, and your friendship—I could not be more grateful. FYW.

To the bloggers who spend countless hours reading, reviewing, pushing, helping, sharing—Natasha, Jillian, Aestas, Wolfel, Angie, Alexis, Allison, Lisa, Holly, Toski, Natasha M., Kara, and the countless others I'm no doubt forgetting at three a.m.—you are absolutely invaluable in both your insane skills and your tender hearts. How did I get so lucky to have your support? Trish, you might not be a blogger but, my God, are you an amazing cheerleader, and an even better friend.

To the person I undoubtedly forgot. I love you. Please forgive my sleep-deprived brain. It's been a long year.

Lastly, again to my husband, the original Flyboy. For coming home to me every time you've deployed. For giving me so much inspiration in our real life that *Hallowed Ground* simply flowed. For this love that has not only survived four deployments, but is all the stronger for them. There's so much of you in here. Your honor, your integrity, your strength. So much of you in every hero I write.

Hallowed Ground is a thrilling follow-up to Josh and Ember's love story with a happy ending. However, the book includes elements that may not be suitable for all readers. Military service and deployment, plane crashes, depictions of war, medical treatment and procedures, depictions of grief and loss, physical injury treatment, and post-traumatic stress disorder are shown on the page. Readers who may be sensitive to these elements, please take note.

*Don't miss the rest of the Flight & Glory series
from #1 New York Times
bestselling author Rebecca Yarros*

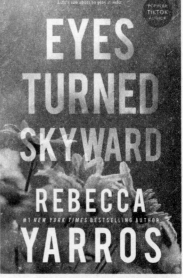

Don't miss the exciting new books
Entangled has to offer.

Follow us!

f @EntangledPublishing

⦿ @Entangled_Publishing

✦ @EntangledPub

♪ @EntangledPub

AMARA
an imprint of Entangled Publishing LLC